"But I miss feeling . . ."

Pepper's eyes softened. "So start again." She plucked the string of Rhett's hoodie. "By feeling me."

"You're beautiful, you know that, right?" He reached and pushed the soft tendrils of her hair back. "If we do this, I plan on doing a lot of looking, Apple Girl. That's part of my deal. I look when I want, where I want, up close and personal."

"So we're going to do this?" she groaned, fingers sinking deep into his hair, pulling him closer. "A summer fling? Right here, right now?"

He tore himself away and glanced around the kitchen. "Yeah. But not here. When I get you naked for the first time it's going to be in a bed." He forced himself to admit the truth. She deserved that much. "The way I've been dreaming about since the day I first saw you."

ACCLAIM FOR LIA RILEY'S NOVELS

IT HAPPENED ON LOVE STREET

"Witty banter, sizzling chemistry, and a romance that captured my heart!"

—Jennifer Ryan, *New York Times* bestselling author

WITH EVERY BREATH

"In this emotionally charged contemporary the protagonists' personal struggles for self-worth and redemption develop into pulse-pounding adventure and breath-stopping romance.... This novel will delight [Riley's] fans and new readers alike."

—*Publishers Weekly*

UPSIDE DOWN

"Fresh, sexy, and romantic, *Upside Down* will leave you

wanting more. I cannot wait for the next book. Lia Riley is an incredible new talent and not to be missed!"

—Kristen Callihan, award-winning author of the Darkest London series and *The Hook Up*

"*Upside Down* is a refreshing and heartfelt new adult contemporary romance."

—*USA Today*'s *Happy Ever After* blog

"Lia Riley turned my emotions upside down with this book! Fast paced, electric, and sweetly emotional!"

—Tracy Wolff, *New York Times* and *USA Today* bestselling author

"Where to even start with this book? Beautifully written, Australia, hot surfer Bran, unique heroine Talia. Yep, it's all just a whole lot of awesome. Loved it!"

—Cindi Madsen, *USA Today* bestselling author

"A rich setting and utterly romantic, *Upside Down* will have you laughing and crying and begging for it to never end. I absolutely loved it!"

—Melissa West, author of *Pieces of Olivia*

"*Upside Down* is a brilliantly written new adult romance that transported me to another country. With vivid imagery and rich characterizations . . . I was completely smitten with the love story of Bran and Talia. I cannot wait for the rest of their story!"

—Megan Erickson, author of *Make It Count*

SIDESWIPED

"I could feel the tension with every page. . . . The Off the Map series by Lia Riley is probably my favorite new adult series of the year."

—Roxy's Reviews

INSIDE OUT

"Riley writes a captivating story from beginning to breathtaking end."

—*Publishers Weekly* (starred review)

It Happened on Love Street

PREVIOUSLY BY LIA RILEY

Off the Map

Upside Down

Sideswiped

Inside Out

Carry Me Home

Into My Arms

Wanderlust

With Every Breath

It Happened on Love Street

An Everland, Georgia novel

Lia Riley

FOREVER

New York   Boston

Copyright © 2017 by Lia Riley
Preview of *The Corner of Forever and Always* copyright © 2017 by Lia Riley

Cover design by Elizabeth Turner. Cover photography © Shutterstock. Cover copyright © 2017 by Hachette Book Group, Inc.

Forever
Hachette Book Group
1290 Avenue of the Americas, New York, NY 10104
forever-romance.com
twitter.com/foreverromance

First Edition: April 2017

Forever is an imprint of Grand Central Publishing. The Forever name and logo are trademarks of Hachette Book Group, Inc.

The publisher is not responsible for websites (or their content) that are not owned by the publisher.

The Hachette Speakers Bureau provides a wide range of authors for speaking events. To find out more, go to www.hachettespeakersbureau.com or call (866) 376-6591.

ISBNs: 978-1-4555-6869-7 (mass market); 978-1-4555-4212-3 (ebook)

Printed in the United States of America

OPM

10 9 8 7 6 5 4 3 2 1

To Poppy Mae, who sat on my lap while I wrote 98.9 percent of this book. You're my sweetest potato. PS: Please stay out of the garbage and toilet. Thanks.

Acknowledgments

No book is ever made in isolation, and I've been blessed to have amazing help along the way. First, a thank you to my new Grand Central editor, Michele Bidelspach, whose gentle challenges and whip-smart insights pushed me in all the best ways. Also, my agent, Emily Sylvan Kim, having you in my corner as a friend and trusted advisor makes me one lucky lady. To my critique partners on this, Jennifer Ryan, Amy Pine, Jennifer Blackwood, and Jules Barnard, thanks for the reads and valuable two cents. To Chanel Cleeton, Megan Erickson, Kennedy Ryan, Natalie Blitt, and everyone at NA Hideaway for having my back. To my family, it's not easy (or particularly clean) living with a working writer, but you are my people and I'm so grateful. Nick, thanks for continuing to teach me what it means to be in an enduring marriage (compromise, family dinners, occasional adventures, Netflix, lol), and for taking me to visit Scotland. There. I wrote it. No takebacks. Packing my bags. Lastly to my readers—yes, you. Thanks for spending time visiting my world and characters. Reading romance is an exercise in hope, an optimistic gesture in a difficult world. Y'all are my tribe.

Excerpt from The Back Fence:

Everland News That You Actually Care About

Classifieds:

Need a Dog Walker? Got a bored pooch sitting around the house full of energy? Let Ruff Love Pet Walkers throw you a bone. One hour, fast-paced (no jogging) outdoor adventures. Call Norma at 912-555-9867. Discounts available for daily clients.

Snug Cottage for Rent: Sunny, furnished one bedroom, one bathroom bungalow available on Love Street. Quiet neighborhood. Contact Doris Carmichael at 912-555-1700—no texting. Please respond with why this ad sounds attractive to you, and when you'll be able to move in. Do NOT contact me with unsolicited services or offers.

Free Lazy-Boy: Earl don't need two and I want room for my sewing table. It's sitting on the curb. 208 Kissing Ct.

Chapter One

One week later...

Pepper glanced around the cul-de-sac, another bead of sweat trickling down her brow. Sun charred the silvery Spanish moss draping the live oaks while the high-waisted Spanx beneath her pencil skirt compressed her organs into diamonds. Good thing she didn't believe in signs from the universe because this shortcut through Hopes and Dreams Way had turned out to be a dead end. Moisture prickled behind her knees, under her boobs, and between her thighs.

Please, Universe. Don't be a sign.

Her judicial clerkship offer had hinged on an immediate start date. The last week was a blur, packing her Manhattan life into three suitcases. She'd stepped off the Greyhound yesterday afternoon with barely enough time to pick up the keys for her new rental house and visit the local Piggly Wiggly, never mind getting oriented.

The absence of a city skyline or a street grid left her sense of direction as broken as the GPS navigation on her smart phone. She huffed a small sigh, blowing up her bangs. Everland, Georgia, appeared to be block after block of grandly renovated antebellum homes, all with jasmine-smothered wrought iron fences, rocking chair–lined verandas, and names like Love Street, Forever Boulevard, Hopes and Dreams Way, and Kissing Court.

Better find a dentist. A year surrounded by this much sugary sweetness put her at risk of a cavity (or five).

A glance at her wristwatch revealed that her Human Resources appointment wasn't for another forty-five minutes. Her shoulders relaxed. It paid to be prepared. Dead end or no, she'd left herself ample time to fire Siri and navigate her own route to the courthouse.

The lace curtains in the gingerbread Queen Anne across the street twitched and a blue-rinsed older woman peered through the slit with a frown. Pepper adjusted the strap on her leather computer bag and bit down on the inside of her cheek. First impressions were everything, and a Yankee fish out of water marinating in a pool of her own perspiration wasn't a great one.

Head down, she quickly backtracked, retracing her steps. Homesickness nipped at her heels. Or more accurately… sister-sickness. Tonight there'd be no cuddle fest over Chinese takeout in Tuesday's Hell's Kitchen walkup, no debriefing about her day before her sister performed—in side-splitting detail—impersonations from her latest Broadway casting call. There wasn't time for a check-in, but she could fire off the next entry of their ongoing Ugly Selfie Challenge and let Tuesday know she was in her thoughts.

Pepper paused beneath the Forever Boulevard street sign, stuck out her iPhone, and contorted her face into a hideous, triple-chinned expression.

And that's when it happened.

The menacing growl sluiced icy dread through her insides, numbing her core. She didn't have to turn her head to confirm what her body reacted to on instinct.

Dog, two o'clock.

Collapsing her shoulders in a protective cringe, arms shielding her face, she recoiled in jerky steps as fast as her tight skirt allowed. A white ball of fluff with matching organza ear ribbons sat on a red-bricked walkway in the shade of palmetto fronds—devil's spawn in a lap dog disguise. It curled back its lips to reveal razor sharp fangs.

Pug or Pit Bull, it didn't matter. Man's best friend was her worst nightmare.

The tiny tail twitched. She swallowed a whimper. *Easy, easy now.* The fence separating them was five feet high. Fluffy wasn't going to spring through the air, latch on to her throat, and gnaw her jugular like a corn cob. Dogs were statistically more likely to lick a person to death.

By a lot.

By a lot, a lot.

But try telling that to her dry mouth and trembling hands.

The growls crescendoed into shrill yaps. Fluffy reared on hind legs, an eight-pound demon cavorting in the seventh circle of hell.

Pepper's stomach responded with a queasy burble. More yowling rose ahead, a Boxer-looking hellbeast tried cramming its fat head through its white picket prison. *Nope.* She veered around a parked minivan and crossed the street, pulse leaping with panic.

"They don't want to hurt me. They don't want to hurt me," she chanted a mantra from Canine Calm, a weekend cognitive therapy clinic she'd shelled out three hundred bucks on after a close encounter with a Shih Tzu in SoHo last summer left her, well, shit-tzuing her pants.

Blink and breathe. Unravel the negative feelings within before they unravel you. Observe fearful emotions and give them space as they arise, watching them float away like soap bubbles. Blink without judgment. Remember, there is no right way or wrong way to blink. Simply be the blink.

Blink that. She'd dropped out an hour into the nonrefundable session. But now her ears were hot and her jaw tight, all the hallmarks of spiking blood pressure.

She could chant "They don't want to hurt me" all day, but the faint white scars on her cheek, one below her eye, and the other to the side of her nose, the exact match to a Doberman pinscher's mouth, begged to differ. Her nervous system issued a warning: *Imminent threat to life and limb. Take cover.*

Two Corgis joined the din, followed by a baritone bow-wow-wow from another backyard.

Which way to go? No direction was safe.

"Is that lady dancing?" a high-pitched voice asked behind her.

"Dunno," another answered.

Pepper turned, and two kids, the girl in a full-skirted pirate getup, the boy in artfully ragged breeches, froze on identical scooters. Their chubby pink-tinged cheeks offset tawny skin, and matching skull-and-crossbones hats perched on top of their thick, black curls.

"Ahoy there, mateys." It sounded like she'd been sucking helium. She cleared her throat, striving for a more natural tone. "Don't you two look cute."

The little girl scratched the side of her nose. "Mama's using us as models—"

"For the Village Pillage ad." The boy fiddled with his eye patch. "She works for Mayor Marino's office, and we gotta beat Hogg Jaw—"

"Village Pillage?" Any distraction from the canine chorus was welcome. Even if it meant hanging out with kindergarteners.

"Memerating Cap'n Redbeard—"

"And Everland's true claim to the lost treasure."

Deciphering hieroglyphics might be easier than understanding those last sentences. Pepper frowned. "You mean commemorating?"

"And Mama promised us ice cream afterward if we smile real good." The girl bared her teeth in an overwide grin or grimace, hard to say which. "Two scoops of Superman flavor for me and mint chip for Will. Daddy said it was bribery, but Mama calls it in-cent-i-vi-zing." She pronounced the last word with careful enunciation.

"Mint chip is one of my favorites, too." Thank God, her ploy worked. The dogs were losing interest the longer they chatted.

"Why do you talk funny?" Caution crept into the little boy's voice, presumably William.

"You mean my accent? Well, see, I'm from Manhattan." A five-year-old had burned her, but who cares? The longer she rambled in the street, the better the chance that awful barking might eventually stop. "Lower East Side. At least that's where I feel that I'm from. I was born in Moose Bottom, Maine, a place even smaller than here, if you can believe that. Located between Podunk and Boondock. No joke. And that's not taking into account Boonie to the south or Timbuktu to the west."

The children's mouths hung open.

Had she spoken too loudly? Too friendly? Too weird? She had no experience chatting up small people. Kids might as well be aliens from the planet Crayon Gobbler, but these two saved her from a public panic attack. She'd had to suck it up and owe them one.

"William John! Katydid!" An elegant black woman appeared on the top step of an ivy-covered house on the corner. Her tailored fuchsia wrap dress popped against her skin's rich bronze, and her long dark hair was pulled into a sleek ponytail. "Get your scrawny behinds back here and brush your teeth. Ah, ah, ah!" She held up a hand, a diamond catching the sunlight. "Don't go telling me that you already did because your toothbrushes aren't wet. Let's go, let's go, we're not going to be late, I'll tell you that much for free."

"Aw, man!"

"Coming, Mama!" The siblings shot Pepper a last lingering look before pushing off on their scooters, whispering as they powered toward the crosswalk.

She gave the woman a *just passing by, I'm a friendly new-in-town stranger who is not trying to kidnap your sweet children* wave. The tentative gesture was met with a distracted smile.

Pepper tucked the corner of her shirt back into her skirt, swallowing an envious lump as the woman reset her Bluetooth earpiece and disappeared inside the magnificent home. Fat chance *she* ate a Pop-Tart for dinner. Imagine having a big house. Cute kids. Effortless fashion sense. The total package.

Must be nice.

Someday she'd meet Mr. Right. One teeny tiny clerkship in Georgia and she'd be off to bigger and better things back in New York. At this very moment, her true love might be staring out his corner office with sweeping views of the East River as inexplicable longing compresses his chest. "You're out there," he'd mutter, slamming a fist against his open palm. "Out there somewhere. And I shall find you, my dearest darling."

Sooner or later, their gazes would connect in a crowded intersection and boom, a part of her soul would lock into his and that would be it. Cue the balloon drop. Blazing meteoroids. Unicorns dancing the fox trot. Rainbows—make that *double* rainbows—bursting over the cityscape. She'd plan a wedding in the Hamptons, stop hitting snooze on her biological clock, and have her own perfect life.

Yeah.

Someday...

But on the bright side, *right now* she was finally heading in the right direction. A statue of Lady Justice rose from the end of the street, keeping watch over the Scooter B. Merriweather Courthouse, armed with a sword, balance scales, and a fierce resting bitch face. Pepper flashed her a thumbs-up. Ahead, her reflection beamed off the courthouse's glass front door, projecting the image of—

Oh. Schnikey.

Desperate times called for a discreet bang fluff. Taming these frizzy, more-brown-than-blond locks into an A-line bob was a battle at the best of times. Georgia humidity required full-scale war with a leave-in conditioner offensive followed by a barrage of mousse, a wide-toothed comb, professional-grade blow dryer, and straightener.

God as her witness, she refused to sport flyaways on her first day. She smoothed her part, shifting left and right, checking for VSL—visible Spanx lines—a real and present danger as her skirt warped and wrinkled.

Wrenching the door open, she stumbled beneath the rotunda, stifling a relieved moan. Got to credit the South's mastery of the fine art of air-conditioning. The wall directory listed Human Resources on the second floor, down the hall from her new boss, the Honorable Aloysius P. Hogg. Judge Hogg maintained a notorious reputation on the law clerk circuit. Whispers hinted that he didn't interview for a Monday-through-Friday job, but expected seven-day-a-week indentured servitude, including all public holidays.

On her way upstairs, the brass handrail cooled her damp palm. This wasn't a dream job, but no one hired professional cupcake testers. And this year of dues paying in Nowheresville, USA, would land her back in Manhattan with a real shot at making junior partner with Kendall & Kline Associates, an elite corporate law firm with an impressive starting salary and more impressive annual bonus.

Her phone buzzed with a text. Tuesday's image flashed on the screen, her sister's full lips pressed in the ultimate duck face as she did that unsettling trick where she crossed only one eye. The message read: Good luck today! You've come a long way, baby.

Pepper grinned. Her sister was right. This courthouse was a far cry from her family's sugar bush farm in Maine's North Woods.

The sticky truth about the maple syrup business was that people didn't get into it to increase their bank account balance. Yes, there'd always been food on the table (provided coupons were cut), (hand-me-down) clothes on her back, and a (sometimes leaky) roof overhead—although prohibitive heating oil costs meant huddling around a cast-iron stove during the winter months.

Dad boasted they were rich in love, but Mom's parting

words before leaving them behind for New Hampshire were tattooed on Pepper's brain. "Whoever said money can't buy happiness must have been poor, honey. Never ever forget that."

And she never ever did.

Dad tried to put a positive spin on the situation: "From now on, girls, we're a trio. Good thing three is my lucky number." But there was no glossing over the fact that Mom had reinvented herself into a far-off Bedford suburb, remarrying a banker and becoming more invested in his stock portfolio than her two girls.

Pepper tried to be a de facto wife to Dad—cooking, cleaning, organizing appointments—and a surrogate mother to Tuesday—nagging her for homework, making lunches, styling her long blond hair before they hurried to catch the school bus.

The more Mom faded from their life, the more Pepper stepped in as Superwoman, self-appointed guardian of the family, and good thing, too. These days Dad was one bad sciatica attack away from being unable to handle the farm's rigorous physical demands, and how long before Tuesday's dreams of Broadway stardom dimmed? Her father and sister were reality escape artists, but someday they'd need her and her pragmatism. Pepper was the third little pig, busily building a sensible future.

Or do you need them to need you?

She lengthened her stride, walking faster than the whisper of doubt. At the end of the hall, Human Resources waited, promising the answers to her prayers. She let out a huge breath, the smallest trace of a smile settling on her lips. *Almost there.* A little routine paperwork and she'd carpe the heck out of this diem.

Chapter Two

⟿

The hum from the fluorescent lights cut through the examination room's silence. Rhett removed his stethoscope eartips with an inward groan.

"Well? Is he gonna pull through, Doctor?" The redhead in the sunflower sundress hitched her breath. No one gave a performance like Kennedy Day. No wonder she'd done well in all those pageants back in high school.

But the real kudos had to go to Muffin, the Bichon Frise valiantly playing dead on the stainless steel surgical table. Still, not even expert training could override a strong, healthy heartbeat.

Proper Southern manners dictated a few words of comfort, but his growing migraine crowded out any chivalrous impulses. "He's going to live to lick another day."

Kennedy clapped her hands without a hint of embarrassment. "Aren't you a regular miracle worker?"

And aren't you one hell of a dog trainer?

He reached into his white lab coat pocket and removed a treat. In an instant, Muffin bounded to his feet with a short but definitive yip. "Seems Lazarus here has worked up a healthy appetite."

"Praise the Lord and pass the mashed potatoes. Come to Mama, Muffin Wuffin." Kennedy scooped up the dog and smacked wet kisses on the top of its head.

Muffin stared at him darkly, telecommunicating, *See what I'm dealing with? Be a bro and hand over a Barkie Bite.*

Rhett passed the treat in solidarity.

"Silly me!" Kennedy's shoulders shook with her tinkling laugh. "Before I forget, I brought you something special." She reached into the bedazzled insulated bag beside her chair and removed a cake, as if bearing a fake dead dog and baked goods were normal occurrences.

Everland, his hometown, could be described many different ways, but *normal* wasn't the first adjective that sprang to mind.

The real miracle to this appointment would be shuffling Kennedy out before getting asked around for dinner. She sported that same determined look while wielding a pump-action shotgun on the opening day of turkey season. She might primp into the textbook definition of a Southern belle but had crack-shot aim when a tom was in her sights.

"This right here is the praline Bundt that's won the Everland Fair's Golden Fork five years running." She positioned the cake to make it impossible to miss the caramel glaze or her cleavage. "You do like a nice Bundt, don't you, Dr. Valentine?" She dropped her voice to a purr. "Or are you more of a sour cream pound cake man?

Dessert had never sounded so dirty.

"Rhett," he snapped automatically. "Plain Rhett suits me fine." The words *Dr. Valentine* made him want to check over his shoulder for his father and make a sign to ward off the evil eye. "We graduated a year apart. My dad coached Sailing Club. Your brother Kingston was on my team."

"Of course." She leaned forward with a suggestive wink. "And might I say you've gone from a dingy to a yacht."

Time to hustle her out before things turned dangerous. He didn't want to lead her on. Not when her megawatt smile gave him flash blindness, even as shadows haunted beneath her eyes. Everyone knew last year's divorce had hit her hard. Breakups sucked. He understood. He even sympathized. But at the end of the day, her failed marriage wasn't his circus.

He had his hands full with his own damn monkeys.

"Listen. About the cake." He handed it back and led her toward the door. "My office policy is never to accept gifts from—"

"Gift?" She halted so fast her heels scuffed the linoleum. "Why it's nothing but a harmless little nut cake!"

"Did Lou Ellen put you up to this?" His sister acted like her fourth term as second vice president of the Everland Ladies Quilt Guild was a mandate to nominate him as the town's most eligible bachelor, as if his single status was due to circumstance rather than choice.

Online dating profiles kept popping into his inbox, as well as invitations to donate a dinner and movie date to the upcoming Village Pillage silent auction, or meet so-and-so's third cousin, niece, dental hygienist, or belly-dance instructor. If he dared to smile at a woman at the post office, the local gossip blog, the Back Fence, posted a poll about wedding cake flavors by sundown.

He'd rather lick one of his waiting room chairs than date under that kind of scrutiny. Besides, bachelorhood came with undeniable perks:

He never woke without the covers.

Never got an arm ache from spooning.

Never had to fake laugh at a chick flick.

And when blue balls struck, well, his right hand had him covered.

Yep, all a man needed was a cold beer, a boat, and a couple of dogs.

And if he ever hit his head hard enough to climb back on the relationship horse, it would be to a low-maintenance country girl who made up for a lack of drama with a love of big bird dogs. Labs would work. Or Chesapeake Bay Retrievers.

"Weeeeell, I *did* run into Lou Ellen last week at the club." Kennedy's cheeks tinged pink as he opened the exam room door. "And she may have let slip that you were in need of a little female companionship. After all, it has been a long time since...well..."

Ah. And there it was. His own personal elephant in its own personal corner.

He reached for the knob, careful not to grind his molars, at least not audibly. If there were a better way to deal with references to that one time he was left at the altar...he hadn't found it.

Once, just once, it would be nice to make it a goddamn week without some reference to Birdie.

"Remember this, Rhett Valentine." Kennedy squeezed his bicep, her thick gardenia perfume exacerbating his headache. "There's no *I* in happiness."

"Come again?"

She screwed her nose like he'd come up a few Bradys short of a bunch. "H-a-p-p-y-n-e-s-s?"

He took a deep breath. She had to go. Now. Before he said something he regretted.

He ushered her and Muffin into the foyer. "Don't forget to grab a Milk-Bone in the bowl by the magazine rack." He shut the door, the loud snick cutting her off mid-protest.

He scrubbed his jaw, eying the locked cabinet that stored the horse tranquilizers. Lou Ellen was going to raise hell once she caught wind of this snub.

Tempting, but nah. "Suck it up, Buttercup," he muttered. If the biggest problem in his life was a bossy big sister determined to sail him off into a happy-ever-after sunset, he should be grateful that things were looking up.

Or at least not facedown in the gutter.

Was he happy? Well-meaning busybodies pestered him with the question, but no one ever quit talking long enough to hear his answer.

Yeah. He was. Happy enough anyway.

He didn't return to his office until Kennedy's Miata convertible screeched from the parking lot. His three Golden Retrievers, Faulkner, Steinbeck, and Fitzgerald, dozed on their respective pillows and didn't flinch when his desk phone rang.

"Valentine Veterinary," he answered.

"The council work session got postponed to next Thursday," Beau Marino drawled in his deep, no-nonsense tone. He was Everland's youngest mayor in a century, son of a Bermudan bartender and local blueblood, and Rhett's best friend since kindergarten. "Weather service predicts it'll be blowing seventeen this afternoon with gusts to twenty."

"Sounds good." Rhett broke into a grin. They jointly

owned the *Calypso*, a bachelor pad in the form of a coastal cruiser moored at Buccaneers Marina. "I don't have an appointment for an hour. I'll swing by home for the marina key and pick you up after work."

"You know where to find me." Beau lived in Belle Mont Manor, the biggest house in the county, but he called city hall home. Worked around the clock.

Rhett hung up and drummed his fingers on the desktop, shedding the irritation from Kennedy's appointment like an onionskin. An evening sail should screw his head on straight. Always did.

As his headache faded, the wall clock chimed ten o'clock. Outside the street-facing window, a silver-haired man in a seersucker suit led a Maltese whose lavender ribbons matched his bow tie. Doc passed the same time each day, a warm and cozy thirty seconds carefully orchestrated to make his only son feel like shit.

And the gambit worked.

Migraine roaring back, Rhett opened his top drawer, shook two ibuprofen from the bottle, and chased the pills with a swallow from the cold coffee in the mug next to his keyboard.

What masqueraded for an innocent pleasure stroll was, in point of fact, a one-man protest against Valentine Veterinary. Doc had made good on his long-ago vow never to darken the door to Rhett's office—going so far as to drive to TLC Pet Hospital in Hogg Jaw for Marie Claire's care—a dick move, but it proved the saying about Valentine men. They did stay true.

Even if it was to words spoken in anger.

Rhett was groomed to study family or internal medicine at Duke and join his dad's practice, not bolt to UGA and become a doctor of *veterinary* medicine.

Mama's death had sent them both to hell, but they dealt with different devils. Seemed his old man was bent on sailing into his final years on a bitter ship.

God-fucking-speed.

As for him, Rhett had his dogs, a growing practice, and low tolerance for bullshit. He was sick and tired of being the bad son for having a different vision of his future. He sank into his leather office chair, shoved his glasses up his forehead, and exhaled.

Next to his computer perched a brass-framed black-and-white photograph of a laughing woman surrounded by two labs, a Siamese cat, lop-eared rabbits, lovebirds, and three guinea pigs.

He grabbed the picture and ran his thumb over the glass. To live with Ginny Valentine meant to love loudly, indiscriminately, and with gusto. Doc tolerated the chaos because it made his wife happy, and she was his sun, the light in all their lives. Rhett's core constricted as if an invisible screwdriver tightened his solar plexus. Did Mama watch over them? He set the frame back down. There'd never been a single sign after her death. No visitation dreams. No soft shift to the air as he turned his shoulder muscles to jelly beating on the speed bag in his tool shed or sanded cedar planks for the fishing skiff he was building in his backyard.

Nothing. Not even during the whole bad business with Birdie.

With any luck, Mama was up there plenty distracted by drinking gin with Margaret Mitchell, her favorite author. Or flying. She always said that's the one thing she wished she could do, fly wild and free like one of the storm petrels that haunted the coast.

His gut twisted knowing how much she'd hate the way

her beloved family had grown apart in her absence. Lou Lou smothered everyone in her path, relentless as a weedy vine. Dad sheathed himself in a thick shell, gnarled and bitter as a walnut casing. And Rhett, well, he grew long "keep your fucking distance" spines like a prickly pear cactus.

He couldn't fix any of that, but so help him, he'd give Mama a fitting legacy—a rescue shelter that bore her name. The Virginia Valentine Memorial Shelter would be her real monument, not that cold slab of ornate granite nestled beneath a dogwood in the Everland cemetery. Her love and compassion for any animal great or small deserved to be made permanent through bricks and mortar.

Or do you want to atone? He rubbed the lines between his brow as if the gesture would erase the gnawing question.

If Mama was a saint, he was another simple sinner who kept on trying.

Word from the Low Country Community Foundation was that the construction loan was as good as wrapped up. The last obstacle before being deemed "shovel ready" was persuading Doc to donate the land. The shelter deserved to be built on the spot where Mama used to take them to play as children, the small rise where live oaks rang with katydids and tree frogs, herons silently stalked the tidal marsh at the bottom, and in the distance the ocean unfurled across the horizon like one of those bright blue ribbons Mama wore in her hair.

He drained the rest of the coffee, grimacing at the final acidic swallow. *Shit.* He'd put off the request long enough, but for better or worse, Doc was his dad. The guy who'd walked him around the back patio on his feet, taught him how to trim a sail, and helped him win third in the state science fair with his stem cell research project.

The guy who'd championed him.

Rhett's gaze tracked the ceiling fan in mute outrage. What the hell? Maybe Doc deserved a thank-you, because nothing ever made Rhett want to succeed at his clinic like the fact his father openly rooted for his failure.

"All right. Let's get this over with," he announced to the dogs. They scrambled to attention as he stood and grabbed the three leashes dangling off the hook by the door.

Doc was a creature of habit. Not only could Rhett set a clock by his dad's morning walk, but the man had a sweet tooth. Right now he must be stopping into the What-a-Treat Candy Boutique for his daily Charleston Chew before joining the Scrabble game at the dog park. With a little hustle, Rhett could catch him by the courthouse.

He shoved on his glasses and adjusted the frames. This conversation was going to be as fun as a poke in the eye with a sharp stick.

But nothing good ever came easy.

Chapter Three

Sorry. I misheard you." Pepper forced a laugh even as her stomach rode a high-speed elevator straight to her toes. "It sounded like you just said that I don't have a job."

The HR administrative assistant's polite smile died a slow death. Two faint lines emerged between her brows. "Pepper Knight, is it?"

"Yeah, that's me." She took out a tube of gloss and smoothed it over her dry lips. In another minute or two, she'd chuckle about the misunderstanding, once the dust cleared and she signed her hiring documents.

The woman tapped on her keyboard before making a series of henlike clucks. "Oh. I see. Oh dear."

"What?" Pepper pressed two fingers against her sternum. The last thing she wanted to do was play "heartburn or heart attack?"

"My boss left me a note before going to Myrtle Beach." Another cluck. "Your offer was withdrawn. I was supposed to follow up, but the notification went into my spam folder. Hand to chest, this computer upgrade is making me crazier than a one-legged cat in a sandbox."

"Withdrawn?" Pepper's heart accelerated from third to fifth gear. Her neck muscles tightened. In pressure cooker situations some people became carrots, limp and lifeless. She was an egg. Hot water hardened her. She focused on the woman's name placard. "Listen, uh, Maryann." The struggle for a smile was real. "Let's be reasonable. Of course I have a position. One that I applied, accepted, and, most importantly, *relocated* for." Pressure built in her skull. She'd jumped at this clerkship rather than holding out for a more desirable location in Boston or DC because it was a guaranteed bird in the hand. A *safe* choice.

"What can I do to make this work? A background check? A drug test? I can pee right now. Right here. Well, not *here*, here, of course, but—"

"I'm sorry, darlin'. This one's out of my hands. The position is revoked." Maryann unscrewed her Diet Coke and took a long swallow before leaning forward, her voice a confidential whisper. "You didn't hear it here, but this decision came from up the food chain, see. The judge's mama is a long-time friend of Senator Haynes, *the* Senator Haynes, chairperson of the Senate Finance Committee, who called in an emergency favor. His oldest grandson has gone wild and needs discipline." She straightened and resumed her loud voice. "But a pretty, smart thing like you? Why you'll land on your feet in no time at all."

"No." The walls closed in like an Indiana Jones movie. The floor dropped out like a sinister Tower of Terror. "This. Is. Not. Happening."

She'd entered a wormhole. This office was a portal to

a parallel universe, a nightmare land where darkest dreams come true. Nothing was as terrifying as the HR assistant's sympathetic expression.

Pepper went to reapply more protective lip gloss, but the tube slipped from her trembling fingers, hit the floor with a clatter, and rolled under a nearby desk.

Looked like the universe had indeed given her a sign this morning. Her hopes and dreams *were* at a dead end.

"My job offer was rescinded." Hot electrical currents zinged through her spine. "Regifted to a member of some back-scratching boy's club?"

"What's the thing all you lawyers say?" Maryann held up her hands. "Time to plead the fifth. I said too much already."

"But this is straight up sexist, nepotistic *bullshit*!" The final word burst out as the beige and cream office decor faded behind a scarlet haze. How many years had she worked her butt off (or rather, grown it through midnight Chips Ahoy stress eating sessions)? NYU engendered a culture of extreme anxiety. Sleep deprivation, tension, and the dream of a social life someday were her constant companions because there was a future payoff. She needed this—no, scratch that—she *deserved* this job and all that went with it. Stability. Security. A chance to build a future on a rock solid foundation capable of weathering any of life's storms.

She earned this.

Her body moved before her brain could register the fact. She slammed out of the Human Resources office, the door reverberating off the stopper with a satisfying thud. At the end of the hall, gold leaf calligraphy spelled out THE HONORABLE A. HOGG.

"Honorable?" she seethed. "Ha!" Judge Hogg didn't

know who he messed with. He was tangling with the person who came in top of the class in oral arguments.

"Miss? Miss!" Maryann shouted in the distance. "I wouldn't go in—"

Pepper stepped into the waiting room. A middle-aged woman in a lavender twinset and pearls glanced up from a file open on her mahogany desk.

"I'm here to see the judge."

The forthright demand garnered a lemon-sucking face. "He isn't to be disturbed this morning."

"Trust me." Pepper clenched her hands into patriarchy-fighting fists, heart pounding like a war drum. "He hasn't seen disturbing."

That's right. Time for justice to be served.

The assistant arched her overdrawn eyebrows in a "your funeral" gesture before shoving on a headset and hitting an intercom button. "Your Honor?" A pause. "Yes, I do, and I apologize. But there is someone out here insisting on speaking with you. A woman, sir." Another pause. "Name?" she snapped.

"Pepper. Pepper Knight." This woman wasn't getting her vote for Employee of the Year.

The assistant repeated the name and nodded. "Yes, I see. Loud and clear, sir."

"Well?" Pepper shouldered her laptop bag as the assistant hung up.

"I'm afraid Judge Hogg's not in."

Pepper refused to break eye contact. "You spoke to him thirty seconds ago."

The other woman didn't blink. "And he says he's not here."

"But—"

"Have yourself a good day."

Unless she wanted to kick in the door, there wasn't anywhere else she could take this. Not right now. "Tell him he'll be hearing from me. I'll write to the governor's office." That's right. Bust out the big guns. She might be a lowly law grad, but she was scrappy.

"He and Governor Merriweather are playing at a charity golf event together next week down at Sea Island Golf Club." The assistant opened up a stick of Juicy Fruit and bent it into her mouth.

"I see." Pepper's shoulders slumped. She was outgunned.

"Now if you don't mind, I have things to do." The assistant snapped her gum, clicking the mouse poised on her "Keep Calm and Carry On" pad.

Pepper pressed her lips into a white slash. How could anyone keep calm when job offers evaporated into thin air, or overused phrases got slapped on everything under the sun?

"Bless your heart." The assistant glanced over again, her disdain dripping from every feature. "You're still here."

"I'm going, going...gone." Pepper tried slamming this door, too, but it was on a hydraulic hinge. No satisfying bang. Instead it closed slower than a Toto toilet seat.

So much for moxie.

She paused at the top of the stairs, leaning heavily on the bannister, dizzier by the second. Shit. The Spanx cut off her circulation. She'd embrace any and all lumps and bumps to be free of this twenty-first-century corset.

The lobby was a blur, and her lungs clogged as she stumbled outside into the humidity. Drowning on air was an actual possibility. A row of ants marched down the sidewalk in regimental lines. They had somewhere to go. A job. Purpose.

Lucky jerks.

She chewed her lower lip, throat aching from all the curse words she stuffed down. The embarrassing-to-admit truth was that she'd harbored a secret fantasy where she'd turn up for this job and everyone would go "Hey, wow. This one's special." Exceptional even. They'd take one look and see all of her promise and the kind of legal pluck reserved for a John Grisham novel.

"On your left. Whoa there. Moving by, moving by, like it or not."

Pepper swung around in time to see a tornado of tails, fur, and tongues. The woman in the middle of the chaos wore a Ruff Love Pet Walkers T-shirt and hurried past, her outstretched arms grappling four straining leashes.

Pepper's blood pressure skyrocketed at the horrific sight. Okay, there were worse fates. She rubbed her temples in a calming circle. She needed to take a moment, have a good long shower cry, and form a new plan. She'd start by drafting a list. Yes, a list—very official thing, a list. Full of options.

She crossed the street and paused, bracing her hands on her knees, sucking in the thick hot air in great, greedy gulps. *Don't vomit. Don't vomit.*

"You know this is what she wanted." A deep voice boomed from behind the hedgerow framing the town green, not a shout per se, but hardly civil.

She heard another man snort. The thick branches blocked any view. "It would have broken her sweet heart seeing you abandon the family practice. Tradition meant everything to her."

"The situation is not that cut and dried and you know it."

"You presume to know *my* wife's mind?"

"She was *my* mother." The hedgerow shook, like someone kicked it.

Pepper backed away slowly. That argument sounded like not her problem. She had enough to worry about without—

Zzzzzt.

Her head snapped up. Thunderheads blotted out the sun. The air smelled like rain.

Zzzzzt.

A dark brown roach rocketed across her field of vision. What was worse than hallucinating? Not hallucinating a flying bug on steroids. Time to turn tail and flee. Except her beloved Miu Mius weren't made for running. Strutting? Yep. Kicking ass and taking names. You better believe it. But not a fifty-meter dash across the plaza's herringbone brick path.

It bombed her like a two-inch kamikaze, passing dangerously close to her earlobe, rustling her hair. Her heart raced, and not just from the unexpected exertion. Breathing was impossible.

No. Nuh-uh. Nope.

She swiveled her head up and down the quiet cross street, seeking safe harbor. Pointless. Scary Bug wasn't going to honor any "Ollie Ollie in come free" code and go cavorting off to the nearest dung heap. Was that truck over there unlocked?

Zzzzzt.

Holy Joe. Cold dread seeped into her bones, freezing her marrow. Her skin tightened. Scary Bug was on her body. Her actual person. First the dogs and now this? *Hello, God, it's me, Pepper. Kill me and make it quick.*

Thick antennae tickled her neck and the ice melted into hot terror. Her heel caught a concrete crack, holding her foot fast even as the rest of her body kept moving. The world tilted. Three Golden Retrievers, trailing leashes, tongues flapping in the breeze, barreled around the hedge.

"Steinbeck, Fitzgerald, I said stay, dammit! Faulkner, come on, man, not you, too."

She turned toward the shout, arms flailing like a Gumby blowup from in front of a car dealership as the leader took to the air, paws landing square on her chest, sending her flat-backed in the gutter.

She curled into a ball, bracing for the moment when teeth bit down. Instead, no crevice remained unsniffed. The torturous waiting grew in intensity until someone—presumably the owner of these hellhounds—ordered them to back off. The commanding drawl was familiar.

The exasperated tone from behind the hedgerow.

The buzzing intensified. No time to put a face to the voice. She ripped her hand through her hair, and Scary Bug struck the concrete, bouncing twice before coming to a stunned stop. She scrambled to a half-sit. It would give her nothing but grim pleasure to drive a stiletto straight through its mother-loving exoskeleton. She raised her foot, took careful aim, and—

"Look out!"

She froze mid-stab, heel clattering off. Scary Bug took to the air with a final mocking *Zzzzzt!*

"Oh no, it escaped."

"Word of advice"—now the deep voice sounded less wound up and more bemused—"step on a palmetto and you'll be sorry. They stink something fierce."

She stared up. "A pal-mett-oh…" The question fizzled on her lips, doused by deep-set eyes framed by a pair of Clark Kent–style glasses. Dreamboat eyes. A shade reserved for tropical ocean photos touting Caribbean vacations, a deep marine blue that invited a person to sit back and float away.

"I don't know what wild hair got into these guys," he muttered. "I've never seen them act that way."

She floated.

And panted. Wait, no, that wasn't her. A wet nose snuffled against her ear and she was back standing barefoot in a gravel road puddle as the neighbor's guard dog barreled toward her, trailing its broken chain.

She yelped, panic twisting her spine, leaving her cowering.

"That's enough. I said back off, Faulkner." He scooped the dog leashes and tugged them close to his side, tousling his messy shock of sandy brown hair. "Are you okay?"

"I—I—I..." She couldn't breathe. Or think. But she wasn't a child. And she hadn't been bitten.

"Jesus. All right. Listen. Breathe. That's it, take another one. Good. And another."

If her fear was a storm, his voice was a life raft. She anchored her gaze on his face. Safer than the dogs at his side. Those fine lines around his striking eyes suggested he was thirtysomething, with a mouth a shade too wide for his angular jaw. But the lack of symmetry didn't detract. If anything, the imperfection had a curious physiological effect, creating a delay in her brain's language-processing center.

"...no idea what bee crawled up their butts," he was saying. "Let me give you a hand." He took hers with his free one and the rough calluses at the base of his fingers caused friction on her skin. It was a big hand, broad and tanned, with freckles smattering the knuckles. The wind picked up, carrying a hint of soap, a little spicy, a little woodsy, and a lot manly. She leaned in, as somehow the smell could wrap her in some sort of invisible shield, keep her safe and protected.

Except he'd turned his focus over her shoulder. She followed his ferocious gaze to an old man in a seersucker suit currently marching across the Main Street crosswalk, a Scrabble game tucked under one arm, and under the other, Fluffy, her lap dog nemesis from earlier in the morning.

"Sorry if I interrupted something." She shuffled a few feet back from his closest animal, slipping her shoe back on like the world's most awkward Cinderella. "I accidently overheard part of your conversation and—"

He snorted. "Way I see it, conversations are an exchange of ideas, not insults."

Before she could make a hasty retreat, the largest dog lunged. No time to scream before a slick heat swiped her wrist. It was official, on this worst of days she was going to toss her cookies in front of a—if not traditionally handsome, incredibly boyishly cute—man.

His irises darkened to a concentrated indigo, and for a moment she could swear he saw her, really saw her. A person who'd had it up to there, but life went right on pouring. She wanted to linger, bask in the unapologetic stare, let the rest of the world blur into oblivion, as indistinct as an expressionist painting.

Except fraction by fraction his brows pulled closer together. His mouth twitched.

A crazy impulse set in to cry out, *Stop! Don't say anything! Don't ruin it.* Whatever *it* was.

She wanted to clutch *it* to her chest, kick and scream, but the moment was gone.

"You're not a fan of dogs, are you?"

Chapter Four

M e? A dog fan?" The guy's bemused question snapped Pepper from her floaty trance. "I wouldn't say that. Not at all. Not even a little." She shook her head three too many times, as if the moment required an extra lashing of awkward.

Spoiler: It didn't.

"Wait," she blurted as he cleared his throat. Some dim part of her brain registered she wasn't about to stick her foot in her mouth, rather cram it in mid-calf. "Before you say anything, I know, okay? I *know*. Admitting to disliking dogs is like declaring ambivalence to bacon or a belief that *Friends* was a terrible show unworthy of ten seasons. But is that fair? I mean, if a dog person made a glancing remark about how they weren't much of a feline fan, cat people would shrug it off as no big deal. To each their own. But not dog people. No, dog people find it impossible to tolerate canine aversion."

Her pause for a breath was met with silence. He passed a hand over his mouth as if erasing a smile. "You've given this a lot of thought."

"Actually no." She pursed her lips. "That was all off the cuff."

"Impressive." It sounded like he meant "scary." One of the dogs whined.

Frowning, she jabbed a hand to her hip. "Stop looking at me like that."

"Like what?" His brows knit.

"You've got the same expression I did this one time a crazy lady tried selling me a bag of crickets on the subway. Look. I'm a stable—very stable—exceedingly sane person and—aaaaaaaargh!" The closest golden retriever slurped her hand. If a horror film score synched with a whale's death song it might match the noise escaping her mouth.

"Faulkner. That's the last time." The guy yanked hard on the leash. "Quit now. The lady's just not that into you." Her not-so-secret admirer wagged his bushy tail, but retreated to a distance that made it possible for her to draw a shallow breath.

At least the dogs were obedient. That helped. Some.

"I'm sorry. Today's been a nightmare. I was fired from a clerkship with the judge on day one. It takes a special sort of talent to lose a position you apparently didn't even have." *Ixnay on the verbal vomit.* This stranger hadn't been selected at random to compete in the pain Olympics. And from the sound of his behind-the-hedge argument, he had his own personal Lifetime drama playing out.

"Judge?" His glare stilled her frantic gesticulating. "Judge Al Hogg?"

Her jaw twitched at the hated name. "Buddy of yours?"

After all, it was a small town. They might be on the same bowling team.

He coughed in his fist. "Not exactly. But the way I see it, congratulations are in order."

"Congratulations?" Her hands flopped helplessly to her sides, her exhale long and shuddering. "What for?" She didn't have the fortitude to withstand him making fun of her. Her field of fucks was barren.

"Know how every village has an idiot? Well, turns out, the same principle holds true for assholes. Trust me, you'd be happier pumping gas at Payton's Pump-N-Munch out on I-95 than spending a day sucking air with that man."

"Are you honestly trying to put a positive spin on this situation?" She could throw sass or burst into tears. At least option A allowed her to retain a scrap of self-respect.

He shrugged.

"Cute. Too bad my funny bone's as broken as my morale." Overhead, raindrops fell, heavy and cool, and her lower lip trembled. *No, no no, anything but this.* Her tears weren't for public consumption. The least her body could do is hold on until she reached her rental cottage and drew the light-canceling blinds.

Pressure mounted against her diaphragm. A flush crept in. Nothing pretty or delicate. Nope. This was a hippo-splashing-in-a-puddle-of-ketchup affair.

"Miss?" He sounded like he'd rather be anywhere else and she didn't blame him one iota. In fact, she'd like to join him.

Hey here's an idea, let's ditch the weird crying chick and grab a pizza.

Instead she was trapped by an expected "the lady doth protest too much" role.

"It's fine. I'm fine." She shaded her eyes. Not that she had to—the sun was cloaked behind a thick blanket of cloud—but because like it or not, waterworks were fast approaching.

She was jobless and stranded in a town where the biggest store was the Piggly Wiggly. Talk about coming full circle. Georgia might be opposite from Maine in terms of geography, but it turned out that a small town was a small town was a small town. And the path that was supposed to keep her moving forward had led her to a place eerily similar to her original starting point.

She sniffled. Her nose had sprung a leak too. More tears welled. The charming street blurred. What more could happen—a giant meteor?

The first defeated sob shredded her throat. It was almost a relief to stand aside and allow the raw moan to expand into a wail.

"*Awoooooo.*" The dogs ceased lunging and howled off-key. "*Awoooooo.*"

Startled laughter bubbled from deep in her belly. Guess today had that little bit more suck to give.

Life. Hideous and yet hilarious.

* * *

The bawling woman collapsed forward, face-planting against Rhett's chest. Her forceful sobs combined with hysterical cackling reverberated through his ribs. A damsel in distress was one thing, but a knockout in a soaked-through shirt quite another. *Shit.* His mouth was like sawdust as he went to encircle her rigid body, drawing her close, trying to keep every movement slow, deliberate, until, at last, she melted, gripping his shirtfront. Slow-boiling awareness spread through his middle. When was the last time he'd held another person?

She felt good. Incredible, really.

It took effort to dig out his arsenal and find the appropriate defense.

Sympathy.

Only a piece of shit would take advantage in this situation. His teeth fastened to his lower lip. He might be a man of faults, but hadn't descended to scumbag depths. With a free hand, he surreptitiously hunted his back pockets for a handkerchief or Kleenex. Nothing but a crumpled—but clean—napkin from Smuggler's Cove. Best he could come up with on short notice.

"Here." He stuck it out.

"Stop!" Her hands warded him off. "Turn around. Don't look. I mean it."

"Excuse me?" The napkin edges disintegrated in the rain.

"Oh God, fine." She snatched the sodden wad and dabbed her nose muttering something that sounded like "so embarrassing." She heaved a heavy sigh. "What sort of bribe would entice you to pretend that I'm not here?"

"Can't do that. And you—quit." He jerked his head at Steinbeck, who halted, mid-belly creep toward the woman's purse. She must have chocolate in there. He answered that question at least once a week. Yes, chocolate was poisonous to dogs; no, it's not an old wives' tale. It contained theobromine, a stimulant that can mimic caffeine that may affect a canine's heart, central nervous system, and kidneys. And he had a greedy-guts of a dog who seemed to have a death wish anytime a Snickers presented itself within a fifteen-foot radius.

"Sure you can," she ground out. "Gather your dogs, keep walking."

"And leave a woman crying alone in the rain? 'Fraid not. Don't blame me, blame my genetics. Too many generations of manners-instilling Southern mamas."

She forced what was an obviously humoring laugh and moved to collect her bag. He got there first.

"Who can I call to give you a lift?" Make her a cup of tea. Take her down a notch, or ten. "I'd offer you a ride myself but I'm on foot. Rain came faster than expected." That's when he realized how long they'd been talking. In public. Where anyone could see.

His jaw tightened as he scanned the road. Empty. Or so it seemed. But one never knew when they were under surveillance in Everland.

Time to get moving before they attracted unwanted attention, but her own stare fixed on a distant point with an unreadable expression. "I don't know anyone less than eight hundred miles away."

Hell. Like it or not, this situation had him by the balls.

"What's your name?" He shoved his hands into his back pockets and addressed the rain, not wanting to gawk when she was this raw. He was damned if he stayed, damned if he left, so might as well be a fucking gentleman.

She rubbed her temples before nodding, the protocol of introductions seeming to help snap her from her stupor. "Of course. Sorry. I'm Pepper. Pepper Knight."

"Well, Pepper. Pepper Knight. Welcome to Everland. I'm Rhett. Rhett Valentine." Her handshake happened so fast that if he'd blinked, he'd have missed it. "There. Guess you know me now."

"Your name's Rhett?" Her brows vanished beneath a thick curtain of bangs.

He bristled at the note of incredulity. *The Gone with the Wind* reference would be coming in five...four...

"Like Rhett Butler?" She made the connection faster than most.

At least she didn't tack on the usual "Frankly, my dear..." quip.

"Margaret Mitchell published that book in nineteen thirty-six, and it was one of my mama's favorites, but truth be told, there've been Rhetts in my family since fifty years before that." He sound snappish, but that's what you get for living thirty-five years as a man named Rhett in the South.

"Only in Georgia." Her gaze slid across his features with fresh interest before she began walking.

He fell in step behind her, careful to keep his dogs under control. *Jesus.* The view from the back was as enticing as the front. Pepper had more curves than the letter *s*, paring the alphabet to the essentials, omitting everything but *e*, *x*, and *y*. Not that it mattered. No, just an observation. "What are you going to do?" he called.

The rain eased to a gentle pitter-patter. "Who knows?" Her shoulders paid a visit to her ears as she wiped her eyes. "Hitchhike to I-95. Apply to the Pump-N-Munch and see what all the fuss is about?"

He hated the quaver beneath her jaunty tone. "Believe it or not, most days in Everland don't end in tears."

She plucked a rosemary sprig poking through a picket fence and twirled it beneath her fingers before glancing over one shoulder. "Guess I'll have to take your word on that."

There was something stubborn about the way she held herself. And the little mole dotting her top lip classified as adorable. An unfamiliar sensation struck hard, like a sucker punch to the ribs. A feeling that had been gone so long that its existence was almost mythical.

Interest in a member of the opposite sex.

He turned lightly away. Took a steadying breath. "Sorry about the rain."

"I don't melt." She dropped the rosemary on the sidewalk and defiantly swiped a lock of wet hair plastered on her cheek.

He got the picture. She wanted to be left alone. Hell, that was his default setting. Except for the present moment.

Surprising.

Too bad he *hated* surprises.

They walked in mutual troubled silence. Her trudging gait nagged at him. It didn't seem fair she should be loaded by an invisible weight, and yet, who was he to offer to carry the load? She didn't know him from the Man in the Moon, and her gaze might as well be blocked off by caution tape. Anyway, he'd soon be turning off, swinging by his house, and grabbing the marina key. After Doc made it clear that it would be a cold day in hell before the shelter was gifted a single acre of Mama's land, Rhett needed the solace of the ocean more than ever.

At the corner, she pivoted, leveling a direct stare. He tried holding her gaze, but kept investigating the planes of her heart-shaped face.

"Hey." Her keen brown eyes narrowed. "Do you mind not following me?"

"Now wait a minute." He bristled at the unexpected accusation. "You're walking in *my* direction. I'm swinging by home to get my boat key."

"Oh." Her shoulders flagged, the self-righteous wind

dropping from her sails. "Go on ahead then." She stepped aside as thunder rumbled in the distance.

"Hatching a plot to check me out from behind?" His teasing tone relaxed some of the tightness around her eyes. The strange feeling returned, stealing around the perimeters of his mind, a wary cat, suspicious and skittish.

Curiosity about a woman.

A dog-hating woman.

Another clap of thunder shook the sky, a boom of divine laughter. Guess someone up there thought the joke was on him.

"Hilarious." Her half smile belied her deadpan tone.

Yeah. Funny as YouTube videos of idiots jumping off diving boards into frozen pools.

"Don't take my word. I've heard it's a sight to behold," he drawled, taking a left onto Love Street with a pang at the impending separation. "And here we are."

Her heel clicks echoed through his brain in staccato pops. He turned back, scrubbing his jaw. "For the official record, who is following who?"

There was no smile in her eyes, just a deepening suspicion. "How'd you know where I live?"

Words deserted him. "Where *you* live?"

She jerked a chin at the one-story white cottage. "That's my house."

"The old Carmichael place?" A FOR RENT sign had gone up in the window a few weeks ago, but he'd given it little to no thought.

"My landlady is Doris Carmichael. She didn't sound that old."

"It was her great aunt Katherine's place. Dot lives Waynesboro way but can't bear to sell. See the red door?" He pointed to the yellow house to the right.

She frowned in confusion. "Yes."

"That's mine."

"You're kidding." The wet, white blouse clung to her chest, revealing fantastic cleavage and the faintest outline of two nipples. "We're next-door neighbors?"

"Looks like it." *Fuck.* What a time for his dick to pitch a tent. Luckily he'd thrown on jeans this morning and not his usual khakis. Good Samaritans weren't supposed to go hard on the job, especially not while looking out for vulnerable women.

The silence dragged. He counted each beat, willing his untouched-for-far-too-long body under control. But when she swung her hair on the seven-second mark, he forgot what came next. Christ. He almost forgot his damn name.

"All right then. Welcome to Love Street," he broke the silence first, removing his glasses and giving the rain-spattered lenses a wipe with his shirt cuff. "Feel free to hit me up if you need more motivational speeches, or job advice."

"Hey. Wait." Her heartbreaking eyes widened as she fiddled with her front gate latch. "Can I ask you something? It's probably stupid, but do you believe in signs from the universe? Or curses?" The next thunderclap lent a certain portentous punctuation to her sentence.

He paused, startled, before a furtive motion in his peripheral vision squashed any budding amusement. Across the street, Miss Ida May's nose pressed against her bay window. Shit. It had been inevitable someone would see them talking. Any second the Back Fence chat room would be lighting up like a Fourth of July firecracker. What would be the headline this time? Some quip about how he knocked a woman head over heels?

"Signs, no," he said firmly. "Curses, yes."

Pepper nodded, holding his gaze with curious intensity before walking toward her porch steps. He shoved his glasses back on. It took him another few seconds to register the fact that he still stood there, staring. Quickly, he backtracked toward his place, raking a hand through his hair. His new neighbor was trouble with a capital *T*. Better get on inside and chug a glass of ice water. That's it. The heat messed with his head.

Everyone went a little crazy in this weather.

Chapter Five

Pepper cringed at her laptop screen. *Eeesh.* Underpaid NSA grunts must be calling in emergency antidepressant refills after checking her recent search history.

- *Law clerk jobs*
- *Last minute opening law clerk jobs*
- *Waiting list law clerk jobs*
- *How to remove a curse*
- *How to break a lease*
- *Tenant rights and responsibilities in Georgia*
- *What to do if landlord has a termination administration charge*
- *Bank of America checking account*
- *Tenant rights law*
- *Can alcohol be delivered to my home?*
- *Best pizza in Everland Georgia*
- *Photos of Hot Guys Drinking Coffee*

- *Photos of Hot Guys*
- *Photos of coffee*
- *I ruined my life*
- *Directions to Smuggler's Cove*

Her chest was tight, like she'd just finished sprinting up six flights of stairs. Each breath came hard, a halting, shallow spurt. No point in teeth gnashing or fist shaking; neither would change the fact that any clerkship worth its salt had been filled. She reached for her third candy bar, but her fingers skimmed nothing but another empty wrapper.

Sucking chocolate-stained fingers, she plucked a sheet of bubble wrap off the kitchen table, popping a row. Not remotely satisfying. She closed the computer and buried her face in her hands. All she wanted to do was live in her favorite city and get stable, career-wise, love-wise, well, everything-wise. Life was happening right now. All around. Except instead of pressing Play, she was stuck on Pause.

No. Worse.

Rewind.

She stamped her feet, punched the empty cardboard box off the table, and screamed. "Fuck!" She hadn't busted tail to escape one small town only to get mired in another.

Now her throat hurt and the neighbors were probably calling the cops. She picked up the phone and set it back down. Talking to Dad was out. He'd spout off feel-good crap like "failure is success in progress," but she was facing down a big, black tunnel without so much as a pinprick of light at the end. Cliché phrases wouldn't help.

Tuesday wouldn't help, either. She'd say, "move back." As if this boondoggle could be fixed by a simple bus ride home to New York. Not an option given the fact her savings account had dust bunnies in lieu of zeroes, her credit card was maxed from the move and buying work clothes, and oh, last but not least, Mount Student Loans was poised to bury her in an avalanche of debt. Combine that with the fact she'd signed a lease that couldn't be broken without a termination fine bigger than her entire current net worth and what did she have?

A whole lot of nothing.

Some Superwoman.

She resumed popping bubble wrap. In law school, classmates clamored for Pepper-in-rural-Maine childhood stories on the rare nights that a happy hour chocolate martini craving overrode her introversion. They hailed from cities and suburbs where events like getting lunch stolen by a black bear at the bus stop or chopping through ice for drinking water were inconceivable.

"Wow. Imagine growing up like that," they'd sigh, eyes bright with idealism of a simpler life.

But her life in Maine hadn't been one big *Little House on the Prairie*–inspired fantasy. It was work. Hard work. Without the benefit of a dashing Almanzo Wilder to whisk her away on nightly buggy rides. Always one catastrophe away from a hungry belly. No, she couldn't return to that life, could only march forward.

She'd be a success, despite the odds, or the fact she had no idea what to do next.

And one day, Mom would flip open the *Times* and see her oldest daughter winning a case or attending a swanky fundraiser, and call to say how proud she was, ask if they could have coffee or meet for lunch.

Pepper would smile and say, "Let me check my schedule. Oh. Darn. Looks like I have better things to do than get my ass kissed by a social-climbing adulterous hagfish. Hope you rot in your McMansion. Thank you and good day, sir."

Or, yanno, some variation on that.

A freshening breeze blew through the window. She peeked through her fingers, palms pressed on her flushed cheeks. Between the crack in the curtains was a direct line of sight into Rhett's kitchen. Hers was a typical shoebox rental kitchen. Plain. White. Boring. His was spacious, full of inviting natural light and exposed beams. Reclaimed wood cupboards contrasted with stainless steel appliances. Simple. Masculine. No sign of a woman's touch. In fact, the only thing on the countertop besides a block of knives was a bowl filled with green apples. Her favorite. Tart but subtly sweet.

Her stomach rumbled. According to Google, the best pizza in town was at a place called Smuggler's Cove. She didn't have access to a Magic 8 Ball, but a twelve-inch pie might go a long way toward improving her current not-so-good outlook.

It was either that or sit scrolling through Facebook posts of people's adult coloring book pages and perfectly organized day planners or click around snapshots of Hawaiian honeymoons and drooling babies, until she became nothing but a numb brain in a jar, beyond feeling or emotion.

Pizza was better for mental health.

The rain clouds had moved on, and it took five minutes to walk to the restaurant. Small wins. But hey, she'd take what she could get. Smuggler's Cove was a red-brick hole in the wall. The placards on either side of the entrance read TWO BEERS FOR THE PRICE OF TWO BEERS and OUR DRINKS ARE COLDER THAN YOUR EX-GIRLFRIEND'S HEART. She opened the door and stepped inside. The cavernous space was crowded; a rousing sea shanty played over the tinny speakers. The décor was *Gilligan's Island* kitsch meets *Pirates of the Caribbean.*

As she approached the WAIT HERE TO WALK THE PLANK sign, the song ended. Someone dropped a fork. All conversation ceased. Her pulse accelerated. Pepper had never been the kind of pretty girl who made a room fall silent. If this was how it felt, then thank goodness for small favors, because it wasn't nice to be visually picked over like a chicken bone.

"Contacts bothering you?"

"Excuse me?" Pepper startled. A vaguely familiar black woman stood a few feet away studying her with large brown eyes.

"You're blinking a lot," the woman said in a sympathetic tone. "That always happens to me when mine get dry."

"Yes. Right. Darn these lenses," Pepper lied quickly. Her vision was 20/20. "I need some of that, um, solution."

"I'm sorry, I didn't get a chance to introduce myself this morning. Would you like to join me and my children?" The woman smiled a friendly, conspiratorial smile as she extended a manicured hand. "I'm Elizabeth."

"Oh, yes. I remember." The woman from the fabulous house near the park, living the dream as Pepper watched, nose pressed to the glass. "I'm Pepper. But it's okay. I'm here to place a to-go order. I don't want to be an imposition."

"Nonsense. Follow me." Elizabeth didn't wait for additional protest, simply turned and sashayed through the maze of tables. Pepper trailed, a frumpy dwarf behind Snow White.

At the booth, Elizabeth gestured for her to sit on the red

vinyl bench. "I hear you've come from New York City, and I'm simply dying to hear all about it. I haven't been up there since having the kids. I believe you've already met my Kate and Will?"

"Like...*the* Kate and Will." Pepper gave the twins an awkward wave. "The Duke and Duchess of Cambridge, Kate and Will?"

"Such a magical couple." Elizabeth heaved a happy sigh. "I'm the biggest royal fan. I crushed hard on that man when a teenager, but now I'm more obsessed with her. Talk about being my style icon! What I wouldn't give to spend an afternoon raiding her closet."

Pepper laughed in spite of herself. "She does have pretty amazing hair."

"And her purses." Elizabeth held up a black tote with brown leather straps. "I bought this Longchamp Le Pliage after I saw her wearing it in a magazine while getting a blowout." Elizabeth wrinkled her nose. "It's silly. You think I'm silly, don't you? Go on. Admit it. Everyone does."

"You're adorable." Pepper grinned. And it was the truth. There was something unrepentantly high-maintenance about Elizabeth. But she wasn't competitive, just a woman who liked to indulge in the finer things and wasn't embarrassed about it.

Will and Kate were elbows deep in their bowls, the sundaes as large as their heads. "Looks like the photo shoot was a success?" When Pepper spoke to kids, her voice went up an octave and took on the beginnings of a Mary Poppins–like accent. It was weird. Especially as she'd never even set foot in England.

"They told you about my bribery attempt?" Elizabeth asked with an unself-conscious laugh, oblivious to the fact she was dealing with a child-fearing weirdo. "Bad mommy here. No shame. I beg and barter with the twins all day. Negotiating international ballistic missile treaties must be easier than convincing my Katydid to smile for a camera."

"Mama said she was going to put you out of your misery when she called you over," Will piped through a mouthful of whipped cream.

"William John! That big mouth is going to get you in a world of trouble one of these days." Elizabeth shot her son a pointed look. "It made my heart hurt to see you standing there with everyone all curious. No one meant any harm, but the limelight can be a lonely place."

"Thank you," Pepper said sincerely. "I'm not used to attention."

"Well, you're doing *me* the favor sitting with us. I needed adult conversation. If I hear any more about bad dreams I'm going to scream."

"Bad dreams?" Pepper knew one or two things about those.

"Nightmares," Will mumbled. "We keep getting 'em."

Kate leaned in, wiggling her sticky fingers. "About a scary hamster."

Pepper pressed her lips together, trying not to laugh in their small, serious faces. "Oh?"

"Henry. Their pet hamster escaped the cage last week." Elizabeth gave her a look that said *the horror, the horror*. "He hasn't been found."

"We think he died and his ghost is haunting us."

"I see," Pepper nodded gravely. "Then there's only one solution."

"Call Ghostbusters?" Will fired off an imaginary blaster.

"Great idea, but mine's better." Pepper flipped over her paper mat. "May I borrow a crayon?"

Kate passed a red one.

Elizabeth propped her chin in her hand, curious.

"Whenever my sister and I used to have bad dreams, we'd come up with Nightmare Action Plans," Pepper explained.

"Nightmare Action Plan." Will pounded a fist on the table. "Yes! Perfect! What's that?"

"You guys keep dreaming about Henry, right? What exactly is he doing in the nightmare?"

"Trying to bite us."

"Of course he is." Pepper drew a picture of a devilish-looking hamster, added in bloodshot eyes for good effect and a gaping mouth full of pointy teeth. "Does he look like that?"

Kate squeaked, covering her eyes as Will nodded solemnly.

"What would you say if whenever Henry made a scary appearance, you took out a slingshot and fired baby carrots? And then, boom! He chews those instead of you." As Pepper spoke she drew out what she described.

"Yeah!" William shouted. "Nightmare Action Plan." He made more gun-shooting sounds with his mouth.

"But does it work?" Kate cut to the chase.

"I'll give you one guess who's the brains of the operation," Elizabeth muttered with a wink.

"Of course it works," Pepper said. And the twins stared as if she was a magical being.

She stared back.

They smiled. She smiled.

"You're pretty," Kate mumbled, eyes wide.

Elizabeth burst out laughing. "Look at that, your own fan club."

"Thanks." Pepper ducked her head, pleased, but uncomfortable with the attention. "I needed an ego boost. And talking about pretty, tell me more about your successful photo shoot."

"My mouth hurts from smiling." Kate popped a cherry into her mouth and flung the stem at her brother.

"Sorry, the ads were for what again?" Pepper broke off as the waitress came over. She ordered a pizza to go. This was fun, but better to eat away from prying eyes and too-loud whispers.

"I'm the marketing coordinator for city hall," Elizabeth explained. "The Village Pillage is a week of fun, the county's oldest and largest summer event—"

"The medallion hunt!" the children shrieked.

"That's what the photo shoot was for today. Getting ads out is my responsibility."

"What's the deal with all the pirate trappings in town?" Pepper glanced around the Smuggler's Cove, making eye contact with a stuffed parrot. "On the surface Everland plays up the romance factor, it's like such a...such a..."

"Sweet, safe community?" Elizabeth raised a brow. "Maybe even boring?"

"Not in a bad way though. *Cute* boring." Pepper made a face. "Sorry, I suffer from foot-in-mouth disease. There isn't a cure."

"That's all right." Elizabeth's grin revealed a deep-set dimple. "You aren't the first to describe us that way, and you won't be the last. But looks around here can be deceiving. Many of the so-called respectable locals have pirate blood flowing through their veins. Our coastline used to crawl with them. The nearby islands provided safe havens, and the riverways provided the perfect hiding places for treasure."

"Interesting." Pepper sat back, fiddling with a napkin. "And all news to me." This town had been nothing but a means to an end; she'd never spent time wondering about its people or history.

Elizabeth cocked her head, taking her measure. "How long have you been here?"

"Two days." Strange. It felt like a lifetime.

"My goodness, brand new." Elizabeth exclaimed. "All right then. Will? Kate? Who wants to tell her our story?"

Kate's hand shot up fastest. "Three hundred years ago Cap'n Redbeard was the mostest feared pirate on the seven seas." She sounded as if she recited a tale that she'd heard a thousand times. "He plundered ships, took gold, and left no prisoners."

"And then—" Will interrupted.

"Hey!" Kate brandished her spoon like a natural. Maybe Elizabeth was right and they did all have pirate blood.

"He hid his treasure where no one can find it," Will said.

"Here." Kate jabbed a finger on the table. "In Everland."

"The General says Redbeard paddled up the river and buried it under a full moon."

"But no one knows where 'zactly. Redbeard told only two people about the secret spot." The girl held up fingers for emphasis. "His first and second mates."

"Then English soldiers caught him."

"He got shot—"

"Stabbed—"

"And his head..." Kate made a neck-slashing gesture that left little to the imagination. "Stuck on a spike on Four Skull Island as a warning to others."

Pepper's head spun and ears rang. These kids definitely didn't know the meaning of inside voices.

"The first mate founded Everland. The second mate, Hogg Jaw. As far as we know, neither of the men ever told a soul about the location," Elizabeth interjected.

"Or if they did, they chopped out their tongues." Will shoveled in another scoop of ice cream, relishing the bloody tale's more gory aspects. "Each town says they have the missing treasure. The General's been hunting it for how long?"

Kate shrugged, scratching the side of her nose. "Long as Mama has been alive."

"Yeah, like eighty years."

"Hey, now! That's enough of all that." Elizabeth squeezed the slice of lemon into her sweet tea. "They don't realize that I stopped counting at twenty-nine," she said with a wink. "Twenty-nine was a good year."

"Isn't that when you had us?" Kate asked.

"That's right." Elizabeth's smile was one of a woman who enjoyed everything her life had to offer.

The sight turned Pepper a pale green. Aspirational pangs were the worst, the art of comparing herself to other women and coming up lacking. It triggered nothing but paralysis, and she was stuck quite enough, thanks very much. She huffed a sigh. Instead of letting icky jealousy eat her up, she'd channel her energy into more productive areas, like demolishing the delicious-smelling "Landlubbers" pizza—mushrooms, peppers, and black olives—that the wenched-up waitress brought to the table.

Pepper opened the box and handed slices to the kids. Elizabeth suggested they'd wash down well with wine, and they quickly discovered a shared love of Zinfandel. When at long last the check came, her insides were full to the brim and not by what was truly excellent pizza, even by New

York standards. How nice to hang out with someone who didn't require anything from her but easy conversation. Elizabeth didn't need money, favors, advice, or coddling. She just wanted to dish about the latest celebrity divorce scandal and the last juicy book she'd read.

"Thanks for asking me to hang out," Pepper said after Elizabeth refused for the third time to let her pay her share. "I needed a…it." She almost said "a friend," but caught herself. Better to avoid rushing to whack a label on their relationship and scare Elizabeth off by looking overeager and—

"Honey, wc all need friends." Elizabeth squeezed her shoulder. "I can tell from this past hour that you'll fit right in around here."

"Oh, I'm not staying," Pepper said automatically. The happy "made a new friend" feeling leached from the moment.

"I see." Elizabeth's expression didn't match her words. "What'll you do?"

"I'm working on figuring that out." She swallowed the sharp pain in her throat. "Top of the list is to find Redbeard's missing treasure and buy a penthouse back in Manhattan."

"What's a pirate's favorite letter?" Kate tugged on her skirt.

"ARRRRRRRRRR!" Will crowed.

"She didn't get a chance to guess, stupid," Kate said.

"Your face is stupid."

"Your butt is stupid."

They dissolved into helpless giggles.

Elizabeth shook her head. "You call me if you need anything, anything at all. Now I'm going to take these two home before I have an all-out mutiny."

"I want to go to bed and dream about Henry," Will shouted.

"Shoot carrots at him!" Kate said. "Nightmare Action Plan!"

"This was fun," Elizabeth said, standing. "Let's hang out again."

"I'd like to." And the thing was, Pepper meant it.

And without warning, the day felt brighter.

Chapter Six

Rhett returned to the clinic and de-mited Alma DeWitt's potbelly pig, treated the bulldog that had stumbled upon a neighbor's rat trap, put an IV in a rabbit, and set the broken wing on a mourning dove that had hit Sweet Brew's front window.

The best part about being a small-town vet was how no two days were ever the same. He'd worked with species ranging from dogs and cats to llamas and ostriches and once performed a cesarean on a cow tied to the back of a tractor during a Cat 2 hurricane. He laughed and grieved with clients almost every day. Each time he stepped through the clinic doors it was a privilege. A privilege to be trusted with the care of such precious family members.

Funny thing was, Dad used to say much the same thing about his own practice.

Their shared love of work should have served as a bond,

not a wedge. The cords in his neck tightened as he locked the front door at the end of the day.

Pointless wishing for something that wasn't meant to be. Besides, he didn't regret his career. He didn't do regrets.

Except one.

He blinked, his eyes tired and scratchy. "Not going there," he muttered before whistling for Faulkner, Steinbeck, and Fitzgerald. They bounded after him with grins so wide that he couldn't help but return the favor. How could his pretty new neighbor not love dogs? He'd had one or two his whole life.

He glared at the sky. Better not to ponder the whys, or Pepper's stray-puppy eyes, or, damn, that body. Curvy in all the right places. Impossible to resist a second, third, hell, even fourth look.

Except he would. No other option. The town biddies had bloodhound-caliber noses for gossip. They'd sniff out details if he emitted so much as a waft of interest. Better to shove her out of his mind, too.

Done and done.

It wasn't until after he picked up Beau from city hall and they idled at the town's lone stoplight that there was a disturbance in the force.

"Who is *that*?" Beau lowered the smartphone that seemed as connected to him as another appendage and whistled under his breath.

Rhett pressed his lips tighter. Pepper crossed the street, still dressed in that cute-as-hell skirt that hugged her in all the right ways. "Lawyer from up north," he muttered.

"How the hell do *you* know *her*?" Beau gave him an expectant look.

"Dude. I know lots of women."

"Yeah? Then how come you're a monk?"

The light flicked to green. Rhett accelerated. He wouldn't glance in the rearview mirror.

He glanced in the mirror. She yanked open the heavy door to Smuggler's Cove.

"I talked to her," he used a carefully casual tone, the same way he'd say "I've got to grab gas." A statement of fact. Nothing important. Moving right along.

"Talked? You. To *her*. Of your own free will?"

Shit. Typical Marino to poke the hornets' nest with zero fucks.

Rhett scowled at the double yellow line, making a conscious effort to relax his jaw. The last thing he needed was to go and trigger another damn headache. "Got something to say, Mr. Mayor? Spit it out."

"All right. I will. You need to get laid."

The pothole came out of nowhere.

"Jesus, man." Beau grabbed his smartphone as it flew from his hand.

"Sorry." Rhett steered back into the lane. "Didn't realize I was driving Miss Daisy."

"You're a funny guy, know that?"

He tipped an invisible hat.

"Funny looking," Beau muttered, returning to his phone.

Rhett reached for his travel coffee mug and guzzled. "Don't you get sick of staring at that damn screen all day?"

"About as sick as you get of chopping off dog balls," Beau fired back. "Besides, I started a mayoral Twitter account and it gets a shitload of interaction. Hard to keep up."

"Twitter?" Rhett chuckled under his breath. "Who the hell in Everland's on Twitter?"

"Try a thousand new followers since I opened the account last Thursday."

"Bullshit."

"I'm a man of the people, promised a—"

"Young, fresh voice. I remember. Had six of your yard signs at my house, and two at the office. What are people calling you these days?" He snapped his fingers. "The Prince of Everland?"

"What people? I know you started it."

"Payback for Cupid."

Beau grunted and returned to his phone.

"But come on, you can't work twenty-four seven. "

"If you don't want to talk, don't," Beau said, flicking up an eyebrow. "But don't pass the buck to me."

"Fair enough." After Beau's wife drowned during a sailing trip in the Bahamas, he'd retreated further and further into himself. Rhett wanted to help but didn't know how to help, except to give space and have patience. "But why sling crap on an afternoon like this? The clouds are moving on. The sun is out. We're going sailing, and no one's watching the clock for us back home."

"Amen."

The two traded fist bumps as they entered the covered bridge.

"Fuck!" Rhett yelled, slowing as they hit the other side. A small sedan had crashed into a tree. Thick, blue-gray smoke poured from under the hood.

"Call nine-one-one," he shouted to Beau, leaping from the driver's side.

"On it." Beau had the phone pressed to his ear.

Rhett's stomach muscles clenched at the familiar bumper sticker. RUFF LOVE PET WALKERS. Shit. No. Not Norma. She'd been Mama's best friend. Practically family.

"Norma!" he shouted. "Norma, you okay?"

"Rhett?" a high quavering voice answered. "Rhett Valentine? Is that you?"

"Yeah, it's me."

Norma was strapped in her seat. The airbag had deployed.

"It was the damnedest thing," she mumbled, pushing back her purple sequined ball cap that read BAD HAIR DAY. "A dang armadillo tried to cross into the road. I swerved and this here tree was in my way."

"How many fingers am I holding up?" Rhett waved two in her face.

"How 'bout countin' this one instead, sugar?" She popped him the bird.

Rhett gave a relieved laugh. She appeared her usual feisty self. "Can you move?"

"My leg." She grimaced. "I think it's broken. And would you talk about terrible timing? I've signed on three new clients. What on earth am I going to do now? Mrs. Johnson is doing the chemo. She can't be walking Ziggy, he's far too strong. Ol' John Drummond has a kidney trouble and Wolfgang is a real pistol."

He liked Norma. She reminded him of Mama, the way she always thought of others. No surprise that she'd be here with a busted leg worrying about her elderly clients. The thought made his gut ache. He couldn't do much about the world's problems, but he could put Norma's mind at ease.

"Let me worry about the dog walking," he said. "Right

now I want you to focus on holding my hand, and if you see any light, stay the hell away from it, you hear?"

She laced her fingers with his and gave a squeeze. "You are a *good* boy," she said, closing her eyes, jaw set tight. "Always were."

As the ambulance siren rose in the distance, an idea formed. His brows drew together as he sat back on his heels.

Guess he'd have to start thinking about his new neighbor after all.

Chapter Seven

I seriously can't stop eating these pickles." Tuesday was out of frame, her phone angled to an unmade single bed and a poster for the musical *Wicked*. "I need an intervention."

Pepper wrinkled her nose at her FaceTime screen. "Is that an innuendo, because TMI."

"Nope." Her sister angled the camera to showcase an actual large dill pickle. She took a noisy crunch. "I bought a jar at the Park Slope Farmers Market. They're artisanal *and* fermented. It's my new thing—the everything fermented diet."

Ah, Tuesday. She'd never met a fad she didn't love.

"Honey. They are pickles. Pickles that probably cost more than your rent." Even as Pepper chided, her heart panged. Today, her high horse had shrunk to the size of a Shetland pony. The Georgia move had emptied her savings account. And what did she have to show for it? Nothing but a closet of discount business attire and debt.

"Remember Granny's root cellar? All the canned beets, green beans, and tomatoes?" Tuesday's leg shot out in a kickboxing round kick, narrowly missing a pile of scripts precariously stacked on her coffee table. She never sat still, even on FaceTime. During their marathon phone call she'd done a hundred crunches, polished off a bowl of oatmeal, painted her toenails purple, and plaited her long blond hair into a complicated fishtail braid. "She was the original hipster. I wonder if Dad still has her recipes. I could sell it to one of the big publishing houses as a retro cookbook."

"Call me crazy, but I can't see tuna surprise or Jell-O pie hitting the *New York Times* best-seller list."

"Oh, shivers. The pie was disgusting. And remember how she'd force-feed you deviled ham sandwiches?"

"Don't make me relive dietary hell." Pepper stuck a bag of kettle corn in the microwave. "Thanks for hanging out. I needed the distraction. All I've been doing is staring at my bank account, willing a nest egg into existence. That and taking long romantic walks to the fridge."

"Why. Not. Ask. Mom. For. A. Loan?" Each word was punctuated by a Rockette-style high kick.

"Ugh. Never." A vein throbbed in her temple at the mere idea. "I'd rather live in a van by the river, or sell Hot Pockets to truckers at the Pump-N-Munch."

"The Pump and excuse me?"

"Don't ask." Pepper punched the microwave's Start button. A few seconds of silence ticked by. They both knew without saying there was no point in suggesting Dad. He'd love to help but needed a new evaporator before the next sugaring season. The old wood-fired one barely made it through last spring. "But I'm serious. Mom will never be the option for anything. I've got nothing left but my pride at this point. I'm content keeping our communication limited to reading her humble-bragging holiday newsletter."

"The worst. Remember the last one?" Tuesday affected a WASPy female accent. "This year has been a whirlwind for Clyde and me. First came the trip to Denmark in February (Brrrr!) followed by the Norwegian cruise and jaunt to Palm Springs. Finally, I threw up my hands and said, enough is enough! We need a vacation from all these vacations. But of course, how was I to know Clyde had booked us in for a French wine tour through Burgundy for our twelfth anniversary? That man! He's a keeper."

"Enough!" Pepper couldn't hold back a laugh, even if it was tinged in bitterness. Lisa Knight had been right about money buying love—er, Lisa Clark. She left Dad and a simple North woods lifestyle to implement a get-rich-quick plan that culminated in a walk down the aisle with a guy fifteen years older and five hundred times more boring. Clyde Clark was human valium with a seven-car garage.

"Moving on. Want to hear the worst thing ever?" Tuesday asked.

Pepper made a face. "Worse than my first day at work coinciding with my last?"

"Terrible in a different way. Angus hit on me."

"Angus who?" She jolted. "Wait. Not Angus—"

"Our stepbrother." Tuesday gave a grim nod.

"But that is—"

"Gross? Nauseating? Barftastic?" Tuesday filled a small watering can at her sink. "Tell me about it. He was in the city on a business trip and Mom called and asked me to play tour guide. He insisted we go to the Empire State Building, at noon, on a Saturday."

"No! But the crowds..."

"I know. We waited in line for three hours." Tuesday watered the basil on her windowsill. "He talked about mutual funds and kept tacking the expression 'if you will' to the end of his sentences until I was stabby."

"Ew."

"And then he asked me out on a date."

"Double ew. Did you alert Mom?"

"No, because which would be worse? Option A, where I tell her and it starts drama, or option B, and she gives me her blessing. He flew back to Bedford yesterday. Guess I'll look forward to most uncomfortable family Christmas ever."

Pepper shuddered. "Just say no to stepbrother dating."

"Amen. Back over to you. Have you given any thought on your next professional move?"

"A little." She traced invisible circles on the laminate countertop as the timer's seconds ticked. "Making cotton candy at Happily Ever After Land?"

"Happily Ever After Land?" Tuesday recoiled. "Do I even want to know what that is?"

"Whatever, Grinch. It's a cute, historic amusement park on the edge of town, like Coney Island but more charming, with a wooden roller coaster and an old-fashioned Ferris wheel. Anyway, I'll stop complaining. I'm fine." Wow, that sounded believably easy breezy. Guess Tuesday wasn't the only actress in the family.

"I have no doubt."

At least that made one of them. "I'm going to go eat dinner."

"Wait, promise you'll consume a food group other than Orville Redenbacher. Give peas a chance."

"Hello? Pop-*corn*. Counts as a vegetable. Plus I love beans. Coffee beans."

Tuesday waved her phone in front of her Terrier's face, her way of ending the subject. "Tell J.K. Growling you miss her, that absence makes the heart grow fonder."

Pepper grimaced as J.K. heaved at the screen, snorting loudly through her smushed-up nose. "I'm like George Washington. I cannot tell a lie."

"For shame." Tuesday stuck out her tongue and clapped a hand over her dog's ears. "Don't listen to horrid Auntie Pepper, Sugar baby, her brains have been rotted by fake butter. She doesn't mean it."

I do, Pepper mouthed. "Wait! Before you go. Show me your view."

"What view?"

"Please," she cajoled.

"All right. All right. Here you go. It's no Park Avenue." Tuesday positioned the camera to catch the brick building across the street, and the alley below.

"It's also not Kissing Court or Hopes and Dreams Way." Pepper sighed. "Oh! A dumpster. And oh! New graffiti. What does it say?"

"Go fuck yourself," Tuesday deadpanned.

Pepper giggled. "Home sweet home. Thanks for indulging me. Be sweet, Parakeet."

"Take care, Polar Bear." The screen clicked dark.

Pepper traded her phone for her e-reader with a sigh. Tuesday once quizzed her on why she still read romances. When not going to casting calls, her sister moonlighted as a kiddie birthday party princess, but scoffed at the idea of happily-ever-afters. At the time, Pepper changed the subject to her latest Netflix series addiction because the truth was tricky to articulate, even to her sister and best friend. It wasn't because like some people assumed—she wanted her bodice ripped or to be ravished. The truth was far more subversive.

These books educated her on how to have an orgasm—life-changing in and of itself—but (possibly) more importantly, had taught her not to settle, reinforced that she deserved to be cherished, mind, body, and soul. Unlike Warren, her last boyfriend, who'd slunk his arm around her waist in the fifteen-items-or-less-checkout-line and announced, "I'm dating someone else and she asked me to choose."

At least Pepper had already paid for the pint of vanilla fudge Häagen-Dazs. Then there was her first (and only) Tinder date with the guy who'd taken her to the movies and moaned under his breath during the steamy scenes.

The only benefit to having a dating closet full of losers was that each one got her another step closer to Mr. Right.

That's how it worked. Hopefully.

The microwave dinged, and she rose to grab a mixing bowl. Time to eat her feelings and the niggling fear that she'd die alone, watching a *Golden Girls* rerun, while clutching the paw of one of her twelve cats.

A knock came at the front door as she poured out the popcorn. Her bare toes curled against the linoleum. Couldn't a girl stuff herself silly on artificial flavoring while finishing her book before watching *The Princess Bride* for the six hundredth time in peace? Plus she was dressed for a self-pity party in her NYU Law hoodie paired with her comfiest yoga pants, the plum-colored ones with the hole in the thigh.

The knock came again. Three insistent raps. She cursed

under her breath. Unexpected visitors ranked high on her list of least-favorite things, right below getting fired on day one. She reached for the light and paused, fingers hovering over the switch. Going dark was too obvious. Should she tiptoe to the bedroom? Pretend not to be home?

Or stop being ridiculous? Her crown might be battered, but she was still queen of this castle. Thrusting back her shoulders, she yanked down her hoodie strings and marched to the hall, tripping on a box of paperbacks. Her forehead struck the door with a bang and she yelped.

So much for dignity.

"Everything okay in there?"

She froze, hands splayed on the wood. That rich molasses voice. She'd know it anywhere. Hot neighbor was on the other side. Here. Now. And she was in the thigh-hole leggings.

Covert breath check. All good. The peppermint she'd nabbed leaving Smuggler's Cove came in handy. With a deep breath, she flung open the door. Rhett stood floodlit by the porch light, dressed in a navy collared shirt that did his eyes all kinds of favors.

"Hello, hello."

"Hey." His hair stuck out behind his ears, unruly and damp as if he'd just stepped out of the shower. The idea of him sudsy and, God, sans clothing caused a tightening below deck. "I heard a crash. You need backup?"

In those Clark Kent glasses he did resemble a secret hero, especially in how he projected the right amount of strength, a rock solid internal fortitude.

"Oh. Right. Well, there was this mosquito. A big one." She gestured vaguely with her hands before clasping them behind her back, nails biting into her palms. "What can I do you for? A cup of sugar?"

"Two things. The first is this." He whipped out a bar from the back pocket of his jeans. "I brought chocolate."

A jolt shot through her with such intensity it became difficult to swallow. "My three favorite words."

His sleeves were pushed up. Holy forearms, Batman—lean, deliciously veined with the promise of delivering sensational cuddles. Her fingers trembled as she took the bar, glancing at the colorful silver foil. When was the last time anyone had given her anything? "My kind of kryptonite."

"I wondered what flavor would be your weakness." His inscrutable gaze locked on hers for a millisecond before bouncing to an indefinable spot between her neck and shoulder. "Ginger over at What-a-Treat makes the best rocky road in the Low Country. The candy shop's an Everland institution, been around forever." His deep drawl performed the sort of sex acts on her eardrums that were illegal in thirteen states. She grinned like an idiot, but it felt too good to care.

"There. Better." He gave a satisfied nod. "Happiness is a good look on you."

Her hand flew to her throat. "It is?" Her pulse pounded beneath her fingertips. As a rule she loathed when a man asked her to smile, but this was different. He didn't sound like he wanted to be all up in her space, demanding her attention; rather, he wanted to cheer her up with a random act of kindness.

"Yoo hoo! Tootle-loo!" A horn honked. Rhett's features shifted into a scowl as the woman from across the street peered through the window of her pink Cadillac. "Why Rhett Valentine, is that you?"

"Not past your bedtime yet, Miss Ida May?" He held up

a hand in sociable greeting even though annoyance underwrote his tone.

"Had Quilt Guild tonight, but looks I got back right on time. Y'all having fun?"

"Being neighborly." He started rocking on his heels, as if shaken off his foundation.

"Bet you are, I bet you are." Ida May pulled her pink Cadillac into her garage. Insinuating chuckles echoed up the street.

His teasing manner from a moment before evaporated in an instant. Rhett's half smile was replaced by a focused look that meant business. "I said I'd come for two reasons. The other is this. A family friend shattered her leg in a car accident this afternoon. She owns a local dog-walking service."

"O-kay?" She mashed her brows. The accident sounded awful, but talk about a random thing to come over and share.

"She needs to hire someone."

"Oh!" Everything was clear. "Like a caregiver…I could do that. Cook meals. Read out loud." She grinned. That wouldn't be so bad.

He shook his head. "To handle her client roster on a temporary basis."

Her smile froze. "Wait." She snapped a loose string dangling off her thigh hole. "You can't mean—"

"You need a job," he said firmly. "And this is a great way to get over cynophobia."

"Cyno-huh?"

"Fear of dogs. It can't be much fun being scared of a common household pet."

"No," she said faintly. "It's not." She *was* desperate for cash to get out of Dodge, but was she this desperate? This opportunity was like wanting a snack, but broccoli's the only thing in the fridge.

"My boys liked you," he was saying. "Especially Faulkner. And dog behavior is predictable if you learn to read their body language. I can help with that."

"I have no problem reading dog body language. They look at me with their beady eyes and say, 'Mmmm. Rawhide!'" She cleared her throat. "Look. This offer is sweet. Really."

He crossed his arms. "But..."

"But you know how the world is divided into dog lovers and cat lovers—"

"And fish people."

"Huh?"

"People who prefer fish."

She frowned. "Huh. Never considered that."

"And snake people. Bird people. Rat people."

"Ew, what? Rat people?" When he made such intense eye contact it was hard to think, but easy to squirm. "Don't make this difficult."

"Rodent lovers. Lizard lovers. Hell, tarantula lovers walk among us."

She shuddered even as an unwilling smile tugged her lips. "If you won't quit destroying my worldviews, could you stop trying to give me nightmares?"

"Never a bad idea to challenge your preconceptions. It's part of my job description to appreciate all creatures big and small."

"So about this job..." She had been spending quality time with fear. What was the harm in sprinkling in more? By the time she'd leave Georgia, she really could be Superwoman. Nothing would ever rattle her again. She'd leap life uncertainties in a single bound. "So, you're a dog walker, too?"

"Me?" He startled. "No. A vet. Valentine Veterinary."

"Wait. Hold the presses. A vet?" The plot thickened. "Rhett...the vet? Like a poet who doesn't know it?"

He frowned at her playful tone before briskly outlining the details of Norma's business.

She regarded him more closely. His rolled-up shirt-sleeves revealed an inked phrase near his elbow. Too hard to read the tattoo at this angle, and she wasn't going to stare. Instead she doubled down on studying his face. That chin. Wow, and that jaw. And hello there, cheekbones.

That scruff would deliciously grizzle against her top lip.

"What do you say?" he asked, no hint in his face that he was secretly quagmired in his own lascivious thoughts. His face was all business. As it should be.

This teeny-tiny crush scared her. Today she'd hit a dead end on her dream of becoming a hotshot law school grad with an out-of-the-gate judicial clerkship. That fact should be the only unsettling part today.

Becoming a clerk was the cornerstone to achieving her dream life. And when one loses one's dream, one should feel crushed like a cartoon character walking under an anvil. There shouldn't be space in her body for lust unless she hoped to salve the disappointment with desire.

Ah. But wait. She huffed a sigh of relief. That could be it. What if her humiliating job loss *had* in fact destroyed her to the point where she now eyeballed the closest decent—fine, more than decent—man in sight hoping for relief, physical distraction.

But she wouldn't grasp for that kind of salve to heal this wound. Facts were facts. She was terrified of being broke and had a childhood phobia of dogs. But avoiding these fears would only make them scarier. She couldn't stand another minute being crushed by impending doom. If she stood her ground and faced them, maybe—just maybe they'd fade.

"Okay, you know what? Why not. You win." She spoke the words carefully. "I'm a gal attached to eating and electricity, so any income is useful. Thank you for saving me twice in one day, Rhett the vet." That poke was impossible to resist.

He hooked his hand to the back of his neck. His rumpled shirt rode up, exposing a flat inch of tanned skin above his worn leather belt. The unexpectedly intimate sight shot her through with tingles, as if she'd brushed up wet next to an electrical socket.

His bright eyes narrowed. "You like pressing buttons, Miss Knight?"

"Not as a rule." She pressed her knees together while he appeared every inch in control.

He cocked his head. "I see."

What exactly do you see? The question danced at the tip of her tongue. Was it a woman crashing and burning following a total loss of control? A big sister whose loneliness grew more acute every hour she spent away from Tuesday? Or a character from *Sex-Starved in the City*, who hadn't romanced anything besides her six-speed vibrator in eighteen months?

She didn't look away. Neither did he.

"Okay then, Miss Knight." He flexed a large, powerful hand. "Have yourself a nice evening."

She gripped the doorway, legs boneless. She wanted to call out "Nothing's okay" as he opened the gate, but her gaze fastened on his ass and her mouth dried. Have to credit a man who didn't skimp on daily deadlifts. She swallowed. Hard.

Enough already.

If she wanted to be a good neighbor, she needed training. First lesson? *Down, girl.*

Excerpt from the Back Fence:

Everland News That You Actually Care About

Classifieds:

Quilt Guild: The Everland Quilt Guild meets Tuesday at 6pm in the Merriweather Common Room at the Public Library. New members welcome. Call Ida May at 912-555-0025

Missing: An "X" Scrabble tile. Last seen at Everland Dog Park. If found, please put in Lucille Munro's mailbox. 102 Hopes and Dreams Way.

Kissing Bridge Work Day: It takes a village to beautify our town. This month the Mayor's office is sponsoring a spruce up of The Kissing Bridge. Help preserve the only covered bridge in the Low Country. Come dressed for work, bring a snack to share and good attitude. See you Saturday from 9am-1pm. Water and sweet tea provided.

Chapter Eight

❧

Pepper sipped her second cup of coffee and ignored her wristwatch ticking down the seconds until she began her new (temporary, but oh-my-God-this-is-happening-what-is-life?) occupation: Ruff Love dog walker. How wonderful that she'd graduated cum laude from NYU Law. Preparing to counsel, strategize, write, advocate, and negotiate would surely be assets in a role where her main responsibilities were keeping pups moving in a forward trajectory and not getting too pooped to scoop.

That second duty should be underlined and highlighted. Otherwise she was liable to be hit with Mayor Marino's new dog waste ordinance, $75 for each offense. A fine that would come out of *her* paycheck. Norma's otherwise cheerful letter of employment didn't mince words in that department.

She wasn't looking to break rules. Or even get noticed around town. If a single solitary word—or worse, a photo—

of her dog walking leaked out in social media, she'd never be able to show her face at an NYU alumni event.

She stood and drained her mug in one long swallow. This was pointless fretting; word wouldn't get out. For the next few months, her life would be simple: head down, walk the dogs, collect the paychecks, save the money, and get the hell out of Dodge by the time her lease expired with enough socked away to put down first and last month's rent in any city in America. Because by then she'd have secured another job offer (please, Sweet Baby Jesus) and this strange Georgia summer could be her dirty little secret.

She glanced out the window, wiped her mouth, and blinked. Then she blinked again, in case "hallucinating half-naked men" could be added to her list of troubles. Nope. This was actually happening. Rhett Valentine sauntered into the bedroom opposite her window, dressed in nothing but a low-slung gray towel, jaw slathered with shaving cream.

She swallowed hard. He didn't look like the gym rat cover of a men's fitness magazine. No pretty boy waxed chest and six-pack here. He rocked a hard torso dusted by dark hair. A strong, capable, male body, built to be used, not for looks.

Especially not her own pervy peep show.

Her heart paid a friendly visit to her lower intestines as he'd reached into his closet, fisted a T-shirt, and disappeared without an inkling of her creeper status.

"Right." She stood. Time for Neighbor Crush Training Number Two. Today's lesson?

Leave it.

Closing the blinds would be too obvious, so instead she retreated to the safety of the kitchen. Every step returned a feeling of control. In her normal world, a silly crush would be harmless. But this was purgatory. Ogling the neighbor's sexy bod wasn't going to get her out of here. Ain't nobody got time for that. What she did have time for was lifting her mind out of the gutter and getting together a game plan. First step, not succumbing to the gut-twisting terror of dog walking. She had faced a serious setback and needed to prove that she wouldn't be destroyed by fear. Her clients were dogs, not hell demons, precious pets to Everland's old and infirm. She could do this.

Correction.

She *would* do this.

Five minutes later, she marched to her first appointment, a soldier heading into the front lines.

"Turn left onto East Forever Lane," a crisp male British accent said. She'd reset Siri's voice last night after watching the lake scene from the BBC's *Pride and Prejudice* twenty-four times (stopping only because her laptop ran out of batteries and she was too lazy to fetch the charger). If one couldn't have a Darcy in the bedroom, why not have a Darcy intone directions?

"Proceed down the route and the destination is on your left."

"Forty-two, forty-three, ah, here we are. Forty-four Forever." She paused in front of the Drummond house. The ornate gables made it look like a wedding cake. Norma had passed Rhett a series of instructions for each client. Mr. Drummond was at dialysis Tuesday mornings, and his Chihuahua, Wolfgang, waited in the backyard.

A perfect first client. Its teeth were the size of Tic Tacs. If it bit her, she could pop it in a six-inch sub and eat it for lunch. Not that she'd do that. Probably.

The garden was neatly ordered, shrubs trimmed to perfection. No leaf out of place. She let herself through the gate and froze. The spotted Chihuahua in the center of the lawn wasn't growling with a look that said, "Death, from the ankles down!" No. He was too busy committing obscene acts on a throw pillow. Moves that might be illegal in thirteen states.

What was the etiquette for hound humping? Should she look away? Shoo it off? She glanced up instead. Not a cloud in the sky. Oh, a butterfly. How 'bout that.

Scratch. Scratch. Scratch.

Scratch that idea. No point focusing on anything when that dog was going at it like this was his last day on Earth. Pepper grabbed the leash hanging next to the grill. "Hi there, Wolfgang. Yoo hoo. Over here."

Scratch. Scratch. Scratch.

She'd sweated blood and tears in law school for this?

Pushing aside a fleeting wish for a hazmat suit, she dropped into a crouch and advanced. Where was she going to grab him? The little fella was gyrating in a manner that would make Elvis eat his heart out. Under his forearms seemed like the safest plan of attack. That was about as far as one could get from the danger zone.

She advanced arms outstretched. One step. Two steps. Three steps. Four. Almost there. Wolfgang froze mid-pump, tail and ears fully alert. His pointed nose turned up, sniffing.

Before she could react, he'd ditched the pillow like yesterday's news, in favor of a new lover. Her left leg.

"No! Bad dog!" This pint-sized pervert made her want to belly flop into a kiddie pool brimming with Purell.

In addition to violating pillows and an innocent pair of LuLaRoe leggings, Wolfgang's other pastime included ignoring dog walker commands, because it took her ten minutes to disentangle the little sucker from her person and wrangle him onto a leash. Another four to reach the sidewalk.

By the time she arrived at the dog park she was dripping sweat. Satan called and wanted his weather back. She took a swig from her water bottle, the ice cubes melted already. If she listened hard enough she might hear her thigh fat frying. Taking another gulp, her gaze connected with a dog—specifically, a brass statue of a one-eyed dog peeing on a fire hydrant. The plaque mounted to the base read DAVY JONES: WHO KNEW WHEN TO GO.

Now there's something you didn't see every day. Then again, Everland, Georgia, wasn't your everyday sort of place.

The park was busy. Every bone-shaped bench was occupied by chatting duos or trios, while a dozen dogs frolicked on the off-leash grass area. Wolfgang hurled himself at the melee, either frantic to play or into autoerotic asphyxiation. The latter was not entirely out of the question.

She bent to unclip the leash and he nearly tugged her arm from its socket. "Sit," she hissed. "Sit down already! Help me to help you."

At last she maneuvered him free and he took off like a shot, bolting to the middle of the pack. He barked a few times and half a dozen furry heads turned in her direction. Wolfgang was no doubt telling a few tales. And the dogs weren't the only ones staring. The park vibrated with a strange tension, the same phenomenon that occurred at Smuggler's Cove a few days ago. No one directly stared, but there was a disorienting sensation of having all eyes fixed on her. The faces weren't unfriendly, but it must be similar to being a new kid at school, standing in front of the class and hoping everyone liked you—or at least didn't actively dislike you on sight.

There was something to be said for the anonymity of a big city. Growing up in Moose Bottom, everyone knew everyone. The bank teller remembered how she'd spent the summer before first grade speaking duck (quack once for yes and twice for no). And it was impossible to take the swaggering deputy sheriff seriously knowing that he had once been kicked offstage for playing "Jingle Bells" with his armpit during the high school talent night. Plus, you always knew who was up or down on life's teeter-totter on any given week.

Right now, Pepper was down. Way down. If there was rock bottom, not only had she hit it but she also was digging to see if she could strike the water table.

Turning toward a shady patch under a wide oak, she recoiled. A hulking razorback boar blocked her path. Maybe it was a statue, an incredibly lifelike statue able to simulate breathing.

Nope.

That was an actual boar sizing her up, snuffling closer as if searching for truffles. A prominent ridge ran down the back of his thick, brown coat, bristly as a wire brush.

No one said a word. Everland's suspicion of outsiders hadn't translated into feeding them to swamp dwellers, right? The boar's tail swished, and she took a step backward, colliding into a wall that hadn't been there before.

"Looks like Dude has taken a shine to you," a voice boomed.

She glanced over her shoulder. The so-called wall was a middle-aged man clocking in at around six-foot-five. A Santa Claus doppelganger, if Saint Nick sported a ginger beard, freckles, and matching thick gold-hoop earrings.

"Who do we call?" she stammered. "The police? Animal control?"

The man cocked his head. "Why'd we do that?"

Was he on something? "There is a giant pig five feet away," she hissed.

"Dude? Oh, that troublemaker's all mine." The man tipped back his leather hat with a friendly chuckle. "And I'm the General." He didn't look the military type, but maybe had been in undercover special ops. Deep, deep undercover. "A semi-professional reenactor, among other pursuits."

She tilted her head to the side. "War reenactment?" Where grown men donned costumes and pretended to shoot each other?

"Revolutionary mainly. The Second South Carolina Regiment is a particular passion of mine, and I make a point of going to Colonial Williamsburg every—"

"That's enough, dear. Unless you want to put her to sleep before you've introduced me." A stocky man with a buzz cut and well-defined brown biceps covered in geometric tattoos came from behind, patting the General on the lower back. "Please forgive my handsome husband. He does go on." He made a *talk-talk-talk* sign with his hand.

"Allow me to present Colonel Jim." Pride tinged the General's voice. "Not your fast-food fried chicken kind either. We're talking actual bona fide military service to this great nation. United States Marine corps, two tours overseas."

"Lieutenant colonel." The man smiled. "Happily retired."

"Hey, does Dude seem hungry to you? I think he looks hungry." The General answered his own question. He reached into his shoulder satchel and removed a plastic bag of peaches. Colonel Jim didn't bat an eye.

"Here, Dude, fetch." He removed a couple peaches and tossed them over the boar's snout. The beast ambled after its prize. "I've had him for near going on seven, no, eight years. Rescued him as a piglet from being roadkill on a backwoods stretch of Florida highway. He was easier to domesticate than this handsome cat." He inclined his head toward his partner.

"You bring a wild animal to the dog park?" Had she forgotten to take her crazy pill this morning? No one else appeared unsettled in the slightest. The creature had tusks, for Pete's sake. Long and pointy ones.

"Don't get him started, darlin'," Colonel Jim muttered.

"How else is he supposed to get his exercise?" the General blustered, glancing between them.

Pepper wrinkled her brow. Maybe it would be best to speak slowly. Use short sentences. "That animal is not your run-of-the-mill pink farm pig."

"Pink?" the General blustered. "Dude's a razorback boar, through and through. But don't worry about him hurting more than a flea. Why he thinks he's a dog himself. Although, to be on the safe side, better not let Wolfgang wander too close. Keep an eye to the sky, too. A red-tailed hawk could swoop in and carry the lil' fella off without so much as a please and thank you."

Pepper's polite smile faded. She'd been so wrapped up in protecting herself from dogs—and boars—that she hadn't considered protecting her clients, especially from being eaten. Add that to her job responsibilities, right below poop scooping.

"Haven't seen you at the store yet."

"Store?" Pepper blinked up into the cheerful face of the pig's owner.

"The General's General Store off Main. Where we sell everything from eggs and milk to Ouija boards and socks."

"He's the face of the operation. I'm the brains." Colonel

Jim placed a hand to the side of his mouth, stage whispering: "He's not allowed to talk to new customers." Returning to a normal volume, he continued, "We're a high-end small goods shop providing Everland with artisanal foods, household items, and books."

"Sounds good. I'll keep you in mind the next time I want to make a milk shake and conduct a séance while keeping my feet warm."

"Ha. You're funny. I like it." The General's grin revealed two gold teeth. "Now tell us what everyone here is thinking but only we're men enough to ask."

Colonel Jim rubbed his hands. "What's the scoop between you and Cupid?"

Her brows knit. "Who?"

"Rhett Valentine, of course."

The General broke in, "The one. The only. The legend."

Pepper shook her head, feigning ignorance. It didn't matter if it was Moose Bottom, Maine, or Everland, Georgia, small-town gossip spread like weeds. Better not to give it fertilizer. "I don't know what you mean."

He rubbed his beard. "You two are front page news."

"Today's front page news is about the sudden spike in pecan prices." Indeed, the headline had read NUTS ARE GROWING. Someone at the paper either had a sense of humor or was completely oblivious.

"Not the birdcage liner." Colonel Jim waved a dismissive hand. "The Back Fence."

"The Back Fe—"

"Well, well, well, look who it is." The General cut her off with ill-disclosed glee.

Colonel Jim practically bounced. "Cupid at twelve o'clock."

Pepper froze at the nickname. "Rhett's here?"

"Walking this way." The General nodded. "Want to wager how many times he's turned up here in the last year? If you bet zero, you'd be a winner. You've caught his attention, missy."

"Stop it," she hissed. "He isn't here to see me."

"Then why is he standing right behind you?" Colonel Jim murmured. "Hello, Sport."

"Nice try." They were playing her. Sometimes it took a while, but she always caught on. These guys were having fun at her expense.

"Wondered if I'd find you here." A molasses-rich drawl drizzled down her spine.

Rhett. He really was here.

She turned slowly. With any luck her flushed cheeks would look like a by-product of the heat and not his inadvertent morning peep show. He wore a dress shirt, vest, and tie with a pair of dark denim jeans, his eyes bright behind his thick frames, his unruly cowlick swooping over his quizzical forehead.

Stop ogling. Speak.

"Hello." Her mouth lifting in what hopefully passed for a casual, neighborly smile.

"You've got something there." His fingers skimmed the shoulder of her T-shirt, brushing her neck almost unperceptively. "There." He held up a white puff. "Cottonwood seed." His lips curled in the corner, the half grin holding no hint that the quick touch was anything more than an accidental brush. It would be easy to dismiss except for the invisible wave of tension that connected their gazes—hot and unspoken.

She stirred and fiddled with her hair elastic. "Checking on me?"

He crossed his arms over his broad chest, a paper cup of coffee in one hand. "I hit up Sweet Brew. Thought I'd come over and see how things were going on your first day." He had perfect posture. Somewhere, once upon a time, a Southern mama had driven all signs of slouch from those shoulders. "Wanted to report to Norma on your success when I go visit her in the rehab center in a few hours."

"Tell her things are under control."

He stared at her a second or two, concentrating, this time the look more concerned than provocative. "Any fear cropping up?"

The fact he asked the question honestly, no trace of submerged amusement that she could be deathly afraid of a Chihuahua, thawed the cold, hard walnut lodged in her stomach, one she didn't even know she carried. "Wolfgang and I are having a great time."

"Yeah?" He glanced around, his brow drawing in. "Where is he?"

"Oh, right over there..." Her pointer finger wilted. "Or at least he was."

"Near Dude?" Concern threaded his voice. The razor-back snuffled amid tree roots.

"Oh my God." Pepper pressed her fingers to her mouth. "That boar moves fast."

Chapter Nine

❡

Hold on, folks. Don't anyone start losing their heads."
The General held up his hands. "Dude wouldn't hurt a flea."

Pepper cupped her hands and called Wolfgang's name.
He had been right there a minute ago, sniffing around her
ankles. "Are boars vegetarian?" she asked Rhett.

"They'll eat anything that fits in their mouth," he answered grimly.

Not the answer she wanted. Wolfgang was chicken
nugget sized. He'd go down in a single gulp. "Form a search
party," she shouted to the growing crowd over her shoulder.
No cause to panic. Yet. But definitely time to be proactive.

The General bristled. "I keep him spoiled on twice-a-day
home-cooked meals. Dude is a friend to all dogs big, small,
and yes, even miniature."

"Too friendly." Rhett crossed his arms. "This is why I
spoke out at city council about letting a razorback boar have
park privileges."

Colonel Jim drew himself to his full impressive height and linked arms with his partner. "Now see here, Sport, the council voted five to four in the General's favor. Dude is legal."

Rhett whirled. "Only after you made backroom promises offering members a seventy percent discount at the General's General Store for three months."

"Rumors and conjectures." Colonel Jim waved a smug hand. "Nothing can be proven."

Pepper blew up her bangs as the bickering grew in volume. Thomas Jefferson wasn't lying when he wrote that all men are created equal. He just forgot to add the "equally stupid" part. Finally she broke out the commanding finger whistle Dad made her master in case she ever got lost in the woods.

Startled silence ensued.

"Focus, people. Please. My client can't be eaten on my first day." There it came, the strange sensation of standing outside herself, the one that accompanied hyperventilation. "To be on the safe side though, how does one give a swine the Heimlich?"

"Honey, look at the shade she's gone. What would you call that, celery root?" Colonel Jim asked, tapping the side of his chin thoughtfully. "That color would look fabulous in a linen set."

"What do you need?" Rhett stepped forward. "Water? A seat?"

"My client, in one piece and undigested." She took off, walking the perimeter of the park, her voice cracking from strain. "Wolfgang? Wolfgang? Here, buddy. Hey you, come on. It's your ol' pal, Pepper. Here, boy."

The park buzzed like a hive. Let them stare. Point. Shake

their heads like she'd lost her damn mind. No humiliation was too great to find Wolfgang. If Dude gobbled him—

"Pardon me. Might I be of some assistance?"

Wait a second. She glanced at the phone. Had British Darcy come to save the day? Nope. This was a real, live person. Be still her heart.

Outside the dog park, on a wooden bench, a dashing man with an inquisitive gaze set down a book titled *Daily Life in the Georgian and Regency Periods*. He dressed in brushed wool trousers and wore oxford shoes like he'd stepped out of her brain as a replica of her fantasy man. Except he wasn't in Manhattan, he was here, in Everland.

Rhett glowered over from across the park—not at all a Mr. Darcy type—except for that bemused frown. He was more an all-American good ol' boy who watched football on Sundays, barbecued in his backyard, and threw around a Frisbee with dogs.

Totally not her type.

This guy, on the other hand...

"Hello." She tried flipping her hair over her shoulder, forgetting it was tied up. Wonderful. Now her hand dangled somewhere behind her head and she was a gesticulating crazy person. "I'm looking for a dog. You might have mistaken it for a swamp rat?" If she talked fast, maybe that would distract him.

"Indeed." He gave his chin a musing rub. "I must say that I harbor a sneaking suspicion on his general whereabouts."

"You do?"

He nodded in the direction of a rustling bush. "Consider directing your investigation that way. A great deal of whining emitted from the foliage a moment ago."

She bent, peering into the undergrowth. Wolfgang

crouched beneath a branch, snout deep in one of Dude's peaches.

"Are you crazy?" she muttered. No wonder the hungry swine was on the move. "Do you have a death wish?"

Wolfgang pointedly ignored her, lapping the pit to a gleaming polish.

If she hadn't been so relieved by the fact the Chihuahua lived she'd have scooped him up from the tail and fed him to the boar herself.

"All's well that ends well?" the man asked.

"Yes. Thank you," she replied gratefully. "You are a life-saver."

"The name's Cedric Swift." His smile revealed deep-set dimples. "And pleased to be of service. I debated taking this bench—allergic to dogs, I'm afraid—but must say, I'm rather glad for it. This is my first week in Everland. I'm letting a cottage near the river."

"Small world." She toyed with her off-the-shoulder neckline. Allergic to dogs? Dreamy. "I'm Pepper and also new in town. But won't be staying."

"Ah." His shoulders fell. "More's the pity," he said. Was it wishful thinking or did a trace of wistfulness color his words?

"You sound a long way from home."

"Ah. Yes. From across the pond." He blinked rapidly. "The Cotswolds in south central England. The land of thatched roofs, cobblestone streets, and teahouses."

"What brings you here?" She was curious, but also curious that her pulse stayed on an even keel. This guy was polished and had a hot British accent. Yes her insides stayed as serene as a morning pond.

"Well, you see, I'm something of a specialist on the

subject of outlaws in the Atlantic. The great age of sail is of particular interest."

Tossing a glance over her shoulder, she captured Rhett's gaze. Not hard, considering he was staring in her direction, one hand shoved deep in his pockets. Sun reflected on his glasses, hiding the expression in his eyes. For not being her type, she found herself more curious about him than her current conversation.

"Ah, I've bored you already," Cedric said. "This is a new record."

She snapped back her head to protest and he lifted a hand. "Not a problem. You won't be the first. Or the last, I'm afraid."

"You're a historian?" Just because she lacked chemistry with this very sweet, very charming man didn't mean she needed to abandon manners.

He nodded. "From Oxford. I wrote the definite account of how Falmouth became a vital part of the empire's maritime strategy during the early to mid-nineteenth century. You might have read it?"

"Um—"

"I was only having a bit of fun," he said with a self-deprecating chuckle. "Not even my own mum stayed awake past the first chapter. Rather dry stuff, I'm afraid. Still, it's allowed me to take a sabbatical for the year. I'm quite interested in the Redbeard lore specific to this region." He reached for the red thermos beside him. "But enough about me. May I interest you in joining me for a cuppa?"

And if there was ever definitive proof that Everland was a parallel universe it was here, in the fact that she'd rather walk back over to a grumpy coffee-sipping veterinarian than stay and take tea with an intellectual Englishman who made befuddled Hugh Grant–like facial expressions.

Notting Hill also happened to be one of her top five favorite movies.

This choice didn't happen lightly.

"Rain check?" she asked, wrangling Wolfgang back on the leash. More concerned about the amorous look in his eyes than his teeth. Progress. Sort of.

"Of course." He took the gentle rebuff in good stride. "I expect to be here most mornings, keeping to this side of the fence, of course. And keeping an eye out for any wayward dogs."

"I'd appreciate that." She smiled before returning to Rhett and the General.

Rhett readjusted a shirt cuff with a stiff nod, not looking her in the eye. "Who was that?" he asked levelly.

"Just a guy. New in town, too." She shrugged. "From the UK."

"England?" Incredulity tinged his words.

"Why are you using that tone?" Pepper stepped under the towering magnolia, seeking refuge from the sun's unrelenting rays.

"Tone?" He frowned down at her. "I have no tone."

She held her ground. "You do, too."

"Do not."

"Well, what *I do* know is that we like seeing you around here, brother. Stop bein' a stranger." The General clapped a friendly hand on Rhett's shoulder. "Why I bet you've the makings of a champion Scrabble player, a regular chip off the ol' block."

"Scrabble?"

"We play here daily." He pointed at a picnic table where a

well-dressed older woman was unpacking a board. Her blue rinse was vaguely familiar. It took a minute for recognition to hit. She was the frowning lurker from the big house along Hopes and Dreams Way, the one who behaved as if her sheer curtains were camouflage yesterday morning when Pepper got lost on the first—only—morning of her clerkship.

"And there he is," the General continued. "Ladies and gents, the current reigning word champion."

The wrought iron gate creaked and in strolled an older man in a suit. At first glance he appeared harmless enough, in his early seventies with a vigorous step. His nose hooked, and his close-set gaze was bright with a fierce intelligence. Not even the fact he matched his bowties to his lapdog's hair ribbons dimmed his dignity.

The fuzz ball glanced in her direction and emitted a low growl in the back of her throat.

Ah, Fluffy. We meet again. Pepper leaned in to Rhett. "If Dude ever did acquire a taste for dog, I know who I'd put on the menu."

Rhett didn't respond. In fact, the blood had drained from his face.

"Hey. You okay?" she murmured. "You don't look good."

"I'm late for my next appointment." He squinted, gaze hard, like they'd been on her front porch the night Miss Ida May had spoken to him.

Pepper quickly put two and two together. That older man was the same guy she'd seen Rhett arguing with near the courthouse. "Fluffy's owner is your dad?"

"Her name is Marie Claire," he snapped. "Now try not to lose any more clients. I stuck my neck out getting you this job."

Ouch. She bristled, taken aback at the tone. "Don't worry, I won't forget..."

But he'd already stalked off without waiting for her response, giving the old man a wide berth.

"Doctor, might I have the pleasure of introducing the Everland dog park's newest member?" The General gallantly signaled toward Pepper.

"Miss Knight, I presume." The old man clicked his heels and executed a stiff bow.

"This is Doc Valentine," the General said. "A living local legend. Delivered half the town. And he's Rhett's father," he added out of the side of his mouth. "They don't get along."

Doc glowered. Ah, there was the family resemblance. That and the way he held himself. No fidgeting.

"Nice to meet you and um, you?" Addressing a dog felt silly but this one seemed to be following the conversation. Wolfgang hurled himself forward, whining, thin tail wagging.

Fluffy growled low in her throat.

"Marie Claire has rarified tastes," Doc said. "She's discriminating in whom she associates with."

Was Doc projecting himself on his pet? Forget pirate history. Someone needed to conduct a dog park psychological study. In the meantime, how was she going to survive this job without losing her damn mind?

Chapter Ten

Rhett stalked the shady, tree-lined street. What had he been thinking? He never visited the dog park. That was Doc's territory. They had marked Everland like two alphas claiming territory. His dad got the park. Rhett got Sweet Brew. His dad got Chez Louis. Rhett got Smuggler's Cove. Dad had a membership to the upscale Ocean Springs Yacht Club, while Rhett kept *Calypso* docked at the more low-key Buccaneers Marina. Today he'd crossed enemy lines and for what? To check on Pepper and see how she did walking a dog?

No. The truth was worse. He'd gotten curious about a woman. Worse, he'd allowed that curiosity to propel him into the park and the interaction hadn't gone unnoticed.

It was enough to almost make him miss the uncomplicated days of the Birdie era. Nobody gave a hoot over a couple who'd gone steady since junior high. There were no surprises between them until she left him standing at the altar while the whole damn town watched with stomach-churning expressions.

Like it or not, Pepper Knight had captured his attention. It wasn't just that she was striking, the thick brows that somehow worked on her otherwise delicate features or the small mole dotting her upper lip. And it had nothing to do with the way her tight pants hugged her hips. Those helped, but it was something more.

When she looked at him, recognition sparked, like catching a glimpse of one's reflection in a window. She'd been hurt deep, too, and he'd never been able to resist helping anything lost.

"Rhett Jamison Valentine, kindly hightail your tushie over here."

Lou Lou had her Suburban parked across the road, glaring out the driver's-side window with an expression that could freeze hell to an ice rink.

"Shit," he muttered under his breath. This day took a sharp turn from bad to worse.

"Keep it PG for the little pitchers. Besides, you know how I feel about foul language." Lou Ellen had the manners of a belle and the ears of an elephant. She also swore like a sailor after her third mint julep, but reminding her of that fact would get him nowhere fast.

As he crossed the road, the back window rolled down and four heads popped out.

"Hey, Uncle Rhett."

"You're in trouble."

"Big trouble."

"Hoo-wee. Mama is maaaaaad."

His four nieces could barely contain their glee. Guess it was another day ending in *y*.

"And you all defended me, right?" he said, giving them a mock glare.

"Nope," they chimed in sweet unison. The little devils.

His sister removed her sunglasses, and a pang slammed through him. Lou Ellen was the spitting image of Mama. The same platinum-blonde hair. And same penetrating take-no-prisoners stare that cut right through a man's soul.

"Butter my biscuit," she sang out, slapping the steering wheel. "The gossip's true. You *are* interested in your new neighbor."

Damn it to hell. How did she always do that? Know exactly what he was thinking. He raked a hand over his head and leaned in. "Can you talk any louder? Pretty sure Miss Ida May only caught half of that, five blocks away, with the windows shut."

"The truth is stamped all over your face," she pushed on. "That's the same expression you used to get on Christmas morning."

Busted. He crossed his arms over his chest. No one ever caught him off guard like his sister. Her Sherlock Holmes–like powers of perception were fierce. It was a shame the CIA never came knocking. Although on second thought, maybe they had, and she was secretly an international spy hidden behind a smear of pink lipstick and blue eyeshadow. "I don't—"

"Don't burst a gullet denying what's obvious to anyone with two working eyes. Word to the wise, little brother. Ida May is ready to start a new neighborhood watch program so get your P's and Q's in order, and"—she lowered her voice to a whisper—"do you have condoms at home? Unexpired ones? Better safe than sorry, I always say."

Overhead, two buzzards circled leisurely. They might get

lucky after his sister was finished with him. "Nothing is going on."

"Mm-hmm. Except that you haven't engaged in a willing, non-work-related conversation with an eligible member of the opposite sex since I don't know when."

"I like my life." He knocked a boot against her tire. "I'm happy." Or at least not in the grip of soul-destroying active unhappiness. If someone would happen to run their fingers over his heart, it would come up coated in thick dust.

"Stop sulking, you big baby. I'd hand over my Macy's card to have that magical falling-head-over-heels feeling again." Her pert nose crinkled. "Instead I've got to text Snapper and remind him that we're out of laundry detergent. Again. And the front hall toilet's not flushing right for the second time this week. I don't know what y'all are doin' in there," she hollered over one shoulder.

"Sorry, Mama!" the kids shouted from the rear, sounding the opposite of apologetic.

Rhett hitched a thumb over his shoulder. "Know what? I'm gonna get going." Lou Lou's long-suffering husband, Snapper, was a far more patient man than him, poor son of a bitch. His sister had the biggest heart in four counties, but also the biggest mouth.

"I'll have to pop by the old Carmichael place and introduce myself. Think she likes red velvet cake? Oh, fiddle dee, what am I asking you for? Who doesn't love my baking?"

Another headache threatened. He'd take a deep breath, but he'd already tried that. No more air would fit into his lungs. He released some in a sigh. This is what he'd been afraid of, other people getting involved, not giving him time or space to figure feelings out for himself. "Don't go poking for trouble where there is none."

"I can't believe Al snubbed her like that." No one got away with calling Aloysius Hogg "Al" except for Lou Lou. She'd briefly dated him senior year. He'd gone too frisky at prom, and she'd dumped him on the dance floor, but not before giving him a knee where the sun don't shine.

Hogg had started rumors, but he picked the wrong family to tarnish. No one had a memory as long as Lou Lou's. She cherished her grudges more than her prized silver flatware, and polished them even more regularly.

Rhett got knocked around in a few fights with the Hogg extended family, meathead cousins egged on by Al. Mama took one look at the boot-print bruise over his kidney and near lost her mind. Doc stepped in and that was it. Game over. His father used his community influence to block Hogg from receiving a local scholarship, and the resulting enmity had endured to the present day.

Lou Lou didn't mind. In fact she was rather proud of the "feud," as she called it, claiming that having a family nemesis was invigorating for the spirit. Rhett thought it was a pain in the ass, but he couldn't respect a man who let others fight his battles, so he let sleeping dogs lie.

"Well, if you're not interested in your neighbor, how about being Mr. Scallywag?" Lou Ellen held up a finger, cutting him off before he finished opening his mouth. "The Village Pillage is next month, and we don't have anyone."

"I'm shocked," he said dryly. The Village Pillage was the annual Everland summer festival, a celebration of the town's pirate heritage. One of the key events was the town silent auction. He always donated a free check-up. But each year some unlucky chump was Mr. Scallywag and was put on the block for a blind date. "Who the hell would want to be Mr. Scallywag?"

"A man who wants to help his sister who is the chair of the silent auction? Besides, the money is going to enhance Everland Green, and that includes your beloved dog park."

"I'm working my ass off to build an animal shelter. My conscience is clear."

"When are you going to come over and play Barbies again, Uncle Rhett? You are the best Ken!" Lilac cried as Lorelai piped from the far back of the van, "Mama, can Santa bring me a My Little Pony for Christmas? I want Applejack."

"I don't even want to hear you-know-who's name until after Halloween." She shook her head. "Whatever happened to it's better to give than to receive? Now what was I saying?"

Lou Lou wouldn't rest until he had enough kids to fill his own soccer team and spent every weekend at Little League with Snapper. He loved his sister, but she drove him crazy. "There's something to be said for peace and quiet." Rhett took a step, then another, backing away.

"What's the fun in that? Oh, go on, walk away," Lou Ellen called. "You can't hide from the truth. This day has been a long time coming, Sugar Booger. An answer to all my prayers."

He scowled at the sidewalk as his sister drove off laughing. The throbbing in his head intensified. For years he'd been the subject of town gossip, and the only way he managed to stay out of the Back Fence headlines was to lie low. Be dull as water. This passing interest in Pepper Knight wasn't worth the hassle. She wouldn't be sticking around, and he had to live here, day in, day out, without going crazier than a peach orchard pig.

Time to fly under the radar and put her out of his mind for good.

Chapter Eleven

⌒

To the telephone line. Come on. Push through to the telephone line," Pepper panted, running along the gravel road the following week. Okay, so not technically running. Senior citizens could outpace her with their walkers, but that wasn't the point. She was out here, putting one foot in front of the other.

At last she passed the telephone pole and threw her arms up in a victory *V*. Mission accomplished. Trouble was, she'd gone a mile and a half, and now needed to make it home. That feat required extra motivation. Popping on her earphones, she pulled out her phone and turned on her new running app, Zombie Sprint. It had been worth the download for the tagline alone: "We'll make you run for your life."

"Let's do this." She hit play and tugged down the brim of her favorite hat, a Christmas present from Tuesday that said WILL JOG FOR CUPCAKES.

"One's coming up on your left, kick it into gear if you want to keep your brain," the authoritative female voice commanded in her ear. She was fond of her brain, so she dug in, picking up speed. *Go. Go. Go.* Her thighs burned. Lungs seared. Okay, no way could she keep this pace up long.

Or for another thirty seconds.

Oh God, it hurt to breathe.

If she were in a zombie apocalypse movie, forget about being the heroine. She'd be the extra who tripped during the scene one stampede and got skull-munched in the background next to the dumpster fire.

"They're coming toward you. The only way out is to dig deep, give it everything and leave nothing behind," the voice faded behind simulated static and zombie groans. On her left, screams came through the forest, from the direction of Happily Ever After Land, heightening the ambiance. Roller coasters left her queasy at the best of times, but the idea of hurling around a hundred-year-old track made her downright nauseous.

She grit her teeth and swung her arms. No one would eat her brains. Not today. Not ever. She rolled her ankle on a loose rock with a sharp gasp.

Holy shit painful. She braced her hands on her knees and squeezed her eyes shut. That hurt. That hurt a lot. Luckily the coast was clear, and no one bore witness as she limped off the road to brace against a tree trunk. Below, the Everland River moseyed along, the current unhurried, sunlight bouncing off the water. She stretched, pointing her toes with a wince. A sweet wildflower scent hung in the air. She gingerly put weight back on her foot. The pain subsided as a gust of wind shook the branches and snatched off her cupcake hat. It floated down, down, down into the scrub brush.

"No!" Her sister felt far away, and that cap was sentimental. Bum ankle or not, she had to get it back. Gingerly, she scrambled down the embankment. The path was narrow and smooth. The riparian area stretched to a wide sandy shoal as thick vegetation blocked the road from view. Alone with the cicadas, rustling trees, and gurgling river, the real world felt far away.

And there was her hat in the middle of the Everland River, perched on a patch of dry bark on an otherwise submerged log.

She'd have to swim out, but if she jumped in wearing these shorts, the homeward run would be one heck of a thigh chafer. But she couldn't walk away. That hat had emotional value, dammit.

She'd worn it on weekend jogs in the city, before meeting up with Tuesday to hit the Magnolia Bakery in Rockefeller Center. The hat conjured up memories of German chocolate cupcakes smothered in coconut, caramel, and pecan icing and people-watching the tourists posing in front of the Prometheus statue outside 30 Rock. It was more than just a hat; it held happy pieces of her past, sweet city days with her sister.

"Ta-weet! Ta-weet!" A nondescript brown bird watched from a bush.

"I'm not leaving," she told it, setting her phone on a flat rock and hiking off her shorts. "I can't abandon it. I won't."

And darned if that little guy didn't burst into woodland song.

She hung the shorts on a low-hanging branch and frowned at her legs, a grooming no-man's-land. Glossy hairs dotted her calves. She hadn't shaved in order to get a wax but was now too broke for a salon. If she buckled down until Halloween, she could go as Mr. Tumnus, the hairy-haunched Narnia faun.

Her racer-back jogging top came off next. It had a built-in bra shelf, which meant that except for her panties she'd stripped almost naked. This felt like the beginning of a bad idea, except that hat flapped out in the river, daring her on.

She eyed the water, hugging her chest. Sentimentality was cold and wet, but she was in for a penny now.

Holding her breath, she dipped in her toe, and huffed a relieved sigh. The water wasn't cold, in fact, the temperature felt nothing short of refreshing. She waded deeper, sweat whisking from her body. Why, she was as good as Tom Sawyer or Huckleberry Finn, splashing around the ol' swimmin' hole.

Except Tom didn't have boobs that floated in water. Time to kick hard before she was spotted. She shoved off the bottom and tried for a decent freestyle stroke. The current was stronger in the middle, but no real challenge. When her fingers closed around the brim, she gave a victorious splash. Unbelievable. She'd swum into the river, tits out, in the middle of the day. That was the most physically daring thing she'd done since leaving Maine, when she used to go frog catching at the pond, or hike Bradbury Mountain State Park during the fall colors, or explore the tidal marshes around Cape Elizabeth.

She plopped the hat down on her head, blinking as water drops rolled off the brim to splash in her eye. Her throat was tight from the unexpected walk down memory lane. It had been a long time since she'd thought about any of that, but she couldn't hang out and reflect, treading water mostly naked. Time to get back to shore and dress before anyone was the wiser.

Halfway back, the strengthening breeze increased to strong gusts. Her shorts swung on the branch, once, twice, and *whoosh!* They took flight, skimming the air, light as a feather, before coming to a rest ten feet downstream, catching the current.

Shit the bed.

In three strokes she'd reached the bank, scrambled out and gotten her tank top safely in hand. But a fat lot of good it would do her without those shorts. She dove in. Good thing they were bright pink. She wasn't sure of the color when buying them on sale, but now the outrageous color shone like a beacon from the dark water.

But the harder she stroked, the shorts stayed ahead, tantalizingly close but elusive. And town was fast approaching. "Stroke," she ordered out loud. "Stroke!" The consequences of failure were too great to contemplate.

The moment of uncharacteristic sentimentality fast retreated behind a gathering shitstorm of reality. If she didn't catch those shorts, doom and hellfire would reign on her nearly bare butt.

The Kissing Bridge loomed ahead, the last stand before town. She kicked double time and remembered. Oh. Shit. For real shit. After the Kissing Bridge was a waterfall. Nothing big. No Niagara. But a respectable ten-foot plunge that wouldn't feel so great clad only in a pink ball cap and pair of cotton bikini briefs. Her legs became eggbeaters, churning the water.

And then...the shorts bobbed beneath the bridge, struck a half-submerged rock, flew into the air with a cheerful farewell and disappeared over the edge.

"Noooooooooooooo!" She grabbed a bridge piling and hauled herself onto the concrete stump, managing a few inches of toehold. Below, her shorts zipped around the bend, heading straight for downtown Everland's river walk. She knocked her forehead against the wood. What did she do to deserve this, run over a guardian angel's halo?

"Pepper? Pepper, is that you?" a low voice whispered. Not any voice either. Rhett Valentine was up on that bridge.

She jerked, releasing her hold on her tank top. It too rocketed over the waterfall with what remained of her pride.

Chapter Twelve

$\backsim$

At first he'd thought it a trick of his imagination. The splashing caught his eye and he slowed as a bare leg shot into sight. Hell of a nice one, too. He knew the exact curve of that calf because it was the same one he'd been covertly checking out all week.

What the hell was Pepper Knight doing swimming under the Kissing Bridge?

He pulled his Bronco to the shoulder and cut the engine, cranking the window. And why was she cussing up a storm, saying words he hadn't heard anyone ever use, expressions he'd never even thought of?

A pink Cadillac pulled alongside.

Rhett cracked a knuckle. Miss Ida May, town windbag extraordinaire, had an uncanny instinct for turning up at the worst time.

"Whatcha doing, Cupid?" She propped her elbow on the window ledge and fingered a string of pearls.

He gave a low whistle, ignoring his bristle of irritation at the nickname. "Why, look at you all gussied up."

Her gaze narrowed even as she gave an appreciative chuckle, patting the salt-and-pepper curls cut close to her head. "You could charm the balls off a bull, boy. But do tell, what's the news?"

"News?" He kept his features stoic. "No news here, ma'am. I'm checking out the river conditions."

Her lips pursed. "Why?"

"Fishing."

"You don't fish."

"Thinking about starting."

There was another splash beneath the bridge. He pretended to cough.

Her eyes narrowed. "Something fishy's going on, though."

Time to take charge of the conversation, drive it in a different direction. "The only thing fishy around here is you, you old catfish."

She batted her eyes. "Another woman might take offense to that kind of talk."

"Another woman wouldn't realize I meant it as the highest praise."

"Rhett Valentine, ooooh, go on." She swatted him away. "You're so cute it should be illegal."

"Make a citizen's arrest." He winked. "I don't mind handcuffs."

"You're nasty and I like it," she said with a throaty chuckle, starting the engine back up. "Now I won't keep you. Got to get on over to Quilt Guild. They're all waiting on my sweet potato pie."

"Quit before you make me want to take up sewing." He

ground his molars. He was laying it on too thick. But she blew him a kiss and drove off.

He waited until she cleared the other side of the covered bridge before creeping to the edge and calling out.

"Pepper?"

Silence.

"Pepper, come on. I know you're there."

More silence.

"Are you okay?" Concern built.

"Don't come any closer!" Her voice was high. Unnatural. "I mean it. Stop right there."

He scrambled down the embankment and froze. Sweet fucking Christ. He'd prided himself on having a halfway decent imagination, but he hadn't made it out of t-ball. Pepper Knight was a major-league home run. And practically naked, water beading on every sexy curve. Except the scowl plastered on the pretty face peeping out from beneath her pink ball cap could douse the most raging hard-on.

Almost.

"Looks like you went and got yourself stuck up a creek without a paddle."

"Don't ask." She was more irate than a feral kitten plunged in a cold bath.

He'd be happy to keep watching her try and fail to cover herself all day, but Mama raised him to be a gentleman. "Let's get you out of here before anyone sees." He strode down the riverbank and held out his hand. "Can you swim?"

"How do you think I ended up in this situation?" Her dark hair shone even in the shadows while that lush mouth compressed into a prim line.

"Trust me, that's high on my list of questions."

Her eyes narrowed at the humor lacing his voice. "I can't come out. Not like this."

She was right. They weren't going to have much time before another car came along, and hell if he wanted anyone else seeing her this way.

He loosened his tie and unslung it from around his neck before unbuttoning his shirt.

"Are you insane?" she hissed, bouncing on her toes. "We can't both be naked!"

"This is called being chivalrous, part of my Southern charm." He stuffed the tie in his pocket and shrugged out of his shirt, holding it out. "Get over here and stick this on quick."

Her gaze lingered on his abdomen. Her eyes were large and round. *Well, how'd you like that, she is perving.* He subtly flexed, not about to turn away from her probing stare. Confusion etched in her face. This time his muscles tightened of his own volition.

"I'm not checking you out or anything." Her glance rose to his mouth, and her bewilderment grew even more pronounced.

"Guess that makes one of us." He winked, baiting her like a cranky kitten.

His reward was an outraged squeak, one he'd like to hear again somewhere more comfortable, like his king-size bed. A fast-sinking sense of self-preservation warned him that this situation would be a serious bite in the ass, but he was in for a penny now.

She licked her lips. "Can you at least try to be mature about this?"

"That's the pot calling the kettle black," he muttered. He couldn't stop poking at her, like a kid with a first crush.

A splash bounced off the underside of the bridge and a moment later she snatched the shirt from his proffered reach. "Ouch."

He turned as she winced, barefoot, from the gravel. Her toes were painted a bold red. Something about that shade was a major turn-on.

"My shoes and phone are upstream." She shoved her arms through the holes and leaning forward to do up the buttons from the bottom. The swell of her breasts teased him through the half-open gap before vanishing from sight.

"I'll drive you to them." His body tensed from both anticipation and nerves. He stepped forward. "Let me help."

"What are you doiiiiiiiing?" she cried as he swung her off her feet. "You have two seconds to put me down."

Her skin felt even softer than it looked, and the strands of her hair tickling his forearms killed him slowly. She smelled like apples, ones that had been bobbing in a river for the afternoon, but apples nevertheless.

"I said put me down!" She twisted this way and that. "I don't need help."

"That's not how it looks to me." He readjusted his grip. *Shit.* That was her ass. He'd accidently grabbed a damn near perfect handful. "And this would go a sight easier if you'd stop wriggling."

"I can take care of myself. I have two perfectly good legs."

God help him, they were better than good. He knew every square inch of those two particular appendages better than the back road to Hogg Jaw. "High school kids party here. There can be broken glass around. You don't want to get cut."

"Okay, but..." She raised her chin a fraction, visibly searching for another excuse. "The hill is steep."

"Pepper Knight, you are the most headstrong, stubborn, bullheaded woman I have ever met, and even that is an understatement." And he meant it as a compliment. She was also smart, direct, and trouble with a capital *T*. But if he told her that, he might let other truths slip out, too, like how his gaze swung to her front door every time he left his house. How a man could melt in those dark eyes, pools of bittersweet chocolate. "But you need to accept help when it's freely offered."

She lowered her lashes, and hesitated, unsure. "I'm not exactly a lightweight."

He drew a long slow breath. Here was the difference between Northern and Southern women. All the ladies he knew—down to a one—would say, "Why, thank you," and accept the act of chivalry as their due.

"What can I say?" Not that her thighs were perfect. Or how all he could wonder was how the weight of them would feel, hooked around his shoulders. "I like a challenge." He started walking. Withstanding the way the side of her ass skimmed his dick going to be the ultimate test of willpower. "Now I have to ask—"

"I'm pleading the fifth." They reached the top and she slipped from his grasp faster than an eel. The sight of her bare thighs emerging from his shirt was the hottest sight he'd seen in a long time.

Guys were supposed to want it all the time. But after Birdie, he'd tried a few times. Not with anyone local—just tourists—but anonymous sex wasn't his thing, and the fact the whole town wanted to spy on his bed had been a boner killer.

He stepped back and reached for the passenger door. His dick had nine lives. "Your chariot awaits."

"Thanks," she murmured, clutching at his shirttail while stepping inside. "Like it or not, guess I needed a hero." Her smile was unexpected, the real deal, and lodged right in his heart.

When he returned to his seat, the cab smelled like a goddamn orchard. He leaned toward the window, sucking in a gulp of country air. Didn't help. Tonight he'd dream of apple pie. "What were you thinking?"

"Long story short, I wasn't." Her brown-eyed gaze bounced around the car, refusing to land on anything. "Enough about me though. Why's this called the Kissing Bridge?" she asked.

He wasn't the Everland Welcome Wagon, but when his audience was a half-naked knockout, it seemed like a good time to fulfill his civic duty. "Back in the olden days, when a young Everland couple went courting, this is where they'd come."

She frowned. It was as if he could see the lightbulb go off. Her whole face illuminated. "Oh! Because it's covered. No one could see what they got up to."

"Guess you didn't earn that fancy law degree for nothing."

Just like that, he blew the moment. Her face shuttered. "Yeah. How about that." She snapped on a seat belt. "You've lived here all your life?"

She was good at redirecting conversation from herself. "More or less. I went to school over in Athens. But it's not here. Say what you want about Everland, and it's probably true. And yet, it's home."

"And how often have you escorted a special someone to the Kissing Bridge?" she poked mischievously.

"Once." The ugly truth slipped out.

She recoiled, as if sensing conversation quicksand ahead. "Oh. I see."

"No." His hand covered her knee. Which happened to be bare. She had peach-soft skin, golden with a hint of blush. "I don't mind. You'll hear it sooner or later. There used to be somebody."

She brushed away a nonexistent mark on his shirtsleeve. "A serious somebody?"

"Somebody I asked to marry me. Somebody who said yes."

"What happened?"

"Got left at the altar." Let her chew on that.

Her mouth twitched, but her dark eyes were serious—weighing if he was joking or not.

He swallowed a sigh. He was a joke, and no he wasn't joking. It had been nice to enjoy the time when she hadn't the faintest clue to his dubious claim to local fame.

He stared at her straight-faced until her half-smile turned into a ghost. "When?"

"A few years ago. Six this month. We were childhood sweethearts. Been together since the Under the Sea dance in the eighth grade. She went as Ariel, red wig, the whole bit." He dragged a hand through his hair. "I was in the relationship for the wrong reason."

"Which was?"

He tried for a smile. "People used to tell us it wouldn't work, but we were both stubborn. Over time, we grew apart. In the end, she made the right choice breaking off the relationship, but the event sent me rudderless. It wasn't losing the love of my life; it was losing a friend, a best friend in many ways, and my idea of how life would look. After that I drank too much. Sailed in storms I shouldn't have.

"The town still roots for me, but I never asked them to fix my problems or fix me up. I don't want a year's subscription to a dating website. I want what anyone outside of Hollywood does, a simple life out of the public eye. I have a job I love, a boat, and trust me, it's all smooth sailing."

"Do you stay in touch with her?"

Pepper pulled the rug out from under his bravado, left him scrambling. The only thing he knew was to plant his feet in the cold, hard, truth.

"Birdie? Yeah, hard not to. We aren't close, but I wish her the best. It took guts for her to do what she did. I should never have proposed in the first place, but we were young and dumb, only nineteen when engaged, and it lasted another ten years while I went off to vet school and started my practice. Not every first love is meant to be your last."

She pondered that a moment, an unasked question scrunching her forehead. "I'll take your word for it."

"What, you've never been in love?" With a face like that, hard to believe they weren't lining up around the block.

After a brief pause, she shrugged. "Do fictional men count? My relationship status is singing power ballads to stray cats."

There it was, conclusive proof that his gender was made up of idiots. "That's the craziest damn thing I've ever heard."

She gave a rueful shrug. "You haven't ventured out of Everland much, huh? The world is a hard place, Rhett Valentine. War. Death. Suffering. Netflix refusing to upload the latest season of your favorite show."

A piece of her flyaway hair bobbed in the breeze. He reached to smooth it and threaded his fingers through the silky tresses instead.

"What are you doing?" She squared her body to face him. Her throat flushed. He liked it. And that small mole on her kissable mouth, too, the one shaped like a heart.

"Looking at you."

Her unexpected smile transformed her whole face. Something passed, invisible, between them. A dark, thick tension burned up his veins, hotter than a whisky shot. Fuck it, he was going in. He leaned toward her. She had the tiniest of freckles on her lower lip. He'd lick it.

"Rhett?" That wasn't a breathy, "take me, sexy baby," tone. He froze.

"Don't look now, but you know the old woman who lives across the street?"

His heart sunk. "Miss Ida May?"

"She is parked across the river spying on us through a pair of binoculars. No, I said don't look."

Too late. Miss Ida May's pink Cadillac was parked on the far side of the river, the hood emerging from the bushes. She waggled her fingers in a cheery wave.

His shoulders heaved with an inward groan. So much for staying out of the spotlight. He'd been damned if he did and damned if he didn't in helping Pepper out of her jam.

Now, he was fucked.

No good deed ever goes unpunished.

Chapter Thirteen

~

A rumble exploded from the west, lightning chasing itself across the inky sky. The Weather Channel forecasted a wild night. Aloysius Hogg flicked the channel with the handheld remote and resumed trimming his toenails on the leather couch. A late-night show flickered on the flat screen. The guy who replaced Letterman interviewed some celebrity hack. He knew both their names, but that fourth whisky on the rocks made remembering a chore. Or was it the fifth? Fourth? Fifth?

Storms made him drink; thunder kept him on edge. He rolled his shoulders. The alcohol wasn't helping release his knotted muscles. Work had been worse than usual. If Tommy Haynes, his new clerk, devoted half the time to improving his legal analysis that he did to his online blackjack addiction, Aloysius wouldn't have to stay up until all hours rewriting his cases.

He wanted him gone, but Mama said to suck it up, that having powerful people in their debt was better than money in the bank. And like it or not, Tommy was a Haynes. That name meant something in Georgia, an old name, and an old-money name. Lifted the Hogg brand through mere association.

Aloysius dropped the clippers to the cushion and studied his hand. It was a hand all right. He flexed. Human. No black hairs on the knuckles, no scars or calluses—nothing like Pops. An average human appendage.

He hated it.

Nothing should be average about him. He tried for extraordinary, worked to a state of perpetual heartburn, but he could never make *her* happy.

In this dog-eat-dog world, only alphas could lead the pack. He needed to have the heart of an alpha. Dante growled as another boom of thunder shook the windows, rain lashing the glass.

His Doberman pinscher had an alpha's heart. But his was weak. Deep down he knew it. Worse, Mama knew it.

She'd taken to her bed a few years ago, after retiring as the organist for Halfway Baptist Church once arthritis got the upper hand. There'd been a time when he thought she'd give up the ghost from sheer boredom.

Until she found a new hobby.

Whenever anyone in Hogg Jaw needed a favor, they drove out here to Founder's House at the end of Gloom Wood Drive. The judge turned a blind eye to the late-night dealings, trusting Mama knew enough to skirt the law but never breach it. She'd driven his career with single-minded ruthlessness for too long to compromise his interests. She'd put him on a pedestal in public, only to knock it out from under him in private.

No. He bit the inside of his cheek hard enough to taste bitter copper. No disloyalty to Mama. She'd done her best by him. Sacrificed everything. *He* was the defective one. Couldn't even continue the family line. Women treated him like he carried an infectious disease, even when he tried to show them he was a winner.

Women loved winners.

But Mama knew best, and *she* said he was a loser. How did she put it the time he'd gone out with Kennedy Day, a divorcée who received a luxury auto dealership in Charleston as part of the settlement? They'd had dinner at Chez Louis, and he'd ordered the most expensive bottle of wine on the menu before rattling off his list of accomplishments and earning potential.

She'd complained of a headache during the main course and left before dessert. Yesterday she'd blocked him on social media.

After he'd confessed all to Mama, she'd clicked her tongue.

"Poor Aloysius," she'd said sorrowfully. "Why are you so difficult to love?"

He picked up his glass Coke bottle and plopped in a few peanuts. The salt fizzed in the carbonated water before he took a swig. Mother hated his favorite snack. Called peanuts in cola common. But what she didn't know didn't hurt him. He smugly took a long pull, crunching on the shells while glancing to the ceiling.

Dread sloshed in his gut alongside the sweet liquid. She hated hearing him chew.

No Hogg should sound like a hog at dinner.

Upstairs, a bell tinkled. He jerked upright, swiping his mouth. Setting the Coke on a coaster, he reached for a butter mint from the crystal candy dish before straightening his collar.

"Coming, Mama," he called.

Chapter Fourteen

When Pepper entered the dog park the next morning, the place went so quiet she could hear a Milk-Bone drop.

"What's up?" She brushed a hand over her face, a quick check for renegade Pop-Tart frosting. "Are my pants on inside out?"

"Suppose we should count ourselves grateful that you've elected to wear some," Doc Valentine muttered without preamble, frowning over the top of the *Everland Examiner*. Today he and Fluffy—er, Marie Claire—were coordinating butterscotch-colored bowties and ribbons. The effect made his skin look sallow and gave Pepper no small pleasure.

Her petty was showing.

Even still, her shoulders slumped like a marionette whose strings were unceremoniously cut. Hard to be snarky when every single person here must know that she'd spent yesterday afternoon lurking under the Kissing Bridge like a half-naked troll. Two ways to play this: act dumb or do a mea culpa. This crowd didn't seem the type to fall for an "aw shucks" routine.

Mea culpa it was then.

Loins, prepare to be girded.

She unclipped Wolfgang's leash. He dove for her leg, but she cut him with a sharp "Sit," coupled with a tough look that promised *On your butt or you'll be coated in batter and deep fried.*

He dropped to his haunches and she resisted the urge to fist pump. *Cesar Millan, eat your heart out.*

"Now what's this about skinny-dipping?" The General clutched his heart with a good-natured wink. "Got to say, girl, I didn't think you had it in you."

"Rumor has it that your boy was involved," said an older woman in tailored slacks, a patterned blazer, and kitten heels. She gave Doc a prudish frown while stroking the haughty Scotch terrier on her lap.

People do look like their pets.

Doc sat back against the bench, resting his interlaced fingers on his small paunch. "I can assure you, Lucille, that whatever undesirables my son fraternizes with is of no consequence to me." His pompously adenoidal tone made it clear that not only did he harbor an opinion, but it was a bad one.

Undesirables?

Oh, for the love of Gosling.

She hadn't danced naked around a bonfire on the solstice; she just hadn't wanted to lose the physical reminder of happy memories. But no point getting sentimental about cupcake hats with that sourpuss.

What was it like for Rhett to grow up in the shadow of this grim-faced guy? Her own dad thought everything she and Tuesday did was the best, most amazing thing ever.

Finger painting. Playing right field on the second-string softball team. Moving to New York for university. Or her sister's off-off-*off*-Broadway roles. His pride was as reliable as Target's ability to make her drop a hundred bucks when all she meant to buy was conditioner.

A rapid movement snapped her out of navel gazing.

Shitake mushrooms.

Wolfgang mounted the butterscotch-bowed Fluffy by the drinking fountain. His tiny hips thrust faster than a seventies porn star.

Doc followed the direction of her horrified gaze and made a strangled sound. "This isn't the grand seraglio of the Ottoman sultans, Miss Knight. Everland, Georgia, is home to God-fearing folk. Get your hound off my Marie Claire."

"He's not my dog. He's my customer." That sounded worse. "Wolfgang." She clapped her hands. Her authoritative voice lost in the tug-of-war with his libido. "Stop. Stop that right now. Wolfgang, I said get off. Down. Go on." Eventually, he dismounted, and tucked his small pointy tail as if to say *thanks for killing my mojo*.

"Guess what?" the General said as the Chihuahua proceeded to clean himself with excruciating thoroughness.

"I despise guessing games," Doc boomed over the noisy slurps. He folded the paper and rapped the Scrabble box. "Are we going to play, or should I gather my things and return home?"

"Can we let her in?" The General nodded at Pepper. "Jim's doing stocktake at the store all morning, and Norma's out of commission while she recovers."

Lucille and Doc exchanged loaded glances.

"No one replaces Norma," Doc answered at last.

"That's okay," Pepper said hastily, whipping out her

phone. Technology, saving victims of casual ostracism in the twenty-first century. "You go on and have fun with your board game."

"A game? Is that what you said? Scrabble isn't a game." The General wheezed, taking a seat next to Doc at the picnic table. "Here in Everland it's a way of life. Think of playing as your initiation into local culture."

"You'll vouch for her, General?" Lucille gave Pepper a censuring stare as she took her place. "If so, then I'm prepared to grant an exception. After all I *am* a Christian."

"Do try to remain clothed," Doc muttered under his breath as he pulled out a tile from the cloth bag. "*Q*."

"Okay. Question. Is this that famous Southern hospitality everyone goes on and on about?" Pepper put her phone away and tiptoed closer.

Besides the General, no one so much as cracked a smile. Her own cheeky grin wavered. "Tough crowd."

"Stop hovering or you'll give me hives." Lucille selected her tile. "*V*."

The General glanced at his. "*S*."

All three turned to Pepper with expectant expressions. Smothering a smile, she sat and plucked one out. "*P*. Like my name."

"You're up first," Lucille said witheringly. "Are you at least passingly acquainted with the rules?"

Pepper debated whether she should own the truth or not. Her letters were *T, E, S, A, R, I,* and *P*. A shimmer of excitement took hold. Best play it cool. "I think so. We spell words, right?"

Doc and Lucille exchanged another look.

Oh, yeah. This was going to be fun.

"Yes," Doc said carefully.

"And while bragging rights are well and good, we prefer to spice it up," Lucille continued. "That is, if you have no moral objection to a little harmless amusement."

"Spice?" Pepper's tone was innocence personified.

"Aw, go easy on her, you two," the General said.

Lucille opened up her handbag. "Five-dollar stake. Each."

"Winner gets twenty bucks?" Pepper sat on her hands to prevent clapping.

"Gambling keeps us young," Lucille said. But her leer conveyed *I've flossed bigger things than you from my teeth, small fry.*

The General cleared his throat. "I don't think we should take advantage of—"

"Count me in." Pepper tugged out a crumpled fiver from her hip pocket. Abraham Lincoln stared from the table with an uncertain expression that said *I hope you know what you're doing.* She tapped her lower lip. "Let me try to remember. If I use a few tiles, then do I replace them?"

"Yes," Doc said.

She furrowed her brow. "What if I use all my tiles in the first go?"

"A bingo?" Lucille said. "That's fifty extra points."

"Interesting." Pepper grabbed her *P* tile and twirled it between her fingers. "One more question. I'm new in town, but what's all this I'm hearing about Captain Redbeard's missing treasure being hidden in Everland? You guys sure have a colorful local history." Inwardly, she cringed. She was going to blow her cover by overplaying this aw-shucks routine.

"That's no rumor," Doc said. "His first mate, Joseph Elleselle, founded Everland and took the secret to his grave. Of course Hogg Jaw wants to take the credit, but what can you expect from a den of hustlers and shysters."

"You're asking the wrong gal." She placed the *P* over the center star, then *I, R, A, T, E, S.* "Bingo." She smiled at their stunned faces. "One benefit of growing up in Moose Bottom, Maine, was that the winters were loooooong. That meant a whole lot of Scrabble. My sister and I won the junior state championships and came in third and fourth in the New England Young Masters Tournament."

The General whistled under his breath. "Lady and gent, we were had by a professional hustler."

"Or amateur pirate?" Pepper winked.

Doc's jaw clenched as Lucille actually snarled. "There are two books I value in this world. One is the good word. The other is this." She slammed *The Official Scrabble Players Dictionary* on the table. "Let's roll."

The scores flew after that. The game full of tricky two-letter word placements. *Za. Xi.*

Pepper laid her final tile, an *O*, beneath the *Y* in *stingy*.

"Yo?" Lucille said disbelievingly.

"Challenge!" Doc fired a shot across the bow.

"I don't think you want to be doing that," the General said. "Yo is a word."

"I said challenge, damn it," Doc repeated.

"They're right." Lucille consulted her book. "Yo is listed right here."

"Final five points to me." Pepper rubbed her hands. "How about a score check?"

"Pepper is at six hundred and twenty-seven, Doc is five hundred and ninety, Lucille is five hundred and three, and I am bringing up the caboose with four hundred and sixteen." The General pushed the wad of bills toward her. "To the winner, her spoils." The gang looked on with begrudging admiration.

Pepper pocketed her reward—twenty bucks would fund a few indulgence pints of Häagen-Dazs—and checked on Wolfgang, snoozing beneath the shade of Davy Jones's statue. "One more history question. What's the deal with Davy Jones?" she asked.

Three pairs of eyes bored into her. "The deal?" they cried in shocked unison.

"Why, it's a tale of heroics," the General replied solemnly.

"Of loyalty," Doc added, placing a hand on the General's shoulder.

"A story of love." Lucille dabbed at her eyes.

The General began: "A long while ago now, Hurricane Angelica struck the coastline. She was a mother of a storm. Cat four. The winds were so loud it sounded as if Everland was a train depot. All through the night the river rose. Davy was a mutt. No one knew where he came from, and no one ever owned him. I guess he was what you'd call a drifter. He'd show up sometimes downtown. Always friendly. He had a way about him, didn't he?"

"Indeed he did," Lucille said. "Except for the fire hydrant fascination."

The General gave an indulgent chuckle, scratching his beard. "That dog couldn't walk past a fire hydrant without taking a piss. Pardon my language."

"None taken," Pepper said.

"I'll take her offense and lump it with mine. Kindly clean up your talk when regaling us with tales about such a noble beast," Lucille said.

"My apologies." The General wiped his grin away and

reset his cap. "You're right. Absolutely right. Now where was I?"

"No one in town had seen Davy Jones in some time," Doc said. "Weeks."

"And here was this storm on its way, and everyone was boarding up buildings, and gathering supplies," the General jumped back in. "No one had a second to spare. The storm moved faster than the meteorological forecasts predicted."

"And no one stopped to say so much as a hello to dear old Davy Jones," Lucille said in a choked voice.

Doc cleared his throat twice with evident emotion. He was grumpy, but he seemed to have a soft, sensitive underbelly.

"The storm rocked and rolled. I've never seen nothing like it," the General said. "Before or since."

"Sometime around three in the morning, the howling started." Lucille shivered. "I can hear it still."

"A sound to wake the dead," the General continued. A few folks finally banded together and went out. Couldn't even stand upright because of the wind. There was Davy Jones, up on the river levee off Main Street, right near my store. The rain and storm surge meant that Everland River was about ready to overflow. Burst the banks and flood the town. Alarms were sounded and people braved the storm. Sandbagging until dawn. Anything they could do to keep the water out. It took all night but the town was saved. Thanks to Davy Jones."

"What happened to him?" Pepper asked.

"No one knows. He wasn't seen again." The General consulted the great oak above them. "I like to think he was a manifestation of Everland's community spirit, there to help in a moment of need."

"More likely some Hogg Jaw no-account snapped him up to use as a hunting dog," Doc grumbled.

"And that brings us to Hogg Jaw," Pepper said curiously. "What's the problem, besides the fact they claim to possess a likely fictional three-hundred-year-old pirate treasure?"

"The problem with Hogg Jaw is that it's full of Hoggs," Lucille stated with a matter-of-fact tone, reaching into her purse to remove a hand mirror. "I'm meeting Earl for a late lunch at Chez Louis," she announced, checking the state of her stylish gray pixie cut.

"They are liars. Thieves. Classless cheats." Doc snuck in a last word, punctuating each word with a fist on the table. "The whole lot."

"'Course, Hogg Jaw thinks much the same about us," the General said with a live-and-let-live shrug. "The two towns don't see eye to eye. Never have. Never will. Used to settle differences with muskets and powder kegs. These days the competition stays on the high school basketball courts and football fields. Mostly."

Pepper jolted as the clock tower chimed noon. Where had the time gone, and how was this possible? She'd been enjoying herself in a dog park. A. Dog. Park. With small-town strangers chatting about phantom savior dogs.

Who *was* she?

The idea sank in, sending ripples through her puzzled brain. What if she didn't know herself? She had so many ideas for so long, and what if she'd never taken the time to look right where she was, at the woman she was, not the woman she wanted to be?

She took her time on the walk back to Mr. Drummond's. The sun might be hot as a branding iron, but the air from the coast was cool, clean, and tinged with a hint of salt. Wolfgang didn't attempt any sexual deviancy. The time passed peacefully.

No sirens. No horns. No pressure to walk fast to keep up with the crowd. No sensory overload from hot dog stands, buskers, billboards, or the idea that you lived cheek to cheek on an island of millions of people.

Yes, there was a part of her that craved the city's endless excitement, the fact that she could be Super Pepper, head-quartered near the NYU campus, ready to seize success, gain stability, and have a future brighter than the sun hitting the glass panes of the Freedom Tower.

Except the super secret of Super Pepper was that her invincibility cloak felt more and more threadbare. Like the time she'd fainted after sitting for the bar exam, and while she sat in urgent care getting an IV of electrolytes, Tuesday called in tears afer losing out on a commercial. Or when her Dad *again* evaded pointed questions about whether or not he paid the farm's property taxes.

Or Mother's Day.

She huffed a small sigh. How quickly the satisfaction of coming to the rescue—of being needed—could morph into feelings about being overextended, overwhelmed, and un-derappreciated. And that's when she loved the city the most, how she could step on a crowded rush hour subway, or sit in Union Square, and lose herself. Be nobody's hero. An anonymous face in a crowd. At least for a few blissful min-utes.

She could never take off the cape for long, because what if Tuesday and Dad tried to fix their problems while she was off-duty? Batman couldn't take extended vacations because Gotham might organize a community crime watch, take down the bad guys, and realize they didn't need him after all. In some ways he needed them as much as they needed him. Maybe more.

The unsettled feeling lasted all the way home. When she got back to Love Street, her mailbox was empty except for a postcard. It was a picture of a roaring bear and read, "What doesn't kill you will make you stronger. Except for bears. Bears will kill you."

On the back, scribbled in Dad's messy handwriting, was a short note:

Chili Pepper,

Dropping a quick line to let you know that I had a tumble last week. Hurt my back again. Nothing serious. Tried to patch up a broken window screen and slipped off a sawhorse. Stayed in the hospital two nights but back home now and fit as my favorite fiddle. Fitter even. Please pass the message on to your sister. Miss you.

Her arms fell to her sides and she sank to the top stair, burying her face in her hands. "Yeah, Dad, of course I'll handle telling Tuesday," she muttered, hating the bitterness curdling her tongue. "Of course, I'll handle everything."

Seriously—a sawhorse? Dad wasn't a spring chicken; he should be using a stepstool. But trying to urge him to make practical choices was like trying to read a blank piece of paper. She could try and try, but what good would it do? She'd only drive herself crazy.

Hospital stays meant hospital bills. She rocked in place, calculating the costs. This required more than Batman skills; it needed a Bruce Wayne fortune.

At least she'd gotten him on a health insurance plan two

years ago because he didn't qualify for Medicare for another year. How on earth would he pay for the deductible?
The short answer was, he couldn't. A cold wind blew
through her, even though the wind was warm. He was an
overgrown kid. A fiddle-playing grasshopper who kept on
laughing and hitting his homemade moonshine even as winter drew ever closer.

His carefree attitude to life was charming, but his fi-
nancial negligence rankled. Right now her plate was full—
jam-packed—without extra room to hold this news. Except
filial responsibility meant making room, even if that required her shoving her own stuff to the side.

Even if it came at the expense of her own sanity.

She walked inside the house and slammed the door behind her with too much force. Real life wasn't dog park
Scrabble, river swimming, or cute Southern gentlemen. It
was her thought-out, meticulously organized plan. She
couldn't goof around. Not when Dad would have to count
on somebody, someday soon.

A place like Everland could never be home, and she
couldn't get comfortable. She was just here visiting.

Chapter Fifteen

Pepper snuggled deeper beneath her quilt, halfway through the world's best comfort food (God bless Entenmann's raspberry danishes) and the second disc of the BBC's *Jane Eyre*. There were many fine Mr. Rochester renditions in the world, but this particular incarnation left the others all behind.

Dad's cryptic postcard had dealt her peace of mind a crippling blow that even starched cravats, repressed passions, and sugary frosting struggled to repair. She reached for her wineglass as her butt buzzed.

She lurched forward to grapple with her cell. An unfamiliar number. *Ugh.* Who used phones for talking these days? She hit the green Answer button with a rumble of displeasure. "Hello?"

"Isn't it past your bedtime, Miss Knight?"

Heat radiated through her chest, like she'd slugged a shot of Southern Comfort. No mistaking the owner of that molasses-slow drawl, rich as peach cobbler. "Rhett?"

"Your light's on."

Whoa. That was an honest to goodness rumble. Her hand wandered to her inner thigh, her fingers tracing lazy spirals over the sensitive skin. "You spying on me?" Talk about the pot calling the kettle black.

"Not hard when your bedroom window's across the fence from mine."

"I know," she murmured. Her wandering gaze might have drifted back to his window, one or two (or twenty) times since the towel incident, by accident, of course. Line of sight and all that. Unfortunately, his curtain had remained drawn.

Wait a second. Her nails drove into her skin. What if he knew she'd peeped on him in the towel? A Danish crumb stuck in her throat.

"Busy?"

"No. Rewatching a movie," she wheezed, her dry mouth making it hard to swallow. "Brooding gentleman in a scary English manor keeps a mad wife locked in the attic while he falls for the young governess."

"Romantic." His drawl went heavy on the sarcasm.

"Shut up! It is. There's pain. Lots of sweet, sweet pain." She hit Pause on the computer, freezing Mr. Rochester's face in a shiver-inducing scowl. "Sorry, lover," she mouthed.

His low chuckle sent a jolt of heat through her. "Remind me never to hire you for marketing."

"It's more than pain, though. It's watching two lost people find a home in each other, you know?"

The other end went silent. Because what was the appropriate response to that level of blurt?

She licked her lips and fought for composure. Her foot-in-mouth disease had progressed to stage four. The only corrective course of treatment was a total tonguectomy.

A chair creaked on his end. "Can I come over?"

"Wait?" She quit writhing, frozen with surprise. "Now?"

"It's late." He sounded chagrined. "But there's a situation that I need your help with."

He *needed* her? "Yeah. Yes, of course." That magic word sent her scrambling from bed, yanking up the coverlet and cramming the Danish box into her nightstand drawer before reaching for her trusty lip gloss. "Come on over. I'm just sitting around." She smacked her lips. Nothing like Peppermint Kisses to restore composure.

"I'll meet you at the back door," he answered. "The fence is easy to jump. Keep your yard light switched off."

She frowned at the strange request. "Why the stealth?"

His response was a muffled grunt. "Never know who is watching who around here."

She stared down at the phone, the call ended, before glancing to her window. Was that an insinuating comment?

She snapped up her head. No time for worry. Not when she had sixty seconds to appear like she'd spent the night doing something more attractive than stuffing her face with two thousand calories' worth of jam-filled puff pastry. Lurching to the dresser mirror, she fluffed her bedhead and pinched color into her cheeks.

Not helping. She looked like someone who'd chased a bus.

Taken as a whole, her features were incongruent parts of a jigsaw puzzle forced together. The faint dog-bite scars. Eyebrows too thick. Mouth too thin. The weird mole on her lip. The perpetual frown in her forehead. A truly underwhelming chin.

She blew up her bangs and spritzed a little No. 5 into her palm, and briskly massaged the fragrance into her knees and elbows. Coco Chanel had once said a woman should never smell like *just* a rose, or *just* a lily of the valley. We were complex creatures and deserved to be treated accordingly. "Damn straight," she muttered, hiking up the straps on her super-soft pink cotton sleep slip.

All this fuss was a little silly. This wasn't some Hollywood rom-com where Rhett crept over to hop aboard the tongue train to Saliva Swap City, population two. He needed her help. Time to drop-kick her mind from the gutter, don her Superwoman cape, and oh, fine, what the heck, her sassiest underwear.

She shimmied out of her white cotton briefs and opened the drawer, fingering her silky-soft, rarely worn scarlet string bikini.

Within a minute, she'd unlocked the back door, tiptoed to the stoop, and glanced toward his yard. The moon was almost full and offered a pale spotlight to the half-built boat hull balanced on two sawhorses in the corner of his patio. Wayward fireflies flitted over the stern, illuminating the darkness.

Two thumbs up for the whole sweaty, brow swiping, cold beer drinking, honest labor, building a boat in the backyard routine. Total competence porn.

Did her imaginary corner office dream man ever use power tools while dressed in a ratty Under Armour tank top and carpenter jeans?

No.

Talk about a glaring fantasy oversight.

Rhett's side door eased a crack. He shushed one of the dogs before snicking the screen shut and padding across the grass to hurtle the fence in a single confident motion.

Even that. That move right there. Such a major turn-on. Did he have a single idea how hot that gesture was, as if beneath the good-guy demeanor was a coiled tiger waiting to spring into the sheets and devour her whole?

From the lost-in-thought frown, no, it wasn't right on the forefront of his mind. He dressed in head-to-toe black. Dark hoodie. Dark sweats. More ninja than amorous. In fact, he looked perturbed.

"What's up?" she asked, acutely conscious that beneath her no-frills sleeveless short nightie was a scrap of red lace that put the *f* in *fundies*.

"Not here," he glanced around as if the rosebushes were bugged by security cameras. "Even the trees have ears in Everland."

He stalked into her kitchen and drew the curtains.

"Stop. Breathe," she ordered, realizing before he did that her nipples puckered from the cold and folding her arms. "Unless you robbed a gas station and the cops are five minutes from busting down my door, take it down a notch."

He crossed the room, close enough that there was no ignoring his woodsy-scented soap. His face half-masked by shadows, panting hard, a no-frills guy, unapologetically take-it-or-leave-it. And right now? She kind of, sort of, please-God-just-this-once wanted to take it.

"Hell, Pepper." He dragged a hand through his hair and held up his phone. "We have a bona fide unfolding crisis on our hands." He stepped back and flopped into a kitchen chair, leaning back onto two legs and resetting his glasses.

She frowned, registering his words. "We? What's this we?"

"Has anyone filled you in on the Back Fence yet?"

"The town blog? Yeah, I used it to find this rental, in

the classifieds." Why was he asking such random questions, and, more important, why was there a gap between his hoodie and sweats, and a line of *V*-shaped muscle. Her tongue explored the roof of her mouth. What she needed was some chocolate. Or a cold bath. Or a spare AAA battery for battery-operated boyfriend.

"It started last fall. Folks act appalled by some of the more gossipy articles, but the monthly site visits are through the roof. Must be the single reason why everyone over the age of seventy owns a smartphone around here."

She let the fact sink in. "I had noticed a remarkably technology-forward senior population."

He passed over his phone with a groan. "This popped up this evening. My friend Beau gave me the heads-up."

She peered at the screen image. It was grainy but clearly the outline of their bodies, leaning together in Rhett's Bronco near the Kissing Bridge. Heat stole up her neck, sending warm tendrils toward her jaw. "It's a 'Caption This' contest." She squinted and read a couple entries. "Romeo Rhett Finds His Juliet?" Inadvertent laughter erupted from her chest. "Oh, wait, this one's even better. 'Randy Rhett Ruts at Last.' And 'Rhett Needs to Rub-a-Dub after Getting Racy at the River.' Okay, that one gets my vote, no contest."

"This isn't funny," he bit out.

"It's a little funny." She snorted. "And that's some truly terrible alliteration."

She jumped at his growl. "Go ahead and think of Everland as a joke, but it's my home. I was born here, I'll die here, and in between those two milestones, I have to live here, preferably without everyone's nose in my business. Hey!" He glanced to the window, pressing a finger to his lips. "Hear that?"

She paused with a slight frown. There was a subtle scratch on the weatherboards. "Oh, that's nothing," she said waving him off.

"Doesn't sound like nothing to me." His eyes were wild.

Of course the first guy she was attracted to in a year had a crazy streak. "Trust me. The first time I heard those scritchy-scratchy sounds I freaked, but it's one of the old rosebushes brushing up against the side of the—"

Rhett tackle-hugged her to the ground before she could finish her sentence. Even though he hit first to break the fall, it was disorienting to go from standing up to straddling a hard male body in less than a breath.

"Are you insane!" Her nose pressed into the side of his neck. Up close the notes of wood sap and spice were even headier. She wasn't sure what made her more outraged, the fact he'd sacked her like a quarterback or the pesky detail that up close and personal he smelled even better. "Let me go."

"Shhhhh." He lifted his head and listened intently. "You never know who's watching," he muttered. "After all, why settle for a caption contest when there can be documented proof of us together, in your house, after dark?"

She must have hit her head in the fall. That was the only explanation for why she was gripped by a sudden, over-whelming desire to lick his Adam's apple. "Remind me to make you a tinfoil hat, Mr. Paranoid."

Using him as a human mattress wasn't unpleasant, and that was part of the problem. A shiver moved through her. It made her feel strange, and not a little trembly. "The only thing out there is an overgrown rosebush. You're jumping at shadows."

"You don't understand people in this town," he fired back. "They're relentless when it comes to gossip."

"Let me tell you what I understand even less." Besides the whole urge to lick his neck.

"What?" he asked, dryly.

"You." She bit the tip of her tongue, because that little word was the equivalent of an iceberg. It didn't look like much, bobbing there, alone on the surface, but dive below and more met the eye.

He shifted his weight, but that meant his hips rolled over hers, their stomachs pressed together. She wasn't the only one breathing fast. Her core tensed as a tremble ran through her legs. Hard to say if the realization was comforting or nerve-wracking.

Maybe both.

"This was a mistake, coming." He stilled, as if registering what he'd done for the first time, his ears deepening to a fiery red. "I should go."

"Not so fast." The fact she could make this guy blush would be cute if she wasn't so furious, with herself, with him, with this whole situation. "You reached out to me, remember? Barged into my house, into my peace and quiet, into my life, into all my thoughts. Do you have any idea how that feels? Freaking confusing."

He jerked as if struck with an undercut. That gave her the opportunity to roll free, to scramble to her knees, get some much-needed distance. He followed suit.

"You're the only one confused?" He sat back on his feet, voice taut, almost strangled. "Is that what you think?"

"Let's review the facts." Her chest heaved. "First you hand-deliver me rocky road and say you like my smile, then the next day barely look in my direction at the dog park. You found me a job, rescued me from public humiliation, tell me life stories, and stare like you want to eat me, but freak out when we're spotted in your car. I'm sorry, am I missing something? Your signals are more tangled than a bunch of old Christmas lights."

"You're right." His simple agreement took wind from her indignant sails. "Absolutely right. But understand, this isn't New York. Small towns are different—"

"Stop. Stop right there." She held up a hand. "Don't think for a second that you can mansplain to me about small towns. I grew up in a place with half the population of Everland, actually less. My senior class took their photo on a log. A single log. So I get the dynamics. Everyone knows everything. Yada-yada. But what I don't know is why you're so paranoid."

"Because..." He scrubbed a hand over his face. "If the Back Fence gets wind of us spending time together, then it's game over. My life would be back in the public eye. I worked damn hard to create an island that's mine and mine alone. No drama. No gossip. Nothing to see. So do I like you? Yeah. Of course. How could I not? But I don't want anyone to know."

She reeled from the impact of his words, trying to absorb the aftershocks. "Wow, you have a way of making a woman feel pretty...pretty bad." She might have a bruised ego, but she'd never let him know. In fact he should leave, now. Better to cut the string on this strange connection fast, before she got too attached. "You know? You're right. You should go. Don't let the door hit you."

"Wait. Fuck. Pardon my French, but this is coming out all wrong." He inhaled sharply, raking a hand through his hair, making it stand up even more wildly that before. "I'm not used to talking to women."

Her brows arched. "No kidding." Still, her curiosity

wasn't killed, only maimed. How exactly was he going to climb out of this hole?

"Let me try again. I don't do relationships."

"O-kay. Glad you dragged me out of bed for that news flash." Did the Brontë sisters ever have to deal with this shit? Probably. That's why they were so full of angst.

He gave a one-shoulder shrug, the cords of his neck drawn tight. "I don't know what I'm doing here."

"At least that makes two of us." She crossed her legs, her tone professional, businesslike. "So you are kind of sort of attracted to me. And maybe—hypothetically—I'm kind of sort of attracted to you. Good thing for you my time in Everland has an expiration date. It's not like I'm staying long enough to feed the gossip mill."

"Hold that thought." He walked his fingers over the floor, halting an inch from her leg. "You're attracted to me?" Stiffness made his voice rigid.

She walked her own fingers toward his, almost but not quite a touch. "I think you're hypothetically sexy." Did her tone sound as dry as her mouth felt?

"Here's an idea." He nudged his finger on hers. "Say we—and this is purely hypothetical—enjoyed the…ahem… pleasure of each other's company in the privacy of our homes."

"Hypothetically, kept it casual and under the radar?" She nudged back. "When I leave, there's no heartbreak, no drama, and no one is the wiser."

"Interesting theory?" He reached out, his hand skimming her thigh. "Or recipe for disaster?"

Tingles shot up her leg. His skin was warm, those fingers very big and very male. "I have enough to worry about with my future. If you don't need me for more than a little here and now? I might be persuaded. Hypothetically."

He moved his hand from her knee to the back of her neck. The touch melted her faster than an ice cube in the July sun.

"What are you thinking?" she murmured.

His deep blue gaze locked on hers and there it came again, that curious sensation of floating and drowning. "That I'd like to hypothetically kiss you."

A sudden roaring filled her ears, a whoosh of blood. "Well, there's only one way to test a hypothesis."

Slowly, oh so slowly, he dipped forward. His lips didn't settle on hers like she expected. Instead, he kissed the center of her forehead, softly, experimentally. A tremble rocked through him.

The evening air was sultry, no hint of chill. The idea that she shook this steadfast man sent a shiver of need through the join of her thighs, a throbbing shudder that swelled to an ache as he peppered a light trail of kisses down her temple, then moved lower. He took his sweet time on her cheeks, treating her as something to savor, a delicious dessert you didn't want to inhale in one bite. Tension spread through her body, pulling tighter and tighter, her belly doing fluttery dips and dives.

When he finally reached her lips, it seemed reasonable to expect that the kiss would be as soft as the others. Silly. Because Rhett was full of surprises. He didn't hold back, his tongue was greedy, insistent, and hungry. Their teeth banged together. A chair tipped over. They crashed against a table leg, sent it screeching across the floor.

"In theory, you're a good kisser," she gasped, tracing her lower lip with her tongue. The skin was puffy, aching.

"Let me experiment a bit more. The initial results are promising." He coaxed her chin up and her own tongue slid deeper as she reciprocated. "Fuck," he groaned, voice hoarse, tasting her in long, leisurely strokes.

"Do you mean that abstractly or—" Her giggle turned into a hitched groan as her back bowed. He nibbled her shoulder. Those big, strong hands were...everywhere. All at once. In her hair. Against her small of her back. Under her nightie. Toying with the thin, silky strings. The savage need in his face suggested that not only did he want to take the sex quickly, but dirty, too. That bulge wasn't a study in subtlety.

Her thighs clenched with anticipation, her hips twisting in shameless circles.

"This okay?" He brushed a hair off her cheek, his mouth curled ruefully even as his eyes burned.

"Okay, it's conclusive. You're quite the kisser." Confident, experienced, and just aggressive enough to spin her head.

His mouth curved into a wicked arc. "Must be all those nights I spent practicing on my pillow."

And when his lips returned to hers, the tension in her shoulders eased. For once, she was right where she belonged.

Chapter Sixteen

This situation would end in disaster, and yet Rhett was moronic enough to march into the storm. With his internal logic crushed to dust, all sorts of wild thoughts flew free, like if he went about this right, maybe Pepper would be there tomorrow, and the night after and after and…

"Jesus." He slid his hands under her cotton nightie, and his fingers explored the lacey edge of a pair of tiny panties. Her hips were cool in contrast to the heat of her secret skin. She gasped when he sucked her earlobe. He had her right where he wanted, but the joke was on him because if he was an island, she was a wave, washing away his rules, his need for self-control.

The flimsy strings of her briefs snapped between his fingers. "Shit." He slapped her underwear on the kitchen table. Red lace? *Shit.* "I can't do this."

"You're kidding." She tugged up one of her straps, half-undressed, wholly exposed. Her eyes were huge, bright, shining like a sun-shaft through clouds. A man could blind himself to common sense if he wasn't careful.

"Not here. Not beneath a damn kitchen table. I don't want to take advantage and—"

"Nope." The sun disappeared. "*You* stop." She grabbed a bunch of his sweatshirt and yanked. "Don't feed me BS lines, Rhett Valentine, not when you've broken my underwear."

"I don't want to hurt you," he said helplessly.

"Objection." She held up a finger. "Leading the witness. The truth is that you don't want to hurt yourself." She traced his cheek's clenched muscle, staring like if she strained hard enough she could glimpse his soul. He averted his gaze.

"Whoever you were with last did a heck of a number on you, huh?"

"That was a long time ago." His voice was a pained whisper, a voice so raw it was almost unrecognizable as him. "Ancient history."

"You miss her?" she asked carefully, too casually.

"No." He met her gaze dead on. The best way to erase any flicker of doubt was to stop the bullshit and give the truth. "But . . . I do miss feeling."

Her eyes softened as the seconds passed. Finally she seemed to reach an internal decision. "So why not start again?" She plucked the string of his hoodie. "By feeling me."

The lightning-quick flash of relief shocked his heart back onto beating. "You're gorgeous, you know that, right?"

She ducked, her hair falling like a soft curtain, blocking her face.

That wouldn't do.

"Hey." He reached and pushed the soft tendrils back. "If

we do this, I intend to do a lot of looking. That's the deal. I look when I want, where I want, up close and personal." He moved his attention to her neck, loving the way she hissed when he traced his tongue over her pulse point, sucking the trace of salt off her damp skin.

"So we're doing this?" she groaned, fingers locking into his hair, pulling him closer. "A secret summer fling? Right here, right now, not in theory, but in point of fact? End it in a clean break?"

"Yeah." He tore himself away and glanced around the cramped galley kitchen. "But not here." His chest rumbled with a deep, primitive reverberation. "When I get you naked for the first time it's going to be in a bed." He forced himself to admit the hidden truth. She deserved that much. "The way I've been dreaming about since the moment I laid eyes on you."

* * *

What was life? Nothing made sense. Ten minutes ago Pepper was engrossed in the gloomy English moors, now she was getting whisked off to her bedroom. She framed Rhett's head between her hands, his scruff tickling her palms. "One more idea."

"Got to say, I'm liking our brainstorming sessions." He settled her onto her bed while doing something interesting with his mouth to her nipple through her cotton nightgown.

"They're Nobel Prize–worthy. Oh God!" A swoosh went through her stomach as he worked his hand over her breast, plumping the skin until it was taut and aching. He skimmed again. More pressure this time. More everything. Then lower. Lower. Lower.

"Ah. God." She licked her lips, her vision dimming at the perimeters.

"You doing okay down there?" There was a dark purr beneath the gentle teasing. No skimming this time. Pressure. Firm, circling sweet, sweet, pressure. Tension built as he massaged her in an unhurried and relaxed rhythm.

She brushed fingers over her lower lip and let a trembling moan of pleasure suffice an answer. Hot diggity, he had skills. Most guys went at it like they were sandpapering a wall or pressing a panic button.

He nuzzled the side of her neck. "You smell incredible, you know that, right?" His grin grew wicked. "Do you taste that delicious?"

He slid down and where to look? Would everything appear magnified with the glasses? Or fog up or, oh! He tossed the frames on the bed and pressed firm, the flat of his tongue swiping away any worries.

His tongue speared into her wet heat as he pierced her with the heat in his gaze. He wanted to do it. That much was clear, as he closed his eyes and nuzzled in, all insistent pressure, taking until she had no more to give, reduced to slicked sweat and churning thighs, hips tensing on the edge of release, body begging, begging for more.

He jerked back abruptly, his breathing ragged.

Her stomach quivered madly but she knew the drill. Here came the part where he wanted his. She swallowed a lump of disappointment because the Big Bang was right there, hovering out of reach with the heat of ten thousand suns. But asking was embarrassing. Asking was vulnerable. Asking was admitting to wanting, to craving, to being helpless, weak and exposed.

To needing.

"I'm selfish." He nudged her legs further apart, milking her tender sweet spot. "Wanted to see your face."

"Oh. Okay." That's it. Her heart was going to burst. At least she'd die happy. "I assumed you were done."

Laughter rolled through his chest. "Hell no. I could do this all night." He leaned back in, using his lips, tongue, and the lightest love bites to show her hypersensitive knot of flesh that he was a man of his word.

She lost track of how many times she broke apart as he pushed his fingers in and out, keeping the perfect, rhythmic suction on her clit. All the cheesy magazines in the grocery store checkout lanes touted how-to headlines about attaining multiple orgasms. Pepper never felt greedy in that department, one did her fine, and anyway she normally took over from the guy anyway, relying on her own handiwork with customary efficiency.

When she finally returned to her senses, or whatever was left of them, he spoke.

"Pepper." He made her name sound like a life raft. "Thank you."

She half sat, attempting to rearrange herself and realized quickly that was a pointless endeavor. Her nightgown top slunk around her waist and the bottom skirt hiked to her hips. She shimmied free. "I'm the one who should be thanking you."

He scrubbed his hand through his hair, making the ends stand out. "It's been a long time." He cleared his throat. "Probably not cool to admit that."

"Yeah. Consider my illusions shattered," she said. He didn't look tragic though, or needy. Simply relieved.

"Sorry," he said. "I'm making this weird."

"Not weirder than the situation already is."

He was quiet a moment. "I'm not always the nicest guy."

"But you're a good man." She reached out. "And if you want to be a bad boy tonight, I won't tell." He'd knocked her reservation loose. Her inner sex kitten prowled, ready for banter and a lot more bedding. Why did people refer to this feeling as an itch? Nothing remotely scratchy happened inside her. This was a throbbing, rich pulse.

He gripped her hips, his fingers branding her skin. "Let's find a better use for that smart mouth."

His tongue swept through the seam of her lips, demanding, claiming, left her twisting, writhing. Every indiscernible plea met with a ruthless chuckle, a deep, smooth rumble that fed the fire lapping between her legs. His hands roamed her silhouette, as if he needed to memorize her outline for future sculptures. No dip or flare escaped attention.

He stood and stripped in a steady, assured motion. Normally she glanced away for this part, got busy studying sheet wrinkles or the back of her hands. Anything to avoid the awkward wang unveil. But tonight was about one thing—getting her perv on. Might as well embrace it. Keep her gaze lasered to the lean, hard lines of his body. The typography tattoo on the forearm.

Stay true. True to what?

"You're staring," he said, taking a condom from his wallet. He was as aroused as she was, the hard length of his cock rising against his flat stomach.

"I know." She poked out her tongue. "Why should you be the only one who gets to take their time looking?"

"Troublemaker." He rolled the condom over his big crown before drawing her into his lap.

"Guilty as charged." She threw her arms around his neck, legs encircling his narrow hips, toes curling as his own legs formed the perfect cradle for her ass.

"Pepper I . . . Shit. It's been awhile." He rocked into position. "I'll try to be gentle."

"Who wants gentle?" she purred, opening wider, giving an all-access pass. Warning: Gentle pressure against sensitive wet skin may cause involuntary writhing. She ached to be filled. "For the love of all that's holy, get inside me."

"Yes ma'am." He pushed inside with that broad head. Not all the way, but beyond the point of retreat. This was happening. Inch by inch she stretched, opening for him. The only thing breaking the silence were short, ragged breaths and the telltale mattress squeak. Her skin's hypersensitivity was maddening. This experiment had gone haywire. She had expected good, the chemistry had been there, but she never anticipated blowing the roof of the laboratory.

"Hurry." She needed him to move, to drive away unwanted attachments and remind her body of the deal. This was a fling, not a forever.

Two deep frown lines creased his forehead as he peered into her face. She closed her eyes. Secret sex heightened everything. She slid her ass forward, rocking, begging, but he didn't rush. Instead he tortured her with each slow grind until he was fully inside, embedded to the root. Only then, chest to chest, heart to heart, did he pause.

"Rhett." Her knees bracketed his hard torso.

"I know." His answer tinged with wonder, his eyes dark as indigo. "Jesus. I know."

She bent against his sweat-slicked shoulder, unable to bear the continued scrutiny. Tonight wasn't about relieving tension or floating on the surface, belly-up, face tilted to the sun. No. It was sinking into the dark places full of raw want and animal need, a place where time hung suspended and wild currents pulled.

She needed this—him—and later it would freak her out. She could feel the fear inside, the cold knot pulling tight. The innate need to slam herself shut. Be protective.

But she'd deal with all that tomorrow. Right now the moment was too powerful, she was too hot, wet, and open.

She rode up and down his length, rubbing a tender spot inside. His mouth slanted over hers. Sweat against sweat. Heat everywhere. In traded breaths. In every nibbling kiss. In each lush, deep pump. She burned. There was nowhere he could touch fast enough. Her fingers locked on his muscular back, as they raced each other on, closer and closer to the edge. When she gasped, it was into him, and his answering groan exploded through her as the orgasm exploded.

In the hushed silence after, his reverent gaze skimmed her bare body, leaving a turbulent wake. She didn't know what he saw, couldn't dare a single peek if she wanted a prayer of believing in her "this was no big deal" story come morning.

Because this—whatever this was—felt big.

Huge.

Excerpt from the Back Fence:

Everland News That You Actually Care About

Classifieds:

Village Pillage Volunteers needed: Want to be part of Everland's annual Village Pillage, the annual celebration of our town's pirate "har-rrrrrritage"? Spaces still available to support the Medallion Hunt and Live Auction (this year's proceeds will be benefiting our local dog park and off-leash area). The Village Pillage is the biggest event in Everland's year. Help contribute to this long-standing and fun event. Sign-up sheet outside Elizabeth Martin's office at City Hall.

Everland Library Historical Talk: Avast ye Scurvy Dogs! Sail back through history this Wednesday. Oxford Scholar Cedric Swift will be conducting an informative lecture on the lexicon of seventeenth-century pirates. (Ed. Note: and if you think history is boring, imagine it delivered in a real British accent.)

Smuggler's Cove wait-staff needed: Do you have what it takes to be a serving wench or scamp at Everland's favorite (Ed. Note: only) pirate-themed restaurant? Seeking a friendly, knowledgeable and swashbuckling waiter with a passion for delivering high seas hospitality. See Gunnar behind the bar after five. Two years' experience required. Wannabe mutineers need not apply.

Chapter Seventeen

Rhett woke to an unfamiliar sensation, his right arm asleep, compressed under the weight of a sleeping woman. Dawn light seeped beneath the curtain, buttery rays spilling on Pepper, all bed-wild hair and parted, slightly puffy mouth. Who knew what made the small mole on her upper lip so kissable. But better not overthink it.

Better not to overthink any of it.

He eased his arm free and she stirred, peering through one eye, a slight frown creasing her brow.

"What time is it?" she mumbled.

"Little before seven." He shook out his arm, pins and needles prickling below his skin. The sensation was annoying, but not the torture he'd remembered. It had been a long time since he'd spent the night with a woman, and it seemed there were three options: suggest another round, offer to make breakfast, or head for the hills.

Truth be told, he didn't have a fucking clue how to play

this so kept his face a mask. Better to let her make the first move.

Realization spread over her face as she rolled into a half sit. "Hang on. We had a sleepover?" Her uncertain voice was cue enough; time to get out of Dodge.

"Guess so. Not very fling of us." He made his retreat, rolling out of her warm bed. Once his feet hit the cool carpet an almost tangible force field descended between them.

She tucked the sheet around her torso, modesty returning with the rising sun. "That should go on the list of no-nos, right? No slumber parties."

"Yeah. Smart." He dressed in quick, efficient movements while she studied something of interest on the ceiling. "Hey, so I have to let my dogs out. Want me to scramble some eggs before bolting?"

She smiled faintly. "I'm a big girl and prefer oatmeal anyway. Let's embrace the awkward and shake hands. You don't need to hang around pretending." Her tone was relaxed and sounded authentic, except she wouldn't hold his gaze.

This ma'am was all about the wham bam while he'd hit it and couldn't quit it. His arms tightened into steel bands. Time to get it together. Leaving was the power move, and hell, she'd basically told him to hit the road. She wasn't playing games but keeping to her end of the bargain.

She was cool.

A little too icy. She'd reached for her phone and already moved on with the morning.

"See you around?" He lingered in the doorway, waiting, for what? For her to throw back the blankets and make a come-hither gesture? To bat her eyes and purr, "Come back to bed, Rhett. I need another round."

"See ya, buddy!" She raised a hand in farewell, gaze glued to her screen.

"Yeah." He forced an upbeat tone. "Buddy."

But as he let himself out of her back door, it was impossible to shake the troubling truth. His simple, straightforward path had taken a detour down Complication Alley.

* * *

"Stop." Pepper halted in front of the dog park, dabbing the perspiration misting her top lip. Wolfgang halted at her side, tail taut at attention. She glanced down at him. "Good boy." It wasn't that she was magically cured of her irrational phobia. The old entrenched fear hummed in the background, but repeated daily exposure to a range of familiar pooches helped her relax.

Before leaving New York, she'd have never expected to willingly walk a dog, let alone enter an off-leash area. And never in a million years would she have imagined being calm enough in the situation to notice a penny on the sidewalk, the copper glinting in the sun.

The world divided into two kinds of people: the penny picker-uppers and the penny snubbers. She belonged to Team PPU. A childhood tightrope-walking the poverty line meant never ignoring free money, in any denomination, even when doing a deep breathing meditative walk with a Chihuahua. Even if the coin was turned heads down.

What made tail-side-up pennies bad luck anyway?

She scooped it up and stood. Superstition was for the birds. People made their own luck. A small smile tugged the corner of her mouth. She was getting lucky all over town.

The smug ache between her legs caught her breath, conjuring delicious memories of that night before.

Pulling out her phone, she glanced around. The coast was clear. With a quick arm extension, she contorted her face into an over-the-top porn star pout while posing with the penny, took a snap, and sent it to Tuesday with the one-liner: Look out, Pepper just got lucky.

She didn't add a second part to that statement about how she'd gotten lucky, three times last night, in a range of positions that made her realize you could take the girl out of yoga, but you could never take yoga out of the girl. Her flexibility was still on point, and what's more, Rhett seemed to like it.

A lot.

A tickle stole across her neck, one of those itchy "somebody's watching me" sensations.

She turned, chest heaving and yelped. An older man stared down at her, all up in her personal space bubble. Not too old—forty-something—with smarmy daytime soap star features and perfect politician hair down to the distinguished gray temple bolts holding a glass bottle of Coke.

A word surfaced from deep in her subconscious, a memory from her semester of German. *Backpfeifengesicht.* A face that needs to be punched.

This guy owned one.

"What do we have here? You must be new to town?" If her startled reaction bothered him, he hid it behind a cocked brow and toothy grin. Worse than the fact he towered close enough that she could smell peanuts on his breath was the dog at the end of his leather leash.

A Doberman pinscher.

"Oh my God!" She tripped over Wolfgang. His alarmed

bark faded as the world spun strange, taking on a slowed-down, unreal tenor as panic gripped her neck, throttling off air.

"Where you from?" He waggled his brows as if she found him terribly charming. "Tennessee?"

A short, confusing silence followed. "Huh? No. Maine? Or New York. I don't know." She was too flustered to make sense.

His smile wilted around the edges. Her answer hadn't apparently been the one he'd wanted. "I meant because you're the only ten I see. Get it? Ten I see? Tennessee."

Where was this joker from, Turkey? That cheesy line deserved to be killed with fire. She wrapped Wolfang's leash around her wrist. Her little frenemy wasn't turning into a Doberman's doggie bite on her watch. "Your animal. He friendly?"

"Depends. You?" His voice dripped with slime. "I think Dante would like you very much. His taste is as impeccable as mine. Aloysius Hogg."

Despite the sweat pouring off her brow, her veins flooded with ice water as she gaped at the proffered hand. Sometimes you were lucky in life and sometimes you were hit on by the sleeze bag who atom-bombed your future.

"*Judge* Aloysius Hogg?" If her surroundings had taken on a surreal bent in the last thirty seconds, now they were morphing into a Salvador Dalí painting. She'd imagined the judge as a paunchy Southern villain, short and jowly with a pale complexion and thick lids. At least that's what her brain had cooked up as she plotted an eventual crossing of paths. One where she wasn't wearing high-waisted shorts and black midriff tank top, good for beating the summer heat, but bad when the target of her stored-up withering comments leered at her peeping belly button.

"Pepper Knight, your honor." She accepted his hand, squeezing his knuckles.

His brows mashed. "Why does that name sound familiar?"

"Because you'd offered me a clerkship. You know, before rescinding it to appease a political crony in a clear case of biased nepotism." Yes, good. Total ass kick. Except her eyes burned with unshed tears. Bad, very bad. "I moved from Manhattan to Georgia for your job." Her voice cracked. Worse and worse.

The judge went from defense to offense in the blink of an eye. His quick shock smoothed over as he moved in closer, the entitled body language communicating one thing: *I'm a man and I deserve to be here whether you like it or not.*

And she didn't like it, not one bit. Her heart accelerated from third to fifth gear. Her neck muscles tightened. She didn't like him or that pasted-on smile that didn't reach his eyes or that dog ripped out of one of her childhood nightmares.

"Please move. Next time I won't ask nicely." Tough words paired with a pathetic, high-pitched, wobbly tone.

He swiveled his head, no doubt seeing if they attracted unwanted attraction. "Don't go getting your pretty panties in a wad," he hissed through his frozen, wide smile.

Her brain short-circuited. "Your honor, I shouldn't have to remind you that title seven of the Civil Rights Act of nineteen sixty-four states—"

"Oh, come, come." Venom dripped from his words. "I'm all for the whole hiring women thing. After all, who doesn't like a good pair of honkers?" His gaze dropped to her chest, ruling out any misinterpretation. "But you're not my clerk. That position belongs to Tommy Haynes. You? Well, you're nobody at all."

Hot electrical currents zinged through her spine, like tangoing with a moray eel. "Sir—the law—"

"Does not prohibit innocuous differences in the ways men and women routinely interact with members of the opposite sex," he said, pompously. "In other words, teasing is permitted. You might be so good as to note that I didn't make a crude remark about your honkers, just a general observation."

"But you're a judge! You can't go around saying…" Her lips were dry. God, her tongue balked at forming the stupid word. Hadn't she learned her lesson by now, that life was hideous, life was hilarious, and she was unhappily squashed in the middle.

"What are you going to do? My family is connected. You're a no one. A no one that no one cares about." Despite the tough talk, there was a restless, jittery tension running through him, a current that was almost visible.

He knew he'd done wrong and was covering it up with bully tactics.

"Now if you'll excuse me, I just remembered that I have better, more important things to do than stand here, chin wagging" he said. He stared through her as if she didn't matter, as if he couldn't wait to get out of there. She'd seen that empty look before, on her mama's face when she left them without a backward glance.

This time she'd be seen.

She'd be noticed.

"Stop right there. Not another step." Pepper stepped forward. Pushed into his personal space. Fists clenched. Activate *Backpfeifengesicht*. Fight the patriarchy. "You owe me an apology."

"You might be right." His hardened gaze belied the easygoing tenor in his voice. "I'm so sorry."

She took a deep breath, off-balance. His words didn't match his expression, but maybe he had a natural jerkface. Everyone deserved the benefit of the doubt. After all, he hadn't known who she was when he checked her out. In bad taste, yes, but maybe he panicked while on the back foot and—

"Sorry *you* don't have a sense of humor." He pantomimed her look of shock and made a low honking sound.

Holy shit. No more excuses. Sweat prickled her hairline. Her senses sharpened. A chorus of "Ramblin' Man" rose from a passing car down on Main Street. Her mouth tasted like the unfamiliar brand of toothpaste she'd picked up at the Piggly Wiggly. A frothy bubble of spittle nestled in the corner of Judge Hogg's sneering mouth.

He *honked* at her.

Her body knew what was coming before her brain. Her arm flung out in a blur, snatching the Coke from his hand.

When she blinked again, the judge's perfect hair was plastered to his broad forehead. Cola dripped from his chin.

Pepper glanced at the empty soda bottle. Did she just—

Yep. She did.

That drenched piece of human garbage staring in stunned surprise was supposed to be her boss. This wasn't how she'd expected the morning to go, but God, did it feel good.

Elizabeth appeared at her elbow, horror stamped on her pretty features. "Oh! Oh my! What on Earth—"

He removed a handkerchief from his pocket and swiped his glowering face. "Miss Knight." There was an edge to the way the judge spoke her name, as if he had carved it in his mind's dark recesses. He glanced toward the dog park, where everyone swiveled their heads away in unison, acting natural, as if they weren't putting up antennae to tune in to the conversation. "Take a good look at your future." He crushed the ruined hankie in his fist and tossed it in the closest trash bin before straightening his tie. "You'll never be accepted for another clerkship so long as I'm sucking air." The Doberman's eyes gleamed, twin black pools of doom.

"Yeah? Well the eighties called and want their hair back." Pepper spun on her heel and dropped the empty Coke bottle into the recycling bin on the way. The eighties? That's what she went with?

She walked fast, Elizabeth's heels clipping along behind, but it wasn't until she reached the statue of Davy Jones that the enormity of the situation crashed on her head like a cartoon anvil. She halted, grinding fists into her eye sockets so hard blue stars cascaded past. She looked up into the dog's one-eyed bronze face.

What. Had. She. Done?

Her heart tripped. Her teeth chattered.

"Are you okay?" Elizabeth asked quietly.

"That back there, that's not who I am. I have common sense. I respond promptly to RSVPs and yield my subway seats to the elderly. But he honked at me. He *honked* at me. Too bad I didn't have a two-liter."

"Whatever he did, you can be sure he had it coming."

"The funny thing is, I could have sworn today was my lucky day." Her palms dampened. A solution must exist. She was strong. Resourceful. She'd clawed out of Moose Bottom and reached New York on her own gumption. That plastic-faced intimidator wasn't going to be her Waterloo.

Chapter Eighteen

After Rhett left Pepper, he jumped the property fence, fed and watered the dogs, took a shower, and walked to work. His pace was quick, Faulkner, Steinbeck, and Fitzgerald barely keeping up. But he couldn't outpace the uncomfortable feeling nipping at his heels.

Weren't men the ones who were supposed to crave sex without the emotional connection? Why was he defective? It left him uneasy how Pepper took his departure in stride, even though he'd promised to keep it on a friend level, not puss out and go heart eyes after the first round.

It wasn't until he leaned against the counter at Sweet Brew, waiting for Delfi, the barista, to grind his coffee that he processed his situation. Last night he hadn't simply opened Pepper's legs; he'd opened a part of his heart that had been cut off for years.

He wasn't an island anymore; now a narrow isthmus connected him back to the Land of Feelings.

Fuck.

He picked up his drink and took a careful swallow. The bitter French roast seared his tongue. *Don't be an idiot.* The isthmus was temporary. He'd drown it under a rising ocean of stone cold realism soon enough. He was here for the wham and the bam, too. Simple. Straightforward.

Three women leaned in close at the nearest table. "I'm telling you the man was soaked, covered in head-to-toe Coke."

He snorted under his breath. Sounded like someone had a rough start to their day.

He fiddled with the lid and returned to his thoughts. The ugly truth was that he'd come dangerously close to losing his goddamn mind inside her sweat-slicked skin. Her astonished look as they fell over the edge together was branded on the back of his lids. Every time he closed his eyes it was all he could see. Already need was building back up in his cock. A hunger that had been repressed for too long.

He'd done it this time. Fucked himself in the head.

He'd had sex, screwed, and even made love over the course of his life, and knew the difference between the three. The thing is, what happened with Pepper was something else, something different, a connection that had a class all its own.

But she came with an expiration date, and who knew, maybe that was the attraction. The old adage of wanting what you can't have. He didn't think he was that kind of guy, but maybe fate needed to take him down a peg.

Consider his ass humbled.

He stalked to an empty chair by the window, grabbed a copy of the *Everland Examiner*, and pretended to scan the headlines.

"Judge Hogg won't take an insult without retaliation," Maryann Munro whispered, or at least gave it her best attempt. "That poor girl."

The table murmured in sympathy.

Speak of the bastard, the judge's shiny face offered up a smarmy smile from a black and white photo on page two of the paper. The connecting article claimed he was the newest board member for the Low Country Community Foundation.

Rhett lowered the paper, staring at the opposite wall in stunned horror. Hogg had joined the LCCF?

God. Damn. It.

Last spring, Rhett had applied to the foundation for a construction grant to help fund the Virginia Valentine Memorial Shelter's capital campaigns costs. The board was to be making a decision this month. He'd already led two member tours, shared blueprints, and talked about community benefits and public health and safety issues. He'd jumped through every hoop and was three-quarters of the way to the shelter's funding goal. But construction grants needed to be approved by the unanimous board, and Hogg had hated the Valentines ever since he ran afoul of Lou Ellen back in high school. No doubt he'd relish this opportunity to be a prick.

Rhett tore a hand through his hair. The dryness in the back of his throat made swallowing painful. His nuts were in a noose and the judge had the power to kick out the chair. A few folks glanced over with curious expressions, and he checked his features. It was like living in a fucking fishbowl around here. For the first time he could understand why Pepper might be attracted to the city.

Times like these made him wish for invisibility.

He tossed the paper on the counter and trashed the coffee—his stomach was acidic enough—before walking out. Pepper might be doing a fantastic job keeping… whatever this was…a secret. But for a few seconds, he wanted to see her, even from a distance. Maybe she'd still be at the dog park.

Please let her be at the park.

If he could set eyes on her he'd be able to reassure himself that these feelings were skin-deep. That he'd had abstained long enough, so of course great sex screwed with his head. Once he could confirm that fact, the waters could rise and he could return to being an island.

He froze.

Pepper stood in the center of the park chatting with Mrs. Lee and her Cocker Spaniel. She threw back her head, laughing, as the General joined in, animatedly telling a story that involved a mock fistfight and what appeared to be a helluva dramatic chase scene.

"Hey there, stranger."

His shoulder tensed on reflex. That sweet voice was a blast from the past.

He waited a beat before turning and smiling at Kate and Will on their scooters. "There's double the fun." He winked at the twins.

"Not today," Elizabeth said grimly, shouldering her purse. "Mr. Will here received a yellow card at preschool and got himself sent home today."

"I didn't mean to head-butt Tommy," Will protested.

"What's this?" Rhett bent down. "You attacked a kid?" He wasn't exactly Uncle Rhett to these kids, but he did his best to play a friendly role.

"We were playing dinosaurs." Kate jammed a finger up

her nose and unself-consciously mined for gold. "He was a T-rex. I was a triceratops."

"Can't argue that logic," he said.

"Stop." Elizabeth laughed. "You're encouraging them."

Pepper glanced over and slowly raised a hand.

Elizabeth waved back before giving him the side eye. "What was that about?"

"Nothing. A wave is a universal form of greeting," he replied peevishly.

"I know that, you donkey. But there's more to that story. You two have met?"

"She's my neighbor," he said as casually as possible, trying not to make a deal out of it, forcing his eyes off of Pepper.

A frown marred the space between her sweeping brows. Elizabeth wasn't on Lou Ellen's level of mind reading, but still did a damn good job. "There *is* something."

"Leave it, Birdie." He didn't use his old nickname for her much these days. Only when he wanted to make sure he had her full attention.

"Hear what she did earlier?"

He didn't take another breath until he realized the answer wasn't *him*.

He shook his head.

"You look different." She lowered her chin, giving him a solid once-over. "Happy. It's a good look on you. One I haven't seen in a long time."

"Yeah, well, work's going well." He shoved his hands in his pockets. "So is sailing."

She narrowed her eyes. He'd clearly set off her bullshit meter. "That's not what I'm talking about, and you know it."

"Heard Chez Louis had a good write-up in the AJC."

"Yes, the newspaper came out. That was a big food critic too. Very exciting." Elizabeth's husband, Jean-Luc, owned the local French restaurant named for his father. After calling off the wedding, she'd returned to Everland a year later, engaged to and pregnant by a handsome chef from St. Barts.

The first time he'd seem them together, he'd known in an instant that it was different. He and Birdie never traded secret hungry stares, crackling the air with unspoken tension. He'd proposed too young and felt honor bound to see the deed through. Stay true to his commitment. Birdie wanted to be adored, not merely respected. When he was too stubborn to hear reason, she fled.

At first he'd fed himself the usual lines. Good guys finish last. She was a commitment-phobe. He'd thrown himself a pity party night after night with his good friend Captain Morgan. Until a better friend intervened. Beau was the one who dragged him down to Buccaneers Marina and talked him into splitting the cost of a boat.

Sometimes it sucked living in the same town as his ex-fiancé and first love. On lonely days it sucked a lot. But that wasn't her fault, and when she applied to be Everland's marketing manager in Beau's office, she'd called him first.

"I won't do it if you mind," she'd said.

"You've been married almost five years and have two kids with a great guy. If I minded, I'd be an asshole and you should ignore me."

"You are a good guy," Birdie had said. *"One of the best."*

Pepper glanced back again. He didn't like her expression. Her smile was trying too hard to be relaxed. She kept touching her hair in that nervous way.

"Poor thing had a heck of a start to her morning, bless her heart," Birdie broke into his thoughts.

"Yeah. You mentioned before." He blinked impatiently. "What's that supposed to mean?" For one brutal moment it seemed not only possible but *plausible* that Pepper blurted out the story of last night to Birdie. Because fate would be that big of an asshole.

"I like her," Birdie said in her usual decisive manner. "And Judge Hogg is a giant ass, pardon my French."

Kate slammed the brakes on her scooter so hard her colorful braided pigtails bounced. "*Ass* is French, Mama?"

"Go on you, and don't let me hear you use that word unless you want to suck a bar of Dial." She clucked her tongue. "They don't look it, but they're always listening."

"What happened?" He was in full protective mode, the conversation from Sweet Brew snapping into place. He might not know how he felt about Pepper, but one thing was a guarantee. Nobody'd messed with her.

"I'll let her tell you what happened. It's her story. Not mine."

Classic Birdie—one of the only people in this town content to mind their own damn business. It had been one of the things he loved about her, way back when, so long ago that memories were sepia-toned, almost as if belonging to another person.

She set a hand on his shoulder, not a flirtatious caress, but a grip so he couldn't get away. "You can fool this town, Rhett Valentine, but it'll be a cold day in the bad place before you get one over on me. We go too far back."

"We do," he answered grimly. Back through broken dreams and bruised hearts.

Her smile faded as if she read his thoughts. "Guess I should go back to minding my business."

"Guess so," he answered gently.

Her hand slid down his arm and she squeezed his elbow. Nothing suggestive. Just a quick reminder of their old affection. His body didn't flinch, nor did it twitch down deep, the way it reacted when Pepper got within a few feet. "You deserve your own happiness, Rhett Valentine," she murmured, locking him in with her eye contact. "A forever love."

Her warm, fixed gaze held nothing but a wish for the best, and that realization steadied him.

Her look said: *Find what I found.*

And for once, just quietly, he'd admit—at least to himself—that fine, he was jealous as hell of Birdie. Not because he wanted her. No. But because he wanted what she *had*.

"Heya, Doc Valentine." Kate buzzed him with her scooter. "I got an animal question."

He steeled himself at the "Doc" reference, but wouldn't correct a kid over misidentifying him as Dad. "Shoot."

"Do goldfish like pink castles or blue ones?"

"Depends." He rubbed his chin.

"On if it's a boy or girl?"

"Nah." He kept his features solemn. "On what's their favorite color."

Kate giggled. He winked.

"Mom, I'm huuuungry," Will groaned. "Let's go home."

"Come on, sugar. Daddy's cooking tonight—*gratin dauphinois*. That's fancy for cheesy potatoes," she said to Rhett with a grin.

"Sounds good, gang." He saw them off with a half-wave. Six years ago it hurt to watch that woman walk away, but it was nothing compared to the pain if they'd stayed together, never able to fully be what the other person wanted deep inside. No. He didn't glance back as Birdie walked away.

That wasn't the way he was going.

He whistled under his breath, striding to the dog park, but the song died on his lips as he pushed open the gate. Pepper was gone.

Chapter Nineteen

~

Pepper's alarm clock ticked on the nightstand, each passing second drilling into her brain.

Tick.

Loser.

Tick.

Failure.

Tick. *Pathetic.* Fifteen minutes past ten. She picked up a pillow and crushed it against her head with a groan. Was Rhett showing up? Was the second hand getting louder?

She rolled over, scowling at the motivational sticker quotes she'd stuck to her day planner during the Greyhound ride south. "Believe it to achieve it!" "Clear your mind of can't!" "The path to success starts with the choices you make!"

Ugh. Talk about the disempowerment of positive thinking. All those chipper, generic phrases left her empty. She threw back the sheets, stalked to the dresser, and slathered on hand lotion. After the slimy run-in with Judge Hogg she'd taken a hot shower and had looked forward to seeing Rhett, to the distraction of sex, the salve of an orgasm—or two.

Three if it wasn't too greedy.

She nibbled the edge of her thumbnail. Waiting wasn't the only option. Here in the twenty-first century, when a woman wanted a booty call, it was her prerogative to dial one up.

She moved on to biting her pointer nail. But all her life she'd chased everything, was always in pursuit of one goal or another. For once, *she* wanted to be pursued, to be the goal, to be chased by a man who'd improve a crappy day with the delicate flick and twirl of his talented fingers.

Honk.

"Ugh." Her groan slipped out on its own accord as the memory crowded away all others. The judge couldn't have genetically engineered a more perfect insult. She'd never be able to repeat the story and be taken seriously. It was too laughably bad.

She snapped the lotion lid and wandered to her window. Light flooded between Rhett's verticals blinds. Faulkner must have caught a whiff of her pathetic yearning. He flew through the curtains, paws scratching the glass with a "Heya neighbor!" woof.

Busted! She hit the deck, glimpsing a flash of Rhett's arm on her way down. Her chin grazed the shabby gray carpet. Did he see her lurking? And second, what business did he have taunting her with such a stupidly, sexy forearm? Her heart leapt from her chest like a darn cartoon.

Tick.

Tick.

Seventeen past ten. She commando-crawled beneath the window to her bed and raised an arm, fumbling for her e-reader. This might be crossing the invisible line separating sane from crazy. Time to breathe. Regroup. If Rhett blew her off, so be it. No more mooning around, spying, or impersonating a soldier in the trenches. She'd hang out here on the carpet, read her book, and make her own fun with a deliciously depraved duke.

Except it was impossible to follow the plot's rapid-fire drawing room banter when her mind kept wandering from Regency London to present-day small-town Georgia. Plus the floor made her back hurt.

She tossed the duke book beside her with a muffled groan.

Life had screwed her, and she'd lain there with teeth-gritted endurance, thinking of England. But then Rhett came along, took her into his arms, urged her to ride faster, harder, deeper, and a realization slammed through her at the same time as her fourth orgasm. She wanted to be back in life's saddle.

She froze at the sound of furtive rustling outside. Heart thumping, she rose to her knees, head cocked.

There it came again—muffled steps—either Rhett or an axe murderer. Her pulse accelerated. Someone rapped on the back door and she bounced to her feet, heat flooding her core. Bad guys don't knock, but Southern gentlemen do.

Before entering the kitchen, she mussed her hair and artfully tugged her sleeping shirt to one side, exposing a shoulder.

Show time.

Rhett stood on the top step holding a brown paper bag, a gleam in his baby blues. Her knees involuntarily flexed.

"What happened today?" he asked in a firm, low-pitched voice.

She crossed her arms. "Hello to you, too."

"Sorry. I heard you had a run-in with Judge Hogg." He strode inside, setting the bag on the table. "Lots of rumors, but no facts. What did he do to you?"

"It's more what I did." She swallowed, flushing with shame, as she recounted the story in as few words as possible. When she reached the end, his blue eyes had taken on a steely gray glint.

"What do you need me to do to that asshole?" he asked. "Teach him a lesson?"

She'd like nothing more than for Rhett to crack open a can of whoop-ass on Al Hogg. Rhett didn't walk around in a 'roid rage, but he carried a latent strength in his big frame, a subtle *don't tread on me* signal that promised pain if he was messed with.

He was big. Masculine. Eager to help. If she needed a white knight, he'd be the guy for the job. But that wasn't in his assigned job duties. Flings don't get called on to fight for honor. "This is my mess, I'll deal. I don't need your protection."

"But I like you." He caressed her face, tracing a finger from her temple to chin. "And that liking extends to your messes, too. And jerks who hurt you."

The flash of his grin stopped her heart.

This was getting dangerous. She couldn't let him fight her battles, the next thing you know she'd start needing him, worse, relying on him. Better to nip it in the bud.

"Last night, shmast night." She waved a careless hand and hopped up on the counter. *Yes, good, easy breezy.* She didn't need him. She was the one other people needed.

"Hey." He stepped forward and tilted up her chin. "What's spinning around that pretty head of yours?"

"Flings are fun." She dropped her head, a curtain of hair blocking his face. Better because staring meant seeing, and who knew what he might find if he looked hard enough. "But you don't have to come over to talk about my day."

"Listen." He pulled out a chair, flipping it around to sit backward. "I did have fun last night with you. The sex, well, it was good—amazing, actually."

"Yeah, but?" Because that part was coming. The *but* rose over his head like an invisible cartoon dialogue bubble.

"But…" A muscle in his jaw twitched. "I don't know. I keep thinking about how I've been this self-protected island. And you? You're a tsunami."

"So what, you need to head for higher ground?" Her pulse leapt with panic even as she strove for levity.

"Dammit." He made a frustrated noise. "How about you quit joking, be serious? I'm not going to bullshit. I like you," he said frankly. When she did nothing but gape, he continued. "Jesus, you're cute, funny, sexy as hell. I want to do more than have sex. Hang out. Talk. Watch movies. Keep it casual, but connect." He reached in his bag and removed a familiar board game. "I hear you're quite the Scrabble player."

"I know my way around a board," she said dubiously, fighting for equilibrium. Too many compliments in rapid succession, she couldn't process them all. Why'd he do that? Because she seemed needy?

"You look like a deer in headlights," he said rapidly. "I'm not trying to push you, or complicate anything. We can keep it as straight sex." He scuffed at the floor. "But I like you. We're friends, right?"

"And you want to upgrade to friends with benefits?" She raised a brow. "Have you never watched a romantic comedy?"

He blinked. "No? Should I have?"

"Nora Ephron is the shit, but as for fling plots, they all go more or less the same way." She braced her hands on the kitchen table. "It starts casual, but by the middle everyone in the audience is throwing Junior Mints at the screen and shouting, 'Good God, people, kiss already.'"

"You have big feelings on the subject." He smirked, not missing a beat. "But if you're the expert on the subject of fling pitfalls, then you should have the answers for how we could avoid them."

He had a point. She swung her legs, thinking a moment. "First, no sleepovers, like we agreed last night. Second, no friending each other on Facebook."

"Easy." He gave a curt nod. "I don't do Facebook."

"I see." Not that she knew that from trying to social media stalk him. No. Not at all. She shifted her weight on the counter. "Exchanging bodily fluids is okay, but no deep feelings."

He shrugged. "Don't have those, either."

The way he stared in her eyes while entering her last night made that claim doubtful. But all kidding aside, she did have a final point that needed to be put on the table. "And last but not least, save the compliments."

His eyes widened. "What's that mean?"

"I don't need a fuss."

"What is the fuss, people being kind to you?"

She shrugged. "There's probably twenty different deep-seated neuroses to unpack here, but that would mean talking about feelings, and that means referring to rule number three." They'd teetered on the edge of something big, and she yanked them back to safety.

This was a temporary solution to a long-term sexual rut. That's it. End of story.

"Even with these ground rules, friends-with-benefits is a recipe for disaster, unless you added a key ingredient. In my case, it's the fact Everland isn't my forever. That means we can keep this fun."

"All right then, lil' buddy. Have it your way. I won't pay a single compliment about you or your perfect breasts." His tone was light, but that probing stare was dangerous.

No more talk. Time to put the *fuck* in *fuck buddy*.

She nodded to the board game. "How about a rousing round of strip Scrabble?"

"Strip Scrabble?" He gave her a bemused smile.

"Yes. I just invented it." She rubbed her hands. "Here's how to play. Every thirty points, the loser loses an article of clothing." She waggled her brows. "And if you spell a body part, the other person has to kiss it."

"Careful, Trouble." He leveled a crooked smile. "I aim to play dirty."

She jumped off the counter, walked to the table, and opened the lid. A shiver of anticipation coursed through her as she removed the board. "I'd have it no other way."

Who knew Scrabble could be sexy?

Five minutes later, Rhett placed an *H* in front of the word *eat*.

"Well, sir, looks as if you have got some of this." Pepper set an *S* tile next to the word *kill*.

"Some guys are breast men—and like I said, you'd make me a convert—but I prefer..." He bracketed the word *high* with a *T* and an *S* and gave a rakish smile. "What were the rules again? That I have to kiss you there?"

"I do like to follow the letter of the law-ahhhhh," she moaned as he parted her legs, head dropping low. "That's not my thigh."

"Oops," he glanced up with a rakish smile. "Aimed too high." He didn't purposely try to sound seductive, but with that molasses-rich accent, he could make reading the instructions for a toaster oven sound hotter than a Southern night.

"Darn," she pouted, both at her letters and the fact he stopped that thing he was doing with his tongue. "I'm like Old McDonald. So much *E-I-E-I-O*."

"You'd make a good farmer."

"Is this a reference to my fertile hips?"

He gave said hips an approving squeeze. "No, I meant you love corn."

"Guilty as charged. Still, there's something else I love even more." She dropped an *S* onto *ex*.

"Never let me be the one who stood between you and what you wanted," he said, before he showed her not only what he could do with his tongue, but also his fingers, and a few other clever body parts.

Afterward, she curled up, sated, lazy, and happy as she could remember in his lap. "I feel something," she whispered.

"Me too." He nuzzled her hair.

"I meant on my butt." She reached and plucked off a *Z* tile. "Guess we earned ten points."

"That's it." His low chuckle sent heat through her belly. "Now you're in trouble."

But, as Pepper realized somewhere between "God, oh God" and "yes, there, yes" that the trouble with trouble is sometimes you want more of it.

* * *

The next day at the dog park, Rhett sent her an invitation for online Scrabble and they played a secret fast and furious game. During her walk back to Mrs. Johnson's house, with Ziggy the seven-year-old St. Bernard on the leash, her phone buzzed.

> *Rhett: Good game*
>
> *Pepper: I killed your butt—holla!*
>
> *Rhett: Excuse me?*
>
> *Pepper: Damn you autocorrect! Kicked. Kicked your butt*
>
> *Rhett: Should I be scared to come over?*

Scared or not, he did. And the night after that. And quite a few more after that.

"How come you're always coming here?" she asked from the cover of darkness.

He tugged a lock of her hair. "Far as I know, you come, too."

"I'm serious. I've never stepped foot in your house."

He remained quiet a minute. "Guess I don't like the idea of making you sneak over in the dark, creeping home."

"Let me get this straight." She grabbed a sheet and sat up against the headboard. "The idea of me walking twenty steps home from a booty call compromises my honor."

"It's not the action of a gentleman."

She tickled her toes on his calf. "And what you did to me ten minutes ago was?"

"Different," he drawled, giving her a light spank.

She shrieked, giggling. "I don't see it that way."

"You're putting me in a hard place."

"No." She lightly ran her nails between his muscular thighs, giving his shaft a caressing squeeze. "*You're* already in a hard place."

He groaned, his hips bucking. "That's not fighting fair."

A gentle twist of the wrist. "Say, 'you're invited to my house, Pepper.'" She increased her speed.

His eyes rolled back in his head as he thickened in her grip. "You're invited to my house, Pepper."

"Tomorrow." She stroked from base to tip.

"Yes. Christ. Tomorrow is great."

"And you're beautiful." Up and down, increasing the grip.

"That's true." His fingers dug into the sheets.

"And smart."

He leaned in, breathing hard, low growls vibrating in his chest. "Smart ass, you mean."

She froze, mouth pursed. "I can stop."

He jerked. "I meant as smart as a whip."

"Is a whip smart?" She leaned in and nipped his bottom lip, gasping as he cupped her still tender sex.

"Genius smart." He brushed his nose against hers, his tongue teasing the seam of her mouth, a sexy direct provocation.

"And...and..." It's a trick to be witty with a finger massaging your lady button. "Wha-wha-what else?" she stammered.

"Humble?" Amusement laced his voice, and something

more, affection, and, God, she didn't want to give name to what else for fear of breaking the spell.

He rolled her onto her back and positioned himself above her on his elbows while she grabbed the box of condoms off her night dresser. "There is only one left. How'd that happen?"

His teeth caught the lobe of her ear, his hot breath making her moan. "I have a theory."

"Shut up." She grinned even though a foreign feeling lodged deep inside. Nothing about the situation felt like work, or compromising. She suspected the unfamiliar sensation had a name.

Contentment.

And it scared her to death.

"What're you thinking, Trouble?" he asked after another hungry kiss.

"Nothing," she demurred. "It's too hard when you do that hand trick, that, with the fingers, and oh, that pressure there." She rested her lips against his cheek, inhaling that addictive woodsy smell, unable to resist adding, "This is good. You and me."

"Come over tomorrow," he said at last. "I'll make you dinner. I make a hell of a steak."

"Sounds like a plan. On one condition. Can I come now?" He flickered over her swollen sweet spot, answering her question.

Afterward he rolled to face her, walking his fingers over the swell of her hip. "Let's get serious about tomorrow."

"Serious how?" Her smile wilted. "Second thoughts already?"

He made an *are you kidding* face. "How'd seven suit?"

Chapter Twenty

At 6:58 the doorbell chimed. Pepper was punctual.

Rhett opened his front door, promptly gripping the knob to keep from slamming it shut. "What are you doing here?"

"The better question is, where are your manners?" His big sister smacked his chest with the back of her hand. "That's a fine way to talk to family."

He glanced over her shoulder. The sidewalk was empty, but Pepper would be arriving any minute.

Lou Ellen sniffed, nostrils flaring. "Mmm...Smells real nice in here." She waltzed into the house.

"What do you need?" he muttered, glancing toward Pepper's place setting. Dinner for three wasn't what he had in mind, but it was time to speed through anger, denial, and frustration and get right to acceptance, because this situation was about to happen.

"I'm here to talk details about Mr. Scallywag. The Village Pillage is coming up, and that means the silent auction.

The Quilt Guild's predicting your turn as Mr. Scallywag will raise more money than any other item besides Kingston Day's timeshare in Cocoa Beach. Did I tell you we chose the dog park to be the recipient of this year's fundraiser money? Miss Ida May wanted to do..." Ellen trailed off, her gaze lasered on the tossed salad and bottles of IPA on the table. "Am I interrupting something, little brother?" she said in a tone of delight. "Why, it looks like you're ready for a hot date—"

The dogs raced toward the door, barking up a storm before the doorbell chimed.

"I'll get it!"

She was quicker.

"Hello?" Pepper lurked, uncertain at the door. "I...can come back later...or...not...just wanted to..."

"Come on in." Rhett had all the enthusiasm of a man marching to the gallows. "Pepper, let me introduce you to—"

"Hello, there. I've been dying to meet you," Lou Ellen extended a hand, bright rings on every finger. "Lou Ellen Woodall née Valentine. Rhett's big sister."

Pepper glanced between them. "I see the family resemblance."

"Do you now?" Lou Ellen touched her cheek.

"The eyes."

"Inherited from our mama," Lou Ellen replied in a softer tone before regrouping. "Now, who is going to tell me what's going on?"

"Back off, Lou." He used his best authoritative tone, one that garnered an instant response from even disobedient dogs.

His big sister was unimpressed. "I think I have a right to know what's going on under my baby brother's roof."

"No, you don't," he pushed back.

"I'm the oldest female in the family," she protested. "Mama would expect nothing less."

But there was a world of difference between being a caring matriarch and a nosy nuisance. Rhett went stone cold silent. Hard to say if anyone even noticed. The dogs were carrying on around Pepper, yelping, tails hitting furniture.

Their gazes connected.

You doing okay? he asked silently.

A hint of tightness strained the skin near her eyes, but her smile reached her eyes. *Yeah.*

"I've never seen those three behave like that before," Lou Ellen remarked.

"Pepper brings it out in them." And no way in hell would Rhett add what she brought out in *him.* Dammit. He loved his sister, but he wasn't ready for anyone to intrude in this Pepper alternate reality. Besides, flings don't meet family.

"I stopped by to get some professional development tips. Rhett's been helping me out with that."

His chest heaved with a silent groan. Pepper sounded as phony as a presenter on a late-night infomercial. Her wide-eyed innocent act might fool a stranger on the street, but not his sister. But he didn't want his sister getting the wrong idea.

She glanced to Lou Ellen, who was practically rubbing her hands, and asked, "Will you be staying for dinner?"

"No," Rhett answered right as Lou Ellen said, "Why, I'd love that."

Silence reigned in the dining room. Even the dogs padded to their individual pillows, ears cocked at attention, no doubt picking up on all the unspoken tension.

Lou Ellen took a seat at the head of the table and crossed her ankles. Her unruffled smile belayed the *I'm getting to the bottom of this* gleam in her eye.

When push came to shove, Lou Ellen would never leak his love life to the Back Fence, but that didn't mean she wouldn't want the lowdown dirty details as kickback. She made his business *her* business, and nothing to the contrary made a dent in her thinking process.

"What are your four monsters doing tonight besides burning down the house?"

"Snapper's coaching their soccer game." Lou Ellen turned to Pepper. "My three big girls are on the team, and the littlest thinks she's the assistant coach. I don't have the faintest idea where Lorelei gets her bossiness from."

"I do," Rhett muttered.

"You're too funny for words." Lou Ellen bared her teeth.

As Pepper took a seat, Rhett fetched an extra plate and cutlery, plus the broiled oysters he'd prepared as an appetizer.

"I want to know everything about you. Tell me a fun fact." Lou Ellen leaned in on her elbows, propping her chin on top of her folded hands. "Something nice and juicy."

"I don't know." Pepper fiddled with her fork. "I'm pretty dry."

An awkward pause. If Lou Ellen was less of a lady, she sounded like she'd cough the word *bullshit* into her fist. Instead she settled for a tight smile and "I doubt that."

Rhett leaned back in his chair. "Leave it, Lou Lou."

"What? I'm simply stating a fact. There is nothing wrong with a little getting-to-know-you chitchat, am I right, Pepper? Rhett doesn't do girl talk."

"Let me tell you what I *do* do." His patience frayed to a

thread. For someone who'd worked hard to be an island, it was starting to feel damn crowded here. "Eat." He picked up his fork and shoved an oyster in his face. "These are a local variety. You know, I read in the *Examiner* that Georgia could well be on its way to being considered the Napa Valley of oysters. Go on, try one, they won't be good once they're cold."

"I have a sister." Pepper spoke over him even as she offered a reassuring smile. "Tuesday and I the best of friends and the worst of enemies."

Lou Ellen nodded slowly, a ghost of a genuine smile on her lips. "A good way to look at sibling relationships."

"Now you asked me to tell you something about myself. I was once in a movie," Pepper said. "As an extra."

Rhett dropped his shoulders a fraction. Score one for Pepper. Unexpected pride warmed through him. If there was one thing Lou Ellen loved besides her family, her Quilt Guild, and her Monday nights watching *The Bachelor*, it was movies. She had a subscription to two celebrity magazines and was up to date on all celebrity gossip, and she shared who dated who or who wore what where, like it or not.

Besides, it seemed important for Pepper to make a good impression on Lou. The realization stuck in his throat, along with the bacon-wrapped oyster, and he reached for his beer to force it down.

"You're kidding. Who? What? Where? How?" Lou Ellen looked rapt.

"*Summer Can Wait.*"

"No! No, you were not!" Lou Ellen stamped her heels on the floor, squealing so loud Fitzgerald whined. Rhett shot him a look of sympathy. His own ears were ringing. "That one is coming out next month. The trailer looks so good."

Pepper's cheeks turned an adorable shade of pink. "I might have been cut from the final version. It was a general city shot."

"Okay. Name your favorite book." Lou Ellen sat back, tossing out enough rope for Pepper to hang herself. "You may or may not happen know that my brother is an extensive reader."

"I'd suspected as much from his dogs' names." Pepper sipped from her pint glass. "But is this a trick question where I'm supposed to answer 'the Bible'?"

Lou grinned. "I'll amend. What's the last thing you read?"

"Essay fifty-one from *The Federalist Papers*."

"For fun?"

"Constitutional ratification is a hoot." She shrugged. "Told you I was dry."

"Good Lord, she is a lawyer, isn't she?" Lou Ellen announced to Rhett. "But she's got pluck, and that counts for a good deal in my book."

"I also have this plucky pet peeve about being discussed like I'm not here. Your turn to get cross-examined." Pepper fired back, chewing the corner of her lip, although her dancing eyes told she enjoyed herself. "Tell me something about Rhett, when he was a little boy."

"Oh. Yes." Lou Ellen clearly relished the chance. "Let me see. My favorite memory would have to be the time Rhett lost his first tooth."

"Not that one," he said with a groan. It was surreal sitting here shooting the breeze with these two. He loved his sister, and he, well, he liked Pepper. A lot.

"It's not every day someone decides to rid themselves of a tooth by jumping off the roof."

"I'm not the only kid who ever believed it." Fuck. What if he more than liked Pepper?

"Believed what?" Pepper knitted her brows.

"Superman underwear could make you fly." How could he be thinking about love and his childhood underwear in the same thought? Any second his sister was going to take one look at him and know exactly what was in his mind. The hairs on the back of his neck prickled.

"You went on your roof in your underwear?" Pepper asked, still too confused about his childhood antics to notice that he was sweating bullets.

"Thank you!" Lou Ellen drained her bottle and raised it in a "cheers" gesture, relishing the moment. "Rhett, honey, kindly illuminate us on your eight-year-old thought process."

He crossed his knife and fork on the edge of his plate. He was willing to play along if it kept the focus on his internal crisis. "Fine. I jumped."

"Why?" Lou Ellen prodded.

He raised an eye at Pepper. "Does this qualify as leading the witness?"

She covered a hand over her mouth, smothering a grin. "Sustain. It's relevant to the story."

He feigned a heavy sigh, playing up his embarrassment. "Turns out Superman underwear doesn't help you fly."

The doorbell rang.

"Now who?" he muttered under his breath.

"Goodness." Lou Ellen poured another glass. "It's like the Atlanta airport around here, little brother. And here I've been worried sick that you were turning into one of those bearded recluses that you read about." She turned to Pepper. "You're good for him."

"Me? I'm just here for professional development." Pepper repeated guiltily. But she was trying to cover, for him, and that meant everything.

"Yeeeeeees. Dog walking. I imagine there's a lot to learn," Lou Ellen deadpanned.

Rhett wanted to signal to Pepper there was no point pretending. Lou Ellen saw through their façade, probably took her all of three seconds. But as long as she thought he was having a fling, she'd miss that part where he might well be falling in love. Better to lose the battle and win the war. "I'm going to get the door."

As he left the kitchen, he overheard Lou Ellen saying, "Tell me, how many children do you want? Three? Four? Nine?"

Jesus. He coughed. His sister was a Russian doll of nosiness. But he couldn't help but be curious. Did Pepper want kids? Did he?

What the hell was going on?

He opened the screen door. No one was there. At the end of the street, an unfamiliar car tapped the brake lights before taking the corner too fast.

With a sinking heart he walked to the bottom of the porch stairs. Sure enough, there was a cardboard box. It thumped twice.

He squatted and opened it up. Inside a gray puppy stared up, blinking in the porch light. His neck corded as his chest heaved in a deep sigh. This happened more than he liked. People got into life trouble. Money got tight. Eviction notices. And it got too hard to support a pet. Word had spread around the town that you could drop off an animal at Rhett's house, no questions asked. There wasn't a rescue shelter in easy driving distance.

Yet.

He scooped up the puppy. Tonight the little girl would stay with him. Faulkner, Fitzgerald, and Steinbeck wouldn't mind. They were used to small frightened animals.

He walked inside as the puppy wiggled once, then collapsed against him with a relieved sigh. Her pulse was normal, and she appeared well fed.

He strode back into the kitchen and his three dogs glanced from their pillows, ears perking. Lou Ellen rose, clutching her heart. "Oh my heavens. Look at that. Isn't he the cutest thing?"

"She," Pepper announced to no one in particular.

"That she is." The oven timer beeped. "Let me go put her in a crate and—"

"Let me hold her." Pepper extended her arms.

"You?" he said.

Pepper flushed. "She looks like the dog statue from the park."

"Davy Jones?" He stared at the little puppy's face. Pepper had a point.

"Now that's spooky," Lou Ellen said with a perceptible shiver. "She's the spitting image. You're going to call someone from the rescue hotline?"

"What's that?" Pepper asked.

"Volunteers who take rescue animals into their homes. We don't have a shelter in the town."

"Yet," Rhett added.

"Yes, yet." Lou Ellen nodded. "Rhett's hard at work raising the funds to get one built locally."

The image of Hogg's smug face shining out from the *Examiner* flashed through Rhett's mind. The foundation hadn't returned his last call. But right now there was a more pressing one staring him straight in the face. Pepper's normally guarded eyes glowed.

His gaze fixed on her tiny top-lip mole, seized with an impulse to lick it. His whole body tensed, ratcheting up with desire, the near painful need to take her in his arms.

He'd seen her drop her closed-off look a few times, especially when he did a certain move with his fingers, but this was something else entirely. He knew how it felt, had suffered from the affliction all his life.

Puppy fever.

Chapter Twenty-One

I don't know who I even am anymore," Pepper announced to the cute wiggly fur ball. "This isn't me. I'm not a dog person."

The puppy gazed from her lap, all innocent eyes, and tried to nip her nose. The sweet little bundle couldn't cause any harm unless it affectionately slobbered her to death.

"There you go, you're doing it again," she cooed. "That face. How can I resist you when you make dat widdle face." It was as if being with Rhett had expanded her heart and now there was room for even more surprises. Like baby-talking to a puppy. Good lord, if Tuesday could see this she'd catch hell.

Pepper frowned. Speaking of her sister, she hadn't returned her last two calls or three texts. She grabbed her phone and checked again to make sure she hadn't missed anything. Nothing. The last message—Hit pound if you're still alive—from last night sat in the message box delivered but unread.

"Coast's clear." Rhett sauntered back into the room. He headed to a well-stocked bookshelf, fiddled around, and music filled the room, a virtuoso acoustic guitar. "Lou Ellen's left the building."

"Speaking of your sister." Pepper tucked her feet up under her legs. "Is she always so...inquisitive?"

"That was her best behavior." He grimaced. "She liked you."

"I liked her, too." And she did. "We're two bossy dames at heart. Big sisters unite." Hopefully she didn't come on that strong to Tuesday. She only ever meant well when advising her sister, but sometimes had an "I know best" attitude.

"She means well, but likes to get a rise."

"I prefer getting a rise out of you more." She traded her moment of sisterly worry for a teasing flirtation. Hopefully fluttering her lashes would drive away the uneasiness.

"I'm partial to it myself." His drawl didn't have a hint of humor. The hot look in his eyes made her cross and recross her legs.

"Careful now." She covered the puppy's ears with a wink. "Kitty has big ears."

When she said the name it felt perfect.

"Kitty?" he rasped.

"I'm keeping her." There's a sentence she never expected to be saying.

"But..." He blinked. "You don't like dogs."

"I know." There was no way to explain the feeling filling her heart near to bursting. This was her pet. Hers and hers alone. The truth sank in to a bone-deep level. It didn't make any sense, but that didn't mean it was any less true. Her fur mama hormones kicked in to hyperdrive. "But she's not any dog. She's Kitty."

"You sure you're up for that?" His forehead crinkled skeptically. "You don't know anything about having a puppy. It's hard work. Lots of responsibility."

"Good thing I live next door to a really smart vet." She waggled her eyebrows. "And he's a looker to boot."

He sank beside her on the couch. "If you're serious, then here are a few tips. First, there's going to be lots of chewing. You ready for that?"

"I can hide my special shoes."

"Vaccinations, a bathroom routine, food, obedience, socializing."

She nodded. "Not a problem. Routine is my jam."

"But why do you want to do this?" He looked inquisitive.

There it was. The million-dollar question. "I don't know," she said. "It's that...she needs me. But it feels healthy rather than co-dependence. Like we can help each other." She screwed her nose and ducked her chin, embarrassed to open up. Deep inside was a part of her desperate for unconditional love. But that was heavy stuff, and flings were light as air. Weigh them down and pop—the magic would vanish.

She liked Rhett, and Rhett's magic, too much to want to kiss it goodbye just yet.

Take the awestruck way he watched her. Like she was this fun, relaxed, confident woman. Boy, she had him fooled. The last thing she wanted to do was remove the mask like a *Scooby-Doo* villain and say, "I'm actually a neediness vortex. Hah hah. Fooled you!"

Kitty heaved a contented sigh, blissfully oblivious to her new owner's internal turmoil, and drifted asleep.

Dog care was a breeze compared to her confusing feelings toward her secret fling. "What should I do now? I

can't hold her all night, but it's a shame to wake her up."
Faulkner, Steinbeck, and Fitzgerald crept under the table,
tails thumping against the floor, checking on what all the
fuss was about.

"Nestle her on this for tonight." Rhett went to the corner
of the room and returned with a corduroy pillow. "I'll grab a
crate from my tool shed in the morning. Right now though,
I'd rather hold you."

After Kitty was tucked in for the night and the dogs
padded off to their cots, Pepper crawled into his bed and his
big, strong arms. He lazily unbuttoned her top button and
then another, and then one more. Enough space to ease a hand
in, caress the soft swell encased in flimsy lace. She'd worn a
good bra tonight, one that set the girls off to perky perfection.
Every other guy she'd been with always did a cursory rush
job, groped as if tuning in Tokyo or kneading bread.

But Rhett. *Oh, God, Rhett.* He took his time gliding his
thumb around her outer nipple, not content to simply let
it harden, no, he kept up the maddening circles until her
flesh ached into a sharp peak, her cheeks flamed, and sweat
sheened her chest.

Then, only then, did he lower his head and suck.

Her head rocked back, her eyes sank closed. Her first
bona fide fling was going to ruin her for all others.

Rhett understood, without being told, the complex
mashup of nerve endings. The way the build needed to
come slow, through delicate touches and ever increasing
pressure. He built momentum until by the time he swirled
his tongue over the nub, her body arched on reflex, ready
for more, but he skirted away.

"You're a tease," she gasped.

"And you love it."

"I do, but I want…"

"Tell me." His lips were against her ear. He traced up the shell with the tip of his tongue, nibbling on the sides.

God, even that. How much he did with just an ear.

She rolled to face him, her mouth dry. It was so darn hard to ask for what she wanted. What she needed. To take up space. If she made herself a bother, no one would want to stick around.

But Rhett wasn't staring at her like she was a bother. In fact, he was the one who looked hot and bothered. The sight gave her courage. She licked her lips. Here goes nothing. "I want you. Again. And again. And again."

"Four times in a row?" He smirked, nuzzling her neck, tracing her clavicle with the point of her tongue. "I'm willing to try if you are."

Her breasts grew full and heavy from his attentions. "I like your house."

"Tell me what you like about it." He drew the skin at her throat into his mouth, tasting, before opening her shirt all the way and running his cheek over her swells, the rough grit of his scruff causing her skin to break into goosebumps.

"That picture," she whispered, tangling her fingers in his hair. The image was framed in silver and hung on the opposite wall. It was a black and white image of a young woman holding a little boy.

He stopped moving and looked up. "Me and Mama."

"I haven't met her. Lou Ellen made it sound like she wasn't around." It seemed a terrible thing to wish, that he'd been left, too.

"She's dead." He said the words simply, but something fell over him, an invisible cloak, impermeable to outside elements.

"Oh no." Her throat clamped shut. He walked a path she couldn't even imagine. "I'm so sorry."

He shrugged, but with so much effort it was obvious that it was more than a simple, casual gesture. "It happened fifteen years ago. I was twenty." Silence stretched over a few seconds. "The strange thing is, I'm near the point where I've lived longer without her than with her."

"You don't have to talk about it if you don't want to," she said, so softly she wasn't sure he'd heard.

But eventually he spoke. "Her name was Virginia, but everyone called her Ginny." A ghost of a smile played on his lips. "You know, she was a lot like Lou Ellen except minus the sarcasm. Those two were a headstrong pair, always arguing but in a way that you knew meant that they loved you. Doc adored her. Thought the sun rose and set just to bring her joy."

"How'd she die? Cancer? Car accident?" She'd passed so young.

"A bee." He folded his hands behind his head. His voice stripped of any emotion. "Simple fucking honeybee."

Oh no. "An allergy?"

He nodded once. "No one knew. Guess she'd never been stung, or she developed it later in life. I'd come home from my first year at UGA. It had been rough, Doc pressuring me to do pre-med, but I wasn't sure. Mama said to stay true to my own path, but Doc was stubborn. He wouldn't pay another cent unless I did the degree. That it's what Valentine men did, became doctors. He was right, too. He was, his daddy had been, and at least the one before that.

"We had a fight and I stormed out, found Beau, drank a few beers, went fishing, and cooled down. But I didn't close the back door on my way out and one of our dogs escaped. She was a new rescue, skittish. Mama carried on fretting until Doc said he'd go help find the dog.

"They hiked through the forest. She bent to pick a Carolina lily and a bee stung her on the back of the neck. Didn't take long for her to start wheezing. Told Dad she was out of shape. Laughed it off. But it progressed quicky."

Rhett broke off, scrubbed a hand over his face. "He never spoke about what happened next, but over time Lou Ellen and I pieced together the facts. He didn't have an EpiPen—why would he?—and they didn't carry cell phones. And so she died at the edge of a meadow, right at sunset, choking for breath, in his arms."

"Oh, Rhett. There are no words." Her voice dropped to a pained whisper. Her heart fractured at how broken the tragedy had left him. Even all these years later, self-hatred shook his voice. Grief was isolating. While her own family tragedy wasn't of this magnitude, in some small way she understood why he'd built such an iron-clad protective casing, despite having such a kindhearted nature. "Your poor mom. Your dad. What happened, it wasn't your fault."

"But if I'd behaved differently, had better control of my actions, she'd still be here. Doc grew into a different person without her. Mama teased him in ways no one else was allowed. She'd call him a windbag, but then they'd kiss. They touched each other all the time. When I was little, I hated it, thought it was embarrassing if friends were over. But now, I know what they shared was rare and powerful. In my last relationship I tried to force something that wasn't there. At the time I thought it was because I owed Birdie to keep trying, but now, who knows, maybe the truth was I didn't want to lose anyone else in my life."

He held himself so carefully still, as if the alternative was cracking into countless pieces. "Come here." She opened her arms. "Rest your head a minute."

He lowered to her chest. "I hear your heartbeat."

She stroked his hair. Eventually he continued to speak. "After Mama passed, I quit pre-med. Doc went nuclear, tried to bully me into seeing things his way. But I wouldn't have it. Told him that staying true to myself, becoming a vet, was my way to honor Mama."

"That's sweet. What did he say?"

"That I wasn't his son. So I thanked him for raising me. For providing for me until that point. Then I went out. Got this tattoo and drank myself senseless with Beau down by the river bottoms."

The dull hurt in his voice made her physically ill. "How could he treat you that way?"

"With hindsight and a decade of maturity, I'd say Dad was wild with grief, but too stubborn to retract his words. After I opened my practice he told me, via Lou Ellen, that he'd never darken the door to my clinic. I sent back word that I wasn't going to lose sleep over the fact. We've never spoken since unless absolutely necessary."

"Why's he so angry?

"He's mad that Mama's gone, and he can't be angry at her, so I'm the emotional punching bag. It's fine. I can take it." He sighed. "Besides, I'd rather have him pissed off at me than at her memory. Let the old man have that much at least."

"But it isn't fair." Her brain cells misfired at the illogicalness of it all, the sheer waste of a precious family relationship flushed down the toilet. "Any father should be proud to claim you as his own."

"It's the way it is." He shrugged. "Some things never change."

"But that's it." She needed him to feel better, she had to find a way to help fix this, to make him see. "People do change. Look at me falling for Kitty. I'm proof."

"This is more than getting over a fear of dogs, Pepper." He didn't sound angry, more resigned.

"People can change. It's just easier not to." Her quiet protest fell on deaf ears. He wasn't ready to hear it, and that fact had to be okay.

"I can think of lots of other topics I'd rather discuss," he said dryly. "Like how to best get you naked for starters." He rose and braced his arms on either side of her. His woodsy smell was as delicious as ever, but had grown familiar, too. A comfort. And if he wanted distraction, she could offer him comfort in kind.

She played up her exasperated huff and was rewarded when the tension around his eyes eased. His gentle exhalation was felt rather than heard, and she purred as the delicious heat from his breath stole up her neck.

"And I like all these little sounds even better." His mouth curved in a soft, sexy smile. "Hey, I have a confession to make."

He sounded deadly serious. "Her heart stuttered as the emotional barometer shifted. "What?"

"A few nights after you moved in, I got home late. I'd been sailing with Beau and was wiped. I intended to crawl straight to bed. Didn't even bother brushing my teeth or turning on a light. And there you were, over that fence, in your room in a pair of tiny pink shorts belting Gloria Gaynor lyrics into a hairbrush, how you would survive."

"You heard that?" She clapped a hand over her mouth.

That might have well been the night she YouTubed the "Tw-erking for Beginners" workout video. The only silver lining to this situation was absolution. Clear the air.

"This is mortifying, but I have a confession as well."

She owned up to the towel incident, and his chest lifted with a chuckle. "We've been dumber than a bag of rocks. But we've grown smarter because now we do this." He kissed her to the edge of crazy and slid a hand under the back of her skirt.

The trouble was that as Pepper let him deepen the kiss, stroking her tongue against his with a raw-edged hunger, she didn't feel all that smart. It was like she'd popped the lid off Pandora's box and all the emotions she'd kept locked away were breaking free. Self-sufficiency and autonomy had sailed her through many a life storm, but the more Rhett dropped his guard and exposed his sensitive underbelly, the more her own vulnerability grew.

She was uncertain where they were headed, but eventually they'd hit a dead end. Because as much as she adored Rhett's companionship, his gruff humor, that ragged sound tearing from his throat as she worked her hand under his belt and teased her fingers against his hot velvet skin, thick with throbbing veins, this wasn't real life. It was a summer fling. And soon, she'd have to leave Love Street.

He nipped the edge of her earlobe with a sweet sting that made her cry out. Yes, she'd be leaving, but until that day—she gasped as he drove her back against the headboard—she'd focus on coming. Every other option came with some kind of string. And if they tangled up, it would be hard to break free.

Chapter Twenty-Two

⟋

Rhett stirred, sleep-hazed, frowning at the pins-and-needles sensation shooting through his fingertips. He flexed his hand, getting used to it. During the night, Pepper had rolled close, the weight of her head cutting off his arm circulation. His ass was freezing. She'd hogged the covers, turning herself into a cute burrito, and even then, her feet remained the temperature of icicles.

What was it with women and cold feet?

He wrapped an arm around Pepper's waist and drew her closer, breathing in her hair, savoring the fruity smell of her shampoo. They'd passed out after a round of marathon sex ending in lazily watching the last half of an eighties flick Pepper claimed as her favorite. "I have this weird love for Billy Crystal," she'd said, cuddling against him. "He is cranky but adorable in *When Harry Met Sally*."

Weird but even weirder was the fact the movie wasn't terrible. He might have laughed a few times.

How had he gotten here? Gone from trying to convince himself he was better to actually being better. To being great. This situation smacked of crazy, like someone snuck into his pantry and moved around all the cans. Trouble had rearranged his simple, straightforward world into something strange and different. Happy even.

The sun rose high enough to fill the bedroom with light. Slowly Pepper stirred. A nose twitch. An eyebrow flutter. Next an eyelid twitch, followed by a wide yawn. She woke halfway through, her startled gaze locking on his. A piece of her bangs stuck straight up while sleep stuck to the corner of her eyes. She wasn't trying to be anything other than who she was right then. His heart gave a painful lurch. Because the truth was that she was beautiful, inside and out, and for some magic reason wanted to be with him.

"Hey." He took a steadying breath, fighting for levity. "Nice tonsils."

"Hi there." She hiked the sheet around her breasts, staring around, trying to gain orientation. "So…guess we've had another sleepover."

"Yeah," he said gruffly, smoothing her hair. "Guess so."

"Is that okay? We never discussed going beyond a booty call." She scrutinized him, gauging his reaction. "This wasn't fling-y of me."

It wasn't. And he didn't care. This was good. Better than good. Waking up with Pepper was fucking incredible, even if she made his arm fall asleep and his ass freeze. "Know something? You talk in your sleep."

"Say what?" Her brown eyes widened.

"You recited a bunch of old man names."

"The presidents." She half-sat, full alert now. "The presidents of the United States."

"Millard Fillmore was a president?"

"Yes. The thirteenth. Preceded by Zachary Taylor and succeeded by Franklin Pierce."

He stared. Not only was she a knockout, she'd be able to KO the competition at Mad Dawg's trivia night. "What else is stored in that brain?"

"Don't even ask." She grimaced. "I memorized the presidents when I was a kid and would recite them when falling asleep. Somehow they implanted into my subconscious. My sister used to complain about me reciting the names at two in the morning."

He swallowed, dropping his gaze to her sweet mouth. "That's sort of cute."

"Oh? Grover Cleveland does it for you?"

He brushed his lips over hers, kissing her with a measured, intense rhythm, drawing the moment out until they both shivered. "Who?"

"Grover Cleveland. The twenty-second and twenty-fourth president, the only one to be unelected after four years and then regain the White House."

"I thought you were talking about the Muppet."

"Ha, no. And anyway that Muppet had nothing to see under his matted blue fur." She ran her tongue along the seam of his lips before whispering in a husky voice, "Looks like Grover's a grower and not a show-er."

"I don't know whether to be disturbed or turned on," he said, rolling on top of her. They laughed into each other's mouths.

What the hell had his life been before her?

There'd always been a usual ebb and flow to his Sunday. He woke. Chugged a protein shake. Ran with the dogs. Came home, cooked a plate of scrambled eggs and bacon and zoned in front of sports cable until Beau quit working enough to take the boat out. He'd never had a morning like this, in bed with a woman he wasn't meant to get serious about, who made bad jokes about dead presidents and somehow looked sexy doing it.

He was so fucked.

A faint whine wafted up the hall.

"Crap. Kitty!" Pepper broke from their kiss and jumped from the bed, stumbling because her underwear had been pulled around her knees. "I have to let her out. Go do all the jobs. I am the worst pet mom ever, forgot I even had a dog. Maybe I should have gone for a fish instead. A nice geriatric fish looking to live out his or her final weeks from the comfort of a bowl on my kitchen counter. What was I thinking? I can barely be responsible for myself, and am still sorting out how to fix a bungled future, not to mention the seriously confusing feelings for—"

"Pepper. Breathe." Rhett stood and threw on a gray shirt, walking after her. She was going to pass out if she didn't stop talking. "Kitty is fine."

Sure enough, her puppy sat alert, watchful but not frightened. Steinbeck and Faulkner flanked either side while Fitzgerald guarded the front like a sentinel.

"They were guarding her. Look! They love her." Pepper clapped her hands, clearly touched.

He zoned out at her, before giving his head a half-shake. No point letting a single thought drift in the L-word direction. "Grab Kitty and we'll take her in the backyard for a pee. It's Sunday. Everyone on Love Street will be at church except for us heathens."

"Good thinking," Pepper said, opening the latch. Once in the yard, Kitty bounded to the fence and sniffed along the perimeter, the three retrievers attending her every step.

Pepper paused to admire his kayak before glancing through the tool shed's window.

"Your dog house is pink?"

"Got left on the curb not long before you arrived. I figured I'd use the wood for a beach bonfire at Labor Day."

"Or you could give it to me for Kitty. Or, I don't know. Maybe not." She frowned thoughtfully. "I'm not looking to stay here and put down roots. In fact becoming a fur mama gives me courage, because wherever I go, now I won't be alone."

There it was. An unexpected downside to her falling head-over-heels for a dog. "But you could stay," he blurted, the words flying out like they had a life of their own. "You know. If you wanted. Check out local opportunities."

Her mouth went as round as her eyes. "In Everland?"

He shrugged. "Not the worst idea I've ever heard. This *is* a semi-not-awful place."

"Yeah." She appeared to mull it over. "Inhabited by semi-okay people." She shook her head. "But let's be realistic. There's nothing here for me to do. The only firm is well established, and the remaining lawyers are independent contractors scooping up the scraps."

He wanted her to stay, pure and simple. All he had to do was figure out some genius plan.

"Let's dig out your dog house," he said. Not exactly genius. But a start. Putting down a rudimentary foundation.

He had a lot of shit in the shed. The doghouse was half buried behind some punching bags and wedged between old plywood odds and ends. When he maneuvered it toward the door, it wedged on an old windsurfer propped against the wall.

"Push harder." Her soft grunt fell straight to the dirty side of his imagination. "Put your back into it."

"I'm doing my best. It's too big." He cocked a brow. "Won't get out. It's stuck." He hammed up the last two lines until she collapsed into a pool of helpless giggles.

"It can't stay like this forever." She cackled even as she grimaced from the weight. "Go back or come out."

"Hello?" A woman's voice drifted from inside Pepper's house next door.

Pepper froze, going whiter than drying plaster.

"Hellooooo?" A rusty squeak carried over the fence. The back door to her house was opening. "Pepper? You home?"

"Oh no, oh no, oh no." Pepper ducked, covering her head as if to avoid a punch. "It's Tuesday," she hissed.

Confusion swirled through him. "No, it's not, Trouble. It's only Sunday. Easy, before you give yourself a—"

"No." She took his face between her hands. The whites of her eyes rang around her amber irises. "Listen. You aren't hearing me. It. Is. Tuesday."

Had she knocked something on her head in his shed? "Last night was Saturday. You came here for dinner."

She slapped a damp palm over his mouth. "There's no time to play Who's on First. My sister's name is Tuesday. She is here. I heard her calling my name from the house."

"Tuesday?" He frowned. "You're sister's name is Tuesday? What sort of a name is Tuesday?"

"I know, right? Especially if you were born on Friday," a husky feminine voice drawled.

He glanced over one shoulder. A striking, platinum-haired young woman peered over the fence. She plucked the Dum Dum sucker from the corner of her mouth and hiked up her gold aviator sunglasses to reveal a pair of eyes that had a familiar tilt at the edge. "Heya, sis," she said; arching a brow. "And nice shirt there, handsome."

He glanced at his bare chest and low-slung sweat pants.

"What on Earth are you doing here?" Pepper squeaked.

Tuesday popped the lollipop back between her lips, her curious gaze boring into them. "I think the real question is *who* are you doing here?"

Chapter Twenty-Three

Tuesday grabbed a handful of grapes from the fruit bowl, tossing one after the other into her mouth while maintaining a brush-and-strike tap dance rhythm. Her sister was a category four human hurricane and a born performer. "Here I kept thinking poooooor Pepper," she was saying. "Pooooooor Pepper stranded in Georgia. Pooooooor Pepper all alone. Meanwhile, poor Pepper is off doing the nasty with the cutest neighbor in recorded history. You did see his abs, right? Glorious. Wait. Of course you have. You've probably licked each muscle. Oh my God. Have you? Was it amazing? Tell me it was amazing."

"Stop." Pepper ducked her head. "It's not like that. We're friends."

"Uh-huh. I have friends. But not ones I canoodle around with in their backyard."

"Anyway, change of subject." Pepper withdrew a coffee

mug from the cabinet, slamming the door. "Are you going
to tell me what happened in New York or what?"

Tuesday geared up for a big finale. *Ginger Rogers, eat
your heart out.* Watching her sister made Pepper tired. She
never stopped moving. "I'm done with the place," Tuesday
replied flatly, with one last heel click for evidence. "Over.
Finished. Done. Finito. Caput."

Kitty scampered across the kitchen floor, skidding on the
linoleum and crashing into the garbage can. J.K. Growling
sat in the center of the room, staring, unsure whether to join
in the fun or run for cover.

"What do you mean, *done*?" Pepper demanded "You
love it in the city. Broadway has always been your big
dream—"

"I can't believe you adopted a dog." Tuesday snatched
the conversation and dragged it into another direction.
"J.K. Growling finally has a cousin. Who are you and
what have you done with my sister? It's the romance here
isn't it? All the Love Streets and Kissing Bridges. A quin-
tessential coastal Southern town up front, with the sexy,
scurvy-dog pirates in the back. Put like that, I can see the
appeal."

"Stop. I'm not staying past summer. Now stop deflecting.
Are you going to tell me what happened in New York, or
what?"

Tuesday's arms fell to her sides and something in her
face broke. "Do you trust me?"

"With my life," Pepper said. Her sister was wild, free-
spirited, but most important, loyal.

"Trust me when I say that I don't want to talk about it.
And"—she held up a finger—"don't start worrying about
worst-case scenarios where I was mixed up in a mob murder

or anything. I'm not fleeing anything illegal, so don't feel like you're complicit in a crime."

"Let me braid your hair." Tuesday had amazing hair. Fixing it before school was one job Pepper never begrudged after Mom bailed. Her sister plopped to the floor with a younger sibling's innate instinct for being pampered and cared for.

Pepper couldn't even envy the concept. It seemed so foreign. Her hands worked in quick, efficient twists, as she spun her sister's locks in a complicated fishtail. "If you're trying to make me worry less," she said at last, "I have to say, the strategy isn't working."

Tuesday pushed off the floor, plopped into a chair, and drew her knees up to her chest. "I know you. I love you. Leave it. Please."

Her sister craved the spotlight, but from the edgy way she glanced around the room, it appeared she wanted to hide under a bed or in the closest closet. It was out of character, and for a character as big as Tuesday, it worried her.

"You wanted to perform on Broadway since forever. It's part of the reason I attended NYU and planned to live in Manhattan long term. You said there was no point living anywhere else."

"Chalk it up to a long list of things I shouldn't have said." Tuesday blew a piece of hair off the side of her face. "Do you have a spare shoe handy? One I could stick in my mouth?"

"I'm Team Tuesday, all the way. During winning seasons and losing streaks."

"Even mafia murders?"

"Except for mafia murders. Maybe. What the heck, I'd probably end up handling your defense pro bono."

Tuesday's eyes sheened. This must be bad. "It hurts when your dreams crash and burn."

Her sister must have lost a dream part. "Aw, honey. You have more talent in your little finger than anyone I know."

Tuesday opened up the breadbox and tore off a piece of baguette. Elizabeth's husband ran the popular upscale French restaurant in town, and her new friend kept dropping off fresh baked bread.

"Talent doesn't always matter." Tuesday took a bite, chewing carefully before continuing, "I could work as hard as I could, day and night, until my throat was raw, but that doesn't guarantee anything. The world is what it is. You get on a lucky streak, or a losing one. And sometimes luck doesn't matter and success feels like a game, but you don't even know the rules and..." She took a shaky breath. "Never mind. I'll be fine. How many people get to live their dream? I'll have to tweak mine."

"This isn't like you."

"This is exactly like me." Tuesday examined the kitchen. "Like you living here in Georgia and working as a dog walker, of all things. Why can't it be okay to modify your dreams?" Her voice suggested that she'd been telling herself this for some time.

"It absolutely can be." Pepper stood and walked to the teakettle, pouring the hot water into her ceramic coffee filter. "But, honey? If you ever want to tell me what happened, I'll be here."

Tuesday remained quiet. In this case, Pepper knew silence was an admission of guilt, but what's more, her sister didn't want to talk. And she was going to have to respect that.

"What do you think about Chicago?"

Pepper shrugged. "I never think about Chicago. Except for deep dish. Yum."

"That's where I want to move. They have a theater scene. It's cheaper than LA. Lake Michigan sounds pretty. Are there any other dog-walking jobs going in these parts? I could hustle up a bit of cash, too, and be on my merry way."

"Not really. I've cornered the market. You could find the Village Pillage medallion."

"What's that?"

"Nothing. I'm kidding." Pepper grabbed a copy of the *Everland Examiner* and held it up. "It's a weeklong festival. One of the big events is a silent auction—neither of us have cash to worry about that—and the other is this town treasure hunt."

"Stop the presses." Tuesday jumped off the counter and grabbed the paper, speed-reading through the front page. "You are a genius! So every couple of days they put in a clue, and whoever finds the medallion first wins ten grand?"

"Yes, but we'll never—"

"Listen to the first clue, it's cryptic . . . *In the summer, fall, and spring, you can hear them sing, at the place that has a bed and never sleeps and a mouth that never talks.*" She lowered the paper with a frown. "Ugh. I hate riddles and brain teasers."

"I know." Pepper had always tried to get Tuesday interested in the *New York Times* cryptic crosswords to no avail. "There's a twisted logic to it. But don't get your hopes up. There will be references to local folklore that we don't know."

"It doesn't matter," Tuesday said. "You have the brains, and don't forget my secret weapon."

"An encyclopedic knowledge of show tunes?"

Tuesday stuck out her tongue. "I'm scrappy."

Pepper shook her head, realization dawning. "We do have a secret weapon. Rhett."

Her sister clasped the paper to her heart. "Your secret, oh-so-sexy boyfriend?"

"Stop. He's my next-door neighbor."

"What he is is yum." She pressed the back of her hand to her forehead and feigned a swoon. "Call me peanut butter and jealous."

"Listen. You can't breathe so much as a word about Rhett and me to anyone," Pepper ordered in a menacing tone. "Wait, on second thought, don't mention Rhett at all. In fact, don't speak, full stop. I'll tell people you're visiting from Helsinki and only know Finnish."

"I do love secret drama, but you are both grown, consenting adults. Why the secrecy?" She clapped a hand over her mouth. "Holy shit, Pepper. You are kidding me." She leaned close and frowned. "Is he married? I can accept a lot, but not that. That's a terrible idea. You have to break this off immed—"

"No! Who do you think I am? Of course Rhett isn't married," Pepper hissed, sitting to inhale the coffee in her cup. This was going to be a three-cup morning. "But you don't know this town. Everyone is in everyone's business."

"Who cares? Look at him. I'd want to walk around getting high-fives at the corner store."

Pepper shook her head. "A few years ago he was jilted the day of his wedding. The whole town bore witness. The emotional fallout and gossip shut him down."

Tuesday wrinkled her nose. "First, who would ever leave all that A-grade cuteness? And second, who gets jilted at the altar? That stuff only happens in movies."

"And Everland. This place, you don't even know. There is a couple here with a pet pig. And a neighbor with a pink Cadillac who creeps around with binoculars and runs a gossip blog. And competitive Scrabble games in the park? And pirate treasure and—"

"Okay, okay, jeez, I get the picture. And circle back to the pirate treasure? Like what amount are we talking about? Scrooge McDuck level riches, doing backstrokes through golden coins?"

"I guess." She smiled. *DuckTales* had been one of their favorite programs as kids. "But I'm serious. No one needs to know about Rhett and me. This is a fling. The last thing he wants or needs is to be the center of more town drama."

"You don't do flings. It's not part of your DNA."

She bristled. "How do you know?"

"Let's see." Tuesday tapped her chin. "Besides the fact you've been my big sister and best friend, since, hmm, let's see, my whole life?"

"Who says I have to be the same person every single day?" She ripped out her hair elastic and slipped it around her wrist. "The one who prefers vanilla to chocolate—"

"Still never understood that."

"Or coffee to tea. Or James Stewart to Humphrey Bogart."

"Oh, no you didn't go there." Tuesday clasped her hands to her chest in mock horror. "You want to debate the sexiest leading man in Hollywood's golden age of cinema? Because *Casablanca* beats *Mr. Smith Goes to Washington* in terms of sexy men—"

"My point is that maybe you're right. At least sort of."

"Wow, what a ringing endorsement."

"I mean, look at you and Chicago. It's a new you, but it

makes sense. Maybe I am not going to scrap my entire identity. I can tweak stuff. But no matter what, I have to practice law, and make money because..." There was no way to say "so I can look after you and Dad someday" without making it sound like a guilt trip. "Because it's practical."

"It's pointless for me to say that I'm not your problem to fix." Tuesday leaned forward, bracing her forehead in her hands. "I can talk until my vocal cords snap, but you'll never hear reason. Mom messed you up so much. Add that particular resentment to my therapy list."

"It's how I'm wired. I can't live without knowing where I'll get my next paycheck, or constantly reacting to external forces rather than being proactive. My chosen path puts me in the driver's seat. Maybe it's boring, like driving a Toyota, but hey, it can be a red Toyota."

Tuesday giggled. "If law doesn't work out, you should consider doing gigs as a motivational speaker."

"Shut up."

"How to live your best life with a practical dollop of daring." She shook her head, still chuckling. "A red Toyota. Only you."

"My point remains valid. Why can't I have a summer fling?" Her voice rang a little hollow, so she kept talking as if she threw enough words at her heart, eventually some would stick. "I'm not staying around Everland past summer's end. Rhett will live here long after I'm gone. I'm never naughty. So why can't I transform this temporary dead end into a chance to sow some wild oats and spread a few branches? There's time enough for roots down the road."

"You can." Tuesday didn't look convinced. "Absolutely. It's just out of character. You're too practical for a friends with benefits arrangement. You'll get involved. I know you. You take a good easy-breezy game, but give it another week or two and you'll be trying to fix his life, assist in any crises, be there, offering a shoulder to lean upon. This is what you do. Because..."

"Go on." She forced herself to take a deep breath and release it slowly. "Don't hold back on my account."

"You're afraid that if nobody needs you, they'll leave."

Pepper sat there, reeling. Part of her wanted to hit back. After all, Tuesday wasn't Little Miss Perfect. One week she'd be splurging on organic chia seeds and kale chips, self-identifying as a vegan, but wait two weeks and she'd be sniffling over a plate of kalbi ribs in Koreatown because she lost a part by "*this* much, Pepper. *This* much." Look up *flaky* or *hot mess* in the dictionary, and would be her sister, hunting for her missing apartment keys or staying up all hours watching miniature cooking videos or never making it anywhere on time, despite sending a heads-up "I'm running ten minutes late" text. Or not. Because maybe her phone was lost. Again.

She had so much ammunition that all she needed to do was open her mouth and she'd take her sister down Rambo-style.

But one thing stopped her.

Tuesday was right. It hurt like hell to hear, but it was nevertheless, the truth.

Finally, Tuesday broke the silence but walking to the kitchen and coming back with a bottle of merlot and two mason jars. She filled them both to the brim.

"Here." She passed one. "You're my sister. You drive me crazy, but you're my best friend on the face of the Earth. I don't want to fight."

"Me neither." Pepper ruefully clinked her glass.

"Now. Where were we? Ah, yes. The medallion prize money. Your Rhett—sorry, Rhett the random friendly neighbor—can assist with deciphering any clues referencing local knowledge or place names. Then we'll find the medallion, grab the money and be off to start new lives in the Windy City."

Pepper frowned. "We?"

"Me? Go to Chicago alone?" Tuesday feigned shock. "Plus, look at J.K. Growling and Kitty. They love each other."

The two dogs were curled up together in a sunny patch of morning sun.

"Chicago," Pepper whispered, tasting the possibilities. It was one thing to tell herself that she was leaving. Quite another to have an actual destination. "You think we'd like the Midwest?"

"We'll take it by storm." Tuesday let free a contented sigh. "No ocean, but hey they have those big lakes. It's a perfect plan."

"Yeah. Perfect." Pepper refused to look out the window at the house next door. Rhett would never leave Everland. His family was here, his whole life. And she couldn't sacrifice hers, or abandon them. The little fantasy she'd allowed to dance around the edge of her mind about finding a happily ever Everland was just that. A story to be told in the dark between kisses and cuddles.

It wasn't real.

Chapter Twenty-Four

⟋

Rhett glared at his desk phone. He'd had to treat a lizard for stomach parasites a few hours ago, an unpleasant business, but this call would be worse. The community foundation had gone radio silent—a bad sign. The idea of groveling to Hogg, hat in hand, sucked, but if it meant securing the shelter's funding, there wasn't anything he wouldn't do. Time to touch base with the grant officer and get it over sooner rather than later.

Steinbeck barked. Fitz and Faulkner joined in.

"Hey, guys, quiet in the peanut gallery," Rhett ordered. Was a squirrel taunting them from the window?

"Hello, is this a bad time?" Pepper poked her head in through the open door.

"No!" He leapt up. "Not at all. Come on in."

The dogs clamored for her attention. She gave them each a quick pat on the head, looking more or less fond. "They're excited."

"Must have gotten a wild hair over something." He suspected it was the same thing making him grin like an idiot—this woman here, in her navy blue sundress with red strappy sandals and toes to match.

"Because I can come back. Or talk to you later or—"

"Shut the door." He pulled out a seat. "What do you need?"

"Nice place." She did as he invited while checking out the office. "Very you."

He glanced at the bookshelves, framed degrees, and photographs. "What's that mean?"

"Has your vibe, open and bright."

He lifted his brows. "Bright?"

"Yeah." She sat, crossed her legs, and regarded him a moment. "You know how sometimes it looks overcast until you go up in a plane, and once you pass through the clouds, the world is blue skies and sunny? That's what you are, deep down."

He swallowed the unexpected lump in his throat, but it refused to budge.

"Here's why I'm here. My sister and I want to win the Village Pillage medallion hunt and the ten thousand dollars."

"Good luck with that." He leaned back in his chair, twirling a pen between his fingers. "So does the whole town."

She jerked a hand to her hip. "Never bet against the Knight sisters when a treasure is on the line. All I know is it's going to be located near the river. The first clue is 'a bed you never sleep on'; that's a riverbed. 'Something that has a mouth but never talks.' River again. I'm not sure on the scream part, but I think it will come together after the second clue is released. But if there are obscure references to local history or places, I can't figure that out alone. Will you help me?"

"Why's this so important?" Pepper hadn't expressed a peep of interest in the hunt before now.

"Tuesday has left New York for good. For that to have occurred something terrible happened, she won't say what. Now she wants a fresh start." She spoke faster and faster, the way she did when wanting to outrun powerful emotions. "Me too. I am looking for the same, a clerkship somewhere far away from Judge Hogg. The medallion money could get us on our way. We're thinking Chicago."

"Chicago? Halfway across the country?" Then what the hell did he want to help for? Helpless anger settled in his gut, growing like a cancer. Three women in his life he had felt something for, and all three had left without him having a fucking say. But look at the hopeful eagerness in her face. Despite a few passing comments, she had been nothing but honest with her intentions of leaving.

He could help her. Sure. Why not? After all, everyone knows good guys finish last.

He pushed up his shirtsleeves and glanced at the ink written on his arm, knowing in an instant what he'd have to do. She might not want to stay, but he'd wavered on the long ago promise he made himself.

Stay true.

He loved that Pepper loved her sister, and while he didn't believe in any instant love-at-first-sight magic, this was a woman he could come to care deeply about. If he could figure out a way to make her stay. But Dad had inadvertently taught him one last lesson: you could never make a person choose a future they don't want.

He had a choice. He could put himself out there. To hell with the Isthmus, he'd build a goddamn suspension bridge to his island and set the speed limit to seventy. This was his chance. To offer himself. Take it or leave it.

"You ever been sailing?" Buccaneers Marina was ten minutes from downtown Everland. A few locals lived down there full time in a small houseboat community. They'd be spotted. But fuck it, go big or go home.

"Sail?" Her eyes widened. "My sister is afraid of the water."

"Why?"

"One, it's big. Two, it's deep. And three, it's full of sharks."

"And you?"

She shook her head wryly. "No. That would be a rational fear. I prefer hyperventilating over Chihuahuas."

"All right then. How about this, you me and dinner on the boat tonight? We can grill, watch the sun set. A date, Miss Knight. I want to take you on an official date."

"You do?" She stilled, a softness coming into her eyes. "That sounds nice. Really nice. Oh, and they'll be releasing the next clue at four so we can decipher it over dinner."

"It's a date." Although the real riddle was convincing a big-city girl to give a small-town guy a real shot.

After she left, he punched in Beau's number.

"What?" his friend barked.

"Is there a mayoral congeniality training program? I'd like to set up a crowd-sourced fund-raising page."

"Sorry, man." Beau heaved a sigh. "It's been a shitty day. Ever hear of Discount-Mart?"

"The big box store?"

"They sent their people over to make contact this morning. These guys were barnacles in my ass but still, it might be worth the hassle. Turns out Everland's on their short list for a new site. A hell of a lot of local job creation potential."

"You're in favor?"

"Don't know. They're being cagey on the locations. Need to hear more. But what's up? That's not why you called."

He rocked on his heels. "You using the boat later?"

"No. Why?" Beau went from work mode to suspicious.

Fuck. He didn't have a story lined up. Oversight. "Just checking."

"Liar. Who's the lucky lady, Cupid?"

Rhett gritted his teeth. He loved Beau like the brother he never had, but that nickname made him nuts. What the hell, though, why not tell Beau what was going on between him and Pepper? He could even offer up advice.

"It's complicated," he began.

"This about you and a certain brown-haired dog walker? What was her name again, Miss Ida May?" There was a muffled response. "That's right—Pepper. What's in the water over there on Love Street? I'll have to talk to the water department."

Rhett's internal axis flipped its magnetic poles. "Miss Ida May's with you?" If Everland was a hurricane of gossip, Miss Ida May was the eye at the center.

"Doing a piece on me for the Back Fence. You're on speaker, by the way." An implicit warning not to say anything too offensive about his favorite love-to-hate neighbor.

"Hey, there, Cupid," Miss Ida May cooed. "I'm doing a sweet and sexy mayor profile. You're the next profile, sugar. Date or no, we at the Quilt Guild have our hearts set on you being Mr. Scallywag this year. Would you be amenable to a shirt-off photo shoot? Or no, I can do better. A tight T-shirt spritzed in the front with enough water to show off all those washboard muscles. Why it's enough to inspire me to do laundry."

"Maybe some other time." Rhett's tone said *when pigs fly*. "Hey, man, can you watch my dogs tonight?"

"Sure thing."

"Rhett Valentine, you're up to something aren't you?" Miss Ida May butted in. "Might as well come clean, sugar. You can run, but you can't hide. It's my mission in life to see you two fine boys properly paired off."

"If there's no smoke, don't go starting fires," Rhett replied blandly. "Sorry to be disturbing you at work, mayor." He clicked off the phone and shoved it in his back pocket before smoothing a hand over his tight jaw.

That wasn't anyone's business but his own and Pepper's. No one else had any part. They might dare to differ.

He wanted Pepper for more than a fling. But what sort of date would knock the strappy sandals right off her feet?

* * *

The *Calypso*'s dock lines squeaked and creaked as the sea breeze kissed the back of their necks. Normally the peacefulness of the waves was calming and comforting, but not tonight.

"Can I pour you another?" Rhett glanced at the bottle of wine.

"I'm good." Pepper raised her still full glass.

"Great." He leaned against the side of the boat. This was going terribly. He hadn't been on a first date in a long time.

The air was thick with pressure, filled his lungs like concrete.

Pepper set aside her fork and knife, steak half eaten next to the baked potato and salad. He'd grilled for her on the small barbecue attached off the back. "I like you."

He frowned. "There's a *but* coming next, isn't there?"

The corner of her lip turned up. "But, what's with this music? I've never heard you listen to saxophones. And the meal is wonderful, but I have never seen you drink wine. Do you even like it?"

"No," he admitted. Wine never tasted like blackberries, clove or yellow apple to his taste buds. More like bitter acid that left behind an unpleasant film.

She set down her plate. "Permission to speak freely, Captain."

His mouth twitched in the corner. "Go ahead."

"Good, I was going to anyway." She glanced at his speakers. "Is this what you listen to out here?"

"It's a playlist that I found online." It was called "Romantic Dinner," and the tunes sounded as bland and uninspired as the name.

"What are you into?"

"I like music, all kinds, lots of country, folk. The blues. But on the boat, I prefer quiet."

She picked up the remote and clicked off the music.

"Hear that?" Rhett asked. A stout offshore breeze batted the rigging against the mast. Water lapped at the hull. In the distance, waves broke against the harbor mouth. A bird gave a mournful cry. "Oystercatcher."

She closed her eyes, going completely still. "In New York, the city sounds became my white noise, helped me think. In a crowd I could become anonymous. Cities are great for introverts. I never had to be the center of attention, but never felt isolated."

"I never thought of it that way." He hooked his arm around her narrow shoulders, drawing her closer as they propped up their feet on a cooler. Venus appeared in the west.

"I haven't ever had even the remotest desire to go to New York. Seeing the ball drop on New Year's in Times Square? No thank you."

"Times Square?" She shuddered. "No way would I take you there, avoid it like the plague. Although, want to know a piece of trivia?"

He grinned. "By all means."

She wrinkled her nose at him. "It was the eastern end point for the Lincoln Highway. The first road to span the United States, and one of the earliest transcontinental highways after the invention of cars. It was nicknamed the "Main Street Across America" and crosses thirteen states before ending in San Francisco. It still exists, but the function's been replaced by I-80. Takes you from San Fran to New Jersey, but it's not the same. I wish I could do a road trip along an old highway, visit all the towns dotting the way. It's not the same whizzing along the interstate with the fast food franchises and billboards."

"Why don't you?"

"Because I don't have time."

"We all have the same twenty-four hours in the day."

"But not everyone has the same obligations or is willing to assume the same responsibilities."

He brushed the side of her cheek, over her small white scar. "I've never asked. What happened here? Chicken pox?"

She grimaced, her shoulders turning inward. "Gideon's love bite. He was our neighbor's guard dog."

Along the shore an oystercatcher called again, a keening cry that sent a shiver down his spine.

"That's why you were afraid of dogs?" So much made sense, all at once. His mind reeled.

"Yeah." Her voice faded into silence.

"This whole time you never said."

She stiffened. "I didn't need sympathy."

"Tell me what happened."

She shrugged. "He was big. Mean. I was in the wrong place at the wrong time. We lived out in the country. Miles from town. The Francis family had a compound. Lots of trucks that didn't work. Lots of guns that did. My guess is they had a meth lab or grew pot, something where they didn't want prowlers. That's where Gideon came in.

"Before Mama left she went through a funk. That's what she called it. But looking back, it was serious depression. One Saturday she didn't get out of bed no matter what Tuesday and I tried. Dad was out on the property. He was always out then. I think because home was so hard. I must have wandered too close to the property line, looking for him. Gideon went into protective mode and broke his chain. I ran, but he caught me at the gravel road. Dad arrived right as his teeth closed down. It could have been worse. A lot worse. But I still remember how hot his breath was, how much it hurt, and how I couldn't get him off, no matter how hard I punched and kicked."

A shiver moved through him, despite the sultriness of the night air, followed by a burst of anger. It would be a long time before he'd be able to get the image of a young Pepper running through the Maine woods, a no-doubt abused animal closing in behind.

He rested his cheek on her hair and breathed in the faint apple scent of her shampoo before catching her hand and lacing his fingers through hers.

She stared at their connection. He did, too, loving to see them joined in a tangible way.

"I want to make it better," he murmured.

"Then how about a beer?" She elbowed him lightly. "I've been eyeing the cooler."

She danced away from the painful memory, and he understood. Tonight the sky was filled with stars. How many galaxies had died billions of years ago, only now hitting Earth with the last gasps of a fading twinkle? There was a somber magic in the air, fed by the gentle pulse of the sea, lapping the breakwalls in a rhythmic caress. It was easy to buy into the concept of the interconnectedness of all things, the universe tied together, everyone serving a mystical, mysterious purpose.

What if there were no coincidences? Maybe Pepper had been placed in front of him for a reason. A light in his long darkness. And God help him, he'd put some shine in her world, too.

He cleared his throat. "I've got a few types. Want me to list 'em off?"

"Nah." She hugged her knees. "Surprise me."

"Now you're talking." He grinned. "I like a challenge." He ran his fingers over the different craft beers he and Beau kept in their shared cooler, before settling on the right one. She was more of a lager girl. Crisp. Clean. No-nonsense. "Try this." He plucked a bottle. "It's a Czech-style pilsner."

"Yes! For real, my favorite."

He took out his keychain and popped the top. "Tell me what you think."

She took a sip. "Hoppy."

"Yeah. I know a few guys who give the variety shit. Say it's too industrial, that it's what gets made en masse. But if done right, the taste is perfect in its simplicity." He drew in to kiss the tip of her nose. "Effervescent. Brilliant in clarity. A little like you."

Her pleased laugh came from deep in her throat. "I never knew beer could be romantic."

"Neither did I." God, all he wanted was to remove the bottle from her hand, take her below, and see how bright he could get her, but something she said niggled at him.

"Tell me more about your mother."

Her sigh was soft, barely detectable except for the light brush of heat against his neck. "What's there to say? She left. A long time ago now. She wanted to look after herself, but that meant there was no one to look after my dad or my sister."

"What about you?"

She bristled at his soft question. "I manage *myself* fine. It's the rest of my family that I worry about. I mean, Dad makes maple syrup for a living. It's not exactly job security, plus if anything happens to him physically, how would he survive? I don't have a clue what, if anything, he's saved for retirement. As for Tuesday, up until a few days ago, all she ever wanted to be was a Broadway star. I'd like to have a unicorn and a tree that produces toffee apples, but I live in the real world. Neither of them have any form of safety net...except me. *I'm* the one who anticipates the future, makes plans. I don't hope everything will magically work itself out. A person has to make their own luck."

"You're the safety net? That's a lot of pressure to put on yourself."

She took a long pull from the bottle and drew her knees in. "Yeah. They both drive me crazy, but they're my family and there's nothing I wouldn't do for them. If they fall, someone has to catch them."

"And what about you?" he asked softly as he pulled her closer. "Who catches you, Pepper Knight?"

Chapter Twenty-Five

"No one catches me," Pepper choked down a rising panic. "I'm the one that can't fail. It's why this career cul-de-sac has been nothing short of a disaster. There is the real world. The one I planned for. And then there's Everland. I've tumbled down a rabbit hole to a place where nothing makes sense. I don't like dogs, yet I am falling in love with Kitty. I grew up in a small town and counted the days until I could get away. I dreamed of meeting a city guy, and here I am with you and it's better than anything. But it's a dream. A lovely detour. And I can't stay here forever."

"Why?" It's all he could get out. Otherwise the hurt was too damn much.

"Because it's not real life. Not *my* real life at least. But that doesn't mean I want it any less." She slid her arms around his shoulders, his protective heat a shield against the cold night. She'd hold him now, enjoy this moment, because reality was creeping in, and soon these stolen moments would be nothing but a memory. "It doesn't matter, though. I have to figure out what's going on with my sister. Start networking for new clerkships. My plan didn't work. It wasn't perfect out of the gate, but hey, neither was the U.S. Constitution. I need to make amendments."

"You could stay. You're happy here, and happy is a good look on you." He smoothed the space between her brows. "There've been less wrinkles here."

"Word of advice there, buddy," she playfully nipped his thumb. "Never point out a woman's wrinkles or gray hair." Her sigh came from somewhere deep, a resignation she'd never had to accept because it had always been there. "It doesn't help to talk crazy. I can't stay. I can't be Pepper in Everland."

"Why? In case you haven't noticed, we're all a little crazy around here. You fit right in."

"Rhett..." She didn't know what to say. It was long past time to logic herself to safety. "And even if I am a little crazy—and for the record, I admit nothing—you aren't."

"Ah. That's where you're wrong," he murmured, brushing a thumb over her cheek. "Don't you see? I am crazy. Crazy for a dog walker who claims she doesn't like dogs even though she does, who talks too much, recites dead presidents in her sleep, smells like apples, and steals the covers." The emotion in those easy words touched her deeply.

What would she do if her life was hers to live, any way she saw fit, free of fear or worry? The notion was equal parts terrifying and exhilarating.

"Who're you calling cover stealer?" She gasped as his hand slid under her shirt, palm cool against her skin. The contrast was good, better than good, and brought necessary distraction. Goose bumps broke out even as fire licked her skin.

"I want." He traced his tongue over the sensitive shell of her ear, exploring all the tingly nerve endings, not accepting one gasp when he could obtain two. "I want for you to let go. Not forever. Not for the rest of your life. Just tonight. Just for now. Let go, and I'll promise to catch you." He nuzzled her neck and pulled her onto his lap, arranging a thigh on either side of his waist. The skirt of her sundress gathered high around her hips, and she found the thin sheer silk of her panties made the rise in his denim more interesting.

"Can you do that?" he asked. "Trust me to take care of you?"

"I want to."

He kissed like there was no time. Nowhere else to be. Only this moment mattered. His mouth on her skin, pulling at her like the rising tide, his lazy tongue working the curve of her breasts until she had to press her palms through her shirt, over her nipples, to cope with the sweet ache.

"Someday I want a short dirty fuck out here on the deck while you wear nothing but moonlight." His gaze scorched. "But tonight," he rasped. "Tonight, I'm taking you below. Tonight, I'm taking you so hard that you forget everything except for the fact you're mine. That I've got you. That I'm here to keep catching you. Let go for once, see if you fall, or if you fly."

He exhaled harshly and stood, clasping her ass and walked to the short flight of stairs, taking each one without hesitation, ducking as they slid into the cabin in the bow. One snug triangle-shaped bed was framed by two small portholes.

He settled her on the mattress, the springs jolting as he

eased on top of her, his braced elbows keeping some weight off as his strong fingers sifted her hair.

"Pepper." He claimed her mouth in a fierce kiss, his tongue massaging hers in lush, decadent swirls. Yes. God. But the urge to have those clever hands everywhere grew unbearable.

"Please, I need…" She trailed off, not even knowing where to begin. God, she needed so much. Her greedy hips pumped as tension wound through her body, pulling so tight she might snap.

"Let me take over, sweetheart," he whispered with dominating confidence. "You have one job right now. Lay back and enjoy."

"Okay." She exhaled, still unable to fully relax her tense stomach muscles. This was crazy. Why not sit back and accept someone doing for her, doing to her, wanting nothing more than to give her pleasure, bring her joy, make her quit worrying for two seconds about every single thing?

A tremble rolled through him. "I didn't know I'd been waiting. I didn't know I'd been wanting. Convinced myself what I had was enough. But you, this, I'll never get enough."

His mouth returned to her throat's hollow, his lips lightly sucking before winding its way along the contours of her shoulders to the plane of her chest, pausing when he provoked even the smallest reaction, attuned to every caught breath or half-spoken plea. This was heat, sweat-slicked, open-mouthed kissing, soft but unbearably urgent.

Desire rolled through her like breakers. She floated and sank all at once. The more she let go, the more she sank into what she wanted, opening herself, offering her body without hesitation, self-doubt, or insecurity, the more he took care.

Every new sensation felt inevitable, but it didn't make it less of a surprise.

Of course he'd do this to her. Of course she'd feel this. Her body was made to feel this way. All her life she'd been waiting to belong to a place, a tangible physical space.

And here it was.

Here was home. Where she wanted to be. Where she wanted to stay.

Forever.

He captured her mouth with a fierceness, tongue thrusting inside, only to tease, to draw out, to say *take it, take what you want because it's right here waiting for you.* It was so much to realize at once. Too much to take in. She tried to pull away but he seized her wrists, pinned them above her head, deepening the kiss. This was to be victory by surrender then. In trusting him with her power, he made her feel more powerful than she'd ever been.

They'd taken pleasure in each other's bodies for a fleeting moment. But something was different, deeper, realer. He hadn't forced her capitulation before, always sensing her natural inherent defenses and never challenging them. Tonight he was making it clear with each inexorable gesture that he intended to plunder, to raze, to tear down her ramparts.

There was no room for flight or fight. She couldn't retreat to herself because he was everywhere, and she couldn't fight back because he dominated her with every gesture. But the whole time she was in control. This was happening because she wanted it. He had the strength but used it in service to her. He took nothing without giving tenfold.

Her dress had evaporated along with his clothes. The salt-sweet scent of sweat and sex intoxicated her.

Part of her brain registered her leg plant over his shoulders, his hands skimming down her outer thighs, his face dipping between, pushing his tongue deep in her cleft, probing, tasting exploring. The first lick came slow, and his moan sent vibrations through her sensitized skin. A storm brewed, darkly dangerous and thrilling.

Every time he passed over her clit, her legs convulsed. Over and over. He didn't miss a spot. She was going to pass out. Any second the light at the end of the tunnel would appear, not a bad way to go.

"Holy shit."

She half sat, unsure if she spoke the words out loud. Her orgasms normally snuck through the back door. They were nice but didn't stay long or make a fuss. This one was the equivalent to a bull in Pamplona after drinking a trough of sangria and ready to plow through a brick wall.

He sucked again.

She saw the light. Her hips rose toward it.

He sucked harder.

Many lights. Stars. She saw stars.

He eased two fingers inside her, and she forgot the whole kit and caboodle, everything, including her name, as her body exploded in one long sonic boom.

She was falling, falling hard without moving a muscle.

"You okay?"

She tried answering. It was a moan at best.

He was hard against her. Wait. She tensed. No. Not that she didn't want it. She did. But she also wanted to eat an ice cream cone with twenty different scoops. It didn't mean she should. But a little indulgence wouldn't kill her.

"I've got you," he murmured into her ear.

Yeah. He'd gotten that right. He had her in a place she wasn't sure she'd ever be able to leave.

He brought out a condom from somewhere. It couldn't have been magic but felt like a sleight of hand. A minute later he was inside her with deep, insistent thrusts. There was no place her attention could wander. He pinned her and groaned.

"You. Are. Incredible." His hands braced her hips, leading her to the Land of Lost Her Damn Mind. This was the *ah* to the *ha*. A light switch flicking on. What it meant to fall. And it wasn't scary. Once you gave yourself over to the rush, the adrenaline surge, it wasn't falling after all. It was flying.

And with Rhett, she soared.

Chapter Twenty-Six

Early the next morning Rhett parked the Bronco in his driveway. He killed the ignition and glanced over. Pepper drew a star on the window condensation.

"Time to go see how Kitty managed with Tuesday and J.K. Growling," she murmured. She'd been quiet for the drive back. They both were lost in their own thoughts.

He cleared his throat. "I have to swing by Beau's to collect the dogs and King Henry before opening the clinic. But first, Pepper—"

"Thank you." She set her hand over his denim-clad thigh, squeezing the muscle. "Last night...you gave me something I didn't know that I needed."

He laced his fingers with hers. "Same."

A rolled-up newspaper was on the floor next to her feet. "Oh no, I was supposed to ask your advice on the second clue." She'd grabbed the *Examiner* from the service station where he'd stopped to grab gas and two black coffees on the way home.

"We have time. Shoot."

She opened the front page and cleared her throat: *"You know you're going right when you take a left. There is a place like nowhere on earth."*

Rhett whistled between his teeth. "That's a doozy."

"It's diabolical. A place like nowhere on earth?"

He frowned. The answer danced somewhere in his subconscious, teasing the tip of his tongue. "I need time to think this over."

"Stop. If lightning strikes, I'll be at the dog park all morning." She leaned in for a kiss and froze halfway. "We're being watched."

"Dammit." He knew without looking. "Miss Ida May?"

"That woman has a bloodhound instinct for drama. I'm going to scram before she barges over with a recorder and tries conducting an interview. I need at least two more coffees before I can face that situation."

He waited until Pepper slipped through her front door before backing out. Yep. There stood Miss Ida May peering over the rim of her glasses, at the end of her driveway.

He gave Miss Ida May a short wave before hightailing it out of Love Street. Who knew what the Back Fence would have to say about that? Funny that the harder he tried to steer clear of town gossip, the more he steered into it headlong.

As he drove to Beau's, he took the longer, prettier way, winding high over the river bluffs, passing Mars Rock Park. A thought struck him and he pulled onto the road's shoulder. The medallion clue—*it's out of this world*—and when you combine that with a previous reference to a river bottom.

Bingo.

He texted Pepper a quick message about his theory. The medallion was in or near Mars Rock.

The moment he stepped from the truck Fitzgerald, Faulkner, and Steinbeck tore around the side of Beau's sprawling, two-story home.

Pepper texted back: Thanks for your help. I think you're onto something. Tuesday is ready to run out the door this second, but you know me, I'd prefer a deliberative approach ;) Time for some additional research.

A lot of happy memories packed into that winky face emoticon.

"Not like you to be an early riser," Beau said, the dogs bouncing around his legs.

Rhett cleared his throat. "These troublemakers behave for you?"

"Of course not." His friend tried to look irritated to no avail. "Steinbeck attempted to steal my stash of chocolate chip cookies." A little-known fact was that the mayor was one hell of a baker. If voters tasted Beau's peach pie, he might have a road to the White House.

"Thanks for watching them."

"Sure thing." Beau passed over the bag of dog food. "But I'm concerned about rumors. You—"

"And Pepper, I know," Rhett said.

"Al Hogg," Beau finished at the same time.

"The judge?" Rhett retorted. "What's that creep done now?"

"Maryann Munro said that he was bragging about how it was up to him whether or not you'd see a dime for the construction grant on your mama's shelter. And he laughed afterward, laughed and laughed."

That weaselly fuck. "I'll handle it," he said curtly.

"No blood baths now. He sits on the philanthropic board of the most respected grant-making institution in our region. You know how he is. He'll want to make a trade."

"Remember how he always had the best food in his lunch box at school, and those deals he'd cut with the St. Clair boys?"

"Not likely to forget." Beau made a face. "He'd trade Hostess cupcakes for them to give me swirlies in the locker room toilet."

"It was sick, the way he'd manipulate people."

"He's been like that his whole life."

"Well, Gunnar St. Clair grew up all right. Smuggler's Cove provides him a good living. He can afford his own treats these days."

"Ever wonder how a St. Clair got money for the loan?" Beau crossed his arms. "Personally, I'd rather sleep under an overpass than climb into bed with the Hoggs. So go, hear what Al has to say, but agree to nothing."

"Don't need to tell me twice." Once in the car, the dogs safely loaded, he backed out, rolling down the window. Needed some fresh air to survive the stink for this call.

He hit his Bluetooth and called.

"Hello?"

"Judge Hogg, Rhett Valentine." Best to humor the power-hungry worm with formalities.

A beat. Followed by a noticeable exhalation. "You were on my list of calls to make this afternoon. Aren't you an early worm."

"I want a sit down. Should I come by the office?"

"Oh no, no, no," the judge said laconically. "This conversation is off the books."

"My office then?"

Hogg snorted. "And lure me to your quarters? No, I don't think so."

"Jesus, Al." Rhett dropped all pretense of formality. Al had won state debate and made a habit out of mocking kids who spoke slower, became tongue-tied. "It's not like I'm going to—"

"I propose we make a trade."

Excerpt from the Back Fence:

Everland News That You Actually Care About

Classifieds:

Tea Leaf Readings by Delfi: Have questions about your future? The Ancient Art of Tasseography is at your service! Email me at teawithdelfi@hotdrinks.com or stop into Sweet Brew to make your date with fate today (pls remember that I'm not available by phone).

Free Sewing Table. Sitting on the curb. 208 Kissing Ct.

Wanted: One Laz-E-Boy. I'll pick up. Call Earl. 921-555-9741.

Chapter Twenty-Seven

Pepper meandered through Everland Plaza with Tuesday who was rummaging through her oversize purse. "Want a stick of gum?"

Pepper glanced over and snorted. "Um...that's a tampon, hon."

"God, it's a mess in here." Her sister dropped the wrapper and continued rummaging. "ChapStick, teabag, emergency underwear, more ChapStick, ah, gum!"

Pepper shook her head, and Tuesday popped the proffered stick into her own mouth, then folded the silver foil into a neat square.

"What's up? You only chew gum when anxious."

"Me? I don't get anxious," her sister scoffed.

"Oh. Right." Part of Tuesday being Tuesday was her insistence that little things like basic human emotions didn't apply to her. She didn't feel sad Mom left. She didn't get stage fright when having an audition. She didn't fret over her bills. She never worried.

Her sister was a liar or a cyborg.

They resumed walking. Pepper kept control of Kitty's leash like Rhett's *Puppy Master* book had instructed. She was to show the frisky puppy who was the alpha. Easier said than done when all she wanted to do was scoop her up and smother her face with kisses. It was nice to be able to show open affection somewhere.

"Have you spoken to Dad lately?" Tuesday inspected a long strand of her perfect blond hair for a nonexistent split end.

"Uh, no." An invisible antenna poked up in the back of Pepper's head. The one attuned to the frequency of potential disaster. "Why?"

"No reason. Just wondering."

They continued walking, but the relaxed, summery, isn't-it-great-to-wear-sundresses-and-strappy-sandals feeling had disappeared. The sidewalk felt as safe as a river of rapidly thinning ice.

Pepper's mind rewound and replayed the last couple weeks. All the scenes were focused on Rhett. A few times, after finishing with a dog-walking client, she'd called Dad for a casual check-in but never heard back.

Her chest tightened at the realization.

He hadn't called back.

It wasn't uncommon for his answering machine to pick up. Dad wasn't the type to sit indoors. Or sit. Ever. He and Tuesday shared a boundless capacity for movement, while Pepper had taken after Mom. They preferred curling up on the couch. Reading. A party was a new book, glass of wine, and a few squares of dark chocolate.

But he'd call back.

Always.

What if he tripped on the property? Fell down a ravine? Had a heart attack? Had a heart attack, tripped, and broke his leg out of cell phone reception?

"Earth to Pepper. Stop catastrophizing." Tuesday gave a friendly arm squeeze. "He's not in a ditch somewhere with a broken neck."

"I wasn't thinking that." Not technically.

"You should see your face. It's doing that worried twitchy thing."

"I'm scared something is wrong." This wasn't the time for sisterly banter. "He hasn't called me back even though I left messages."

"Me neither. But he mentioned he was taking a vacation."

"A what?" Pepper tried processing this unexpected information, but it was like her hard drive was full. "Dad doesn't take vacations."

Tuesday shrugged. "Guess he does now."

"Where'd he go?"

"He didn't say."

"Who'd he go with?" She pushed.

"Do I look like the Spanish Inquisition?" Tuesday glanced at her yellow and blue romper. Only she could make an outfit like that stylish. "I told him to have fun. That's it. End of story. We'll hear from him soon. He's an adult and doesn't need us baby-sitting him twenty-four seven." Tuesday gave her a teasing push. "I need to scoot to the *Examiner* office. The next clue should be out soon, and I want first dibs."

Tuesday was gone in a flash, and Pepper stood alone, anxiety bubbling inside.

Kitty raised her nose, tail wagging.

"Well, looks like it's just you and me, kid." Pepper smiled. "When in doubt of what to do next, why not have a coffee?"

Inside Sweet Brew, Elizabeth Martin hunched over a laptop at the corner table and waved her over with a bright smile.

"I'm not interrupting, am I?"

"No, all done. Great timing." The pretty woman shut the laptop. The afternoon light fell just so through the window, making her thick, black hair extra glossy. "Mayor B asked me to proofread one of his articles. He's started a monthly column in the Back Fence and takes it very seriously. It's going live tonight, and he didn't get it to me until twenty minutes ago."

"Oh dear. One of those moments where 'a lack of planning on his part shouldn't be your emergency' sort of things?"

"Guuurl." Elizabeth's smile widened. Her dentist must love how well she represented their business. "Enough about my boring work." She leaned closer, her voice taking on a conspiratorial air. "I hope you don't mind me prying. But it appears that you've captured someone's heart."

"I have?" Pepper tried playing dumb.

"Rhett Valentine."

"Oh? Hah. No. He just gives me tips for the dog-walking service," she responded by rote. "We're neighbors. It's a geographical proximity thing."

"That's the official word on the street, but I'd hoped that you and I were becoming better friends," Elizabeth wheedled, dropping her voice. "What's the unofficial version?"

Pepper hesitated. Elizabeth exuded such a friendly, inviting air. It was tempting to open up, confide. "Rhett's private." She hesitated.

"Can't fault him for that." Elizabeth smoothed a finger over one perfectly sculpted brow. "The town means well, but they've been—how do I put this—enthusiastic about championing his love life."

"I guess they feel bad that some harpy left him at the altar."

"Harpy?" Why did Elizabeth squint like that? "Was that *his* choice of words?"

"No." Pepper hesitated. "He didn't use that exact turn of phrase." She'd stuck in that flourish to the narrative, because how could a woman leave Rhett alone at the altar? It made no sense. Birdie existed in the background of Rhett's story, a ghost of lovers past. A series of unexplained questions because there were no photos, no hints around Rhett's home. Had she been taller, shorter, fatter, thinner? Was she prettier? Sexier? Just...more?

"Good. Because that so-called harpy was me."

Pepper laughed uneasily. "Yeah, right."

"Hardest thing I ever did." Elizabeth sounded serious. "Trust me, girl, when it comes to confusion and love, I wrote the book."

"But he was engaged to—oh my God..." Pepper stared, gobsmacked. Her breath vanished in a gust. "Elizabeth, wait. Are you Birdie?"

"His old nickname for me." She shrugged. "Look, it was a long time ago now. I panicked. It was stupid. I don't regret calling off our wedding, but wish it could have been under better circumstances. I had to do what was best for me. And him. And neither of us regret it."

A short awkward silence ensued.

"But…" Eloquence flew out the window. Pepper was at a complete loss. "I like you."

"I like you, too." They stared at each other. There was warmth there, and friendship, but also that moment of tacit understanding where it's silently acknowledged that they'd both touched the same man.

"You're not awful," Pepper blurted through a pang of jealousy. "In this scenario you are supposed to be a home wrecker or deranged."

Elizabeth laughed, a trifle uneasily. "Trust me, after two kids, I'm deranged all right."

"But how do we do this?"

"Do what?"

"Be friends."

Elizabeth gave her a long look. "Honey, Rhett Valentine is a good man. He simply wasn't my true love. And I wasn't his."

An awkward silence grew and grew.

"You think I'm terrible, don't you?" One more good thing about Elizabeth, she wasn't a word mincer.

"You couldn't be terrible if you tried," Pepper answered simply.

"Oh, believe you me, I've had my moments." She smiled faintly. "Except that's when I tell myself, 'Elizabeth, you know what? There's not a woman alive who hasn't.'" She straightened, rapping the table with her knuckles. "But you seem confused. You know what I do when I get clouded thinking these days?"

"Have a drink? Four drinks? A lobotomy?" Pepper held Kitty tighter. It was either that or start pacing. "Nothing in my life makes sense."

Elizabeth cupped a hand to her mouth and called to

the barista, the woman behind the counter with the pink shoulder-length hair parted down the middle. "Hey, Delfi! Can you brew one of your famous cups of Earl Grey? I have a friend who needs a reading."

Delfi glanced at the clock with her preternaturally wide, unblinking eyes. "There is time." She signaled to a hand-painted beaded curtain depicting Botticelli's *Birth of Venus*. "Enter there," Delfi intoned in her softly modulated voice. "I'll join in a moment. Begin emptying your mind."

"I'd have better luck licking my own elbow."

"Trust me, this will help. Delfi possesses remarkable insight," Elizabeth said, reaching to take Kitty from her. "Well, trust me as much as you can trust an evil ex who has sinister designs on your future happiness."

"I see where you're going with this." Pepper grinned despite herself. "When I step through that curtain I'm going to fall inside a big hole that's been cleverly concealed by well-placed tree boughs, huh?"

"Darn, you found me out." Elizabeth shook a mock fist. "But seriously, go on. I'll take good care of your puppy until you get back."

"Don't you mean *if* I come back?"

"Muah-ha-ha." Elizabeth mimicked a cartoon villain's evil laugh.

Pepper stood and approached the curtain. She'd been kidding. Sort of.

Chapter Twenty-Eight

Pepper entered a nondescript storage room lined with industrial steel shelves full of disposable coffee cup lids, coffee bags, and bottles of hazelnut and vanilla flavoring. The aroma of coffee beans infused the air, rich and aromatic.

The beads swished and Delfi entered, holding a silver tray. "Take a seat," she said, nodding to the room's far corner. Beneath a small window was a circular table with two red plastic chairs. "Have you ever done tasseography?"

"Tasseo—sorry?" Pepper sat and crossed her legs. "Sorry, I have no idea what that is."

"Tea-leaf reading."

"Um, no. Never." This was Elizabeth's big plan? Fortune telling?

Delfi arranged a white pot and matching ceramic cup and saucer. "The first thing you need to do is steep the tea and quiet your mind."

Pepper picked up the pot and poured as Delfi closed

her eyes. Looked like they were going to get right to it. The barista's posture was perfect, and she drew deep, measured breaths. They were about the same age. Her nose was pierced, and glitter sparkled on her cheekbones.

Delfi opened up one eye. "You're not concentrating. Here." She slid the cup over. "Sip and find your center." Pepper reached, and Delfi captured her wrist. "Stop. You're right-handed?"

"Y-es."

"Then you'll need to lift the cup with your left hand. And I can see that you're distracted. This only works if you focus."

"Right. Oops." Pepper smashed her lids together, palming the warm cup and taking a slow careful sip. It was perfect. Hot. But not too hot.

"Drink the liquid carefully, avoid consuming too many tea leaves."

Pepper did as she was told. "What's next?" she asked when the cup was half-empty.

"Relax. Breathe." Delfi flicked a lighter and procured a stick of incense from a hidden pocket in her voluminous emerald dress. She lit one end and set it onto the table edge. "Is there one question that is coming to the forethought of your mind? Take your time. Pretend to be a sieve and let feelings pass through you."

"I don't get this. Is the tea supposed to be magical because—"

"It's not about the tea. Or even the water. You left traces of your psychic energy in the cup. That's what we shall now read."

Psychic energy? Oh come on. This was nonsense, but she was stuck. To bolt for the exit would be incomprehensibly rude. The only choice was to breathe in, breathe out. Grin and bear it. She closed her eyes. The first image was Elizabeth's pretty face framed by her sleek, perfectly styled dark hair. Then Judge Hogg crumpling that Coke-splattered legal brief. The way Tuesday refused to meet her gaze when questioned about New York. Kitty's sweet eyes. Miss Ida May in her pink Cadillac. And then Rhett, over her, under her, consuming her. Dad's postcard. Subways. Traffic. Everland's Main Street. The dog park. More Rhett. Kissing Rhett. Laughing Rhett. Those adorable eye crinkles. The way his collared shirts clung to his shoulders. The innate affection he gives to his dogs, his sister, her.

What should I do? Where do I fit in? Where do I belong?

Belong.

Rhett's mouth on hers, his tongue tasting of home.

Dad needing her.

Tuesday needing her.

Rhett curled beside her in bed, watching a movie, feeding her popcorn bite by bite.

Where do I belong?

"Good," Delfi murmured. "Now sip. Concentrate on the flavor of the tea. Leave a small amount at the bottom of the cup."

Pepper complied.

"I want you to swirl the liquid around three times. Yes. Like that. And then dump the remaining liquid into the saucer. Perfect. Take a few more deep breaths and turn the cup back over."

Pepper did everything asked. "Now what?"

"We read the tea." Delfi stared. "Lines. Interesting."

Pepper's lungs flooded with the incense. It left her lightheaded. "What's that mean?"

"A journey. The lines are crooked, which means complications."

"Is this a future trip or one I've taken?"

"Both." Delfi cocked her head. "There's a woman in the center of the cup. She reaches forward and behind, tearing herself in two."

Pepper squinted her eyes and froze. Mother of God. There *was* a shape of a woman there, fracturing into two equal halves.

"See these stars?" Delfi waved a hand over a few specks. "They signify that you're scattered. Homeless. Rootless."

"What's that? In the distance? There on the...on the..." What was that? "The hill-looking thingy," she ventured.

"What does it look like to you?"

"A person," Pepper replied, awkwardly.

"What are they doing?" Delfi goaded.

"I don't know. Who is that supposed to be?"

Silence fell like an invisible axe. "Only you can say," Delfi answered at last in her calm monotone.

"That's not fair. You're the expert in tea-leaf reading."

Delfi idly toyed with the amethyst pendant hanging from a thick silver chain around her neck, unfazed by Pepper's perturbed tone. "Look deep inside yourself. You have the questions you seek. You know who this person is."

But that was the whole problem. She didn't. She was scattered, tearing herself in two. Who was that up on the hill? Her dad? Her sister? Rhett? So many people wanted something from her, all of them pulling in different directions until she didn't know which way to go to please all of them.

"How about a hint?"

That didn't garner so much as a smile. "Only you know your own truth."

"Gotcha. Thanks for your time," Pepper did her best to sound earnest. How pathetic that she'd let herself be taken in by mumbo-jumbo. What was going to be next? A palm reader? Tarot cards? Her life wasn't hidden in a teacup. There was no secret detour. Only the path she'd set for herself after Mom left. The road felt long and lonely, but she was committed to the course of action.

When she emerged through the backroom beads, Elizabeth was cooing over Kitty, holding the puppy like a baby. Kitty's paws were tucked in, and she gazed at the pressed tin ceiling with an expression of blissful contentment.

"Get clarity?" Elizabeth asked with a quizzical gaze.

Pepper gathered Kitty into her arms and pressed her cheek to her silky soft fur. "Confirmation that I'm more muddled than a mojito."

"Ah." Elizabeth nodded. "So it's not going to be that easy for you."

"Truth can be dimmed, but it never gets extinguished." Delfi strode to the counter right as the bell chimed and a group of customers flocked in.

"I know she's a trip," Elizabeth said, eyes kind. "But Delfi is wise. She's been touched by something big and mysterious."

"You mean something crazy," Pepper muttered under her breath.

"Before you go poking fun, stop and consider this. Look around," Elizabeth waved out the window. "Everland's not like anywhere else. There's something to the air here. I like to think it's magic."

Pepper sighed. "It would be great to believe you. I love the idea of magic, fate, and destiny." She buried her face into the top of Kitty's head, right between the ears. "Ugh. I don't know. Maybe this is where you're revealed to be the evil ex-girlfriend after all. You've charmed yourself into my circle of trust, and are whittling away what little remains of my sanity."

"Oh, girl." Elizabeth laughed long and loud. "Give Delfi's reading a few days to sink in. What I'm saying is think about it while trying not to think on it."

"Yeah, that makes total sense."

Elizabeth wagged a finger. "You can poke fun all you want, but please trust me on this one thing. You can know a lot and still not understand the secrets to your own heart."

When Pepper left Sweet Brew, she paused on the sidewalk and kicked at a pebble. Kitty glanced up, looking for a lead on their direction.

Turn left, turn right, or go straight ahead? Too many directions tugged at her heart. Dad's absence. Tuesday's secrets. Maine. Rhett. New York. Chicago. Everland.

People needed her. But the image in the cup of the woman tearing herself apart rose up in her mind's eye.

Maybe the time had come for her to ask, *what is it that I need?*

Chapter Twenty-Nine

Rhett strode into his backyard with one simple desire: to perform a mindless, uncomplicated task. Sanding planks for his boat project fit the bill to a "T." The noise was rhythmic. A *shh, shh, shh* sound that he could lose himself in. Almost. The conversation with Al Hogg niggled in the back of his mind. The request was strange. In order for Al to clear the way for the shelter's funding, Rhett needed to have the Quilt Guild to nominate *him* as Mr. Scallywag for the live auction.

Rhett had almost laughed himself off the road. No woman in her right mind would spend a penny to go on a date with that man. In fact, he'd be able to hold a fundraiser all on his own if he made a public promise never to ask out another woman.

Lou Ellen would never agree to it.

He sanded harder. Sweat sheened his shoulders. Anyway, no good having a construction loan if Dad wasn't going to cough up the land rights.

He worked his arms hard, his back muscles numb with exertion as sweat flew off his brow. What sucked wasn't just the personal blow—yeah, that stung, but by this point he was almost numb to his father's behavior. The real kicker was that animals would suffer needlessly, and for what? A grudge that at this point was being held purely out of default. No way could Dad still feel butt hurt about Rhett's career decision. Not anymore. At this point he maintained this stupid-ass stand-off out of a sheer lack of imagination.

"Rhett!" Lou Ellen's voice startled him.

He dragged a forearm over his brow. "I didn't hear you knock."

"That's because I didn't." She sashayed close, plopping her handbag on the sawhorse. "But I've been calling your name for a better part of a three minutes. And look at you. What bee crawled up your bonnet?"

"You can't come waltzing in here like the Queen of Sheba, Lou." He picked up his water bottle and drained it in four long swallows. "I thought that we'd agreed on boundaries?"

"That only people who need boundaries are those with something to hide." She glanced around the backyard like there was a trapdoor leading to a secret sex club.

"We're going to have to agree to disagree there." He scrubbed a hand through his hair as if the gesture could smooth out his troubled brain. "Warm day."

"Hotter than two rats humping in a wool sock. Now find some manners and offer me a glass of sweet tea and a seat in the shade."

"Coming right up." No point arguing sense with Lou Ellen when the mercury rose over ninety.

He went inside, splashed cold water on his face, cleaned

his hands, changed his shirt, and fixed her a glass of tea, how she liked it, six ice cubes, lemon zest, and a healthy glug of Southern Comfort. Walking it back outside, he set it down on his bistro table and took the opposite seat. The veranda provided respite from the sun's rays, and the air held a faint lilac-ish tang from the giant butterfly bush towering over his toolshed.

"All right then." He slapped his thighs. "Tell me what you need."

"Ah. That right there is my favorite thing a man can ask." She removed a hand mirror from her purse and checked her lipstick.

"Has anyone made your husband a saint yet?" Rhett huffed a sigh. "Snapper should convert to Catholicism. He'd be in like a shot."

"Hardy-har-har." She took a sip of the tea, made a face of approval, and took two more. "I came by to drop off a suit. It's hanging in your closet now, fresh pressed at the cleaners. I took the liberty of selecting one of Snapper's. He has excellent taste, seeing as I've picked them all out myself."

He regarded her steadily. "Who died?"

"The auction, silly. Mr. Scallywag."

Shit. Without intending to, he'd ended up in the middle of yet another "damned if you do, damned if you don't" situation. The last thing Rhett wanted to do was inflict Al Hogg on the town. Except he didn't want to fall on his own sword in the process.

The best thing to do would be to level about the whole situation with Lou Ellen. She'd be apoplectic, but at least half her rage would be turned to Hogg.

"Don't give me that look." She glared, crossing her legs

and tapping one pointy heel against the table leg. "I didn't want to have to resort to this."

"Easy now." His nuts crawled inside. Those suckers could do serious damage. "I'm not currently looking to have kids, but don't want to take that off the table."

"Please." She flicked a wrist. "I am a lady. If you don't give me what I want, I'll blackmail your ass, pardon my French."

He jerked back, recalibrating. Did he have an EASY MARK stamp today? "What the hell are you talking about? You've got nothing on me. I'm an open book." The way to beat Lou Ellen was to admit no weakness. She sniffed out ammunition like an airport bloodhound.

"It's not what I have on you. It's what your sweet little neighbor doesn't." She jerked a thumb toward the house. "As far as I know, those panties on the kitchen floor aren't yours, J. Edgar. They have a name printed on them. The name of the woman who lives next door."

He froze. Shit. Pepper did have a pair of panties with her name on them, combined with a cartoon chile pepper.

Lou Ellen smiled in triumph. "Whatever dalliance you two have going is all well and good, but that doesn't change the fact you're going to be Mr. Scallywag for the live auction. I've promised everyone at the Quilt Guild. It's the coup of the event! Bid on Everland's most eligible—and elusive—bachelor for a night of dinner and a movie." She dropped her hands. "And if your pretty Pepper has an issue with that, tell her to be the highest bidder, although she'll have some competition against Kennedy Day. This is a done deal, Rhett. The live auction bid sheets have been set up, including one that says "A Night with the Love Doctor.""

"The what with the what?" he sputtered.

"Don't let me down on this."

"I'll think about it," he said grimly. Not that he had a single intention of following through. Worse come to worse. He'd twist Beau's arm. There was Everland's real eligible bachelor. Rich. Handsome. Corner office at City Hall.

Lou Ellen cared a great deal about other people's opinions. The family feud between him and Doc caused her more pain than she'd ever admit, but beneath that tough steel magnolia was a heart that could be soft as a peach.

He didn't want to let her down, but he didn't want to do it, either.

"Thank you." She blew an air kiss. "I owe you one."

"How about never threatening to blackmail me again?"

"Deal." No one could lie as smoothly as Lou Ellen. She meant well, but Christ, the road to hell was paved with good intentions.

He walked back inside as she bustled out to the driveway and froze. The kitchen floor was empty. He glanced around. Not a stitch of underwear in sight. Could she have taken it? No, never in a million years. A white flash caught his eye out the window. It was Pepper's washing line. Her clothes were hung up, flapping in the breeze, soaking up the summer sun. Right in the center of the line was a white pair of panties that said PEPPER in a fancy calligraphy font.

A bemused chuckle shook his shoulders.

He'd been played so hard. His sister had got him to admit his secret relationship status.

Oh, she was good. Cover CIA counterterrorism good.

Steinbeck padded up and nudged Rhett's thigh with his nose. He scratched his buddy behind the ear, right in his favorite spot. "What am I going to do, man?" He wasn't going to make a deal with Al Hogg. Never in a million years. But he wasn't going to let Lou Ellen railroad him, either.

For being an island, he certainly had a lot of people walking on his beach. Time to pack everyone up and send them on their merry way.

He heaved a sigh. He didn't know how to fix any of that. Or what to do about Pepper wanting to leave. But he did know one thing. The shelter might take longer. More blood, sweat, and tears. But there wasn't going to be a shortcut to success, nor would he sacrifice an ounce of integrity or cut a single corner to get done the project that was going to bear Mama's name.

He stepped back inside and made a call.

"Judge Hogg's office," the administrative assistant said in a reedy voice.

"Hi there, Lois. This is Rhett Valentine, and I want you to pass along a message to the big guy. Tell Al that I've thought over his offer and am going to pass."

Chapter Thirty

⌒

The house had been quiet all night. Aloysius sat at the kitchen table watching condensation trickle down the side of the pitcher of sweet tea. The bell hadn't rung once since he'd gotten home. There'd been the low, murmured sound of voices punctuated by periods of gospel music. The back door opened and shut. The heavy clomps of boots on the side stairs.

Mama had been busy with her business.

At last, the house was empty and the silver bell tinkled.

He glanced to the antique hall clock. Ten after ten. She'd kept him stewing long enough.

He trudged up the carpeted front stairs one by one, and when he reached her bedroom he was startled, as always, by how someone so ruthless appeared in the guise of fragility.

Mama rested atop a pale silk pillow, a gold-leafed Bible on her nightstand. Inside the back cover she kept the

IOUs—when townfolk approached her with a problem, she found solutions, for a price.

What that price was, he didn't know. Nor did she want him to. Deniability of your mother's potential criminality was important when you were the local judge.

"Cop a squat, sugar." She reached for her remote control, fiddled with a button, and turned down the chorus to "Swing Low, Sweet Chariot."

He walked to her recliner, the one where she made a *tut-tut* sound. "Not there, dear. There."

He shuffled to the tiny stool by the bed, heart sinking. The stool's third leg was broken, making it impossible to sink your weight down. The result was a thigh-crunching balancing act to keep from toppling over.

Mama reserved this stool for those in the proverbial dog house.

"Sugar," she murmured in her breathless way, reaching out and taking his hand between hers. Her skin was paper thin. You'd never think those were the hands that wielded a wooden spoon to strike fear and pain into a young boy's hindquarters. "You disgraced yourself at the Everland park."

The muscles of his stomach tightened. "Dunno what you're taking about." How had she heard about his interaction with Pepper Knight? He hadn't known who she was, just that he liked the way she filled out her shorts. Bitterness bubbled inside him. He'd have been able to look his fill every day if Mama hadn't forced him to let her go to hire that idiot Tommy Haynes.

"You gave that town cause to laugh at us." Mama squeezed his hand harder and harder. For someone with arthritis, she had a constricting grip, like a python, choking off his blood supply. Her voice hardened. "When Everland laughs at you, they laugh at me, and when they laugh at me, they laugh at Hogg Jaw."

"I'm sorry, Mama. I tried to make a plan—"

"Trading your support in the Low Country Foundation to become Mr. Scallywag? Have you been in the moonshine again?"

She knew about that? Why was he even surprised? Of course she did. This was Mama. She knew if he was going to take a crap before his stomach rumbled. All he'd wanted was for her to see he was a man women would throw money at in order to spend the evening with. Not a laughingstock.

But her hoarse chuckling revealed he'd been kidding himself.

She pounded her chest. "It's my life's curse that the Good Lord only saw fit to bless me with one child. More's the pity, you take after your father. Weak. Cowardly. A disappointment."

Aloysius recoiled, impossible to move back on the wobbly stool, especially when she held him fast.

"But, Mama," he whined. "I've done everything you've ever asked. Every time. I thought if I came up with a plan all on my own it would make you proud." His whole life that's all he ever wanted. She's the one who pushed him into law, trampled all over his desire to be a dentist. Then she'd orchestrated his campaign to be judge. She had the vision for his life, and he'd stayed the course.

"People despise you, sugar," she said bluntly. "That's different than fear. I thought getting you installed as judge in the county seat would be a way to bring that high-horse town under our thumb at last."

He wasn't sure if Mama loved him, but she did care

about her hometown. She and his father both were distant descendants of its founder, Redbeard's second mate, Henry Hogg. Pirate blood flowed through her veins.

His too, he supposed.

She took her heritage seriously.

"But you hated the Valentines. I thought you'd like it if I played hardball and—"

"Son. Let me tell you a little story. Virginia Valentine was from Hogg Jaw, did you know that?"

He shook his head slowly. Mama recycled her tales to where he knew most by heart. But had never heard this one.

"Ginny was my childhood chum. We used to do everything together. And then she went and defected upriver. Married the man I set my cap on. The man that should have been mine, not your daddy, who got me pregnant on the rebound. Because I let hurt make me stupid.

"But not anymore. For far too long Hogg Jaw has been darkened by Everland's shadow. But they've grown soft, complacent, weakened by their romantic whimsy, forgetting their legacy, turning their proud pirate heritage into a cheap sideshow." She gasped, a wheezy crackle echoing through her chest, and motioned to the orange pharmacy bottle on the bedside table.

He undid the lid and shook out a small white pill, handing it over with her glass of water.

"Forget the Valentines." She swallowed with a sigh. "They are small fish, and a much bigger one has swum into our river. Everland laughs at you today, son. But Mama's here to fix it, same as always. Plans are in motion to stop their laughing once and for all."

He leaned in. "How?"

Mother smiled, a gentle, sweet smile that belied the terrifying gleam in her rheumy eyes. "Steal their community spirit. Siphon it bit by bit, so slow and so steady that they won't know they've been emptied until it's too late. *Now*, son, I'm happy to share that you've been selected for leading the first task. Time to make Mama proud."

Excerpt from the Back Fence:

Everland News That You Actually Care About

Classifieds:

Reward: Everland Quilt Guild is offering a $500 reward in addition to a rare Chinese lantern pattern quilt for information leading to the recovery of Davy Jones, Everland's beloved town mascot. Any leads can be sent to Lou Ellen Woodall at 4kidsandcounting@woodallhome.com

Listen and Learn: Mayor Marino is opening up his doors and wants to hear from YOU. Every Tuesday he'll be meeting with members of the public for fifteen-minute intervals. Let him know how he can work for you. And don't forget to follow his new Twitter account: @MayorBeau for all the news from City Hall.

Medallion Hunt: (note from your humble editors) The Everland Examiner asked us to remind everyone to keep an eye out for the Medallion Hunt's third clue. This family-friendly event runs in conjunction with the Village Pillage. Solve the clues and be the first to find the Medallion hidden somewhere on public land and worth a whopping ten thousand dollars. Of course to do any of that, you'll need to buy the paper (think they're feeling the heat from us? Haha!).

Chapter Thirty-One

For once Pepper blended in at the dog park, her black outfit a match to everyone else dressed in mourning to pay their respects. The somber mood was conveyed poignantly by the General and Colonel Jim as they approached the concrete pillar where the Davy Jones statue used to be and laid a single red rose on top.

The General opened his mouth to speak, but his broad shoulders shook as if he'd been overcome by an emotion too powerful for words. Jim pulled him into a tight embrace.

"Dear Lord," Lillian whispered in a choking voice. She dabbed her eyes with a lace-edged handkerchief. "Must be my allergies acting up."

"But who would do such a thing?" Pepper asked nobody and everyone. "Who would want to steal Davy Jones?"

"Someone without a soul," Lillian responded with vehemence.

"We're starting a neighborhood watch." The General approached, finding his voice. "Doing evening patrols."

Colonel Jim nodded. "The mayor's come to pay his condolences. Maybe he has an update."

Beau Marino entered through the wrought iron gate dressed in a rumpled suit. Despite his olive skin, there were dark circles under his eyes.

"Any leads?" Lillian called out.

Beau shook his head. "Not yet."

"No surveillance footage?" the General asked.

"The park isn't outfitted with cameras."

"The police should be conducting door-to-door searches," Colonel Jim said with feeling. "Can you authorize the funding?"

"You think someone in town has Davy Jones?" Pepper asked.

"Everyone is a suspect," Lillian replied firmly.

"Everyone?" Pepper was dubious. "That means anyone here. We have to be able to rule some folks out."

"Perhaps. Or perhaps he was snatched as a prank by an out-of-towner who thinks that hometown pride and traditional values are something to poke fun at," Lillian retorted, glaring at her over the top of her tiger-print bifocals. "Oh, I wish Doc were here."

Pepper glared back. Someone was still bitter about losing all those Scrabble games.

"Ladies, ladies." The General stepped between them. "We can't fight amongst ourselves. The enemy wants grief to tear us apart. Fear can't win today."

"How can you be so sure what the enemy wants?" Pepper asked.

Beau crossed his arms and regarded her blearily. "I

suppose you've heard about Davy Jones by now?"

"Yes," Pepper said, uncomfortable under the full force of the mayor's scrutiny. She knew who he was, of course. The distance between elected Everland officials and the electorate was often the person ahead in line at Sweet Brew. Still, he was Rhett's best friend, and until this moment he had never directly spoken to her. Plus, he was good-looking, in an intimidating way. Not like he was going to throw a punch, but he looked like he could. And he'd make it hurt.

"Then you can appreciate how he is a well-beloved town mascot."

Everyone murmured in agreement.

"Which raises the question, why would someone from town steal it?" Pepper asked, hoping to get them thinking in the right direction.

"You're asking a lot of questions. What were you doing last night?" another voice called out.

It took Pepper a moment to realize that the question was being leveled at her. Worse still, she knew exactly what she'd been doing last night, and the fact it was dirty deeds with the beloved town vet wasn't an answer she could toss out. Her cheeks heated.

"That's a guilty look," Lillian muttered. "Look at that. I know a guilty look and she's got one."

"How could I have stolen that statue? It would weigh as much as me." Pepper bristled with impatience. They were chasing their tails and missing the bigger picture. "And more important, why would I even want it?"

"To boil down and pawn the bronze?" Lillian fired back. "Your sister has been leaving no stone unturned with the medallion hunt. All I hear out of that girl's mouth is money,

money, money. Mayor, I demand you take them both in for questioning."

"This is a witch hunt," Pepper cried. "What about being innocent until proven guilty?" Typical small-town mob.

"People." Beau raised up his hands. "Calm down. We're getting to the bottom of this dognapping. It's my highest priority, I can assure you. Miss Knight?" he said without glancing over. "A word?"

Funny how silence can sometimes sound exactly like "Oooooooh, someone's in trouble."

Pepper glanced at Ziggy, her charge for the day, who romped with the dog pack without a care in the world. "Sure." She trailed the mayor across the park. He was a big man. Football player big. The sun brought out the copper highlights of his strong cheekbones. His hair was thick, wavy and a shade lighter than black. He paused next to an out-of-the-way picnic table.

"Look, you have to know that I didn't steal—"

"I'm not here for Davy Jones," he said. "I know you didn't steal the dog. Last night I called my best friend three different times. He didn't pick up. I know he wasn't on the boat, because I was there."

"Oh." She examined her shoes.

"Let me shoot straight. Whatever you and Rhett get up to is your choice. You're consenting adults. If it's fun for you to run around pretending it's a big secret, then who am I to judge?"

"We aren't pretending," Pepper said. "He doesn't want the gossips to know."

"And I can't fault him for that," he shot back. "But what I need to talk to you about is Tuesday. She's your sister?"

"Yes?" Pepper blinked. This was the last thing she expected Beau to bring up. "Don't tell me she's a suspect."

"No." He grimaced. "She's a royal pain in the ass."

Pepper chewed the bottom of her lip. When did Tuesday cross paths with the mayor? And what gave him the right to talk that way?

"My turn to be straight," she snapped. "Only I'm allowed to talk trash about my baby sister."

"I respect that." He stood a moment in uncomfortable silence. "Can you introduce us?"

Pepper lifted an eyebrow. "Excuse me?"

"Introduce us," he said with gritted teeth.

"You smack-talked my sister, but haven't personally met her?"

"I don't even know what she looks like," he muttered.

"I'm sorry, back up? I wasn't aware that Tuesday's skills had developed to the point where she was making people she's never met crazy."

"The Back Fence," Beau blurted.

"The gossip blog?"

"I have a new column there. Mayor Musings."

"Catchy."

His jaw twitched. "I didn't name it. Anyway, she baited me."

"What do you mean, like a troll?"

He nodded slowly. "I wrote a post and she...she poked fun at it."

"My sister isn't mean." Pepper tried to imagine her sister being a troll who hangs out in the comments section. She didn't have an angry bone in her body. Plus, she'd never lurk online. If her sister had something to say, she'd make sure she found the person's face and said it to them, straight on, damn the torpedoes.

"The comments weren't mean." He rubbed the bridge of his nose. "They might even be funny. The problem is that my job is serious. My messages are serious. And she's turning them into a joke."

"So you want me to introduce you to her so you can ask her to play nice."

"I have important meetings coming up. I can't be made a laughingstock," he seethed.

"Aren't politicians supposed to have thicker skin?"

"Arrange a sit-down. When you have a time, call my assistant, and she will put you straight through." The mayor stalked away.

Chapter Thirty-Two

Forty-five minutes later, Pepper met Rhett at the front door of her house. They tumbled inside, a tangle of tongues and limbs, and were met with a loud throat clearing. Tuesday draped over the back of the couch. "I'd ask you to get a room, but Kitty and J.K. Growling are napping on your bed, and I've commandeered the spare one."

Pepper adjusted her top, her throat tightening at the expression on Tuesday's face. "What's wrong? Is it Dad? You heard from him?"

"No. It's hopeless." Tuesday raised the paper. "The next clue doesn't even make sense. *'Go deliver a dare, vile dog! Murder for a jar of red rum. Do geese see God? God saw I was dog.'*"

Rhett and Pepper exchanged glances as she read the clue in a dramatic voice. "Does it sound like a reference to any place name you can think of?" she asked at the end.

"Doesn't sound like much of anything," Rhett answered, turning to furtively tug up his zipper.

"I hate riddles, my preciousssssss," Tuesday hissed in her best Gollum voice, rolling up the *Examiner* to shake it like a stick.

"Hang on a second. Red rum?" Rhett frowned. "Isn't that from a Stephen King book?"

"No idea." Pepper shook her head. "The only genre I can't read is horror. I get that man is talented, but he sets his stories in Maine. Too close to home. I'd never sleep at night."

"That's so true. You're a wimp when it comes to horror," Tuesday said with a laugh. "Remember when you watched ten minutes of *The Shining* during that high school Halloween party and—"

"Red rum. Red rum." Pepper snapped her fingers. "Murder. Wait. Read the clue back for me."

Tuesday repeated it. Twice.

"Murder? Red rum. Dog? God. Dog. Of course!" Pepper clapped her hands. Excitement built through her, the way it always did when she untangled a thorny mental knot. "These sentences are palindromes."

Rhett grabbed the paper and his eyes locked on hers. "You're right."

"Pali—what's that?" Tuesday tipped her head to the side, confused.

"Words or phrases that are spelled the same in either direction. Do geese see God? It's spelled the same if you read from left to right or right to left."

"Hot damn!" Tuesday threw her arms up into the air in a victory *V* shape. "You're a genius."

"It's only part of the puzzle." Pepper shook her head with a frown. "They are palindromes, but I don't understand the significance."

Rhett cracked a knuckle. "Clue one. It's by the river. Clue two indicated it was near Mars Rock. Wait. Give me a pencil, quick!"

"Pen?" Pepper reached into the basket on the kitchen counter.

"That works. And some scratch paper."

She passed him a notepad and he jotted down a few words. "I got it. Elleselle Memorial, that's where you'll find the medallion. It's near the river, in Mars Rock Park next to the National Wildlife Refuge. Elleselle is a palindrome, too."

"Can we go?" Tuesday executed a flamboyant pirouette. "Right now?"

"Let's load the dogs into my Bronco." Rhett tossed the pen on the pad. "I'll drive."

Fifteen minutes later, Pepper had organized six dogs, a vet, and one hyperventilating sister into the Bronco.

She paused outside the passenger door. "Do you think anyone else is there?" She spoke low, out of Tuesday's hearing range. Her sister was so excited, she didn't want to raise her hopes only to watch them dash.

"Not sure," he whispered back. "There is still one more day before the final clue releases. We're ahead of the game."

"But you're smart. Both of you," Tuesday piped in, rolling down the window.

So much for protecting the innocent.

As Rhett drove off, Tuesday crowed, "Ten thousand dollars! For some people in the city that's a couple pairs of shoes and a Friday night out. For us? It's a fresh start."

Pepper rubbed Rhett's suddenly tense shoulders. How did he feel about all this? If they won the prize money, his reward would be losing her.

Her thoughts drifted back to the teacup and Delfi's gentle question. *What does your heart tell you?* She gave an internal shrug. Tea leaves—logical decision-making method there, Pepper. Jesus. She was the one losing something— her damn mind.

"Hey, I forgot to ask. Has anyone found that missing dog statue?" Tuesday popped her face between the two seats.

Pepper twisted in her seat, grateful for a distraction. "How'd you hear about that?"

She shrugged. "The mayor's column."

Beau's conversation from the dog park came flooding back.

"I need to actually have a word with you later about that," Pepper said. "I hear you've been quite the trolling commenter."

Tuesday blanched.

"What's this now?" Rhett asked.

"Nothing," Tuesday said, right as Pepper replied, "Secret sister business."

"Sounds like a whole lot of I don't want to get involved," he replied. They hit the edge of town, and Rhett turned onto a bumpy road. He rolled the windows down, and the cicada song increased in volume. The dogs jockeyed for the best place to hang their tongues out.

"Why aren't we going to the river?" Pepper said, studying the fields.

"We are in a roundabout way. Mars Rock is above the wildlife refuge. There's a historical monument here, too, honoring one of the region's early settlers. Joseph Elleselle was a British soldier, marooned by Redbeard on the nearby coast after his ship was plundered and set alight. He led a group of survivors upriver to this spot. They lived here for another year before the English navy finally rediscovered them, and in that time they only lost two of their party. Elleselle founded Everland, and a few of the other men returned with their families.

"My mama could trace her roots back to that period. It's the whole reason why I know about the memorial. She used to take me and my sister out here and make sure we'd never forget our history."

"Only one other car's here," Pepper said, examining the lone Subaru with a trailer in the parking lot.

"That's a good sign, right?" Hope infused Tuesday's words.

"Those guys are probably mountain bikers here for the river single track. Lots of riders come here. But if it's otherwise empty, I'd say that is a very good sign," Rhett responded. "The 'out of this world' comment threw some people. Most folks are honing in to the crater crash."

"Crater?" Tuesday asked, jumping out the back door with J.K. Growling's leash.

"A myth that's been debunked. A few scientists from Ithaca came out couple years ago. I don't know how they tell one sink hole in the ground from another, but guess they took one look and knew it wasn't from anything from outer space. Still, locals are stubborn, and plenty are combing that area."

Tuesday hugged herself. "But if locals are stubborn, wouldn't the Pillage organizers have hidden it there, believing the story was legitimate?"

"Trust me, I'm right."

"I trust you." Pepper swallowed back a flicker of self-doubt.

Tuesday said nothing.

It has hard to tell if Rhett noticed as he was busy letting out the dogs.

Once everyone had their boots laced and a leash (or three) in their hands, they set out. At one end of the parking lot was a hand-painted wooden sign. The words ELLESELLE MONUMENT were faded but legible, as was the arrow. A half mile out, the trail dipped downhill, narrowing from a flat, easy boardwalk into a steep single-file gravel path cutting through waist-high grass. Furtive rustling sounded as small creatures fled at their approach. Butterflies abounded. In the copse ahead rose a stone tower. "There," Rhett pointed.

Tuesday broke into a run, but Pepper hung back, taking Rhett's hand. The medallion hunt had been distracting fun, but what would happen after her sister found it? Ten thousand dollars could be enough to restart life somewhere new.

Was Tuesday serious about her Chicago plan? Would she go with her? Did she even want to?

Don't count a medallion before it's found.

Screams filled the air. Not Tuesday. Lots of happy screams. Of course, the amusement park, Happily Ever After Land, was through the forest.

Just like the riddle had described.

This *was* the place. A wash of certainty flooded Pepper, confirmed a moment later when her sister whooped.

"Got it!" Tuesday brandished the medallion in the air. It had been stuck under the historical marker. "We did it. We did it." She ran toward them, arms flung out wide.

"You did it," Pepper whispered.

"Not without your help." Rhett drew her in. "We make a great team."

"Now we have to get this bad boy over to the *Everland Examiner* office and claim the prize. Decide what to do."

The smile slipped from Tuesday's face as reality sank in. Fun and games were over. Time for real life.

So many decisions, but which was the right path?

"Honey, are you sure you don't want to go back to New York?"

Her sister's headshake was adamant. "There's nothing for me back there."

"Except for oh, say, five hundred theaters," Pepper persisted. She couldn't stop pushing this line of thinking. If her sister reverted back to her original plan, it would be easier to follow suit.

"Do you need me to hire a skywriter to write 'New York won't make me happy'? What about you? Your happiness?"

"I'm working on it." Pepper was unable to meet Rhett's gaze. No fun being in the hot seat.

"Let's call Dad. At least he'll be excited." Tuesday slammed the phone to her ear and after thirty seconds rolled her eyes. "No answer."

"This is weird." Concern skimmed Pepper. "I'm starting to worry."

Tuesday shook her head, her mouth twisting wryly. "Imagine a world where a sixty-plus man doesn't feel the need to check in with his daughter like she's his mother." Her tone was light, but the intent was not.

Ouch.

She saw Rhett's sympathetic expression out of the corner of her eye, but shrugged it off. He didn't have to swoop in. Nothing to rescue. Move along. Nothing to see here. Her footsteps grew louder; she'd started to stamp. With a deep breath, her gait resumed something less militantly annoyed.

So much for fun.

The walk to the Bronco was silent. Even the dogs were subdued. It was a ten-minute drive back to town and the modest two-story brick shopfront a block from Main Street, home to the *Everland Examiner*. Pepper and Rhett hung back, allowing Tuesday to pose for the check. She enjoyed the spotlight, and Pepper found her own mood too unsettled for celebration. The deep furrow between Rhett's brows, coupled by the fact that he kept his hands balled in tight fists, told her he felt the same.

After he took the dogs for a stroll around the block, a stout reporter wandered over.

"Nice day," he said. He wasn't much taller than her. Unfortunately that meant it was harder to avoid his direct eye contact.

Pepper gave a polite smile that faded as he brought out an audio recorder.

"Oh no, please," she protested. "My sister is the one you want to talk to about finding the medallion."

"What do you want to know?" Tuesday bounded over.

"What next?" He clicked the play button. "Do you have special plans for the prize money?"

"Indeed we do. My sister and I are going to move to Chicago as soon as possible. We'll stick around until the end of the festival and then it's off on a new adventure."

"I see. We can't entice you to stick around longer?"

"Don't get me wrong. Everland is great. Beautiful. Romantic. Quaint. But there's nothing for us. Not in the long term."

"Ah, Rhett, just the man I'd hoped to see," the reporter broke in ahead of Pepper. "Do you have any comment on these women leaving town? Rumors have been flying you've gotten involved with one. A Miss Pepper Knight, allegedly from Maine by way of New York City and soon to be Chicago."

A crowd gathered, humming with speculation.

"No," Rhett said automatically.

"Are you prepared to go on the record?"

"I am prepared to tell you to back off and leave me out of any town gossip. You're with the *Examiner*. Why not cover real news?"

The reporter cleared his throat. "Well, numbers have been falling with the launch of the Back Fence. I've been ordered to sex things up."

"Well, there's none of that here."

"Care to sit down then for a round of twenty questions tomorrow afternoon?" The reporter pushed, undeterred. "Build up the buzz before the silent auction."

Pepper frowned. "What buzz?"

"Every year the Village Pillage holds a silent auction. All the downtown businesses donate. Plus, there's always two popular extras. The condo timeshare in Key West and the Night with Mr. Scallywag."

"What's that?" Tuesday asked. "Sounds tempting."

The reporter chuckled. "That's the idea. An eligible local bachelor is auctioned off for a real date."

"I see." She didn't, though. Rhett was auctioning himself off as Mr. Scallywag?

"Do you have anything to say about that?" The reporter shoved the voice recorder back in her face. "Confirm the rumors of a secret fling?"

"Rhett and I are good friends. He offered me a job and helped me through a rough patch."

"So there's nothing romantic between you two?"

"Me and Mr. Scallywag?" She glanced to Rhett. In the

top secret corners of her mind, hidden behind caution tape and classified stamps, she'd kept a hope that their so-called fling meant as much to him as it did to her. But he'd signed up to be put on the chopping block for all the single ladies in Everland. Agreed to go on a date.

A date!

Perhaps they'd made a pact to keep their fling a secret, but they hadn't discussed seeing other people.

"I'll be going to Chicago and looking to restart my planned career in law," she set her jaw and announced firmly. "Like my sister said, we have no future here."

"Over to Rhett."

Her stomach tingled with an unexpected fluttering, the lightest gossamer kiss to her core. Tiny hope taking flight. It was so stupid. So impractically stupid, but for a moment it seemed possible he'd do the thing she couldn't. Recover the situation. It was like they were at a Choose Your Own Adventure cliff-hanger and he had the power to get them to the next chapter. She rose up on her toes. Leaned in.

Please.

A wordless whisper, a word written in white crayon on blank paper. This was the chance. The chance for him to prove—

"Pepper Knight is my neighbor." His growl was so rough that the words were barely comprehensible. "She's a dog walker. That's it. End of story."

Their gazes locked. All the butterflies from her stomach flew into a pesticide cloud of practicality and dropped stone dead. She locked her face, erasing all emotion.

Rhett was absolutely right.

This was the end of their story.

Chapter Thirty-Three

Pepper held it together until they got home and Tuesday wisely announced she was going into the backyard to try calling Dad one more time.

"Chicago. Really?" Rhett said as the kitchen door slammed.

"What's wrong with that, *Mr. Scallywag*?"

That innuendo struck home. He raked a hand through his hair. "Listen. Pepper, I didn't—"

"Oh my god. Holy shit. Pepper? Pepper!" Tuesday stumbled in with J.K. Growling and Kitty in hot pursuit.

"Now what," Rhett muttered under his breath.

"It's Dad! He's in the hospital," Tuesday panted, pacing in front of the stove.

"What?" Pepper was halfway across the kitchen before she realized her legs were moving. She grabbed her sister by the shoulders. "Details. Everything. Now."

"I just checked my voicemail bank. There was a message

from two days ago. A nurse saying that they were trying to reach next of kin."

"Next of—oh my God." Pepper fisted her sister's shirt. "Two whole days?"

"I didn't know. I hate checking messages. If anyone wants to get in touch with me they can text."

"Tuesday!" Her adrenaline, pumping from the fight with Rhett, threatened to replace the blood in her veins.

"Look, I'm sorry, okay?"

It wasn't her sister's fault. The impulse to strangle her lackadaisical neck was coming from a place of pure panic. "Why didn't the nurse call me?"

"I don't know. I don't know anything except oh, she said that it's his back."

Of course. The great ticking time bomb. "Is it the community hospital near Moose Bottom? Did you get that much at least?"

"No. Portland," her sister murmured.

"That's nowhere near the house." Dizziness set in. "What if he was air-flighted? We have to think. You call the hospital. Try to figure out what the hell happened. I'm using part of my medallion money to book a flight. I should be able to get on a red-eye."

"A what? You're booking now? Wait a second. Let's get a handle on the situation first."

If she waited another second she'd scream and start walking north.

"Tuesday is right. Get more facts before doing anything," Rhett said gently.

She shook him off. "I don't need to have every scrap of information to know my father is a thousand miles away with no one to look after him. I knew this would happen!" She didn't mean to shout, it just happened. "I knew it."

"What did you know?" Tuesday glanced up, scrolling through her phone contacts.

"That I'd have to take care of him. That it would come down to me."

"And everyone says that *I'm* the drama queen," Tuesday muttered under her breath. "Cool your jets. Everything will be okay in the end, if it's not okay, it's not the end." Tuesday's blithe assurance didn't improve the situation one iota.

"I have so much to do. I have to pack. I have to call Norma and quit. Forget Chicago."

Tuesday lowered the phone and stared. "What?"

"Dad has his whole life in Maine. A farm doesn't pick up and move. And if he isn't able to run it anymore, it will take time to dismantle, and I'll have to find a law practice close by, and he can live with me and—"

"Stop," Tuesday said. "This is crazy. You don't even know what happened."

"I know that if this isn't serious—and right now I doubt that—then at some point it will be something else."

"You can't live your whole life afraid of bad things happening. Dad would never ask that of you."

"Maybe not, but I can't live if I don't ask that of myself."

"Being a martyr," her sister spat.

"Who else is going to help him?" Pepper dropped her voice to a menacing whisper.

"Um, last time I checked, I was still his daughter, too."

"And what will you do? Community theater?" She hated making her sister flinch, but there was no time to pussyfoot around sensibilities. "I know you love being an actress. You are great. You can sing, dance, it's so fun. I want you to have that. But let's be honest. It's not exactly going to pay the grocery bills."

"Wow. Ouch." Tears pooled in the corner of her sister's narrowed eyes. "Tell me what you really think."

"This is why I have made every decision I ever have." Pepper's pulse pounded, sending tremors from her wrists to her temple. "Because you want to be an actress, and Dad wants to make maple syrup. I want you both to be happy."

"Let's get one thing straight," Tuesday snapped. "No one ever asked you to sacrifice your happiness. Not once."

"Someone has to be practical."

"I think what Pepper is trying to say—" Rhett began.

"Stay out of it, Valentine," Tuesday snapped, her color high. "You are trying to tell me that you never wanted to be a lawyer? Pepper? Is that what you're saying?"

"Wanting has nothing to do with it!" she shouted. "What I want doesn't matter."

"What you want is always important!" Tuesday raised her voice to match.

"I want you to be happy." Pepper closed her eyes and drew a deep breath. "I want Dad happy. I want my family to be safe and okay. Screw Chicago. Take your part of the medallion winnings and, I don't know, go to Hollywood." She opened her eyes back up and looked pleadingly at her little sister. "You have more talent in your little finger than most people have in their whole body."

"Stop with the martyr routine. You're acting like that tree from *The Giving Tree*. I hate that book."

"I love that book." The tree was selfless, gave everything until she had nothing left, and then the boy came back.

Granted she was a stump, and he sat on her, and never seemed very grateful...

Huh.

"And what about him?" Tuesday jabbed a finger at Rhett. "Do you even look at yourself in the mirror these days? You're different. Lighter. Smilier. That's what's different about you. You are happy, on the brink of finding passion."

"Passion is self-serving," Pepper shot back. "Obligation is what matters."

"Can't you do what you love, be what you love, and still meet your selfless responsibilities?" She flicked her brows up, and her small smile was devoid of its usual warmth.

"Ha." Pepper tried for a joke. "And I thought you were the one who didn't believe in fairy tales."

"Stop!" Tuesday's foot stamp shook the floor, crushing any attempt at flippancy. "Remember senior year? You worked at the hardware store that whole winter. I magically scored a scholarship to theater camp in Boston even though I didn't apply. And you said you put your money toward college. Did you think I was stupid? I knew it was you. But I couldn't even say thanks because you didn't want me to know you were helping. And it made me feel guilty."

"That's not what I want." Pepper's shoulders were stiff. What was wrong with helping? She cared about her sister and was good at solving problems. "I never meant for you to feel that way."

"There's a fine line between a hug and squeezing so tight that I can't breathe from the force. I appreciate support and encouragement, but don't want to be disempowered in the process. It feels like you don't believe in me, like you always know better." Tuesday studied her face, her eyes burning. "Let me make mistakes. Trust that Dad has a plan. We aren't stupid."

"I don't think either of you are stupid. But..."

"You know who you don't trust? Yourself." Her chin lifted slightly. "You worry about us so you don't have to worry about yourself, afraid what it means to look at what you want deep down because that means you'll have to own it. And once you admit what you want, it's scary as hell because it means you have to make the real choice. To go after it or not."

Pepper reeled like she'd been struck, and flexed numbing fingers. Her mouth dried. It took two swallows before she could speak. "Tuesday—"

"Go." Her sister's tone was calm, but hard. A stranger's voice. "Leave this place, that guy standing there. But remember you aren't doing it for me. Or for Dad. You're doing it because you're afraid that you aren't enough, that the moment you stay, that you admit that you're the one who is human with needs, just like the rest of us, he'll go. And you know what? Maybe he will. Because this is life, not a Disney movie. But you know what? Maybe he won't. Maybe you and he will live on Love Street forever. Take walks down to the Kissing Bridge. Live out the most disgustingly happily-ever-after that's ever been. Here's the thing. You don't know which way it's going to go. But don't use me as an excuse, because I am *sick* of it."

Tuesday turned her back and walked down the hall. The slam from the spare room door rattled the framed quote—I LOVE THE SMELL OF AMBITION IN THE MORNING—hanging on the wall.

* * *

"I'm sorry you saw that," Pepper said after a long moment. "No one fights worse than sisters. It's gloves off."

"Hey, I've got one too," he said slowly. "They can strike right to where it hurts most." Even still, everything those two just shared rocked him to his core.

"I wasn't being hyperbolic. I need to book a flight and go. Tonight. Tuesday is wrong to underplay the situation. My dad has no one else, and he can't be left alone, hurting. Anyway, we knew this was coming, right? It's a fling, not a forever. And in some ways the timing works out great. I get to move on. You get to move on, Mr. Scallywag, you." She knocked his biceps with a playful punch.

"Stop." He caught her hand, traced a thumb over her clenched knuckles. "Drop the act and be real a second. This is it, Pepper. Tuesday was right. You do need other people. For a long time I tried living the opposite way. It's not all it's cracked up to be. There was a reason Tom Hanks started talking to that damn volleyball in *Cast Away*. We're human, but we're animals, too, social ones. We thrive in relationships. In being together. In needing and relying on one another."

That stupid smile stayed stamped on her mouth, even as a single tear escaped down her cheek. She yanked her hand away and swiped it away. "We can't give each other what we want. I can't stay. Let's agree this was an almost-to-be, not a meant-to-be."

"You are right, and wrong. So fucking wrong." He smoothed a stray hair back from her hot temple. "I get that you have to go. You want to check in on family, and nothing is more important. But come back."

She gave a disbelieving laugh, pulling her hand free and swiping her eyes. "That makes the least sense of anything. You're a vet. I still get nervous around dogs. You're small town, and I'm big city. My happy ending will never happen if I sell myself short. Not only did you not admit our relationship, you will never leave Georgia." Her voice sharpened, each word striking some inner stone lodged in her heart, honing the edge. "This is your home," she spoke faster, slashing indiscriminately now. "Your practice is here. You are part of this place. You live on Love Street, and your last name is Valentine. You're a pirate in the sack and sail a boat. This place is in your blood, and you help make this town the way it is."

"You're here too. Way I hear it, you're the Scrabble queen of Everland Dog Park and have the folks there eating out of your hand. You took a guy who thought he didn't need a woman messing up his world to being grateful she did, because he loved being with her more than having a simple life. Let's face it. Simple sucks."

Her hands shook as her lips stitched together. He couldn't tear his gaze from the slight vibration. "Rhett—"

"Stay." The raw word tore from him. "Stay here and get complicated. Let me be what you need." Heat flared in his gut. "You're sarcastic, but I like it. You dress blacker than a raincloud half the time, but always manage to brighten my damn day. You make me crazy, because when I'm with you the impossible feels sane. You need to wake up every day knowing you're amazing. And fall asleep each night knowing that you're adored. Give me half a chance and I can make you happy, because one more thing. I think I'm in love with you, Pepper Knight. And you need to know that, too."

He'd done it. His heart wasn't on his sleeve. It was cut out and offered, throbbing and raw. No cute little geometric preschool shape, but the real thing, in all its pain and all its potential.

She slowly blinked her nut brown eyes, a thousand amber colors trapped there and yet revealing nothing of her mind. Her mouth opened. She was going to say yes. His heart pounded, his vision dimming on the edges as his world narrowed down here to this moment, this woman who'd blown up the walls he'd kept around his heart. Let him believe that it was worth risking everything one last time, because when it's right, it's so fucking right.

She licked her lips. The word was right there. She bit her top lip, heaved a sigh, as soft and final as a falling leaf through autumn air. "No."

Pain laced the heavy silence. The walls around his heart were smoking rubble. His heart defenseless from the assault. "Pepper—"

"No. No way. Can't you see? I—I can't." She broke away and swept her hand in the space between them. "I'm not a mess for you to fix. I graduated from NYU Law, for God's sake. I need to get it together and land a real job. Be professional. Stop playing pretend."

"And that's what you want? To be a lawyer?" He knew the answer, but needed to hear her say it.

"Why doesn't anyone understand? It's not about what I want!" she screamed. "My sister doesn't get it. My dad doesn't get it. And you…you don't get it. You stand there saying all the right things, but what happens after the happy ending? Books, movies, they all stop right at the best part, and there's a reason for that. Because after that moment it all grows ugly. I'm doing both of us a favor and getting out before we get to that point. Everland was a dead end. A cul-de-sac. It's time for me to make a U-turn and get back on track."

He sniffed, his mouth tugging into a bitter smile. He'd

given her his fucking heart for safekeeping, and she chewed and spit it out. The space between them had felt so close a moment ago; now it was a gulf. A void. They stood as if on two icebergs slowly drifting away on an implacable tide. "And me? I'm a dead end, too?"

Masochist. He had to hear her say it. Otherwise he'd dive in, try to rescue them in one final reckless attempt.

"Don't do this." She grabbed her hair in two fistfuls. "Don't make it worse than it has to be."

He should be more careful what he wished for. Her non-answer was reply enough. The pleading was plain in her eyes. For him to stop. To relent. To pretend this wasn't wrenching. "It's already worse, Pepper," he snarled, a chill lapping up his back, icing over his insides. "So go on, then go. Have yourself a great fucking life. Enjoy getting everything you never wanted."

And because he needed to watch another woman he loved walk away like he needed his nuts staple-gunned to the wall, he left first.

Chapter Thirty-Four

Pepper took the window seat flight in front of the wing. The only good part to a last-minute red-eye hacker-fare flight was the near empty plane. With any luck, no one would claim the space to her right. Once they were in the air, she'd curl up into a tight ball and give herself over to the numbness. Her core was so cold she might never get warm again. Sleep? Yeah, right. But if her cheeks happened to mysteriously dampen over Virginia no one would be the wiser.

A rheumy-eyed woman in a purple and yellow tracksuit shuffled past. Then a guy with impressive mutton chops. A few bored-looking businesspeople. A visibly exhausted mom ducked into the empty seat in front of her, a baby whimpering from the sling. Then no one. The flight attendants locked and armed the doors.

She sighed and pressed the heels of her palms into her eyes and took a deep breath. "And away we go."

The takeoff was smooth and uneventful. Pepper zoned out the window, the lights below fading from town, to country, and the blackness of the sea beyond. Everland was down there somewhere. Right now Tuesday would be sleeping while J.K. Growling and Kitty snored from their crates. The only thing her sister said before Pepper left was a curt agreement to puppy sit. Rhett would be home, in the bed where they'd gone from a fling, to a sexy friendship, to something that pushed up on the edge of forever.

Was he asleep? Or out in the backyard, sanding his kayak in an insomniac haze, regretting everything that transpired? Did he see her passing overhead, not a star, just a blink, soon gone? The flight time to New York was two hours, and each minute passed like a lifetime. At the descent, she squeezed the armrests. There was the Hudson. The familiar city lights. The vast forest of steel and windows. The Freedom Tower rose high and proud and behind it the first hint of dawn lit the horizon, a red line of fire cutting through the darkness.

Below stirred millions of people, and not a single one was Rhett.

Enjoy getting what you never wanted.

Her forehead knocked against the window, the glass cold against her hot skin. No matter what happened with Dad, if she ended up living in Maine or back here in the city, she'd never belong, because it would never be home. Because Rhett wasn't there.

Tuesday had been right. The sob Pepper had been holding back for hours choked her. She didn't trust herself to be happy, because vulnerability scared her. All air sucked from her lungs. Her chest ached. The world seemed unreal, as if she were looking at it through the surface of the waves, trapped underwater.

What if she gave voice to the hunger buried deep down inside, and was rejected? What if she went all in with Rhett but she wasn't enough and someday he left just like Mom?

How could she withstand that level of pain?

All she'd ever wanted was a home, a place to feel safe and loved. The rest was mere details. But what if home wasn't a place?

Home was together. She braced her hands on the airplane seat, fingernails sinking into the cheap gray vinyl. Inside her shoes, her toes flexed and relaxed, flexed and relaxed as if kicking through the murk and up toward an invisible surface. The wave of realization broke over her, tumbling her senses. Her head spun and her mouth tasted of salt.

Home was love.

She gasped. Home was Rhett.

The truth smacked her in the face like a rogue wave. She'd been the one to leave and it was the worst mistake of her life.

* * *

Rhett took another pull from his beer. Shit. Empty already. He set it back in the pack and searched for another one. All six were drained to the dregs. When the hell did that happen? The wind hit the mast, knocking about the rigging, a lonely sound of metal chinking off metal.

Pepper was gone.

He'd asked her to stay, put himself out there, and what did he get?

A no.

"Rhett? Hey, man."

Shit. Beau. He didn't feel like talking to anyone. Not even his best friend.

"How'd you know to find me here?" he grunted, rubbing his eyes in a stupor.

"You're drunk." Beau jumped into the boat.

"Tell me something I don't know."

Beau crossed his arms and leveled a long hard stare. "Girl trouble?"

He wiped his mouth with the back of his hand and swayed. "No."

"Liar." Beau crouched next to him. "I've known you since you had that crush on Britney Spears in the schoolgirl uniform. Never told anyone about the poster you hung up in your closet."

"Jesus. I'd forgotten about that. Those pigtails were so damn wrong, and yet so right." He folded his hands behind his head. "But I'm not in trouble. Trouble is what happens when you forget to put gas in the car. Or you forget a Sharpie in your pocket and before doing wash. This isn't trouble, my friend."

"A shit storm then. I heard about you and the dog walker from Elizabeth."

That secured his attention. "What's Birdie got to say about this?"

"You know her—lots. Guess the two of them were becoming fast friends."

"Of course. Because God hates me."

"Hang on." Beau made a show of glancing around. "Have you seen where I put it?"

"What?"

"My tiny violin."

"Shut up."

"No, no. I want to compose a concerto in your honor. Too bad I spent more time in middle school orchestra trying to peek up the first chair flutist's skirt."

"Stop."

"She had pigtails, too."

"Come the fuck on."

"You're in luck because I'm in a tell-it-like-it-is mood." Beau was warming up. "You live in a small town where people give a fuck about you and your happiness. The Back Fence is a bunch of older ladies who have known you since Sunday school and hate seeing you alone and miserable. They want you happy, with a wife and a minivan and two-point-five kids. Same as your sister. Except with less rugrats."

"My sister's uterus is a clown car."

"She's gotten what she wants. And meanwhile you act like people caring about you is a burden."

"I'm trying to stay—"

"True? Stay true to what? I loved your mama like she was my own. But if she could, she'd come back from the grave and kick my ass for not kicking yours. What she wanted was for you to live. Not to suffer or sacrifice."

"And what am I doing?"

"Making excuses."

Rhett responded with a fist.

Beau took the punch. "I knew it was coming, still, damn, didn't make it hurt any less. Feel better?"

"Not really."

Beau slugged him, cracking his lower jaw. "Now?"

Rhett saw stars. "Fuck. What's that for?"

"Trying to see if there's any sense left in there." He

passed over a stainless steel bottle. "Don't get excited, it's only water. Drink up."

"I asked Pepper to stay." Rhett slumped over, elbows on his knees, head ringing from the punch. "Stay in Everland."

"The answer wasn't yes?"

"See her here?" Rhett drank deep. "She's on her way to Maine. Her dad is in the hospital, and she wants to look after him."

"You can't fault her for doing the right thing."

"I'm not. But she's not going to come back, either. Her sister's packing up. They're taking the medallion hunt's ten grand and leaving town. She told me it was over."

"It wasn't meant to be then."

"That's bullshit." Rhett sat back, staring at the sky. Under the moon, a tiny red light blinked, a northbound plane. Beyond the light was a darkness that threatened to take what was left of his heart. "I told her to stay. I told her that I loved her. But I didn't offer anything to meet her halfway. It was my way or nothing, and now I've lost her forever."

"Can I say something?"

"Can I stop you?"

"I'm never getting another shot with Jacqueline. I lost her before I could put our relationship to right, if that was even possible. Your girl is in Maine. See the difference?"

"Shit, man—I—"

"No." Beau held up a hand. "I don't want your pity. I want you to pull your head out of your ass. If you don't chase that girl, then you're going to be chasing your own tail for the rest of your life. So what's it going to be? You want to seize the moment or go in circles?"

"I can't drive. I had six beers."

"That's your excuse?"

Rhett shook his head. "This is me, asking my best friend to forgive the fact that I'm an idiot and help me out. Drive me to the airport?"

"Let's go."

Chapter Thirty-Five

Pepper had never spent much time in a hospital, but if she was blindfolded she'd be able to pick out *eau de medical facility* in an instant. It was a scent that put her on edge, made this moment real.

A bad thing had happened. She'd worried about Dad for so long, and the day arrived that she'd been dreading. She hit floor three in the elevator. The doors shut and there was just enough time to squeak out a few frustrated sobs. Dammit. She wasn't ready for this to have happened yet. And how stupid and selfish was that?

Because there was no convenient time for disaster, and accidents never occur when you'd expect. So much for being prepared so that when the inevitable day came, she could swoop in with her superhero outfit and save the day. What a joke. She wasn't Superman. Or Batman. Heck, she wasn't even Robin.

She was a broke daughter with a fancy degree who

walked dogs for minimum wage. But she'd figure something out. She'd have to move in with him, of course, but
hey, the sugar bush farm was a pretty property. He was her
father. She wasn't going to abandon him.

But what about Rhett? Delfi's tea leaves were right
on the money. She was pulled in so many directions
that any second she might be ripped apart like the paper
doll she'd once destroyed during a sister squabble with
Tuesday.

The elevator stopped and she'd composed herself before
the doors opened.

"I'm looking for Josiah Knight," she said to the nurse at
the station.

"Room three two four," came the reply. "Down the left
side hall, second door from the end."

"Thank you." She turned to leave.

"He's such a hoot," the nurse said. "We all enjoy his
company."

"Yes." Pepper feigned a smile. Dad must be faking happy
and brave. No big surprise there. But he didn't have to be
strong anymore. She'd take over. Each step felt weighted by
a hundred pounds. She was ready for the worst. Poor Dad,
all alone. God, she hoped he hadn't been too lone—

"Honey!" Dad propped up in a hospital bed surrounded
by a dozen heart-shaped balloons. No Grim Reaper in sight,
all sunshine and smiles. "What are you doing here?"

"Hey!" She dashed forward. "Who brought the circus?"

"Me." A plump, friendly-looking woman answered from
a recliner, looking up from her pile of knitting. "Hospitals
are such dreary places. I felt like this was an easy way to
add pizazz to the room."

Pepper opened her mouth but nothing came out. Who

was this woman sitting here clicking needles like she belonged to the place? "Hi, I'm—"

"Chili Pepper," Dad broke in. "This is my . . . Susan."

"Pepper, it's so good to meet you!" Susan hurtled out of the chair and launched at Pepper, clasping her to her ample bosom.

"Good. Yes." Pepper took a muffled breath. "I . . . sorry . . . I don't mean to be rude, but who are you?"

Dad laughed. "Susan and I met a few months ago. She came on our land, birdwatching. She's the secretary of the Maine Ornithological Society."

"I was trying to spot a rusty blackbird." Susan chuckled. "But found Josiah here instead. And you know what they say about a bird in the hand."

"Susan's taken me all over the state. Although I got over-ambitious, which is how I came to hurt my back."

"You hurt yourself birdwatching?" Pepper fumbled for the doctor stool in the corner.

"Hiking out to a puffin colony," Susan added solemnly, heading back to the recliner to resume her scarf.

"Hold on." Pepper held up a hand. "I'm confused. I thought you hurt your back on the farm."

"The farm? Heck no. In fact, I found out this morning that it sold, and for a pretty penny."

"Another reason for the balloons." Susan's needles kept clacking. "We're celebrating."

"You sold the farm?" She choked on a gasp. "No more maple syrup?"

He nodded with a relieved expression. "It was all catching up with me. A nice family from Portland stopped in a few months ago looking for a "tree change" and asked if I'd ever consider leaving. I'd been feeling like a change. They came back with a price that was more than fair, and now your old man is sitting pretty. What a week," he said, reaching out to take Susan's hand. "And we're going to tour the country in Susan's Airstream. Hitting up all the hotspots."

"I had it renovated two years ago," Susan chimed in.

"A real adventure, Chili Pepper."

Pepper didn't know how to react to their expectant stares. "First dog people, now bird people," she mumbled.

"They gave him a steroid shot." Susan nodded like everything was in hand. "He should be getting discharged this afternoon."

"I thought that you'd need me to look after you," Pepper said softly.

"Honey, no! I didn't want you or your sister to worry about me. I didn't mean for the hospital to call."

"We're your daughters. Your blood. We worry about you."

"That's what I told him." If Susan didn't quit it with the sage nods, she was going to get a neck crick. "See, I have two of my own as well. Wren and Robin. Twins about your age. They're working for a wild bird rehabilitation center in Massachusetts."

"So a big Airstream trip, okay, okay, um, that sounds..." Pepper shook her head, completely out of her element. She didn't know what to think about Susan, Wren, Robin, or bird nerds. "Impulsive."

They both laughed, giddy as teenagers. "At our age, what's the use in waiting? We aren't getting any younger."

"Life is for the living," Susan added. "After Dom passed I made a pact that I wasn't going to waste another moment. If I want to check off every bird in the Sibley North American bird guide, who is going to stop me? If I want to do it beside this handsome hunk o' spunk who makes melt-in-your-mouth buttermilk pancakes, then life is good. I'm going to say yes. Right, Pepper?"

"Yes!" Dad punched the air. "Yes to it all."

"So what are you doing all the way down in Georgia?" Susan asked. "We'll have to come down and see the scissor-tailed flycatcher, and then go south for the Florida scrub jay. I've always wanted to visit Georgia. You must love it."

The dam broke in her throat and Pepper burst into tears.

Five minutes later Susan had her set up with a lukewarm cup of Lipton while Dad rubbed her back like he did when she was a kid afraid of the dark.

"I—I-I-I'm supposed to take care of you." She hic-cupped. Great. She never could stop once she started.

"Chili Pepper, I'm going to say a few things that need saying. I am a grown man. And I love and appreciate the way you always want to look out for me. But stop using me as an excuse."

"For what?" Another hiccup.

"Not living your own life. Now, don't interrupt. I've let it go for too long because I thought you'd grow out of it, but let me be crystal clear. I am not your responsibility. I have set funds aside for myself, sweetheart. But I'd never ask you to shoulder my burdens. All I want in this world is for you and your sister to seize life with both hands and do what you love."

Pepper's shoulders slumped. "I do worry, though."

Dad laughed. "Honey, I'm happy. My life is wonderful. Every day might not be good, but there is something good in every day. I've had the astounding fortune to have the two best daughters that anyone could have hoped to have. How many thousands of generations have conspired to produce you? How many chance meetings, and love, and sacrifice and hope? You are a blessing."

When Pepper sniffled, she wasn't alone.

"This man," Susan said, mopping her eyes with her ball of wool. "This dear, dear man."

"I know." Pepper stood and kissed him on the deep crease in his forehead. "Promise that you'll take it easier going forward."

"Never," Dad said. "Because what is life but a grand adventure?"

Pepper glanced to the corner table. It was covered with maps and guidebooks.

"I'd rather spend my retirement collecting moments than dust," Dad said. "We are reading up on Niagara Falls, Graceland, the Black Hills, saguaro cactus, the Grand Canyon, San Francisco, redwoods, the Pacific Ocean, but once we hit the open road, we'll go where fancy takes us. The only definitive place we'll be going is Georgia, of course."

"How do you do that?" Pepper said.

"What, honey?"

"Live without a plan."

Dad laughed. "What makes you think I don't have a plan? I have one right here." He tapped his forehead. "Wake up each morning, look around, and figure out how to live as much life as I can right now."

"It sounds good in theory, but—"

"No buts, honey. It's not a theory. It's a fact. Today. This very moment you, me, your sister, Susan, we are alive. This is our time."

"Excuse me?" she said, bristling.

"I'll let you two have a father and daughter chat and go check on lunch," Susan said, leaving the room.

"How can you mock my plans, my goals and dreams? Not everyone can jump in a van and roam the country looking at birds."

"Honey." Dad pushed himself up, wincing and rubbing his shoulder.

"Hey, we don't need to talk about it. You should rest."

"I'm fine. My shoulder will heal back to normal. Or it won't. But what's the point of me worrying? And I'm not making fun of you or your goals. You impress the hell out of me. You always have. But sometimes I worry about you, honey."

"Me?" Pepper stared. "When have I ever given you cause to worry about me?" She never caused anyone to worry. Mostly because she spent so much of her time worrying about everyone else.

"You lived in New York, the most exciting city on earth. Did I ever hear you once talk about visiting the Met, or taking in a show on Broadway—"

"Do you know how much it costs to—"

"Honey, the specifics don't matter. What I'm trying to say is that you always were focusing on the future, the castle on the clouds."

"Because it's good to make a goal, and work toward it."

"Of course it is. Of course. But what happens if the goal becomes the excuse? You get so busy planning that you stop living."

"And you think I do that?"

"Do you?"

"Maybe." Another hiccup.

"Stop looking at the life you're busy planning and see the life you're living. Or could be living."

She shook her head and walked to the window. "I feel silly."

"Why?"

"Because I have spent my adulthood worrying about my dad, who is apparently one of the smarter people I know."

"What would make you happy?"

"Not being a lawyer," she whispered. And once she said the words they climbed off her chest and she could breathe again. "I don't think I ever wanted to be one, but it was a stable choice. It felt safe."

Dad wiped his eyes. "I'm sorry if I ever gave you cause not to feel safe or stable, sweetheart."

"It wasn't you, Dad." Blood pulsed through her ears as something warm and wet trickled from the corner of her eye. "It was Mom," she sputtered. "Mom, when she abandoned all of us to chase a better life." The word *better* tasted bitter, stung her tongue like nettles.

Her father held her gaze with his deep-set, unruffled expression. The kindly one that always made her feel anchored during life's coldest, howling winds. "What if that wasn't the reason, honey?"

"But she as good as told me that was the reason. We weren't enough. You weren't enough." A ripple of pain spread over her chest. "How can you possibly think of defending her?"

Dad didn't blink. "Your mother may have convinced herself of that reason, but it doesn't make it true, Chili Pepper." He shrugged. "There is always the story we tell ourselves, and then the truth. From where I sit, you look like enough. You—you look like plenty. Every day I wake up and the first thing out of my mouth is thanks. I'm a lucky man to have such fine daughters. A damn lucky man." Dad's eyes darkened with intensity. "What's your truth, honey? The one no one can take away?"

Pepper closed her eyes and a face appeared, not the deeply chisled man from her old fantasies. No. None of them wore glasses, or had a steady blue gaze hinting at a dry sense of humor, a down-to-earth demeanor, and an intelligent mouth. An intelligent mouth that could do some seriously dirty tricks.

"Rhett."

She didn't realize she'd said the words out loud until Dad repeated, "Rhett. Rhett Butler?"

"Nope." She grinned. "Better. Rhett Valentine."

After she told the story of the last few months, he stared at her in stunned silence.

"I only have one question," Dad said. "What are you waiting for?"

The rest of the day disappeared in a haze of phone calls to airlines, boarding, takeoffs, and landings.

When Pepper finally ran up to Rhett's house and pushed the hair out of her face, rain threatened. The misty air probably made it look like she'd stuck a finger into an electrical socket. Whatever. Time to stop sweating all the stuff that didn't matter. So her hair was in a frizzy half ponytail. She was powered by airplane coffee and three bags of salted peanuts, was in the same pair of jeans she'd worn the last forty-eight hours. She might not be the image of a stereotypical princess about to kiss her Prince Charming (at least she kept travel toothbrush, toothpaste, and deodorant stashed in her purse at all times), but this was her own story, her big happily-ever-after moment, so who the hell cared about hair.

She reached for the doorbell. Forget butterflies in her stomach. She had a chimpanzee cage. They were swinging on ropes and juggling bananas.

Twelve paws crashed up the hallway. She smiled at the barking from behind the door. He was home, she loved him and his crazy wolf pack. The door swung open and she stepped forward, arms open, ready for the big embrace and...

"Beau?" She froze, arms out before her like she was Frankenstein's monster in a game of charades.

"What are you doing?" He glanced over her shoulder. "Where's Rhett?"

"Isn't he here?"

"No." Beau's brow wrinkled. "He went after you."

Chapter Thirty-Six

Rhett didn't know whether he was coming or going. There'd been a quickie layover in Newark and a glimpse of Manhattan. Jesus. Pepper wanted to live in a place like that? And yet, why not? He'd be able to get a job there. It wasn't what he was used to, but neither was love. By the time the plane had touched down in Maine he'd amped himself up so hard that it was practically impossible to wait for a cab to take him to the hospital address Tuesday had begrudgingly provided.

"My sister's too good for you," she'd snapped while Beau idled in the car.

"I know."

"Do you? Mr. I Hide the Best Woman Ever under a Rock So That My Small Nosy Town Doesn't Know What a Catch I've Made?"

"I was stupid."

"You were."

"I want to make it right."

"I am seriously considering Chicago. If I asked her to, she'd come with me." Tuesday's voice held a challenge.

"What if I asked her to stay?"

"You want to see who she'd choose?" Tuesday taunted.

"No," he said after a moment. "I wouldn't want to hurt her like that. If she wants to live somewhere else and she'll have me, I'll go."

Tuesday went silent. "I'm impressed, Valentine," she said at last. "You might live up to the romantic promise in your name yet."

"I'm working on it," he answered.

But when he reached the hospital—no Pepper. He met her dad and the girlfriend. They were kooky as hell, but nice people. Everland types. The realization warmed him deeply. He and Pepper were from two different parts of the country, but their roots were the same. Before he raced back to the airport, her dad had clapped him on the back, called him a "good guy."

He was trying to be.

His phone had died and he hadn't packed a charger in his hurry, so he couldn't call. All he knew was that she was heading back to Georgia. He had to find her. A sympathetic agent found him a last-minute ticket on the flight from hell. He visited Pennsylvania, Virginia, and North Carolina before catching a puddle jumper home.

There was a pay phone at baggage claim—the damn things still existed—and he called Beau, who came and grabbed him but shook his head at the request to be delivered to Love Street.

"No can do. It's the night of the silent auction fundraiser. I have to be on hand, and you're coming with."

"Shit. I forgot. And Lou Ellen is going to kill me because there's no way in hell I'm going to be Mr. Scallywag."

"It's fine. She found someone else." His tone was tight, repressing something that sounded curiously like laughter.

"Who?" Rhett glanced over at Beau. "Not you?" Beau wouldn't be laughing if he'd been roped in.

"Hell no." Beau grinned. "Your father."

"Bullshit." Rhett made a strangled sound. "Doc?"

"Yeah. I saw them at Smuggler's Cove at lunch. And here's the surprising thing: the surly old bastard looked upbeat about the opportunity. Anyway, you don't want to go home. Pepper's at the auction, too."

"How could you possibly know that?"

"Her sister's been posting photos of them on Instagram."

"Tuesday?" That took him back. "You two are friends?"

"That drama queen? No." Beau flexed his fingers on the wheel, as he turned them into an open parking spot by Everland Plaza. "Why? She say something about me?"

"Not a word." Curiouser and curiouser. "It sounds like you want her to, though."

"This conversation is over." Beau threw open the car door. "Now let's go get your girl."

Beau was hiding something, but right now his focus was finding Pepper.

As they drew near, a local string band, Empire State, was playing in the gazebo, filling the air with guitar, mandolin, and dulcimer. Fairy lights were strung through the live oaks and magnolia, and the temperature had dropped to the sultry low eighties. A perfect Georgia summer night. Friends and neighbors dressed in their Sunday best waited in line for the oyster bake, sipping sweet tea. He sought her out, looking for a smudge of black amid the pastels, but she wasn't to be seen.

His heart sank. Had she left?

"They're over there." Beau nodded to the left, without glancing over. "See? By the gazebo. The sister's making a spectacle of herself."

Ah. Tuesday was dancing, her white-blond hair swishing over her shoulders as she let the General lead her around the dance floor. And behind her, studying a table of silent auction bids, was a knockout in a white sundress.

He'd know those legs anywhere.

He didn't have to call out. She was turning as if already sensing his approach. The lively song ended and a slower, more romantic song came on, a cover of an Iron and Wine song.

"I'll leave you to it," Beau muttered. Rhett didn't turn to watch his friend go. Beau would know he was grateful for his help. But he knew Beau would kick his ass if he delayed a second longer.

"May I have this dance?" he asked, not reaching for her supple waist until her shy nod. As he interlaced his fingers with hers, he dipped his head, breathing in her familiar apple scent. Murmuring rose from around the dance floor. He was dimly aware of flashes going off. He didn't care. He didn't have a care in the world except to never let this woman out of his arms.

"You came back," he murmured.

She nodded slowly. "Turns out I needed to wrap up some unfinished business."

"Yeah. What kind?"

"Me." She pulled back, pain etched on her face. "I didn't mean to hurt you by leaving. It was selfish. The worst thing I could have done. I was terrified by the feeling of needing. Of needing *you*. I've done everything I could to never need anyone."

He twirled her around. "I know. I know. But you know what? None of that matters. Not one single stupid thing we've done in our pasts."

"Why?"

"Because every step and every misstep has brought us here, right here, to this moment." He dropped his head, resting his cheek on hers. "And now I'm a small-town guy, dancing with a big-city girl to one of my favorite songs."

"It doesn't feel too complicated?" she teased.

"Making a decision to be with you is the simplest decision I've ever made." As he pressed a kiss to her ear, smiling at her happy sigh, his gaze met Birdie's across the dance floor, where she danced with her husband and twins, the four of them holding hands and turning in a laughing, tripping circle.

She winked at him and he winked back, warm to his toes. Thank God she'd let him go all those years ago. Because it made space in his life for this moment. And as the song finally came to an end, he couldn't feel regret, because his and Pepper's melody had just begun.

Lou Ellen stepped up on the stage, striding to the microphone and giving it two brisk taps. "Good evening, Everland. I think you'll agree with me when I say this has been our best Pillage yet, am I right?"

Whoops and cheers erupted around them.

"The oysters are going to be coming all night, so eat, drink, be merry, and on behalf of all of us at the Quilt Guild, go make bids. There are gift cards from a range of local businesses from What-a-Treat Candy Boutique, to the General's General Store, to Smuggler's Cove and Chez Louis, plus many more! There's also the always-popular Florida condo and, saving the best for last, Mr. Scallywag. This year we have a fine man—not that I'm biased—a little older than our usual vintage, but aged like a fine wine. Dad, come on up and let the ladies see what they'll be bidding on."

More cheers, especially from Miss Ida May and Maryann Munro, who threw elbows as they good-naturedly jostled to reach the Mr. Scallywag bidding table first.

"Get out of the way, cougar! He's five years younger than you."

"Who you calling cougar, you horny old saber-tooth!"

Doc stepped up the stairs, and despite the perfection of everything else, a shadow passed over Rhett's heart.

Pepper must have felt it because she rose on tiptoe to kiss him on the cheek. "His loss," she whispered.

He was glad Doc was willing to go on a date, even if it was for charity. He knew Mama would never have wanted him to grow old, alone and bitter. Mama loved to rescue lost souls, and she'd hope a good woman would come along and save his dad from living alone except for Marie Claire.

Speaking of the Maltese, she didn't look right. His gaze dropped down to the small white dog peeing on the bottom step of the gazebo. Strange. He frowned. *A case of nerves?*

Doc stepped to the mic, not seeing as Marie Claire collapsed to one side, eyes glazed and muscles twitching in herky-jerky spasms.

"Stop!" Rhett dropped Pepper's hand and dashed forward.

"Son." Doc frowned, his bushy brows contracting. "This forum is no place to rehash old—oh! Marie Claire!"

Everything happened in a matter of seconds, but time moved in slow motion.

Rhett knelt down, checking her vitals as the seizure stopped. "Has this ever happened before?"

Sometimes dogs have a one-off seizure and it's not an emergency.

"Three times in the last month," Doc said in a choked voice. "I took her to TLC in Hogg Jaw, and they assured me she was fine. The diagnostic bloodwork they ran came back negative for anything serious."

"The wait-and-see approach is not a good idea with re-occurring seizures. We'll have to bring her to my office for a checkup. Now." He caught Doc's gaze and refused to look away. "You okay with that?"

"Can you help her?" The old man's voice cracked, and for the first time Rhett saw Doc as he was, not the towering father figure of his imagination, but an old man who matched bowties and hair ribbons on his pet. A man who doted on a dog to try to bring a little joy to what was a lonely life.

Rhett's heart expanded in pity. "I'll move heaven and earth."

Doc mashed his lips before replying. "Thank you, son."

All those years ago, Dad had been in the wrong. But hell, he'd lost the love of his life and was hurting. Rhett glanced at the tattoo on his arm. What would Mama say? Stay true to self-pride at the expense of patching things over? Stay true to emotional isolation? To a lonely existence because it guaranteed never being hurt?

Never.

"You should take her home to rest tonight. Keep her under observation, and you can bring her in first thing tomorrow morning. There are many possible underlying causes, so we have to do a lengthy workup. No stone will be left unturned."

"I can be there first thing."

"Sounds good. We'll make her better, Dad. I promise."

A half hour later, the band was back onstage and the town celebration had resumed. Pepper lifted a flute of Champagne to her lips, smiling as Tuesday and Rhett danced.

"Mind if I have a word?" A crisp British accent, not a slow Georgia drawl.

She turned, blinking into the shadow. "Cedric Swift? Is that you?"

"At your service." The British sailing historian stood in the gathering dark, looking decidedly uncomfortable.

"What's the matter?" she asked.

"What would you say if I told you that I might have some information about illegal activity?"

"In Everland?"

He nodded once. "Stealing in particular." He pointed to the flower-strewn cement base where Davy Jones used to stand. "That dog statue to be exact."

"You know where Davy Jones is?" she asked, shocked, mostly because of the relief flooding her. Who knew that she'd grown so attached to that bronze furball, and yet, he was a part of this town. This place that felt so much like home that her body ached with the promise.

He frowned. "Not exactly. But I think I do know who took him." He undid the top button in his button-down shirt and rolled his shoulders. "I'd been up in Charleston doing research. Found a few interesting leads on...well...a few interesting things. The night the statue went missing, I'd had a hard time sleeping, so I decided that a midnight stroll would do me well. Fresh air and the like. And that's when I saw a man behaving rather peculiarly."

Her brows mashed. "Peculiar how?"

He cleared his throat. "Creeping through the town green in a black ski mask, carrying a sack and a crowbar peculiar."

"That isn't something that you see every night."

He chuckled. "Happily, he didn't see me. So I watched, assuming he was going to break into an automobile. But instead, he headed to that dog statue. It was hard work for him to get it off. Ample swearing. Then it came free, striking him in the face. He ripped off his mask and it was—"

"Hey, what's going on?" Rhett pulled up short, frowning between them.

Pepper made a "quiet" motion. "You've met Cedric Swift. He was just telling me—"

"No, but I've seen him around a few times. Talking to you." There was definite tension to his voice.

She gave him a look. "I did not fly back here like the west wind was at my back to find you only to have you getting all weirdly jealous about the fact I'm talking to this guy."

"This guy?" Cedric pointed at himself. "What's wrong with this guy?"

"Nothing." Pepper gave him a reassuring pat on the arm. "You're perfectly nice. And brave. And knows who kidnapped the Davy Jones statue." She stressed the last part of the statement for Rhett's benefit.

"Who did?" Lou Ellen drew close, emerging from the shadows with Snapper and their four daughters in tow.

"It was that chap with the strange name. Not Kevin Bacon." Cedric laughed to himself. "Although that movie *Footloose*, ah, what a classic."

"Cedric," Pepper snapped, clapping her hands in his face. "Focus."

Cedric startled. "Hogg. Yes, the judge with the swine-like surname."

"Can you be certain?" Rhett growled.

The historian gave a one-shouldered shrug. "As certain as anyone can be who sees a man in the dark. He clocked himself jolly well hard in the face, so if he's the man I think he is, you should see him sporting a sizeable forehead egg."

Lou Ellen gasped. "It *was* Hogg. Today at Sweet Brew, Maryann Munro mentioned that the judge had taken up boxing. I thought it was strange, but she said he'd come into work with a black eye and a mood worse than usual."

Rhett cracked a knuckle. "I saw his car by the courthouse when Beau parked. Let's go have ourselves a conversation."

Folks streamed out of the auction, catching wind of what had happened. Rhett, Pepper, Lou Ellen, the General, and Cedric found themselves flanked by a large and increasingly agitated mob.

"We need to calm everyone down," Pepper muttered out of the side of her mouth.

"Good idea," Cedric suggested. "What do you suggest?"

"Sing 'Kumbaya'?" Pepper was kidding. At least half kidding.

"Stick by me in case the action gets out of hand." Rhett beckoned her closer.

Lady Justice watched their approach. God, she gave good RBF. Her stone face watched the crowd with a calm impassiveness, as if she knew righteousness would win the day, and that would be enough.

Sure enough, the judge's apple-red Cadillac was parked in his designated parking spot.

"I almost feel bad for him," Lou Ellen piped up chirpily. "If I wasn't so pleased that rat bag was finally getting his due."

"I don't." Maryann jogged up. "This man has had it coming for years. Do you know how many times he's made me cry, in the little girls' room? The lord works in mysterious ways."

They filed into the courthouse's marble rotunda. Pepper hadn't set foot in the courthouse since her unlucky first day. She glanced up at the rotunda as the crowd hustled toward the staircase. It was as if she could see herself in her pencil skirt and poofy hair that fated first day when she was chasing a dream that she'd carried for so long.

A false dream that would never lead where she wanted to be.

Rhett turned to her, an apology in his eyes and something else. Something she hoped she wasn't hallucinating through heartsick longing. "After this dies down, we need to talk."

She nodded in assent. "Soon."

He gave her hand a squeeze. They were at the door with the frosted glass.

"Easy now." Rhett held up a hand. "I'll go in alone."

"Not so fast. I'm coming, too," Pepper announced.

His mouth twitched as if he was going to tell her to wait, but as her hands migrated to her hips he smashed his lips together, nodding once in assent.

Rhett walked with her through the door, and then let them into the large back office. Judge Hogg sat at his desk, hands clasped, waiting. Cedric Swift had been right: he did have a black eye and deep bruising on his forehead.

"What's the meaning of this?" His tone of manufactured outrage was exactly the type people use when they must pretend at having nothing to hide.

Rhett cut to the chase. "We're here for Davy Jones. Where is he?"

"The precious town dog? I don't know what you're talking about." But his hands belied the bold statement. They didn't stop moving, adjusting a water glass, moving a pencil. Sweat sheened his creased brow.

"You were seen," Pepper said. "Crowbarring him off his pedestal."

"We don't want trouble." Rhett jerked a chin to the door. "I can't say the same for the people lining up behind that door."

The judge cocked his head. Deep-set lines bracketed his mouth as he took their measure. "Such a pity about your animal shelter. You had worked so hard to honor your mama."

"What's that mean?" Pepper swiveled her head back and forth. The judge was steering the conversation in an unexpected direction. "What's the shelter have to do with anything?"

Judge Hogg blinked blearily. "Doesn't matter. It's not going to be built."

"You have no say in that," she scoffed.

"Actually, yeah. He does. Hogg's on the board of Low Country Community Foundation." Rhett raked a hand through his hair. "He needs to review our grant application and sign off. He tried to strong-arm me, and it didn't work."

"Deal is off." Hogg shrugged with satisfaction. "Construction grants require unanimous approval."

"Listen good." Rhett broke the smug silence with a fist banged on the desk. A glass of water upended, trickled down to the carpet. "There's three things I care about most in this world. One is this town's reputation, and one is my mama's memory. Here's how this is going to go. Another deal. Give me the statue and recommend the shelter funding—in full."

"Or?"

"I open up that door and unleash a horde that will tear you limb to limb like a pack of hounds on a treed coon."

The menacing grumbles outside increased in volume.

"It's not here." The judge's Adam's apple worked up and down. The clockwork gears in his head almost audible.

"Where?" Rhett wasn't fucking around. All patience was gone. His boyish features brokered no weak excuses.

"Hogg Jaw." He licked his dry lips, glancing at his dog's painted portrait. "Let me drive home." Anxiety wafted off him, thin and sour as old milk.

"You're lying," Pepper broke in. "Rhett, Davy Jones is here, and I think I know where."

The judge broke into a sweat as Pepper stalked to the portrait, "There!" She touched the frame and the picture swung open. Inside was a secret cubby. A pair of bronze ears poked out of the top of a flour sack.

The judge bolted to the office door, took one look at the townspeople, and slammed it shut. "Mama's going to kill me," he sniveled. His hands splayed the wood. "She has a plan. Taking that dog was step one."

"Now I have the statue. I still want the grant." Rhett's tone was implacable, even as he opened the window. "Deal or disaster?"

"Yes, damn you," the judge choked. "Deal. Deal. Anything. I'll sign off on the grant tonight. All I'm asking is to get out in one piece."

"Pleasure doing business. There's a thick wall of ivy. Climb down and head for the hills. Tomorrow the shelter will be funded in full, and you'll submit your resignation from the board and job. You're off the bench and out of town. No more lording over the people of Everland."

"Climb down?" The judge's pale face drained of the last

vestiges of color. His waxy mouth went slack with shock. Fists beat at the door. The frame creaked. With a whimper, he kicked a leg over the window ledge and vanished into the night.

Pepper closed the cubby and swiveled around. "What are you going to do to buy him time, uphold your part of the deal? You got the dog and the grant, but this crowd is baying for payback."

"Trust me, Trouble." Rhett's features grew grave. "I'm going to do something I should have done a long time ago. And when I'm done, people will have something to talk about for a good long time."

Chapter Thirty-Seven

❧

Townspeople poured into the judge's office. The gawking expressions were anxious, angry even.

"Hogg, get out here with your hands up."

"We want Davy Jones!"

"Calm down, everyone. Calm down." Rhett raised his hands, his voice deep and authoritative. "Davy Jones will be returned to the Everland Dog Park after a few minor repairs. I'm sure Mayor Marino will waste no time in ensuring that the statue will be fixed good as new."

The crowd hummed, digesting the information.

"But there's another matter to attend to," Rhett persisted. "Davy Jones represents courage. Loyalty. A steadfast heart. In that spirit, I have to repair something else tonight, my relationship to this incredible woman standing beside me. Many of you know that I like nothing better than avoiding the town spotlight. Wanted to steer clear from the Back Fence and any gossip, but—Miss Ida May, are you here, ma'am?"

"Move it, move it. Coming through, people. Step aside. Coming through." She barreled her way to the front. "'Course I'm here, Cupid."

"You have full permission to print everything I am about to say."

She reached into her purse and removed a notepad with an audible squeal.

"Pepper. When I said I value three things, I meant it." Rhett turned to engulf her hands in his. They were warm, so warm, and all she could do was kick herself that she had almost walked away from them forever. His touch was an anchor, and promised to help her steer course through any rough waters ahead. "There's my mama's memory. This town. And you. There was a time this week when I wasn't sure I would ever see you again. And I realized that could never work because if I never saw you, I could never tell you that I love you."

Pepper's gasp was magnified by those of everyone in the room.

"Yeah. I love you," he repeated, his voice rough with emotion. "Once I told you that I thought I did. And I lied. Because I knew it and got scared. But you don't deserve lies anywhere near the kind of love I want to give. And you sure as hell don't deserve cowardice. So now I want everyone in this town to know the truth. No secrets. No more hiding. Because with you on my arm, I'd be the proudest man on the coast, and no matter where you go, I want to stay true to you, and that means staying by your side.

"I love watching you watch eighties romantic comedies and that when you laugh, it makes me laugh. I love that you will drink a beer on my boat and tell me to turn off cheesy music. I love that since you've lived here I've had the privilege to watch you flourish and grow. My dogs love you. Kitty loves you. Hell, the whole dog park adores you. And I love your red underwear and—"

"Hey, son, tone it down. We don't want to lose a PG-13 rating here," the General shouted through cupped hands.

Ida May jostled closer, breathlessly scrawling across a notepad emblazoned with a Back Fence logo. "Rhett spilled his heart. Bared his soul. And what do you say, Pepper?"

"Rhett." Pepper shifted uneasily. The spotlight had never been her favorite place. But when she locked on to his warm blue gaze, the rest of the world floated away. The words came easily, breaking through the flimsy dam. "You're a guy who lets me steal the covers and warm my icicle feet on your legs. Who loves his family and take pride in his hometown. A real man who loves animals, which shows that you are nurturing, responsible, affectionate, and compassionate. And who could ask for a better dream man? I love you, too," she said.

His gaze slid over her face, eyes dark, searching. "Wherever you want to go, I'm going to be there. I'll even leave Everland, just say the word."

The crowd gasped. Someone murmured, "No!"

"I do want to move." She hooked her hands around the back of his neck, inhaling his perfect smell. "Right next door, if that's all right."

The rumble in his chest vibrated through her whole body. "Hell yes it is."

Cheers broke out.

"You, me, Kitty, Steinbeck, Faulkner, and Fitzgerald." She rose on tiptoes and shouted in his ears over the din of whoops and well-wishes. "That's four dogs. Too many?"

"Four dogs is just right," he murmured. "Now brace yourself, because I'm about to make a very public display of affection, Trouble."

"Good, because if you don't soon, you're gonna be in some."

Their lips crashed together to the clicks of a dozen camera phones. But all she knew or cared about was that the man in her arms was with her.

Excerpt from the Back Fence:

**Everland News That You
Actually Care About**

Classifieds:

Community Celebration: All of Everland is invited to the groundbreaking ceremony for the Virginia Valentine Memorial Rescue Shelter this Friday at ten am (4021 Kissing Way, go over the Kissing Bridge and look for the turnout after the first mile marker). This state-of-the-art facility will provide two surgical suites and multiple pre-op and post-op recovery areas, "catios"—outdoor patios to house multiple cats. Don't forget the indoor climate-controlled bathing and grooming area, and the PawsTracking mobile application that will help pet owners find their beloved lost animals.

Help Wanted: Fast-paced careers in the amusement park industry! Whether you're looking for a temporary adventure or long-term employment, you'll be making dreams come true for our visitors at Happily Ever After Land. Now hiring ticketing cashiers, game and ride operators, parking attendants and a Princess Party Host. Apply online at www.HEAland.com or in person at the Park's HR Office.

Chapter Thirty-Eight

T hat's the last of it." Tuesday smoothed packing tape over the seam of the last cardboard box. "Whew! A person could move eighty feet or eight hundred miles. The amount of work is still the same."

Pepper slung her arm around her sister's shoulders, pulling her in tight. "Are you sure about this, me moving?"

"I love this tiny house." Tuesday gave a happy sigh. "I signed the new lease and sent it off to Mrs. Carmichael this morning."

"We'll be neighbors, but you're committing to Georgia? That's a big deal."

"As if I'd run off to Chicago and leave you here." She snorted. "No chance, not when J.K. Growling finally has a fur cousin. Actually, what if we cut a hole in the back fence, and let her and Kitty hang out whenever they want?"

"Five dogs between us?" Pepper said wonderingly. "Can you believe it?"

"Ha! I know. And who said they didn't like dogs again, Ms. executive director of the Virginia Valentine Memorial Shelter?"

"Try saying that five times fast." Pepper hugged herself. She'd finally found a great way to use her law degree, running a place where being needed was an asset. On her watch as shelter director, no animal would ever feel abandoned. "Are you coming to the shelter's groundbreaking ceremony?"

"I can't. I have to start my first day." Tuesday grimaced, gesturing to the tiara on her head. "Princess party host."

"Are you excited about Happily Ever After Land?" Something told Pepper that it wasn't only the job that kept Tuesday from the shelter's ceremony, but the fact that the mayor would be there in an official capacity. She had tried to bring up the fact Beau asked to meet with Tuesday to her sister on two occasions, and each time her sister had rebuffed the idea and redirected the conversation so fast Pepper had whiplash.

"There are a few eccentrics working there, but I guess I'm one, too. I'm requesting my official title be Princess Felicia Ariana Beatrix Ulrike Leila Olympia Ursula Sophia." She waved her hand with a flourish.

"I'm sure the children love meeting you with that mouthful."

Tuesday winked. "It's an acronym."

Pepper paused. "Princess F.A.B.U.L.O.U.S? Sounds wonderful, your excellence, or should I say, your modesty."

Rhett came in, swiping a brow. "Do I bow or kneel in your exalted presence?"

"What about me?" Tuesday folded her arms. "I'm basking in front of Everland royalty here."

"What's that supposed to mean?" Pepper asked.

"You two have been the subject of every single article on the Back Fence bar one, the hottest topic since Rhett confessed his love in front of half the town."

"Your sister deserves hearing her praises sung from the rooftops," he said firmly.

"I do like you, Cupid." Tuesday blew him a kiss.

"I am curious." Pepper leaned in against Rhett, looping a finger into his belt, another giving him a private tickle. "What's the one story not about us?"

"Davy Jones, of course." Tuesday tossed the packing tape and caught it with one hand. "The statue was put back today. No one is calling the judge out directly, but everyone is willing to forgive him, if not forget."

"That's for the best," Pepper said. "I feel bad for him."

"Why?" Rhett asked, mystified. "After what he put you through?"

"He's a coward. And it's a terrible thing to live your whole life in fear."

"Do you think that anyone is going to try to prosecute him?" Tuesday asked.

Rhett shook his head. "Everland wants to move on. But I did hear a rumor from Maryann that he asked her to look for home help care for his mother because he'll be moving, wants to buy a fishing cabin somewhere quick."

"Wow," Pepper said, before glancing to the book on the counter. "*Pirate Lore of the Georgia Coast*? What's this? You taking an interest in history?"

Tuesday snatched it up. "Maybe."

"Honey, we found the medallion. That's real treasure."

Her sister glanced down at the book, rubbing the cover. "I took J.K. Growling to the dog park this morning. The

General was there and that cute British guy walked past, and I overheard them discussing an actual treasure in Everland."

"Too late." Rhett slung an arm around Pepper and kissed the top of her head. "I already found it, and she's right here."

Tuesday pretended to gag. "Is this what it's like living on Love Street? Because I might need to take back some of the money that I donated to get that shelter a state-of-the-art dog rehab pool and invest in noise-canceling headphones and an eye mask."

Pepper laughed. "Someday a guy will awaken your secret romantic side."

"Ha, good luck with that," Tuesday retorted. "It doesn't exist."

"Can I carry anything else over before we hit the road?" Rhett looked around the cottage, clearly not relishing the mushy girl talk.

"All that's left is that box of dishes." Pepper pointed. "My casa is officially su casa, sister."

Tuesday saluted.

"In that case, I might come back for the dishes in a minute. I'd rather carry you over the threshold." Rhett scooped Pepper off her feet.

"Have you lost your mind?" She grabbed his broad shoulders with a shriek.

"Love Street," Tuesday grumbled with a good-natured eye roll.

Pepper and Rhett exchanged glances and laughed. "Yep."

"Let's get you home, Trouble," he murmured, walking outside.

"Home. I like how that sounds." She caught the time on her watch and gasped. "Oh, we have to go, we're going to be late."

"I have something I want to do first." He increased his pace, passing his driveway.

"But I'm the shelter's executive director, and you are the board president. We can't be last-minute arrivals."

"We won't." His tone was firm. "But first, I want you to take a walk somewhere with me."

"Yoo-hoo! Hello, you two." Miss Ida May emerged with a hose from behind her rosebushes. "Now, Rhett, I have a date with your daddy tomorrow night, Mr. Scallywag himself. And hoowee, isn't Maryann Munro jealous!" She waved the garden hose in a satisfied arc.

"That's good to hear," Rhett called. "Real good. Doc needs a night of fun. Just go easy on him, you hear?"

Miss Ida May tilted back her hat. "How is Marie Claire?"

"Going to make a full recovery."

Pepper ruffled Rhett's thick hair. "Thanks to this one," she called. It was pure pleasure to brag about her smart, sensitive man. His promise to leave no stone unturned for Marie Claire was an honest one. He spent hours ruling out diet and exposure to toxins and mold, but rejected giving a diagnosis of idiopathic epilepsy. It wasn't head trauma or an infection. The liver and kidneys checked out. Then he found a meningioma in her olfactory lobe the size of a marble. Fortunately, it was a benign tumor, and Rhett pulled strings to get her seen by a veterinary neurologist contact in Athens. She'd make a full recovery.

"Good to hear." Miss Ida May's smile was as warm as fresh buttermilk biscuits. "I do love a good happy ending."

"Me too." Rhett gave Pepper a sidelong look, a lazy grin slanting his mouth. She squeezed his hand. He had healed not only Marie Claire, but also his relationship with his father.

He ambled—fingers laced—to the end of the street.

"What's this all about?" Her gaze roamed the empty, shady street as he returned her to her feet. "You're up to something."

"Maybe." He jutted his chin at the Love Street sign overhead.

Her thoughts spliced, the ends loose and jangled. "I have lots of questions."

"Me too. Starting with this one." He fished a small black box out of his pocket and dropped to one knee. Inside nestled a simple diamond in a band of rose gold. "Pepper Knight, will you complicate my life forever? I want to live the happy after the happy ever after right here on Love Street. I want to spend the rest of my life making sure you never need anything. Because of you, I laugh harder, smile more, and live more richly and deeply than I ever believed possible. It would be the honor of my life if you'd be my wife."

"Oh." Tears distorted her vision. Her knees wobbled. "Oh God. Oh my God."

His eyes twinkled, warm pools of deep Caribbean blue. "Nah, just a small-town boy offering the woman I love my mama's favorite ring."

"Yes. Yes a thousand and one times. Of course I'll marry you, incredible man. You make me happy in a way no one else ever can." She sniffled as he slipped the band on and flexed her finger. The fit was perfect. "Life took me in a direction that I never saw myself going, but love brought me home."

"You're the beat to my heart, Trouble." He rose, drawing her close. And as he kissed her brow, the tip of her nose, and lingered at her mouth, she knew her detour through Everland was really a shortcut to forever.

Actress Tuesday Knight let go of her Broadway
dreams and moved to Everland, Georgia. But when
she meets handsome Beau Marino, Tuesday begins
to hope for her own happy ever after . . .

A preview of

The Corner of Forever and Always

follows.

Chapter One

There's a convenience factor to owning a pair of heels that goes with everything, except for when they blend into the background like a pair of overachieving chameleons.

"Have you seen my glass slippers?" Tuesday Knight quizzed her drowsy twelve-year-old Boston Terrier. The missing shoe quest quit being funny five minutes ago.

J.K. Growling replied with an offhand snort and returned to the business of burrowing beneath the quilt piled on the unmade bed.

"Great. Big help there, little buddy. You do you." Tuesday scanned the chaotic avalanche of maxi dresses, yoga pants, celebrity magazines, bangles, bohemian scarves, and an empty salt-and-vinegar potato chip bag. Lucky thing musical theater had taught her proper diaphragmatic breathing—a helpful skill when desperate times called for heaving dramatic sighs.

A rooster crowed from beneath the mess—her nine o'clock alarm—and J.K. Growling went belly-up. Even poultry failed to rouse her from Tempur-Pedic-induced torpor. Tuesday kicked items left and right while wrestling with the stubborn back zipper to her fuchsia ball gown. That crow meant *Leave pronto, or you'll be late.*

A vague memory took shape while plucking her iPhone from beneath a back issue of *Vanity Fair*. Last night, following a ten-hour shift as Happily Ever After Land's newest amusement park party princess, she'd collapsed on the couch—smelling like cotton candy, ears ringing from the carousel's Wurlitzer band organ—to play Oregon Trail.

"That's it!" The tension in her body evaporated. She tore down the hall, skidded to a stop in the doorway, and fist-punched the air. Sure enough, the glass—or rather, plastic—slippers were propped against her peacock-print throw pillows. Right where she'd kicked them off after dying of dysentery at mile 947 on that stupidly addictive phone app.

A rhinestone-encrusted tiara twinkled on top of a coffee table book, *Broadway Musicals: The 99 Best Shows of All Time*. Perfect. Saved from the hassle of mounting yet another search and rescue. Tuesday plopped it on her head, adjusted her bodice over her nonexistent bosom, and shoved her feet in the smidge-too-tight heels.

J.K. Growling peered around the corner with a bemused expression.

"It's not easy being a princess," Tuesday informed her. "But hey, if the shoe fits..."

She yanked open the front door, struck, as usual, by the quiet. Typical for Everland, Georgia. Manhattan had been a noisy symphony of jackhammers, cab horns, loud neighbors, and police sirens. Here the coastal breeze rustled the hundred-year-old live oaks lining the shady street, dripping moss from thick, gnarled branches. A bird trilled in song. A dog barked. A neighbor tuned a mandolin on a front porch swing.

Just another warm and sunny, small-town September morning.

She climbed into the orange-colored AMC Pacer (aka Pumpkin) purchased for a song from a Hogg Jaw mechanic with the leftover Village Pillage medallion hunt prize money that she'd won with her sister this summer. Everland residents were proud of their local pirate heritage. The legend went that the infamous Captain Redbeard stole a king's ransom and hid it in these parts over three hundred years ago.

Tuesday got bona fide thrills when discovering five bucks in a winter coat pocket. Imagine unearthing a treasure horde? The only thing better would be scoring front row tickets to *Hamilton*. And a time machine to see it performed by the original cast.

Pumpkin started on the third try. As the old girl wheezed to life, the gas light blinked on, and Tuesday knocked her forehead against the steering wheel. Forget daydreaming about pirate lore. Time to get real and play her least favorite game: Dare the Gas Tank.

"How low can you go?" She muscled the stubborn gearshift into reverse. Payday wasn't until tomorrow, and she didn't have enough funds in her checking account to refuel, not after giving Lettie Sue, a park waitress, her last few hundred bucks.

Yesterday, the single mom broke down in the staff room over her inability to cover next week's daycare bill. Afterward, Tuesday had snuck to the snack bar to make an ATM withdrawal and left an anonymous envelope of twenties in her co-worker's locker.

She didn't regret giving the hardworking woman a single penny, but the ramifications from the impulsive decision couldn't derail her morning obligations. She was hosting a Foster Friends field trip for the local children's charity. If she didn't dilly-dally she'd have enough in the tank to get to work and home. It was all going to come down to fumes and a prayer.

Movement caught the corner of her eye. Her big sister and her sister's fiancé, Rhett, staggered from the house next door, a tangle of limbs and leashes. Between them, the happy couple owned four dogs. A few months ago, Pepper had moved to Everland for an ill-fated legal clerkship. After losing her job on day one, she'd detoured into what turned out to be the right direction, finding work as a dog walker and falling head over strappy sandals for the hot vet next door. Now she was spearheading the opening of Everland's rescue shelter as its executive director.

Pepper glanced at her thin wristwatch, brows wrinkling beneath fashionably cut side-swept bangs. "Aren't you late?"

Tuesday restrained a grimace. The one and only drawback to living next door to such a capable, successful sister was frequently feeling like a hot mess. "What can I say?" She cupped a hand to her mouth. "Lost my shoes again."

Zero surprise registered on Pepper's pretty face. They each played their respective roles well, the responsible, dependable, reliable one and the free-spirited walking disaster. But after Tuesday's world in New York City spun out of control, she headed straight here.

Her big sister was true north even in the Deep South.

"Are we seeing you tonight?" Rhett called. The dynamite duo were hosting a potluck dinner around the theme of

"Southern Comfort." Pepper had entrusted her with the napkins. It wasn't meant as an intentionally insulting gesture, but unintentionally? That was a whole other story.

"Wouldn't miss it for the world!" Tuesday cracked a tight smile before driving away. Downtown Everland was more or less deserted this time of morning. The lovingly restored buildings dated back to the late nineteenth and early twentieth century, but the town was more than a hodgepodge of bright awnings, mom-and-pop storefronts, and cheerful planter boxes. The charm lay not just in the bricks and mortar, but also the bighearted, warm, and welcoming (if eccentric) citizens.

A bay window etched with the words WHAT-A-TREAT CANDY BOUTIQUE stenciled in mint-green calligraphy caused her to gasp as today's date hit home. It was the thirtieth birthday of What-a-Treat's owner, Ginger Reed! She'd been informing everyone who ventured in for a slice of fudge of her intention to enter a mystical time warp whereupon she'd remain twenty-nine forever and ever, amen.

Kitty-corner to the shop sat city hall, the imposing building framed by a profusion of late-summer flowers. "Perfect." Tuesday slammed on the brakes. If she hustled, she could pick a spur-of-the-moment bouquet for her friend and leave it in front of the candy shop's door as a quick pick-me-up.

She climbed out of Pumpkin and raced over the lawn, kneeling beneath an office window and grabbing Shasta daisies, goldenrod, and a few begonias. The blooms were vibrant, like her new friend. In fact, they looked so pretty she picked a few more, and just a few more, and what the heck, now that she had this much, she might as well go the whole hog. After all, forever is a long time to stay twenty-nine.

A throat cleared behind her.

"Morning!" She squinted at a security guard, backlit by the bright morning sun. "Don't mind me, I'll be up and out of your hair in a sec."

"Well, Miss Knight, it's like this see..." He shuffled from side to side. "There's been a report of vandalism."

"Really?" She glanced around, half expecting a lurker to be slinking from oak to oak, clutching a can of spray paint. "What sort of damage are we talking about? Graffiti? Arson? Broken windows?"

The man removed his blue cap and studied the embroidered brim with particular attention before mumbling under his breath.

"Theft?" she repeated, unsure if she'd heard him correctly.

The security official grimaced. "The complaint was about you destroying city vegetation."

She pointed at her chest. "Who'd give the first fig if I picked a few flowers? There's so many." The drape twitched in the window above and her core temperature dropped ten degrees. "Hang on." She pursed her lips and pointed an accusatory finger. "Whose office is that?"

Dumb question.

"Mayor Marino requested that you be informed that this space is public property and not your own private garden."

"For Pete's sake." Her laugh was incredulous. Everland residents were as charming as their town except in one respect. Their mayor had a stick shoved far up his (admittedly fine) ass.

"There's more." The security guard swallowed hard and adjusted his belt buckle over his straining belly. "I'm to confiscate the flowers."

"Oh, come on. They are picked." She waved the gorgeous bouquet under the security guard's nose. "The damage is done."

"Orders are orders, ma'am."

She glanced at the clock tower. Crap. Was that the time? Forget getting all "no justice, no peace." "Fine. Here." She shoved the blooms into his arms. "Give these to the mayor with my regards."

"He was leaving the premises on official business."

"Well, inform him upon his return that he's officially a jerk." She flounced away, fuming. Last week she'd taken J.K. Growling for a walk in the rain. They'd been minding their own beeswax, dancing in ankle-deep puddles on Love Street, when Beau Marino had driven by with a face like she was you-know-what stuck to the bottom of his shoe. He'd rolled down the window and told her she was jaywalking.

She'd told *him* where to stick it.

Balling her hands into two fists, she half smashed a lone Shasta daisy. The sole survivor of Operation: Bouquet Obliteration. Once back in the car, she tossed the flower on the passenger seat and cranked the volume to her beloved *Grease* soundtrack. Pumpkin's main selling point (beside the rock-bottom price) was the unexpectedly badass stereo system. She might look the part of a wide-eyed, angelic Sandra Dee, but she had Rizzo's soul. Letting her vocal cords rip to "There Are Worse Things I Could Do" felt damn satisfying, even if it uncorked emotions better kept tightly bottled.

She increased her grip on the steering wheel as she drove past the once-grand, now-abandoned Roxy Theater, a crumbling eyesore off the otherwise neat and tidy Main Street. Even the for sale sign plastered to the marquee had weathered to tatters. Once someone had built the place with grand hopes, but starry-eyed dreams had a bad habit of fizzling faster than a meteorite striking Earth's atmosphere. Tuesday knew all about that phenomenon thanks to two-time Tony Award–winning director Philip Chandler, who cast her for a part that she hadn't auditioned for—the unwitting other woman.

Mistress.

Sidepiece.

Shack job.

Pumpkin's wheels hit the road's rumble strip, and the tactile vibration warned that she'd drifted too far right. She bit down on the inside of her bottom lip and corrected, taking shallow breaths to work around the asphyxiating knot in her chest. Despite the eight-hundred-mile distance stretching between here and Manhattan, the name—Philip Chandler—made her insides roil. Not every fairy tale had a happy ending, especially ones that started as "Once upon a time, a girl in love with love, was invited out to coffee by a narcissistic, cheating a-hole…"

A beep from the pink Cadillac in the oncoming lane interrupted her navel-gazing. Tuesday couldn't decipher Miss Ida May's face from beneath the wide-brimmed straw hat garlanded with silk flowers but made sure to give her neighbor from Love Street a wave. Miss Ida May administered the Everland gossip blog, the Back Fence, and was constantly trolling for a juicy scoop.

Drive along, ma'am. Nothing to see here.

No one in Everland knew the rumors. The awful story was so common as to be a cliché, an ensemble actress trying to seduce her way into a breakout role. Or so the tale went. And whoever let truth get in the way of a good story?

Philip had been married! *Married.* M-A-R-R-I-E-D. Not D-I-V-O-R-C-E-D like he'd said.

That wasn't all. His shameless flattery evolved into:

You're eating that? Remind me; are you an actress or a pig?

Maybe you're not pretty enough for a principal role.

Jesus Christ, you laugh like a horse.

Pepper could never find out what happened. She'd think Tuesday was lying, an idiot, or both. It seemed impossible to believe she'd let a man treat her with such a total lack of respect.

But she had.

Tuesday's face reflected from the rearview mirror—her brown-gold eyes darkened by guilt and shame. She'd wanted to be a star, and he'd filled her head with fame, luring her in like a stupid fish until she was caught in his lies and unable to escape. Tears welled before she blinked hard, stamping them out.

No pity parties allowed in Scarlett-Freaking-O'Hara country. She'd take a page from that fierce heroine's playbook and not think about that mess now. Not when she could toss her head and sing louder.

One thing was certain. She'd never lose her sense of self in another relationship. Whoever she got involved with next time around would take her as she was, or not get her at all.

The song ended as she passed Happily Ever After Land's main entrance on the town outskirts. A school bus turned beneath the sign that read YO DREAMS START HERE. The *u* and *r* were missing.

The only decent spot left in the staff parking lot was a tight squeeze beside a group of professional-looking people filing out of a deluxe minivan.

Terrific. Reverse parking with witnesses.

Tuesday lowered the volume to "Look at Me, I'm Sandra Dee" with an inward groan as her gaze locked on the tall, tawny-skinned man with a shaved head who towered over the group with intense va-va-voom blue eyes that would be completely sexy if not for the stony glare.

Her toes curled in her fake glass slippers as she fought the unwelcome pyrotechnics detonating in the pit of her abdomen.

Beau Marino aka Hater of Random Acts of Joy.

Although, when not calling security over war crimes against begonias, the man gave good face with his strong dark features, aquiline nose, stern mouth, and an innately haughty air that earned him the town nickname of the Prince of Everland.

She blinked first. Whoops. Worse, her heart did that annoying panicked response where it ran flailing into walls, or more accurately, her rib cage. This man's raw masculine beauty had an irritating habit of setting off a chain reaction of unwanted physiological responses.

Stupid beautiful face.

It took three attempts to park Pumpkin, and even then she ended up crooked. Whatever, good enough. She set the hand brake and fished in the center console for bubblegum-pink lipstick, taking her time with the application.

The stray daisy gave her an idea. Deep breath in. Let it out nice and easy. One more time and equilibrium was restored. Time to get in character. Tuesday might not know how to behave, but Princess Fabulous would.

She stepped out of the car with the flower, righted her cartoonish tiara, and kept her gaze profoundly vacant.

Show time.

"Mayor and friends! Always an honor to have local dignitaries visit our most humble kingdom," she trilled with an inward smirk as a muscle twitched near his ear.

Stupid beautiful ear.

Seriously, there wasn't a single good reason why that ear should look so freaking attractive. But it did. So did the three dark freckles dotting the center of the lobe in the exact same pattern as Orion's belt. It was the second thing she'd ever noticed about him, after the pale blue eyes, the irises cut by white rays. Mesmerizing eyes that matched the sapphire tie, unsmiling eyes that were . . . currently affixed to the wilting blossom.

She broke the stem, creating a daisy boutonniere that she shamelessly stepped forward and popped into his buttonhole. "A token of my esteem." She cloaked the needling tone inside her sweetest pitch. Her fingers grazed hard muscle. What exactly was he packing beneath that suit? She froze.

Say what?

Not cool, body. Neither was the fact that he gazed at her cleavage with barely disguised revulsion. Hey, her pint-size rack deserved an A for effort. Her boobs might not be massive, but they were mighty.

"What *is* that?" Two lines bracketed his pursed mouth.

She glanced in the direction of his frown. A brown sticky blob dangled from the satin bow in the middle of her bodice. "Oh shhhhhhhhhhh—ugar bowl." No hiding she'd inhaled a slice of peanut butter and banana toast for a rushed over-the-kitchen-counter breakfast.

One of the group members, a middle-aged guy sporting an impressive horseshoe moustache, handed over a napkin stamped with the logo from Smuggler's Cove, Everland's popular bar and restaurant.

"Thank you, kind sir." Tuesday dabbed her torso and gathered the remains of her dignity, lifting her chin like the Queen of England, not an underpaid actress in a stained dress and cheap plastic shoes. "Now, to what do we owe the pleasure of your patronage?"

"We're from the Georgia Tourism Commission," a kind-faced, silver-haired woman with funky dangling earrings answered after what proved to be an uncomfortable silence.

"Castles and cauldrons! Then haven't you come to the right place!" She plastered on a saccharine smile and wadded the napkin into her fist. Obviously Beau Marino came to the park in a professional capacity. A man who called security over flower picking wouldn't have fun for fun's sake, not on a workday. "Why, Happily Ever After Land is the best time you can have around these parts with your clothes on."

What the mayor needed was a not-so-gentle reminder that life was an out-of-control roller coaster, so might as well throw up your hands, laugh, and occasionally scream.

The twitch in Beau's temple turned into a pulse. That vein could pop in three...two...

"We're hosting a very special group today," she said in her most singsong voice. "A field trip of foster children awaits a royally good time."

"Now doesn't that sound wonderful?" The silver-haired woman clapped her hands. "My oldest daughter fosters. Mind if we tag along? See how the kids react to the park?"

"I..." The mayor looked like he'd rather trim his nails with a chainsaw, but he was trapped. "Of course, Donna." His lips curved at the edges, but Tuesday knew better. His flaring nostrils gave away his displeasure.

Her own smile, on the other hand, was one hundred percent genuine. Turned out revenge was sweeter than a chocolate chip funnel cake smothered in whipped cream.

Time for Beau Marino to buckle up. He was on her turf now, and she intended to take him on a wild ride.

About the Author

Lia Riley is a contemporary romance author. *USA Today* describes her as "refreshing," and *RT Book Reviews* calls her books "sizzling and heartfelt." She loves her husband, her three kids, wandering redwood forests, and a perfect pour-over coffee. She is 25 percent sarcastic, 54 percent optimistic, and 122 percent bad at math (good thing she writes happy endings for a living). She and her family live mostly in Northern California.

Fall in Love with Forever Romance

DEADLY SILENCE
By Rebecca Zanetti

Fans of Maya Banks, Shannon McKenna, and Lisa Jackson will love this sexy, suspenseful romance from *New York Times* bestselling author Rebecca Zanetti. Paralegal Zara Remington wants to keep things casual with private investigator Ryker Jones. But when a secret military organization starts to hunt them down, her true feelings for him surface—just as their lives are being threatened.

Fall in Love with Forever Romance

TOO HARD TO FORGET
By Tessa Bailey

The "Queen of Dirty Talk" is back with the third book in the Romancing the Clarksons series! Peggy Clarkson is returning to her college alma mater with one goal in mind: confront Elliott Brooks, the man who ruined her for all others, and prove she's over him for good. But she's in for a surprise when this time Elliott has no intention of letting her walk away.

Fall in Love with Forever Romance

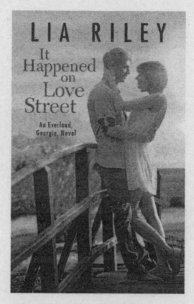

IT HAPPENED ON LOVE STREET
By Lia Riley

Lawyer Pepper Knight finds herself stranded and unemployed in Everland, Georgia, and she turns to the sexy town vet, Rhett Valentine, for help. But when she starts to fall for him, she has to decide: Will she be able to give up her big city dreams for love in a small town? For fans of Kristan Higgins, Jill Shalvis, and Marina Adair.

Fall in Love with Forever Romance

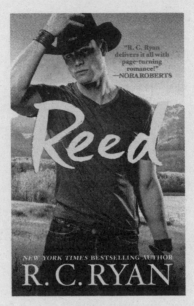

REED
By R.C. Ryan

In the tradition of Linda Lael Miller and Diana Palmer comes the latest from R.C. Ryan. Cowboy Reed Malloy is Glacier Ridge's resident ladies' man and now his sights are set on the beautiful Allison Shaw. But a secret feud between their families threatens their love—and their lives. The heartwarming conclusion to R.C. Ryan's Western romance series, the Malloys of Montana.